One of the Spirits Burning

(A Musical Memoir)
by Don Falcone

Foreword by Michael Moorcock

One of the Spirits Burning

Print ISBN 978-1-960405-31-9
eBook ISBN 978-1-960405-32-6

Visit Don online—https://www.DonFalcone.com
Cover design by Guy Corp—www.GrafixCorp.com
Cover illustration by Hawk Alfredson—
http://www.HawkAlfredson.com

STAIRWAY≡PRESS

STAIRWAY PRESS—APACHE JUNCTION
www.StairwayPress.com
1000 West Apache Trail
Suite 126
Apache Junction, AZ 85120 USA

Dedication

To Karen, my wife, and our pets past, present, and future (dog daughters Sienna, Kiara, and Indy, and our first pet, our cat named Cleo)

Contributors

Don Falcone: Author
Michael Moorcock: Foreword
Edward Kazala: Beta Reader

Hawk Alfredson: Front Cover and Interior Artwork
(The cover artwork "Deep In The Chambers Of A Whale Fish" is oil over egg oil tempera on canvas 1995-2010, 58" x 38", in the collection of Damian Michaels.)

Karen Anderson: Photo Illustrations of Hawk's Artwork
Don Falcone: Cover Redesign of Hawk's "Deep" Artwork
Bridget Wishart: Photo Illustration of Don

Band, Musician, and Other Photos: Karen Anderson, Pau Arumi, Michael Clare, Harry Collison, Don Falcone, Jack Gold-Molina, Michal Skwarek, Pete Stanley

Special Text Entries: Karen Anderson, Steve Bemand, Albert Bouchard, Robin Burns, Kim Cascone, Michael Clare, Joe Diehl, David Falcone, Ernie Falcone, Catherine Foreman, Jack Gold-Molina, Sam Herzberg, Jerry Jeter, Mack Maloney, Pierce McDowell, Jeff Melton, Pete Pavli, Martin Plumley, Donald "Buck Dharma" Roeser, Sunita Smith, Brian Tawn, Pat Thomas, Bridget Wishart, Cyrille Verdeaux

Quoted input in "The Crew" chapter from 125 musicians who contributed to Spirits Burning recordings, including BÖC family members Joe Bouchard, Richie Castellano, Danny Miranda, and Donald "Buck Dharma" Roeser, Hawkwind family members Steve Bemand, Richard Chadwick, Dead Fred, Paul Rudolph, Adrian Shaw, and Steve Swindells, Gong family member Mike Howlett, Keith The Bass, Steffe Sharpstrings, and Harry Williamson, Van Der Graaf Generator family members David Jackson, Graham Smith, and

Judge Smith, plus Robert Berry (3), Andy Dalby (Arthur Brown), Peter Knight (Steeleye Span), Matt Malley (Counting Crows), Monty Oxymoron (The Damned), Pete Pavli (High Tide), Robert Rich, Jonathan Segel (Camper Van Beethoven), Andy Shernoff (The Dictators), Fabienne Shine (Shakin' Street), Darryl Way (Curved Air), and more

Additional Information: Scott Baer, Cindi Falcone, Richard Falcone, Richard Fouchaux, Tim Griesemer, Bill Jordan, Kevin Krause, Randall Orris, Carol Weeks

Special Thanks: Karen, for successfully transferring emails from one Mac to another over the years—the emails were invaluable for reconstructing past events; Michael Clare, for his collection of archive emails; Ed Kazala, for his immense help as a beta editor and sounding board

I'd also like to thank my memories for sticking around. I appreciate their attempt to resurrect the past, even when they might veer from what happened. They have their vantage point, and I accept that.

Foreword

WITHOUT DON FALCONE my musical career might have finished around the time his started in the 1980s. I can say with absolute certainty that without his project my own musical career might have faltered when I quietly ended my fairly long-established association with Hawkwind and my own Deep Fix project around the mid-eighties and when his seriously got moving.

Like me, Don went through the experiences associated with most kids of his generation who wanted to play what for the sake of brevity we call 'rock and roll'. My own story is typical of my time and therefore just a little different. I suppose I came in at the beginning when the likes of Gene Vincent and Buddy Holly were starting to be heard on the radio and touring the US, England, and Europe in package shows reminiscent of the old Louisiana Hayride shows. My story, because I'm a fair bit older than he is, was the story of post-war British rock. I went through the British experience. Unable to afford electronic instruments, I started in skiffle in the 1950s. I found the folk scene through upbeat versions of Lead Belly's *Rock Island Line*. I wrote to Woody Guthrie and Pete Seeger from London where, at the time, their work was generally better known and admired. I got replies from both, probably because their world was then a bit smaller than ours. I played *Pretty Boyd Floyd* and all those others to the chords and licks I learned directly from Jack Elliott, who had played with Woody. This was why Bob Dylan had a better audience for a while via the BBC.

From there I moved into the world of the blues, where, in Soho, Alexis Korner and Cyril Davies established various clubs and taught us all about Clarksdale, Memphis, and Chicago, taught us how to play first acoustic then electric guitars, following in the footsteps of the Delta musicians and enthusing the likes of John Mayall, Jeff Beck, Long John Baldry and then the R&B keyboard players like Graham Bond, Zoot Money, Georgie Fame, and ultimately Elton John, as we started to combine the power of rock and roll into our music and create what ultimately became, in the States, the British Rock Invasion.

Some of us took different paths, giving a twelve-bar feel to the so-called 'psychedelic' music of early Pink Floyd and so on. Zoot Money's Roll Band became Dantalian's Chariot, The Action became Mighty Baby and, ultimately, from The Dharma Blues Band, Dave Brock formed Hawkwind and then, spinning off Hawkwind, impatient with some of those long Grateful Dead-style half-hour riffs, Lemmy ultimately formed Motorhead, influencing other Heavy Metal power trios until there was a whole wide range of super-heated, mind-expanding, lyrically-inspired music feeding back to the mother-lode, to Americana like Commander Cody's truck-rock, or the Beach Boys or the Highwaymen and all the vast variety of music which enriched our world from Liverpool to Los Angeles, enabling us to play every sort of music echoing the choices we had in classical music from Vivaldi to Mahler and Schoenberg to Glass. Record companies and venues enabled musicians to make the same choices, to play, if they liked, in bands that suited every audience and all their own many tastes. And so, we came by Space Rock...

For a while musicians could, if we chose, play so-called 'experimental' music, mixing our taste for science fiction with moody, extended sounds moving well into so-called psychedelia, where one piece could last an entire side of what had been a 12-inch record or give our audience six or seven brief fast-paced numbers reminiscent of early rock singles. The great thing was that musicians could choose to do that, making a living from playing whatever they wanted, depending on the mood they picked up from their audience or how they felt at the time. Audiences, also, could make those choices, even, on the club or pub scene, moving from Hawkwind's long inventive riffs around one number to punk's brief, nervous meth-driven numbers that lasted only a couple of minutes, depending on the mood of the band or the demands of the audience. And then there was the inspired pop-music of the sixties or seventies and the disciplined inventiveness of the three-minute single. It was all ours. And, if we were so minded, we could pick whatever kind we liked. By the 1980s, however, with the fading away of our best sounds from most radio, we had to look for and make our music for ourselves and though we could play whatever we liked, we ceased finding radio stations or venues which allowed us this privilege.

The Golden Age in music was over and for Don that was almost before it began.

Don's tastes were for what has become known as prog-rock or space-rock and ambient rock. After his involvement with Thessalonians, he played in a number of bands, most of them pretty short-lived and typical of the day—Spaceship Eyes being the longest lived—playing keyboards and synth, being signed to Cleopatra in the early 90s when he revived Spirits Burning as first a band and then, like me with Deep Fix, a general project which brought in a large number of musicians from all over the music world, many being associated with Hawkwind, Deep Fix, and Blue Öyster Cult, all bands associated to one degree or another with 'space' or 'psychedelic' rock. He became a sought-after producer doing, for instance, a wonderful job on Deep Fix's *Live at The Terminal Café* for Cleopatra Records in 2019. With his Noh Poetry label, his penchant for getting material before the public extended to his being executive producer on the rough tracks Pete Pavli (High Tide) and I did for *Gloriana* and *Entropy Tango*, two projects which were never finished, due to their expense and our failure to find other musicians willing to play the difficult parts we were writing which owed as much to Schoenberg as Schuman and were originally put out by Brian Tawn, the hard-working editor of Hawkfan. Without Don's skills, those might never have been heard by a wider audience at all. Meanwhile the project consisting of four long complex records based on my *Dancers at the End of Time* sequence continues towards conclusion, an enormously impressive expansion of the three books into something resembling an opera, although perhaps closer to a modern ambient/space-rock musical.

The hopes we had originally held for a broadening taste in music had somewhat narrowed in terms of popular audiences by the 90s so that many small companies found it very hard to support the old space rock bands. The audiences established for the likes of Hawkwind, who could stay alive during hard times by putting out a lot of albums and doing a lot of gigs reminded me of the state of *fiction* in the 1920s and 1940s, supplying relatively few magazines which supported just about enough fiction of one type to fill them—from the so-called 'little' mags usually backed by private donors or universities publishing 'experimental' or 'literary' fiction to pulps barely able to sustain themselves by publishing detective, romance or science fiction. The mass audiences wanted something bland, undemanding, sentimental and largely un-stimulating. Ultimately, however, this began to change.

For those of us in bands still trying to produce what *was* progressive, experimental, fresh and unbland, the old record companies did not exist. There was always a reasonable hope that those companies would return to back what we knew to be stimulating but we could not rely on it happening by magic. We needed audiences and they could only be created by companies and individuals willing to continue putting out the stuff we liked. We had chiefly to rely on idealists, just as magazines like my own NEW WORLDS had relied in the sixties and seventies and eventually got the work we liked into the public arena.

In the 70s, there were companies who managed to stay reasonably alive, like STIFF, who kept people like Elvis Costello, Madness, The Damned, Rockpile and others going until ultimately they became popular with larger and larger audiences and eventually found very large audiences, sometimes by changing the taste of the popular audience or at least kept going for a long enough time to establish a reasonable following. In England, we still had one or two companies like FLICKNIFE, who kept Deep Fix going for a while, but these eventually could no longer support us. If it had not been for Don Falcone's project, we might easily have stopped altogether. Happily, Spirits Burning and Don Falcone saved the day for us and enabled us to continue! Spirits Burning married both established and lesser-known musicians who have wanted to take their own path.

In this sense, of course, Don reminds me more of the NEW

WORLDS magazines project which I maintained for many years, publishing a wide range of work as an ongoing project rather than as a company with a particular commercial taste. Of course, all this work had been unusual, experimental and highly individualistic, bringing together, as NEW WORLDS did, people with a very different approach, yet all unwilling to make compromises to fit in with current commercial demands. To do this, it usually takes the determined and unflinching work of one or two people and a group of fellow spirits burning to maintain a constant momentum.

This is the real Don Falcone story. He has often and almost single-handedly continued to bring the unusual, the unknown, the experimental and the work of enthusiasts to a grateful and highly appreciative audience; one which will remain unwavering and willing to form the core of a concrete group, there to sustain musicians often forced to keep their careers going by performing music not always to their own taste, just as those writers I knew like myself, writing commercial fiction and decent work not wholly to their own preferences or indeed unable to do exactly the music or art they found completely satisfying or perhaps which no longer completely sustains that which they still wish to perform. It takes people of enormous idealism and consistency of vision to do that. There are very few of them to be found anywhere in the world and I am proud to say that Don Falcone, with his many musical skills, is one of them.

This is how I personally find Don and what I think others of us also find in him. This modest memoir helps us to understand the kind of character it takes, the kind of drive and sheer guts it requires, to keep the flag flying, the courage alive and the spirit burning.

It explains what I owe to Don. What we all, as part of the Spirits Burning project, owe him and will continue to owe him for many more years to come. Keep the starship moving, the idealism alive and the crew strong, Don! We all love you and this book shows us why!
—Mike Moorcock
Rue St Maur, Paris
October 2024

About the Author

(photo by Karen Anderson)

MUSIC PRODUCER, SONGWRITER, keyboardist, bassist, vocalist, lyricist, and technical writer, Don Falcone has played on over 40 albums by his bands and music projects. His Spirits Burning collective has brought together almost 300 musicians from classic and underground rock bands, including collaborations with Daevid Allen, Albert Bouchard, Michael Moorcock, Cyrille Verdeaux, and Bridget Wishart. His music journey has touched ambient, drum 'n' bass, space rock, prog, psychedelic, folk, post-rock, and experimental.

As a technical writer, he managed the team that produced Pro Tools documentation for ten years and was the lead writer for Dolby Atmos content creation tools for over a decade. He and his wife Karen are dog parents. He believes we are in a golden age of pizza, tacos, breads, and pastries.

He has spent his Bay Area years discovering and enjoying Thai, Indian, Mexican, and Ethiopian dishes, and many soups and salads.

Table of Contents

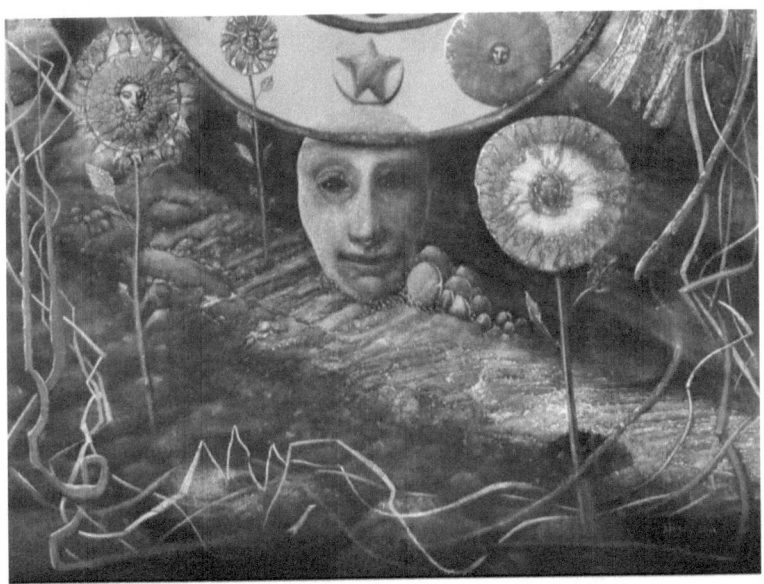

GONZO
Weekly #49
EXCLUSIVE:
Don Falcone from
'Spirits Burning'
reveals a whole plethora
of new projects
EXCLUSIVE:
Orrin Hare on
Krautfolk
EXCLUSIVE:
Merrell Fankhauser's
birthday Jam
EXCLUSIVE:
Steve Ignorant's Slice of
Life get new bass player
EXCLUSIVE:
Clepsydra tour dates
EXCLUSIVE:
Hugh Hopper archive
releases
EXCLUSIVE:
Doug Harr on
Cat Stevens
PLUS:
New EP from
Galahad
Brian May on
fox hunting
The Millenium Falcone

Image courtesy of Jon Downes, Gonzo Weekly

Every Chapter

SO FAR, EVERY chapter in my life has had a years later. I'll keep that in mind while reflecting on the past.

Perhaps this was what I was toying with when I wrote a song in 1981 titled *Future Memories*. I was still immersed in the 70s; Nektar's *Remember the Future* concept album and lines from Peter Hammill like "I want the future now." (The collector in me that continued to buy every album by a music group, or their offshoots, understood the cut of another Hammill line: "I've got every one of your records, man. Doesn't that mean that I own you?")

At 23, I was thinking about my place in a world where poets and musicians thrived. With a lifetime of possibilities in front of me, I was searching for my own phrase, and my own way of describing my thoughts in a past, present, and future way. I landed on *Future Memories*.

I was starting to write lyrics, moving on from the thoughts and interests of my high school and undergraduate years. I was also navigating the blurred lines between lyrics and poetry (and that might be why my poetry blew towards experimental). It would be a few more years before marrying them on a serious level.

One of my early language or sound poems started with the first consonant of a word ("branch"), and then played with the syllables of another word ("forest").

Forest

Ba Ba Branch
       fair in the
for us Ba Ba
       fern in the
base
          It'll
tinsel you Ba Ba
         tie loose
the air in
        you have saved
        for us

The Ba Ba smell
      errand still
until the wind
blow Ba Ba
        soft tine unties
        fern all back
        is pose for
Ba Ba fair branch
      fair while wait
until I sell you Ba Ba
        shore for wind
shore for air
        shore for us

Another poem removed the first letters of some of the words in its opening mantra and continued with the motif throughout.

In A Church

the ass ass mass ass of oof oof roof oof
folds his ong ong song ong
under the ench ench bench ench
Could it be love?

/luther oother an
 lois ois, ooper eroes all/ (2x)
/a pure tan from opper opera one/ (2x)
who owns who owns who owns
a truth from the makers
of a hollar dollar mahler of fistfuls

and how much should a hero get paid?

ipso facto
kribtoe crabtoe
be air fool
where you step

ipso facto
kribtoe crabtoe
be air fool
where you stop

the ass ass mass ass of oof oof roof oof
folds his ong ong song ong
where we

we watch from the ands
with our ands
folded over our ands

These poems worked best when read aloud or performed. Reading
In A Church and raising my voice from the first line onward announced

that it was true and had to be listened to. That was my belief. The physical hand gestures and extended arm movements during a reading invited the audience. Ending the poem by folding my hands over my hands solidified that this was a ritual, albeit a short one, and the plural, inclusive "we" brought it to a peaceful close. With no fadeout.

Both poems were published in the 1986 book that was part of my master's degree. My printed thesis lives quietly at San Francisco State University, far from the view of the outside world. The single duplicate lives in a bookcase in my home music studio. Like other theses of the time, they were composed of 8 1/2 x 11 pages, each character with the same, basic font, the pages bound together by a thick, blue cover with the author's name and chosen title printed on the spine in white.

A year earlier, *In A Church* was included in a poetry magazine called *Five Fingers Poetry*, the brainchild of a group of former classmates at San Francisco State University. Their magazine was a good example of DIY promotion. To get published, start a magazine and include your own work. Plus, by promoting other writers, you add fuel to your work. Strength in quality via your poet and short story neighbors.

In A Church got a space rock reading on the debut Spirits Burning album *New Worlds By Design* in 1999. For that rendering, I invited Knut Gerwers to do the reading. He has a strong, deep voice that seemed more appropriate than mine. Plus, I gave it a new title: *Beautiful Stealth, In A Church*. Perhaps I was commenting on the process—I had taken the fire of art from one place and set it to another.

It wasn't lost on me that much of the music that I listened to was British, and some of the singers didn't fully Americanize to the blues of the past or pop and rock of the present. Instead, they maintained an accent that sometimes hid the first consonants of certain words. At least, that's how their vocals took to my ears. In an inverse world of sorts, I sang my early songs with a British accent.

(Years later, perhaps as a karma rebalance, I was in a band called

Melting Euphoria. The bassist and leader of the band took the influence a step further. He was American and typically talked with a British accent. Some music articles described him as an Englishman; a characterization I never achieved.)

I gave a half dozen or so poetry readings in San Francisco. One of them in the city's North Beach, a few blocks from The Spaghetti Factory, one of the few places that had real Italian ice—like the lemon-flavored kind imported to New York from Italy and then brought to my hometown church in Pennsylvania for Sunday spaghetti dinners the end of every month (excluding summertime). The Spaghetti Factory closed (the restaurant and its market across the street). Gelato, the next big thing, put a stranglehold on the chill side of the dessert market for decades. So began my search for real Italian ice. Success came in the next century and a ride on a gondola down the waters of Venice. Well, virtual waters...at the Venetian in Las Vegas. The end of the ride revealed a virtual town square with food stalls. At the front was a long stall dedicated to Italian ice. The lemon flavor I knew, and many more. I wonder if it still exists.

My North Beach reading was at the Tattoo Rose. It was both a tattoo shop and cafe. Run by Lyle Tuttle, known for his tattoo work on famous people: Cher, Janice Joplin, Joan Baez, Kiss' Paul Stanley. My memory is that he looked tough and had the voice of Truman Capote. Watching him on YouTube reveals the faultiness of that memory. Clips from before my time in the city reveal the voice of a potential late-night host, and a more slender, well-dressed suit and no tie look. With a firm hand on the community and art scene, Lyle booked local aspiring poets for a weekly nighttime reading series.

My reading at the Tattoo Rose and other venues provided a chance to perform in public and move past the fears that are inherent in playing with your art form in front of a live audience. And it did feel like play. Preparation included choosing which poems to read, practicing them out loud, developing any choreography. For example, I read one poem while hitting claves together. *In A Church* incorporated its body motions. These were small, easy-to-apply methodologies. It was a start. Anything was possible.

One night, I brought my bass guitar and Pignose (a tiny brown practice amp and speaker combo with a silver power/volume knob that looked like...a pig's nose). Ready-made for bedroom guitarists or busking. With a bass guitar and its inherent low-end frequencies, it was easy to get unintended distortion and take years off the Pignose's life. For this performance, I had worked out a clean-sounding bass song interweaving two-note chords, whole note pads, and some moving riffs. Between the bass and the Pignose cables was an orange MXR Phase 90; a stomp box that gave the bass an almost watery sound, like the bass sound that Spirits Burning contributor Adrian Shaw used on Hawkwind's *High Rise*, (a song my Spirits Burning project covered on the Hawkwind tribute album *Daze of the Underground* in 2003). On top of this bottom end music, I sang about a love that was not happening.

I wrote two songs for Karen West—not the Karen I would marry years later. One song was utterly awful. Called *Karen*. Started off with me playing bass and shouting, "Kare-in, Kare-in," a little bass riff, and then "Kare-in, Kare-in." The one this night, titled *We Gather in Twos*, had depth, including direct questioning and jabs at her in the song's core. The song ended with the hope and serenity of the main line: "We gather in twos...to make music...in the dark...in the dark."

In retrospect, I should have been happy that the song's central figure was present, supporting me. I should have considered not laying bare my take of the relationship. In the future, I got better at disguising real life in songs, or choosing real life stories that warranted retelling, or avoiding real life altogether. This night, not so much. She had to sit through a long, winding road of a song.

The places I read were scattered throughout the city. Most of them no longer with us.

- The Tattoo Rose (Available North Beach retail site at the time of this writing, with at least four apartment complexes above it).
- The Co Lab (now Core40 gym in lower Pacific Heights).

- Two places in the Mission district:
  - The Eye Gallery (now Souvla, a Greek restaurant).
  - The Clarion Cafe (now a Footwear Express).
- Rising Spirits Cafe (a cafe and bookstore that used to be part of the Ecumenical House, located across the street from San Francisco State University).
- San Francisco State Student Union Basement (the bowels of a student union).

○ ○ ○ ○ ○ ○

In the 80s, the English department and Admissions buildings were the closest buildings to the bus stop at 19th and Holloway. One end of the city. Here, the City by the Bay became a gateway to the peninsula and the string of cities south of San Francisco.

Weaving between the two buildings and walking deeper into the campus revealed the Student Union. A strange, brutalist design. The top of its structure looked like the wings of a futuristic jet fighter that had been tilted up in opposing directions. The extruding winged design on the left highlighted the flat of a downed wing, like it had crashed and embedded itself on an aircraft carrier. From a side angle, it looked like a drive-in movie screen tilted in a way that prevented actual viewing. The design on the right emulated the cool concrete seats of a football stadium. Students sat there, gazing onto the grassy area in front of the union or outward to one of the surrounding buildings dedicated to a subject-based department.

When the weather was nice, many students took advantage of the grass to lie in the sun and study alone or talk about school or other topics with fellow students.

Somehow, maybe because of the Student Union's mysterious, otherworldly design, the building felt inviting. You had to wonder: What was inside? Was it as strange inside as it was outside? Any hidden areas to discover?

Once you entered, you could move past a large assembly room on the left (where a version of Spirits Burning would one day perform), then down a flight of stairs, past a flower stand, and down one more flight of stairs that led to the basement. This area included four food stations and a game room. Sometimes this area felt dark, like you were in a cave. On occasion, the power would be lost, and the lights went out. The pinball machines and pizza oven too.

Chris Mahnken, an early roommate, worked in the game room. In her bare feet. Some of San Francisco's past was still intact. Of the food places, I would eventually manage the pizza one (The Pizza Boat). Rob Burns, the sound person for bands I was in the first half of the 80s, worked two stations over, at The Far East Delight. After college, Rob took his Broadcasting degree and got hired by Telemundo, which was part of NBC. He earned a couple of Emmys there. Those two food establishments? Replaced more than once over the ensuing years, as different vendors got the bid to run the stations.

The Pizza Boat was a DIY of the business world. Two students put in a bid for the space as part of their business degree. When they expanded, I moved from managing the campus Boat to a new one downtown. Then, I moved on, concentrating on my master's degree, combining it with an AA in Electronics at Heald College. (Heald is also no longer with us.)

Most students lived off-campus, somewhere in the city, and then took public transit to the campus. My first apartment was with Jack, a gay teacher in his 40s. My parents, on the other end of the continent, were concerned. After a few months, and wanting to live closer to the college, I moved to a house located a half block from Golden Gate Park, six miles from school, living with two female students. My parents were happier, even if it was with two girls.

They were also concerned about my first job in the city, at a vegetarian restaurant on Polk Street. I told them the street was one gay tier lower than the better-known Castro Street. I had discovered the "Now hiring" sign on my first walk downtown. I bussed to a Tower Records, walked to the next record store on a side street, and then turned right, toward the third record shop. I was now at Polk Street. It was at that point that I saw the sign.

I only worked at the Denebeim Kosher Vegetarian Restaurant for a memorable month; as a combo busboy/dishwasher who did some prep work. I swear I could microwave a quiche for one time setting and have success and then do it for less and always have it explode. Logic says that I imagined that. I was one of two straight people there. I went to a reading of Edith Sitwell poems with one of the two gay owners. A letter to my parents detailing this and other tales probably caused some stirring at my childhood home.

Another employee at the restaurant took me to an EST meeting. The white buttoned-down shirts were my first turnoff. Too many years of Catholic school. I wasn't going there again. When my coworkers introduced an EST member to me, I explained my ideas about life and art. I always took it as a compliment when the EST member responded "well, maybe EST isn't for you."

Within my month at the restaurant, I introduced pizza bagels to San Francisco. That's my story and I'm sticking to it. I had experienced pizza bagels in Philadelphia the summer before on a record store trek to Third Street Records in South Philly. I suggested pizza bagels for the vegetarian menu, and it quickly became popular. Even started to pop up at other cafes. Still, my time there was clicking away. It seemed that everyone except the two owners and main cook couldn't survive for more than a few weeks or a month. I got a tip that I was going to be fired and quit. My parents were happy when I got a job on campus, at a pizza place in the bowels of the Student Union.

The Pizza Boat was crucial to my early years in San Francisco. The female focus of that bass 'n' poetry performance worked here. A future girlfriend, Anita Acquistapace, would work here. Karen Anderson, my future wife, would work here. So did our maid of honor Tracy Williams (who was in the 1987 version of Spirits Burning) and our best man, Ed Kazala (who sang one song— *Bourgeoisie*—with two versions of the 80s Spirits Burning).

There were two drummers of note there too. Sam Herzberg played with Mrs. Green, a band that helped resurrect Beserkley Records, a label that previously included The Greg Kihn Band and The Modern Lovers. Kevin Carnes (who worked at the Pizza Boat after my stint) played with The Broun Fellinis. Sam and Kevin contributed to the modern Spirits Burning in the 21st century.

Ed Kazala Performing Bourgeoisie with Pizza Boat Friends, Clearlake, CA, 1974
Don (Bass), Ed (Vocals), Sam Herzberg (Drums), Tracy Williams (Guitar)

During one 80s stretch, Sam and Kevin's bands practiced across the hall from my band at Hudson Street Studios, Hudson being the H of the alphabetical avenues that dotted Third Street, at one of the edges of the Bayview-Hunters Point district. South of downtown. And an area that was not necessarily safe for a skinny, young, white human being. I remember walking down Third Street with two bandmates, on our way to a local BBQ place. In full sunlight. Hudson Avenue led to Innes Avenue led to Jerrold Avenue... We had to get deeper into the alphabet to reach our destination, closer to Palou Street. The three of us. Bruce Smith and I were the drum and bass rhythm section of Kameleon, respectively. (Bruce turned out to be one of the few musicians of my past that I would never find. Having the same name as a Buffalo Bills lineman or the drummer of Public Image Limited who also played with Bjork and African Head Charge made any search all the harder.) Jerry Jeter was the guitarist. Many of my friends thought of Jerry as the good looking one in the band. He was black, and well-built, with tattoos from Lyle Tuttle's place. Unlike Bruce or me, he maintained a workout routine. This was Kameleon. The three of us. It didn't matter. Our conversation withered away as we passed a black man holding a gun. Eye contact was avoided. It could be scary. However, if you made it to Everett & Jones BBQ, you were safe. The cook yelled out. "Isn't this the best damned BBQ place in the world?" And it was. (They eventually closed, and now have a much larger, more accessible restaurant located in Oakland's Jack London Square.)

I do wonder. How many of us who practiced at Hudson Street Studios knew it was located on Hudson Avenue?

Each room had a latch and padlock that the band (or multiple bands sharing the room) used to secure their room and the equipment inside. After practice, you turned out the light, closed the door, flipped the latch, inserted your padlock, and secured the shackle with a click. To cut to the chase: You could be imprisoned in the room. Thankfully, it never happened. By the time I was no longer in bands renting out practice rooms, and had settled into home studio recording, I did become claustrophobic. On an airplane, I couldn't sit in a last row window seat. (An attendant taught me that a moistened wipe on my neck and water would help, and it did.) I had trouble with the German sci-fi thriller *Dark*, which had caves as part of its core landscape. It didn't affect my appreciation of the series. However, I sometimes had to look away, or take a deep breath, or ask Karen to pause it while I took our dog to the back porch and inhaled fresh air. After having vertigo a few times, I even found it hard to sleep in total, extreme dark. Finding a sliver of light in the darkness helped.

Hudson Street had some bands that made a mark. No Poetry was there. At the end of the hallway, on the left. They were fronted by vocalist Meg O'Leary (a future Pigface member). The band briefly had former bassist Don Falcone (me) suddenly playing a Crumar String Ensemble with an occasional burst of a Big Muff distortion box or MXR Phase 90 box. When No Poetry left, I (Don Falcone) now had a space for my next band.

The studio had an upper level. I'm told that Faith No More practiced there.

Directly across from our room, Mrs. Green shared a room with Adam Sherbourne and his HI-NRG dance-rock band Until December, and then his alternative rock/industrial outfit Consolidated. In the same space was Afro-industrial noise ensemble The Beatnigs, which expanded into punk-industrial improv group The Broun Fellinis. Adam was larger than life to me, and I was 6'2". He frequently wore leather head to toe with silver chains dangling. It was a fashion look that I never attempted. I was more influenced by Steve McQueen in The Great Escape, more comfortable with a sweatshirt. Or a rock t-shirt.

Sometimes the hall exploded with the buzz, swoosh, and blap of multiple instruments and singers. This was the Norman Salant Group, fronted by the saxophonist who appeared on the Romeo Void *Benefactor* album and a Residents album. At some point, the Salant Group in the hallways became the 15-piece ZaSu Pitts Memorial Orchestra. While I would always say hi or tilt a smile, I rarely conversed with most of the people in the building. On a certain level, my bands there were shy, existing in a bubble.

o o o o o o

While some of my music consumption included bands that had what I considered deeper lyrics (Jethro Tull *Thick as a Brick* or *Passion Play*, take your pick, or the two Peters—Hammill and Gabriel), there were plenty of songs with simpler phrases or simpler intent. As a teenage fan of music, and then bass player, I had been pre-schooled in hard rock: Led Zeppelin, Deep Purple, Nazareth, Uriah Heep, Black Sabbath, and eventually Hawkwind.

It took another decade to realize that many of the songs of this generation revolved around fast women and cars; the songs did not age well for the older me with a different ethics about people and inanimate objects. Surprisingly, the early songs of Black Sabbath aged the best of the hard rock lot. Hawkwind is a different story. The songs mutated, whether you were listening to the original recording with one band line-up and their inherent sound, or a subsequent live version with another line-up. A plethora of astounding sounds and amazing music. That happens when you have over 50 members[1] over 50 years. When the next century approached, I created a music collective called Spirits Burning. Over the first 25 years, "we" would have almost 300 members. Strength in numbers!

The younger me comfortably wrote punkier verses, with potential catchy food for thought in the chorus.

Future Memories

The toys you're playing with
Are made to break and steal
The games you're playing out
Teach how to shout and kill
The money in your hand
Will buy your food and clothes
The paper forms you fill out
Each truth and lie they slowly show

> Can you handle the future memories?
> Can you handle them one by one?
> Can you handle the future memories?
> Can you handle them one by one?

The girl you're looking at
You know you want to use her
The girl you're going with
You know you're going to lose her
The only friend you've got
Is leaving in the morn

---

[1] For Hawkwind, Wikipedia 2024 lists five current members, 37 former members (including Ginger Baker), 20 additional musicians—not sure what qualifies one as an additional member—and 12 session/one-off musicians (including Eric Clapton).

The only life you've got
Starts to die when you are born

> Can you handle the future memories?
> Can you handle them one by one?
> Can you handle the future memories?
> Can you handle them one by one?

Years later, *Future Memories* became my first composition to be covered by another band. Austin's ST 37 transformed it into an intense, industrialized, angry experience. I loved that they took it somewhere new. They also asked for permission to use it again, this time as an album title, and I said "of course." Plural future memories sound good.

Even more years later, I flew to that same Austin, and in a nearby city recorded Michael Moorcock for two projects (both with chewy names): the project I led, this time under the name Spirits Burning & Michael Moorcock, and his longtime project Michael Moorcock & The Deep Fix.

○ ○ ○ ○ ○ ○

In late 1980, I was also searching for my voice. It's what artists do, isn't it? It was my first year away from my home state, my first year living in a big city, my first year of graduate school at San Francisco State University. I had a class there taught by Frances Mayes. She became my advisor and helped me weave through the process of getting a master's degree. She would also someday write the New York Times best seller *Under the Tuscan Sun*.

Frances reminded me of Scout in *To Kill a Mockingbird*, all grown up. She had short, cropped hair and spoke with a natural southern accent. She had a gentle nature, with a dose of wisdom that came with experience. She was ready to help the misunderstood streak that runs through the blood of every would-be poet.

She was a teacher I could trust. And respect. Especially when I considered the attention she was giving to my poems, which, when compared to her published works, were very different. Her poetry was more in touch with nature, and the South. I found it calming. Never dark. My poetry went in a different direction, at times experimental. Besides sound poetry, I was honing the John Ashbery infused style of breaking lines of thought, as I had done in my undergraduate school under the tutelage of poet John Taggart. (When I went to see John give a poetry reading in the 21st century, it was amazing. His words were musical, like a sax solo whose ebb and flow took you deep into its weave. This was not the level of poetry I was doing or would ever do. Perhaps, that's why I eventually redirected my artistic energies.)

When Frances' bestseller was made into a film, they chose Diane Lane to play her. This was not Scout grown up. Even the hair color felt wrong. The film reworked her real-life story and had her moving alone to Italy after a divorce. Reality: She and her husband went to Italy and together renovated a villa. She did not do it with the help of young, hot Italian neighbor.

Regardless of how your story is presented, the interpretation reveals a variation, resurrections. (Years later, I remixed a Gary Numan song, titled *Deadliner*. The label gave me access to his vocal tracks only. His fan club held a vote of which remix was considered the most like the original. They had a pie chart. I was proud my Spaceship Eyes solo project had the smallest slice. I hadn't listened to the original and specifically didn't want to do a straight cover. The original served that purpose. Another pie had the Spaceship Eyes remix as the least liked remix on the album. Oh well. I do wonder: What did Gary think of my flirtation with electronica in the 90s?)

In a class with Frances, another student asked, "Is it important to find your voice?" The question surprised me. The class was a mix of out-of-state writers and in-state writers who maybe had an easier journey to a graduate level classroom. It felt like the entrance bar for the former was high. The tuition was higher. It felt like some of the latter were just beginning their journey of writing poetry or prose. Regardless of how my classmates had gotten here, it was a question I didn't expect to hear out loud.

I was a bit jaded, internally, with a confidence built from a recent past. I had been published in the *Reflector*, the literary magazine at my undergraduate school, Shippensburg State College. I was the editor my senior year. Over a three-year period, I had multiple poems, and two stories published. And an article on Hawkwind using a New York Times approach. (Years later, while cleaning his mom's attic, Steve Swindells found a copy of the *Reflector*. This was probably the copy I sent to their management.)

Steve is a singer/songwriter/keyboardist. He had a couple of songs covered by the Who's Roger Daltrey. For me, though, he made a larger mark as a keyboardist for Hawklords, and then Hawkwind, and then a couple of contributions to Spirits Burning). My confidence should have been muted. I had been accepted at two schools only. Then again, a third classmate would later ask "Do you have to rhyme?"

On that other day, my classmate asked, "Is it important to find your voice?" Frances' answer: "Yes, it is important to find your voices." The answer immediately radiated for me. Art was pluralistic. We are pluralistic. And I suspect there were other layers to her answer. I do understand the value of getting one style down before moving on to the next. However, to a student in their 20s, who loved to try anything in the land of poetry and music, this was a literal feast, to be celebrated and shared—and repeated—forever.

○ ○ ○ ○ ○ ○

Life is a series of events you brew. The confluence of others doing the same thing with their lives can create a bit of confusion, luck, disappointment, success. They can fit in the same bucket. Or bucket list.

Bridget Wishart, singer and dancer with Hawkwind, was eating a kiwi on Haight Street. It was Monday afternoon, the day of their show at the I-Beam. I had taken the day off from work. I told Karen (my wife) we should visit the Haight; some band members might be there. Bridget was wearing a leather jacket. Her back was against the wall between two stores, one leg bent with its foot also against the wall. An unintentional band photo pose. (Simon House did a like pose for a Hawkwind photo I had used in my *Reflector* article about Hawkwind.) Unfortunately, this was before the cellphone camera era. Karen and I approached her. We recognized her from the OMNI show in Oakland the night before. Still, I asked if she was in Hawkwind. She confirmed her identity. I asked how the tour was going and what she thought of America.

Bridget doesn't remember any of this when I invited her to contribute to Spirits Burning years later. Between 2010 and 2020, we recorded three Spirits Burning & Bridget Wishart albums and an instrumental album under the name Astralfish. Bridget was a regular contributor to other Spirits Burning albums over that time. Plus, we would be onstage together in 2017.

Karen and I continued up Haight Street, towards the I-Beam. In a thrift shop, we saw Hawkwind's captain, Dave Brock, with his partner Kris. Dave's back was to me as I approached. He was looking through a rack of clothes. I reached out my hand, and said "Hi, I'm a fan of your music." He jumped! I had clearly startled him. I said a few more words, and then retreated. It was safer for everyone.

○ ○ ○ ○ ○ ○

Some of the words we choose or select in our life are embedded in us via work experiences. I was a full-time technical writer from 1989 to 2024.

As a tech writer, I learned that periods and commas always go inside the "closing double quotes." First, I learned that what I had been taught in grade school—the exception of when it didn't—was no longer true. When we started working with other countries, I then learned that UK and elsewhere do the opposite.

We followed the Chicago Manual of Style when I worked at Digidesign, a division of Avid Technology (until the Digidesign brand name was phased out in 2010, and then called Avid Audio in 2011) or before that, when I worked at Orban (a private company when I joined in 1989, then a division of AKG Acoustics Inc, later a division of Harmon International—you get the idea). At Dolby Laboratories, my final full-time stop on the technical writing wheel, we used the Chicago Manual, and then switched to the IBM Style Guide.

At two of these companies, we avoided contractions. To help users whose first language was not English. In the word count war, you can make a case to follow this or not, depending on your goal.

At Dolby, the law of the land was to never use possessives with an inanimate object. Instead of writing "the application's menu," you would write "the application menu."

At Orban, the manuals were very dry and straight forward, except for one word. We used the term nastinesses when discussing pops, clicks, and other digital noises.

When writing personal emails or liner notes for albums—text outside the work microscope—it was impossible for me to not consider the pros and cons of these guidelines.

I created my own rules too. As a kid, I tired of the reactionary phrase "when you assume, you make an ass of you and me." As an adult, I would avoid "I assume," and always say "I presume." That did mean that I needed some level of information so that I really was able to presume.

There are other words I avoid. I didn't like the verb "stress." Instead, I use the word "emphasize." I must work harder to eliminate the verb phrase "has been" or the word "mean."

One rule above all others: Be consistent with whatever approach you take. Even if you are writing a book where each chapter (or chapter section) might use a different approach or genre of writing. Try to be true to that chapter (or section).

○ ○ ○ ○ ○ ○

When preparing to do something for the first time, it makes sense to study those who have gone before you. My brief drum 'n' bass period was spawned after Cleopatra head Brian Perera responded to my self-released Spaceship Eyes CD with a call to do drum 'n' bass. I probably asked Brian for input, as well as Kim Cascone (the owner of Silent Records, who I was doing music with, in Thessalonians and Spice Barons). I used the Alta Vista search engine (which now redirects to Yahoo! Search). The Tower Records store located a few blocks from the university had a drum 'n' bass section. So did the smaller record shops.

The cover of *World Dance, The Drum + Bass Experience* CD caught my eye: A yellow image of Europe and Africa from space, immersed in a sea of orange, with a futuristic gyroscope at the center, its rotor a spiked ball. "Scratched by DJ Hype and Ellis Dee." I bought this CD and a DJ Hype double vinyl album.

The music was enlightening. You could do anything within the jagged landscape of this genre. Rhythms fast and hectic, traversed with deep bass synths and keyboard chutes and ladders, seeded with samples from our world and others.

I proceeded to do an experimental version of drum 'n' bass, weaving in space rock and ethno-ambient approaches I had learned with Thessalonians. Was it good drum 'n' bass? Probably not. It was something more, very different. One of my workmates at the time, Jon Leidecker (a.k.a. future Wobbly) used to say "It just is what it is. It's what you do. Spaceship Eyes!"

○ ○ ○ ○ ○ ○

By 2024, I decided to write a book. In preparation, I read the second edition of Paul Sears' *Angels & Demons at Play*.

Paul regularly contributed drum parts to Spirits Burning long distance, and we were part of the Clearlight *Impressionist Symphony* album I produced. I also read *Chasing Shadows: The Search for Rod Evans* (the first Deep Purple singer), published by Stairway Press, the publisher of Paul's book and eventually mine.

Paul played drums in The Muffins. That band was part of a music scene in Maryland that included my cousin Ernie, who played in Mars Everywhere, and the label that became Cuneiform. (The Muffins' *Manna/Mirage* back cover graphics and postcard were by Ernie's sister, my cousin Diane.)

o o o o o o

When I visited my sister in New Mexico a few years ago, she planned a Saturday night Italian dinner for me and two of her friends. Cindi alerted them ahead of time that I was quiet and shy. After the dinner, and probably by the time I was out of town, her friend told her: "Cindi, your brother is not shy and quiet."

o o o o o o

My thesis is titled *In Case of Ritual*. A basic way to weave my music interests (Hawkwind) and fiction interests (Michael Moorcock) into a scholastic book title. Hawkwind had a song titled *Sonic Attack*, which begins "In case of sonic attack." The lyrics for that song written (and sometimes performed onstage) by Michael Moorcock.

After the title, it reads "a creative work submitted to the faculty of San Francisco State University in partial fulfillment of the requirements for the degree—Master of Arts in English: Creative Writing."

I'm surprised it next says by "Donald Marino Falcone." I never liked the name Donald. I only use it when forced to, for example for licenses and health care. The Marino part: I am not surprised. A nod to my father and his first name.

On the Certification of Approval page, there are three signatures.

- Stan Rice, Professor of Creative Writing. I took at least one course with Stan. One time, we had his class off-campus, at his house. I remember his wife and son momentarily passing us by and leaving the house. He commented that his wife was working on a novel. His wife was Anne Rice, the author of *Interview with a Vampire* and other vampire diaries.
- Frances Mayes, Lecturer, Creative Writing. As mentioned before, Frances was my advisor. She also helped me immensely on the other requirement: an oral exam. You chose three authors to study and then talk about. Together, we decided that I should concentrate on the works of John

Ashbery, William Butler Yeats, and James Joyce. Yeats was perhaps an odd choice, although there could be a pastoral wave outside the industrial and city side of my poems. Joyce was more obvious, given the journeys and experimentation. I can say that I've read Finnegan's Wake word for word multiple times. I'm not sure if that gets me anything. The oral exam turned out to be more of a struggle than expected. I had to take the exam a second time; after I recovered from an unexpected moment of failure.

- Dan Langton, Professor of English and Creative Writing. I had taken a writing course with Dan in my first semester at SF State.

In October of 1980, one of my classes had an assignment to provide a collection of poetry for the teacher to review. I presented poems I wrote at Shippensburg, including some that had been in the *Reflector*.

My teacher wrote:

> *There is no question. You are a talented poet, bursting with energy, already committed (Especially in subject matter) to paths that make a career possible.*
>
> *I think (I hope) you are very young. At least, most of the things I don't want to see happening are things the very young do.*
>
> *Like:*
>
> *Sometimes you reach for language rather than letting it come from the poem itself (cauldron-lifeblood).*
>
> *Sometimes you have the nerve (usually a good trait) to think you can get away with anything = even that first kiss Laura crap.*
>
> *Sometimes you don't know that you have exhausted yourself and the poem.*
>
> *Sometimes your fine sense of humor (humour?) results in private jokes.*
>
> *Sometimes a sweet ignorance won't let you see the*

difference between a poem and a notebook jotting.
Notwithstanding, they are the mistakes you <u>should</u> be
making. I probably have more sense to write In A Ballad
[one of the poems submitted], but poetry doesn't need to
make sense, and you were right to do it. The remarkable
sense of energy hides so many mistakes.
BUT

  That does not mean the mistakes should continue to
be made.

  I don't think they will be. I think you are coming.

o o o o o o

Six years later, before the acknowledgements and Table of Contents, the thesis includes a brief statement from me.

  Sometimes we lean to the left. Sometimes we step to the
  right. I have always believed the best of these motions to
  be alive and relaxed. Each spoken word is capable of
  easing or exploding into life, into calm. This is the
  setting for the work which follows.

And one more time, Stan Rice's signature; dated 12/4/86.

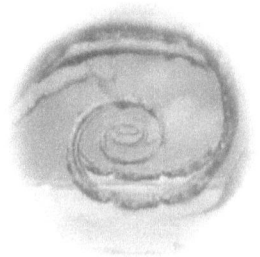

Sending Out Invitations

Calling All Space Rock Artists!

I'm contacting you because I'd like to invite you to be part of a different kind of space rock experience, under the group banner of Spirits Burning.

I've always believed that space rock fans and musicians are a special lot, that inherently believe the world can be a better place, and that it's possible for all of us to join together in our dreams...

I want Spirits Burning to be a place for those who are spirited and passionate about space rock, experimentation, and interacting musically in new, enjoyable ways...This invite is for you, or your group, to participate in any manner that you choose...

Over and out,
Don Falcone

SINCE THE FIRST invite, over 290 people have contributed to Spirits Burning (which I often abbreviate as SB). The 1999 debut album includes Steven Wilson (Porcupine Tree) and Daevid Allen (Gong). The second album incorporates poetry readings of Hawkwind singer Robert Calvert (posthumously) into two songs, courtesy of his wife Jill. Science fiction and fantasy writer/musician Michael Moorcock and former Hawkwind singer Bridget Wishart officially debut on the fourth release. Over the course of subsequent decades, solo artists and family members of Hawkwind, Blue Öyster Cult, Clearlight, and many other bands answer the call.

Considerations

After the first two albums, I reworked the invite. To inspire interest and add resume-style weight, I began listing other musicians on the candidate song (or album). I promised everyone a copy of the CD when released. Starting with the third album (*Found in Nature*), I also promised to give writing credits to everyone on a song. Worthwhile if the song gets airplay or sync usage in film or TV—which equates to money via a performing rights society.

(In the liner notes, I began listing the musicians who started the song first, followed by "with <the names of the other musicians>." To acknowledge who originated the piece.)

Sometimes I provide the in-progress song upfront. Sometimes I wait until an affirmative response. I used to send a compressed file (mp3) or mail a physical CD-R. Nowadays, I provide a link to the song on Dropbox (or other preferred cloud storage service, such as WeTransfer). I typically provide 44.1 kHz/24-bit files: better than the 44.1/16-bit standard established for CDs. I avoid compressed files; I found the invitee's resultant recorded part for it might sound slightly out of time when imported into my session as a clip. When that did happen, I highlighted the clip and moved it in the timeline.

Once onboard, I provide multiple mixes if applicable (for example, for a vocalist to hear my temp vocals separately, or to have the instrumental version to sing to).

Before the invitee records or delivers parts, I tell them that I can accept up to 96 kHz sample rate/24-bit resolution files (although most musicians send 44.1 or 48 kHz files).

Additionally, I request a quick mix of the song with their parts. This is primarily for syncing purposes—to know where their parts fit in the timeline—for example, if they didn't start at my zero point, the place where the song starts in my digital session. The quick mix also lets me hear how they envision their part in context.

Questions

Is this an opportunity to collaborate with musicians and sounds of one's youth, artists who were on albums you bought?

(For example, four of the five original members of Blue Öyster Cult; three musicians from the Van der Graaf *Vital* era, three of the first five Hawkwind bassists, which includes Paul Rudolph, who appeared on the initial Brian Eno albums.)

Will other musicians who have recorded with or played live with major artists be willing to participate?

(For example, Simon House played violin with Hawkwind, David Bowie, and on Thomas Dolby's *Blinded by Science*; singer/songwriter Keith Christmas played acoustic guitar on Bowie's *Space Oddity* album; Vibrators guitarist John Ellis played guitar on Peter Gabriel's 1984 China tour; wind/reed player Theo Travis of Gong and Soft Machine was also part of Pink Floyd guitarist David Gilmour's live ensemble.)

Is this a place to play with like-minded independent artists?

(For example, drummer Paul Williams of Quarkspace, who attends Strange Daze 99; multi-instrumentalist Pierce McDowell of Azigza who gives shelter to Daevid Allen when he visits San Francisco; Scott Heller, who asks for permission to use the word collective as his Øresund Sound Collective begins taking shape; vocalist Erin Bennett of EBB, a band that opens for Hawkwind and is contacted via Facebook.)

Will there be happy accidents, unexpected groupings of musicians (like Eno solo albums gathering musicians from Hawkwind, King Crimson, The Pink Fairies); or the antinuclear campaign single released under the name The Radio Actors, featuring Sting and four future SB contributors (Steve Hillage, Mike Howlett, Nik Turner, Harry Williamson)?

(For example, the song *We Move You* bringing together Hawkwind's Nik Turner, Robert Berry of 3—a band with Keith Emerson and Carl Palmer—Paul Sears, the drummer of The Muffins, bassist William Kopecky, guitarist Jay Tausig and me, on keyboards; *Our Crash* opening the *Starhawk* album with family members of Yes,

Counting Crows, Van der Graaf Generator, Flame Tree, and Grindlestone, with folk artist Nigel Mazlyn Jones on vocals; songs across the Spirits Burning *Evolution Ritual* album showcasing violinists—David Cross, once of King Crimson, Peter Knight and Jessie Mae Smart, from two different generations of Steeleye Span, Hoshiko Yamane of Tangerine Dream, and Darryl Way who played in Curved Air alongside future Police drummer Stewart Copeland.)

Can musicians no longer in the public view, and maybe no longer performing be brought onboard?

(For example, Ursula Pank, formerly Ursula Smith, the cellist in an early version of Third Ear Band, the band that later did the soundtrack for Roman Polanski's *Macbeth*; and Bridget Wishart, who performed with Hawkwind in the early 90s and was no longer actively singing when invited to SB.)

Can writers be included in this collective?

(For example, Michael Moorcock, author of the Elric novels and *The Dancers at The End of Time* trilogy; and Mack Maloney, author of *Starhawk*.)

Will any releases focus on a collaboration with a specific musician?

(For example, Spirits Burning & Bridget Wishart, Spirits Burning & Thom the World Poet, Spirits Burning & Michael Moorcock, Spirits Burning & Clearlight, Spirits Burning & Daevid Allen.)

Would a musician be more likely to say yes if they are a fan of the collaboration?

(For example, musicians like Albert Bouchard and Jsun Atoms, who are fans of Michael Moorcock.)

Can a dog be invited?

(For example, our dog Indy providing growls and barking for a cover of Hawkwind's *High Rise*, based on a J.G. Ballard novel that has a dog in it.)

Can a music collective be an advocate for the space rock genre and its community, bringing that community together?

(For example, gathering musicians from across that community on an individual song, sometimes pairing a musician with another musician they are fans of or are influenced by; promoting a musician by listing in the liner notes their sightings—their bands or other musical adventures.

Could this project celebrate space rock past? And take it to new places?

(For example, the opening song of *Reflections in A Radio Shower* with poetry and samples from Hawkwind's history; the song *Drive-By Poetry* featuring the poetry of Robert Calvert and others, while the music combines a demo song by SF band Kameleon with newer instrumentation.)

Can the definition of space rock be expanded to include other genres?

(For example, progressive rock, psychedelic rock, acid rock, ambient, rock in opposition, art rock, folk rock, post rock.)

Would patience be required?

(For example, a recording session with Michael Moorcock waits until he is back in the states; a musician like bassist William Kopecky must finish a tour; some musicians take a year to deliver their parts for reasons unknown.)

Would rejection happen?

(For example, the quiet after Richie Blackmore's manager is contacted; a musician says their current label will not allow them to participate; a local musician questions the worth of being involved, a musician says no because of the presence of another musician; or Lemmy does not answer yes after a cohort gives him a tape with an in progress song while Lemmy is playing pinball at a club prior to a live performance, and another time a coworker who is in a band with Lemmy's engineer, gives a CD-R to his engineer.)

Would any musicians ever change their yes response?

(For example, David Cousins publicly announces an end to Strawbs live shows due to health reasons and bows out of singing a song for a *Dancers* album, or Arthur Brown says yes, and then loses interest as recording details become complicated.)

Would any musicians ever change their no response?

(For example, former Pink Fairies Andy Colquhoun decides against playing guitar for a Falcone/Kazala song called *Bourgeoisie* because the rhythm of the in-progress mix is bad—it was, I was still learning—and years later is happy to contribute guitar to the Spirits Burning & Michael Moorcock song *Peace and Love*.)

Would any musicians fail to contribute because they died?

(For example, Mick Farren is onboard for singing *Bourgeoisie* or Demis Russos, the voice of Aphrodite's Child and Blade Runner, is about to be sent a song to consider contributing to.)

Will there be new musicians with each release?

(For example, the fourth Spirits Burning & Michael Moorcock album introduces these musicians to the crew: singer Roz Bruce, guitarist Andy Colquhoun, vocalist Mr. Dibs, guitarist Andy Glass, synth player Scott Heller, bassist Niall Hone, singer Susie Loraine, guitarist Nick Salomon, and singer Alisa Wood)

Can a group really be part of this collaboration?

(For example, ST37 does a cover of Don Falcone's *Future Memories*, and provides snippets of jams that are incorporated into the song *Alpha Harmony*; Malcolm Mooney donates a song from his last album; Pat Thomas and Mushroom—with a lineup that includes Jon Birdsong who played with Beck—provide access to multi-track jams that can be reworked to support additional musicians, such as *Logger's Revenge*, which adds the voice of Hawkfan scribe Brian Tawn.)

Can the collective be a global one?

(For example, from Michael Clare when he lived in Hawaii to Melodic Energy Commission's Don Xaliman in Canada to Cyrille Verdeaux when he lived in Brazil to Richard Chadwick in England to G. C. Neri in Italy to Twink in Morocco to Alisa Coral in Moscow to Harry Williamson in New Zealand to Daevid Allen in Australia.)

Would having 40 musicians on an album create unexpected costs?

(For example, the promise of a CD for each contributor affects the budget...postage from the U.S. to Europe and surrounding countries is at least $20 in 2024, such that mailing CDs to 20 musicians overseas eclipses $400; U.S. mailings add dollars, although the media mail designation keeps the cost reasonable; labels now provide less free artist copies, less copies to buy at artist pricing, such that some copies must be purchased directly from the label at retail.)

Can an independent musician build a home studio with gear capable of supporting albums with 30-40 musicians on it?

(For example, by working at audio companies such as Digidesign/Avid or Orban and having access to professional equipment, or the ability to purchase the equipment at a reduced price.)

Can recording be done locally?

(For example, when Daevid Allen or Nik Turner tour the West Coast, or Cyrille visits his daughter, or any local musician—like violinist Craig Fry, guitarist Jerry Jeter, guitarist Doug Erickson, or percussionist Sam Herzberg—is available to record at my home studio; or recording Michael Moorcock reading from his book during a Zoom call.)

Can recording be done remotely?

(For example, flying to Texas to record Michael Moorcock at his home, or having former Avid coworker Nick Pellicciotto who lives near Mike do the session per detailed instructions; giving Daevid Allen Avid hardware and software to let him record in Australia at his leisure; working with any musician who can record their own parts.)

Will record labels be interested?

(For example, France's Gazul likes the mix of space and progressive sounds of the first two albums; Italy's Mellow Records releases SB and two other Falcone projects; Black Widow responds affirmatively to the mix of heavier space rock and Moorcock songs of the fourth album—even doing a double vinyl version; Voiceprint— later reborn as Gonzo—offers a monetary advance and multiple album contract culminating in a boxed package with CDs, posters and stickers; Cleopatra releases SB music in three formats—CD, vinyl, and digital.)

Can albums be instrumental or vocal?

(For example, primarily instrumental Spirits Burning & Clearlight albums that feature keyboardist Cyrille Verdeaux, and the vocal-based SB albums that adapt a novel—*Starhawk* and *Dancers at The End of Time*—or albums showcasing former Hawkwind singer Bridget Wishart.)

Will there ever be an album that requires self-release?

(For example, the SB acoustic-based album *Evolution Ritual*, which some labels dismiss because it isn't spacey, and Cleopatra feels the timing is too close to the previous release.)

Will there be re-releases?

(For example, as SB albums return their rights to its captain, each album is re-released as a digital album on bandcamp.com and then queued for streaming on Amazon Music, Tidal, Apple Music, and elsewhere.

Will there ever be a live version?

(For example, for a 2017 UK festival performance with a band featuring three Hawkwind family members: Richard Chadwick, Bridget Wishart, Steve Bemand.)

Does Spirits Burning survive for decades?

(From 1998 to 2024, 17 studio albums, one EP, four best of compilations—one under the name daevid allen & don falcone—and one live album, with plans for future albums, including *The End of All Songs - Part 2*, a new collaboration with Bridget Wishart, a Spirits Burning & David Jackson album.)

Yes!

Tips—Stage Props

The earliest known use of the term "properties" in English to refer to stage accessories is in the 1425 CE morality play, 'The Caster of Perseverance.' [2]

I WAS THE bass player for Kameleon from 1981 to 1985. I sang most of the vocal songs. I occasionally moved to the left side of our drummer and played a keyboard (a string ensemble, later replaced by a Roland Juno-60 synthesizer).

My keyboard stand was a five-foot-high brown, wooden crate used to carry equipment. It had the drawing of a small chameleon taped to its side, the artwork by Tony Garay. Tony worked with me at The Pizza Boat, first the one at SF State and then the one downtown.

Tony was also the bassist in a punk band called U-Jackal. Karen and I once saw them play in someone's backyard. The hit of the day was a performance of their thrashy original number *I Smoke Marijuana*. Karen thinks it was one chord. I think two. The song is a continuous drive of eighth notes, with the only words an infinite chorus of "I smoke marijuana."

At some point, other people in attendance formed a line leading up to the mic, for their chance to confess that they too smoked marijuana.

Cathartic punk at its best.

---

[2] from Wikipedia (https://en.wikipedia.org/wiki/Prop)

Don on Bass at the Civic Center Gig, 5 September 1983

Years later, Tony joined The Lewd. This band included guitarist Bobby Clic, who was in Melting Euphoria after my time there. Bobby was in the longest running version of that band, and he and I are now admins for the Melting Euphoria Facebook page. We have never met.

o o o o o o

By the Fall of 1985, I had made the switch to keyboards only. I added a Sequential Circuits Six-Trak, often to do left-hand bass parts, and I had to buy a keyboard stand to support two keyboards. Onstage, I was tied to the stand and its keyboards.

There were moments where I sang a song center stage, behind a mic stand, with no instrument near me. It might have been the last version of Kameleon.

I was now playing keyboards, and we had a new bass player; guitarist Joe Diehl brought in a friend of his, Adam Stein. Or, it might have been the next band, an early version of Spirits Burning that had two keyboardists (with the addition of Paul Reynolds from The Employees, a band that had the same sound person).

It was in one of these lineups that I used a prop for a song I wrote.

The Unknown

I choose my place, outline of flesh
remember my name,
purpose of fame
to dance around the spin of birth

Comes the flash,
new lease on life
stir to wake, pause to love
I like the feel for what it's worth
  I like the feel for what it's worth

We take from the hand
and give to the world the unknown

When we like the night
we like the moves
  we know we're right
when we forfeit our dues
we want to hold it all for all time

Control of ease
on top of the world
get to the soul and make it roll
knowing it all makes it fine
  knowing it all makes it fine

We take from the hand
  and give to the world the unknown

What works for years should work for less
What's in your heart is the place to start

and the words you choose should never lose
   because gods they come and gods they go . . .
into the unknown

I choose my place…

We take from the hand
   and give to the world the unknown

The prop: I thought it would be interesting to shower the audience with a bit of "the unknown." For this magic, a handful of Starburst candies could be the perfect visual accompaniment. If you don't know Starbursts, they are small square-shaped chewables of different flavors, wrapped in paper the same color as the intended fruit flavor.

At some point during the song, I had a handful of Starbursts in my right hand. As I sang the final "We take from the hand," my left hand reached into my right hand and grabbed the Starbursts. Then, as I sang "and give to the world," I raised my left arm slightly upward, a half foot or so from my left ear, and continued moving my arm backwards. My left hand now slightly tilted downward. It was all reminiscent of when I pitched as a 12-year-old for the Steelton Coal and Oil baseball team that my dad sponsored and my brother Rich coached. We won the championship that year.

Now, as I sang "the" and the first syllable of "unknown," my windup moved towards completion, as my arm, still above my head, came forward. It was then, and only then, as I sang the second syllable—"known" —that I released the Starbursts into the audience.

I used this prop a couple of times. Each time was at the Mab (The Fabulous Mabuhay Gardens, located in North Beach). Known for punk bands: Flipper, The Dead Kennedys, The Lewd. The owner, Ness Aquino, was open to any local band, though; this was a place every struggling band had to play or could play.

After the lights went on and our band came out to tear down and pack our gear, I remember jumping off the stage and surveying things. There was a yellow Starburst here, an orange one a few feet away, a green one over there. All of them still wrapped. Maybe this wasn't working. Maybe no one was interested.

Still, I persisted. If nothing else, there would be this weird moment where the audience would wonder: Did I see something fly from his hand? There were rows of seats, starting about 10-15 feet from the stage. After one show, I found a Starburst had travelled well beyond the first row. I was gaining confidence.

I always felt it easy to emote during this song. It was in my range. I found it easy to yell the final lines. I would sing *The Unknown* years later at Kozfest 2017, minus the prop, but full of lots of hand and arm motions. Plus, I would change the line "because gods they come and gods they go" to "because gods and goddesses come, and gods and goddesses go."

The last time I used the prop, I had to go to a plan B. I had forgotten to purchase any Starbursts that day. I had a free moment before the gig. I left the club and walked around Broadway—the street The Mab was on, and at that time, the red-light district of San Francisco. In search of a store that had Starbursts, I came up empty.

Until I found another space candy. It seemed perfect. A Milky Way. Truly, a natural accompaniment for "the unknown."

When the set reached *The Unknown* that night, I took my spot at center stage, behind the mic stand. I performed as usual, this time taking the Milky Way from my right hand, winding back, and then lofting it into the audience. I was aware that this wasn't a few small Starbursts, so I made sure to loft it with ease, kind of like throwing a knuckle ball, or a baseball player throwing a foul ball into the stands.

When the set ended and the lights went on, I jumped off the stage and went towards the front row seats to talk to friends who had come to support us. An attractive girl who I didn't know came up to me. I was excited. It wasn't often that this happened after one of our shows. She said "hi." I said "hi." I probably was blushing. She then asked: "Why did you hit me in the head with a Milky Way?"

Taking Off with Me Onboard

IN 2017, SPIRITS BURNING (SB) performed live in the U.K. twice.

Creating a Live Band

You can take your studio project and catalog of songs, gather crew members to form a live ensemble, and then perform at a festival.

About This Task

- Most of the steps in this procedure are applicable for a band that plays live regularly.
- Many of the steps can be done in a different sequence, or can be done multiple times, to taste.

Prerequisites

- Band or studio project
- Catalog of songs

Procedure

1. Get a gig.
   a. Identify a viable gig (such as a UK festival).
   b. Contact the organizers and sign a contract.
   c. (Optional) Add a warmup gig at another venue.
2. Fill out the band line-up.
   Important: Be prepared for changes to the band line-up.
3. Select Songs
4. Practice
   a. Set up practices in the area with the most band members.
   b. Record practices.
      Tip: Consider filming the practice.
   c. For any remote members, share practice audio files, and have them do a quick mix incorporating their parts.
   d. Set up at least one dress rehearsal practice for the full band.
5. Work out travel and housing plans.
6. Do a dress rehearsal.
7. (Optional) Play warmup gig.
8. Get to the festival.
   (Recommended) Enjoy the festival.
   (Recommended): Sell merchandise.
9. Perform.
10. Complete post-performance steps.
    a. Get paid.
    b. Do a band photo.
    c. Return home.

What to Do Next

- Release a live album. This includes collecting audio and video files, addressing any issues, mixing the audio, and finding a label to release the album.
- (Optional) Release videos.

Meeting Prerequisites

By 2016, SB had recorded 13 studio albums, 200 songs.

Getting a Gig

I first thought about a 21st century SB live ensemble when working with Cyrille Verdeaux. When it became clear that I couldn't assemble a band in time for his next visit to the Bay Area, I communicated some future possibilities to Bridget Wishart while we were developing our third Spirits Burning & Bridget Wishart album.

10 June 2012

I can see creating 1 or 2 bands that meet monthly or bi-monthly and slowly learn the songs and each other. I've also thought about doing something in the UK with you (Martin? Jasper? and?) as a one-off someday…a dream.

I returned to the subject 3 1/2 years later, the day before Bridget's birthday.

24 February 2016

Not sure if this qualifies as a birthday gift…Karen and I will be visiting England in 2018. It'll be part of my 'year I turn 60' present.

Besides the social, food, and surroundings side of a vacation, there are some early thoughts, possibilities about playing an SB gig. Getting there a week or so early, practicing, maybe/maybe not doing a club gig ahead of time.

> *So... I have a couple of big quests for you: Would you*
> *be up for performing some of the songs? If you had to pick*
> *four or so SB&BW or other songs, what would they be?*
> *Of the space-based festivals, which would you recommend*
> *(most people, best vibes, etc.)? Off the top of your head,*
> *what musicians might you suggest I reach out to? (I'm*
> *thinking Kev, Steve Bemand, maybe Ken Pustelnik. I*
> *suspect Paul Sears would be willing to travel. It turns out*
> *that Doug E. here might also be willing to travel too.*

Bridget's first thought included Kozfest. Compared to other festivals, they "are more festivally."

Due to other ongoing life and music priorities, we didn't discuss the idea of a UK gig for seven months.

3 October 2016

Bridget informs me that Chumley Warner Bros. (her project with her husband Martin Plumley), have a slot for the July 2017 Kozfest festival. Plus, her and Ian Abrahams will be there for a signing of their *Festivalized* book. Martin suggests that he, Bridget, Steve (Bemand), and I do some SB songs that the Chumleys regularly perform, and then have a larger SB line-up continue from there.

This is a year ahead of my schedule. I had wanted more time to coordinate work schedules, vacation plans, managing ongoing music projects (albums), and getting a band together. Bridget can't guarantee that Chumleys will get a 2018 slot. 2017 seems like a better opportunity, having Chumleys and SB play on the same day, if I can get the gig.

7-9 October 2016

Bridget contacts Paul Woodwright (who does Kozfest booking) and tells him I'm interested in a gig. While waiting to hear back, I share with Doug Erickson online reviews and YouTube performances from Kozfest past. We discuss airfare costs and how long we'd stay in the UK.

17 October 2016

Having not heard back from Paul, I contact him directly. Within two days, Paul responds. They have a Friday afternoon slot available; a different day from Chumleys, plus it probably would have less people present. Bridget confirms my concerns. Most people get to the festival Friday night. Disappointed, Bridget and I start thinking about 2018.

22 October 2016

Silence, or my slowness in replying to Paul (mainly due to me being busy) seems to have some level of power. Paul now offers a Saturday 1:50 to 2:50 slot, and more money to cover costs. The gig is on!

Filling Out the Band Line-up

Before we had a gig, I started a discussion with Bridget regarding the band line-up.

5 October 2016

I would need a UK band (or collection of UK musicians) willing to learn x number of songs, and then I can play additional keys, and/or sing a number or two, and add a guest or two.

For the SB/BW pieces, we would need to figure out how best for me and Steve B (if he's a yes) to fit in (and that's a good discussion for another day). I suspect that Doug won't be able to make the trip, but that's still up in the air. He's concerned about committing and then pulling out and its effect on the gig.

Bridget told me there was no contract and all bands got the same pay (although Paul would offer me more, given my travel costs).

Most of our probable band members lived near each other. Bridget, Martin, Steve, and Jasper (Pattison) lived in Bath, and could possibly rehearse with Silas (who played drums in Citizen Fish,

Jasper's band). Otherwise, I had two plan Bs: Invite people closer to California that already play together or bring together Americans like Doug Erickson (California) and Paul Sears (a few states away). Plan C: Look deeper at my contacts in Europe. England's Kev Ellis was a good vocalist consideration too, if we did any songs that he had sung (like *Alien Injection*).

3-4 November 2016

With the gig confirmed, I send emails to guitarist Steve Bemand and bassist Jasper Pattison. I cover the date, payment, and needing a band.

> *Bridget, Martin, and I will play 15 minutes of a one-hour set. The other 45 minutes will be the 'band'. To make this happen, I would like to get a UK-based group together, say guitar-bass-drums.*
>
> *Together, we could pick songs from the SB catalog, and then have the group practice between now and then at their leisure. (I envision the trio shaping the songs, and then sending me rough mixes to practice to, and I can send back what I'm planning on doing.) I could then arrive the week of the gig for a practice or two.*
>
> *I would bring one keyboard and a computer to cover keys, and I'd plan on singing 1-2 songs (maybe Hawkwind's High Rise). Additionally, there is a possibility that I will be accompanied by a guitarist (Doug Erickson), who could handle extra rhythm, fxs, and so on.*

Steve responds the same day. He is in. The next day, Steve tells me that he is with Hawkwind drummer Richard Chadwick, and he would be up for playing drums if I was interested.

I respond. "That would be quite amazing. Let's say yes. Absolutely." As the clock turns to my November 5 birthday, I tell Bridget "I think I'm speechless."

7-10 November 2016

Jasper isn't available for Kozfest. He is in two other bands doing other festivals. Soon after, Steve procures bassist Colin Kafka for our band, and I get Kev Ellis onboard to sing 2-3 songs. Bridget okays having Steve and Colin play on the three SB/Chumley songs with her and Martin.

We have our first band line-up: Bridget (Vocals, EWI), Colin (Bass), Kev (Vocals), Martin (Acoustic Guitar, Backing Vocals), Richard (Drums) Steve (Electric Guitar), and me (Keys, Vocals).

Steve shares that Richard is concerned about Hawkwind scheduling a late July gig. Due to that and other reasons, he recommends we not mention his involvement yet, and investigate a deputy drummer, just in case.

In March 2017, I see a post that Hawkwind may have a Devon get-together in July or August. My fingers are crossed that they steer clear of Kozfest weekend.

Karen decides to not accompany me, to save money, and to stay at home with our dog daughter, Kiara.

Selecting Songs

Early November 2016

With Steve onboard and confirmed as my main band contact, we begin discussing songs for the set. I post to Dropbox 26 songs for consideration. About twice as many as we need.

Vocal Songs

For Bridget, I include songs she suggested.

- *Crafted From Wood*
- *Journey Past the Stars*
- *Earth Born*

For my vocal songs, I choose ones I'm comfortable singing.

- *High Rise* (This is a Hawkwind song that SB did for a tribute album, with Doug on rhythm and lead guitar.)
- *Strafed By A UFO*
- *The Hawk* (I tell Steve the studio version is "a bit dicey. I could have done a better production job. Not really pushing this one, but if it grabs everyone…)"
- *The Real Time* (A song where I can sing and play organ.)
- *The Unknown* (I write "I would love to sing this one live. I didn't do the version here, but have long, long ago.")

Instrumentals

One song here—By Design—is the one instrumental that I absolutely want us to do.

- *Alchemy*
  A Daevid Allen Weird Quartet version, and I used to play it in SB 80s. If we did it…I could play organ. However, it could also be our Born to Be Wild moment, where I play distorted bass—if one is available for me—and start the piece off with the slow part. There are other versions of this…from the 80s that might be worthwhile for you to hear.
- *Augustus*
- *Black Squirrel at The Root of The Staircase* (Steve played on the studio version)
- *Burning Bush*
- *By Design*
- *Rolling Out* (Of all the candidate instrumentals that will not make the set, this one came the closest to surviving.)
- *Second Degree Soul Sparks*
- *Snakebite Serum*

For Kev

*One song here—Alien Injection—is the one vocal song that
I absolutely want us to do.*

- *I Have Two Names*
- *Live Forever* ("This could be a killer piece.")
- *My Life of Voices*
- *Alien Injection*
- *Stand and Deliver* (The original featured Kev and Bridget. Kev
  mentions this is a fun one for him. Plus, if we did it, Bridget
  could join in.)

Other Vocal Songs

*These are here to see if any spark an interest and seem
more interesting than the songs above. If we did any of
these, Kev or I would sing.*

- *Our Crash*
- *JigSaw Man Flies a JigSaw Ship*
- *We Move You*
- *New Religion*
- *In The Future* (The only unreleased song; planned for a future
  Spirits Burning & Michael Moorcock album)

*None of the songs must be the exact length as the studio
versions. I'm open to you and the band rethinking and
reinterpreting them. Whatever can pump new life into
them.*

*When we get to ordering things, it would be nice to
end with something where Bridget (EWI/backing
vocals), Martin, and Kev are involved. Maybe something
that has a great anthem chorus.*

16-18 November 2016

Steve dives into the candidate songs. For each, he deciphers the song key, and marks whether the song can be played live easily or would be trickier. Two of the tricky songs are instrumentals: *By Design* and *Snakebite Serum*. For the former, he notes: It has a "very tricky intro timing." It would take some work.

Bridget verifies Chumley versions of the three SB songs are different than the studio versions. Her and Martin can record their version for reference.

24 November 2016

With the set list in flux, Steve meets with Colin to go through the non-Bridget songs, with plans to connect with Richard the following Sunday. Colin loves *By Design*.

As we discuss whittling down the number or length of songs to a manageable set time, Steve mentions deleting *The Hawk*, although he was drawn to it, and was keeping it in his playlist for now. In response, I suggest dropping *High Rise*, in favor of *The Hawk*, both of which are songs I can sing.

4 December 2016

Steve begins mapping the current candidate songs with chord progressions and lyrics (provided by Bridget and me). This includes the song *Live Forever*, which has these words by me:

They dress me up
With a uniform
Saying if you can get
  From point A to C
        You can live, live, live, live
        Live Forever

They're taking off
  With me onboard

That should come as no surprise
  When you're first to believe
        You can live, live, live, live
        Live Forever

Steve presents an initial set list, the three songs with Bridget and Martin now at the top of the set. (They were briefly in the middle.) Of note, Steve makes sure that we don't play songs in the same key back-to-back.

    The set list is five minutes over our allotted one hour.

Earth Born F#
Crafted From Wood E
Journey Past the Stars F#
The Unknown E
The Hawk Gm
By Design E
Snakebite Serum B
Alien Injection Em
My Life of Voices E
Our Crash G
Live Forever E
    Second Degree Soul Sparks
Stand and Deliver E

(We initially plan to perform *Second Degree* within *Live Forever* and including band intros. As the set develops, the two songs are kept separate; the band intros within a song idea is dropped or forgotten.)
    On the home front, I contact Doug.

> *Let me know if/when you're ready to get studio versions*
> *of the song to listen to, along with any help from me.*
> *Down the line, Steve will send their practice versions.*

13 December 2016

Kev mentions the Daevid Allen Kozmik Stage—where we will perform—provides all the bands with a digital multitrack of their set. I envision a live album.

15 December 2016

Steve completes most of the initial song maps and asks if all the tracks sync to BPMs. He was importing them into Cubase, his Digital Audio Workstation (DAW), and having trouble sussing out the speeds of some songs. He correctly deduces that some songs were recorded differently—typically, the songs from early SB albums (like *By Design*, *Snakebite Serum*, and *The Unknown*, all from the first album). These were from a time before I used Pro Tools and before I recorded to bar|beat sessions. I provide the BPMs for seven songs. I include "one evil thought": *My Life of Voices* BPM goes back and forth between various speeds.

28 December 2016

Steve tries to quantize the analog-based tracks to a BPM. With his tools, the original analog two tracks of songs like *By Design* warp out the sound too much. He decides to re-record the songs with his guitar parts and temp drums to set BPMs. This provides new reference songs for Richard, Colin, and everyone else.

Steve asks: "Who's playing guitar on *By Design*? Brilliant! What great solos." I report back in the affirmative and add: "One Joe Diehl."

Practicing (and Finalizing the Band Line-Up and Set List)

The calendar turned to 2017. We had almost seven months to dedicate to practicing the songs. There would be two types of practices. Acoustic practices at the Plumley's (Bridget and Martin's) house, and full band practices at a practice studio.

Kev didn't live in Bath like the rest of the UK band members.

He would attend less practices. In the meantime, Steve would sub for Kev and my vocals. This often limited what he could play on guitar during a practice.

Six of the practices with five or more band members were recorded, one of which included video. These recordings provided a snapshot of the band at different points in time: mid-February (two recordings), early March, early April, late June, and the fourth of July. We shared the recordings on Dropbox.

January 2017

In January, Steve creates a Facebook Messenger group chat that includes Bridget, Colin, Kev, and himself. Richard isn't on Facebook, so Steve communicates with him directly. Bridget represents herself and Martin.

I'm added to the group in February, representing Doug and myself. Before that, I communicate with Bridget, Steve, and others in separate Facebook chats and email. When I join the group, it is illuminating to read the group discussions prior to my presence.

I go offline the last two weeks of January as Karen and I fly to Asia for a vacation (Singapore, Thailand, Viet Nam).

28 January to 1 February 2017

Bridget confirms singing and playing on *Stand and Deliver*, and EWI on *Live Forever*.

There is concern about the more complicated songs. Steve confesses that he "rooted for *The Hawk* to be included," and although it's not so simple, it's not as complicated as *By Design*, which he can play after much practice. However, *My Life of Voices* is proving difficult for the rhythm section.

Meanwhile, Richard finds a cheap place to rehearse in Radstock—Rockaway Studio. Steve shares "It belongs to The Mob (the band, and not the criminal organization). The studio engineer Magnus is playing keyboards for the Hawks on the up-and-coming tour. It's great, £25 gets us all night if we need it, very cheap. A brilliant find."

Dave and Kris Brock give Hawkwind a few weeks off before their upcoming tour, so Richard is eager to get with Steve and Colin in Rockaway to sort out what they can achieve.

Still on the high seas in Asia, I email Steve: "If you haven't already, can you, Colin, and Richard discuss the set? Are there any songs not working, any too complicated, etc.?"

Steve reports back that Richard has doubts about *Snakebite Serum* and *My Life of Voices*. The latter song is noticeably never included in a practice recording. It will fall out of the setlist.... multiple times.

7-9 February 2017

Bridget suggests adding a Hawkwind song or Demented Stoats song (*So Alone*) that Richard knows.

Steve schedules sessions with Colin and Richard for Wednesday the 15th and Friday the 17th, and Bridget and Martin can make both— the first opportunity to do recordings and hear what the live band sounds like.

Steve and I plan a Skype meeting for the second weekend in February—we will finally meet, remotely.

Revisiting the Song List

Steve sends a revised set list noting vocalists. Three items catch my attention.

"The *Unknown* may have to transpose for Don as original is female voice": I find the comment funny. For Steve, the original is the 1999 album version with Karen singing. In the 80s, I sang it many times. All versions were in the same key—E.

"*Snakebite Serum* (substitute with *So Alone?*)": Steve includes this line twice, with two options for the placement of either song—next to another instrumental, *By Design*, or between two songs Kev sings. I definitely don't want to drop *Snakebite*. I envision it to be one of our best numbers live. I have less interest in doing a Demented Stoat song at the cost of losing an SB one. We will keep *Snakebite* next to *By Design*.

"*My Life of Voices* (may substitute *Images*)": I had already made the decision to ax *My Life*. *Images* made sense. Bridget and Richard did the original studio recording on Hawkwind's *Space Bandits* album. The three of them had performed it together on the tour promoting the album when Steve subbed for Dave Brock, who was unavailable.

12 February 2017

My first post to our Facebook Messenger group:

> *My guitar partner here is named Doug. He'll know within the next week if he can make the gig (he has family events before and after and may not be able to get out of work the week of the gig.)*
>
> *Steve is still holding on to the possibility of doing both Snakebite and My Life of Voices; Plus, I do see above the mention of both Images and the Stoats piece, which Steve mentioned to me.*
>
> *Let's see how the core band does with the two SB pieces this week (as well as the others) to see how they go.*
>
> *If we have room for a song not on the original set, I'm ok with one cover, whether it be the HW or DS piece.*
>
> *Also saw the note about doing a gig Wednesday nightish...I was originally planning on arriving in the UK late Monday the week of Kozfest, in time for a Tuesday practice. If we want to do a gig Wednesday night, and it is official, I can consider coming in a few days earlier, say in time for a couple of weekend practices, etc.*
>
> *Should add I probably need to know asap if we are doing a Wednesday night gig, as I'm working on airplane tix soon.*

Kev reports that SB is getting regular daytime play on local radio "here in Portsmouth" and that *My Life of Voices* is the fave choice.

One of the Spirits Burning

Steve responds:

> *I think the instruments and vocals in Voices are really integrated, counterpoint stuff n all, that's why it's a bit difficult to take it apart to learn. I "know" all the bits now but haven't managed to play it through on my own yet. I don't know if it has been performed live ever?, just gotta trim it down for a single guitar to play.*
>
> *I'm not surprised the track's popular, it's bloody well performed and recorded and produced too (with playback speed tricks!).*

I add:

> *My Life of Voices was originally two songs. The bookends were the intro/chorus of a simple punky new wave number called My Life. The guts (the chordal part and 8th note riff) was a piece called Voices.*
>
> *Both were performed live a dozen times in the 80s. I never thought of either as a complicated piece. Voices just has a bit of dynamics, given the one part is played heavy, then soft. (Otherwise, please ignore my speed tricks in the studio version. That was an evil thing on my part. If helpful, I can search and send a version from an 80's live performance.)*
>
> *Snakebite Serum...was played live a handful of times in the 90s. Two different drummers. One tried to approach it as a rock song and had trouble with it during his one live performance. The other drummer approached it more as a jam piece once you get past the tribal intro and did much better with it.*
>
> *The main point, which is stated above by a couple of people, is let's be flexible. If any pieces simply do not gel during early practices, we can drop them.*

15 February 2017

First almost full band practice. Rockaway has all the basics (stands, mixer, PA, mics).

The band just needs to bring milk, tea, mugs. Steve brings his mic and music stand, which he considers essential for early days of practice.

Everyone is happy with meeting one another and practicing. Steve's recordings have hiss issues. He had forgotten to do a recording check. The waves looked good; they were actually phone noise and not music. Then by chance, the ones the band listened to at the studio didn't have phone noise, or pops, or level issues.

I still enjoy listening to the practice from my home in California. I tell the band it is "kind of like an out of body experience on multiple levels."

I also note:

> *For Crafted: From what I heard on the first practice, it's blossomed into a fuller space folk piece. Really special. The one missing element is a bass (as I'm not hearing it and remember that was the plan.) What's your thoughts on asking Colin to play on it?*

The recording is really Bridget and Martin with Steve and Richard jamming along. I like the fuller sound. My suggestion helps to get Colin officially assigned to the song. (Eventually, he is added to all the opening songs.)

Rejiggering the Band

20 Feb 2017

Doug makes it official. He can't get the time off work. I will be traveling alone. I ask Steve to contact Cary Grace to play synth. We had become Facebook friends, and I notice her band is scheduled to play at Kozfest the day after us. Cary says yes.

I explain to the band that I'm playing "Keys: Some synth. Some organ. Some quarks. Some strangeness. I'm semi-concerned that we are missing a spacey element, as I typically don't do bubbly things. Or, less likely when I'm playing another key sound at the same time. Maybe I'm being overly concerned and we're fine if she's not available."

Steve adds:

> I agree some twitters and bubbles and swooshes are needed, in Timelords I set up long synth sounds and hit keys occasionally but it's good to have "played" synth not just ambience.

5 March 2017

This Rockaway practice is the first time the rhythm section works on *Alien Injection* (and *The Unknown* too). And they will give *My Life of Voices* one more shot.

The practice produces an almost complete set. Steve takes the recordings and uses SoundForge to edit and splice the best of each song to fix mistakes and create solid arrangements.

Steve reminds me that the actual performance takes up more time than the total song length; we should shoot for 55 minutes. I contact Paul of Kozfest to see if we can do 65-70 minutes; the answer is no.

Steve asks if I'm ok to sing *The Hawk*. "I think it's one that's been going well, fun to play." I said yes. He also suggests Cary might be good to sing *The Unknown*. Steve is still used to hearing the studio version with Karen. I reiterate my intent to sing both songs.

> The three of you seem to be clicking. It'll be interesting singing The Hawk. While I sang the studio version, I usually only did the intro back in the club scene day. It almost feels like it would be good to sing with a vocal effect (pitch doubler). Don't know if that would be easy to set up, etc. I always sang Unknown, until the original SB became a female vocal band. I'm much more

comfortable singing Unknown, and was looking forward to being out front for one number. Let's see how my vocals to your practice go, when I get around to recording it. Two, when you count Hawk.

I'm surprised to hear that the band hasn't practiced *Second Degree Soul Sparks* yet.

Cary's first practice with the band is on March 11.

○ ○ ○ ○ ○ ○

We continue our online discussions about whittling down the set list time, while noting which songs each person likes.

2-4 April 2017

Colin doesn't want to drop *By Design*, *Snakebite*, or *Images*, as the band plays them all well. Although *Stand and Deliver* is under-rehearsed and not sounding good, Steve notes that it is a "killer bouncy dancey fun last number," with Kev adding "fastest most rock n roll song in the set. Should be the set finisher I'd say. Also, the only one I sing with Bridget." Richard really likes Kev's singing, particularly on *Stand and Deliver*. And Steve really likes *The Hawk* too.

Steve writes:

Something will have to be dropped tho, as after latest adjustment it's at 1 hour 5 mins, and in "onstage time" that's about 1:10 or more probably. Don should have the veto really.

I respond:

Let's do a couple of things...let's stay the course...let's continue to work on all the songs we've been working on, with the plan to play all of them Wednesday night, and then be flexible on Saturday depending on when we start (5 or greater minutes early, on time, or late).

Second Degree Soul Sparks can be our wildcard. We can drop it on Saturday or play to the amount of extra time available. Let's do everything we can to not start late.

Around this time, I learn that band performances in the two main tents (Daevid Allen Kozmik Stage and Judge Trev Stage) overlap. Paul tells me the band playing before us, on the other stage, is from 1:10 to 2:10. At least a 20-minute overlap (with our 1:50 start time). On our stage, we will be preceded by Shom, ending at 1:10. That gives us a 40-minute changeover window. (Kev reveals he is singing with Shom, part of his effort to be in the most 2017 Kozfest bands.)

21 June 2017

I work out keyboard parts for *Crafted From Wood* as there were none on the original recording. I share a mix with Bridget; her and Martin like the keys I did on the intro a lot, and what I did in the verses. I then write to everyone.

> *I posted a Crafted From Wood wDon mp3 tonight. Bridget and Martin preflighted a listen to the intro, bridges, and verses. I've since done a new chorus part, and something during the guitar solos. The new chorus part mirrors the style of the intro. For the guitar solos...I improv'd a bit with modulated whole notes...emphasis on improv, as I'm not sure what patterns are being played. At the next practice, would it be possible to solidify the chords/roots for the solo sections? I hear the verse and chorus in the solo, but not necessarily at expected places. Thanks!*
>
> *One more item, based on a conversation with Bridget. For CFW, I think it makes sense for her and Martin to handle all the vocals, and I'll stick with keys for this one. That'll simplify our practice and gigs.*

It also means that I won't need a mic near my keyboard.

30 June 2017

We previously discussed me Skyping into practice so I could listen and meet everyone. And get a feel for people's "body lingo." However, the reception would be poor, along with an 8-hour time difference that meant I'd have to take a PTO (Personal Time Off) day at work.

We decide to film the end-of-June practice. Al Spangle acts as the tape operator and does the videotaping using an iPhone 4. This is the most important practice for me, as I can now see the band (minus Cary, who was unavailable). I do have to download the video from work; attempts via our 2017 home setup fail.

Early July 2017

The video and a subsequent audio recording of the 4 July practice provide clarity—what is working and what is maybe not.

I really like Kev's harp on *Crafted From Wood* and encourage him to keep that. The band agrees. However, I don't want him to play harp on *By Design*, which he did at the video practice. It gives a country flavor that feels out of place. Whereas his Kaoss Pad provides mystery and spaciness to each song it touches.

There are some songs that the band plays differently than the originals. For example, with *Live Forever*, there is a section where Steve and Colin play a different chord than my original studio keys. On inspection, I discover my original part was obscured by the mixer—one of the few SB songs I didn't mix. To simplify things, we agree that I'll change to what the rhythm section is now used to playing.

I love Richard's background vocals (especially in every even line of *The Unknown*) and tell Steve to encourage him to keep it up.

One issue I find while playing my parts to the recording of *Stand and Deliver* is Richard's drums. He isn't doing the syncopated kick, and it alters the feel drastically. He plays the whole piece with toms, instead of hi-hat, which is fine, just too straight ahead.

I write: "The last practice version remains the hardest to play to. My intro triplets need "Mickey you're so fine," which sounds really sad to say…"

Band Final Line-up (and Timing Is Everything)

In late February, we procure a warmup gig in Bath, at the Widcombe Social Club. The Wednesday before Kozfest.

5 April 2017

Cary announces that she can't make the Bath gig due to intensive rehearsals for her band and The Luck of Eden Hall band, both of whom are playing at Kozfest. "Hopefully Kev can do some bleeps and sweeps on his phone or something…"

Kev responded: "I will have my bubbles kit for Dubbal with me for the Bath gig, so that will be no problem."

15 June 2017

Our Kozfest time changes to later in the day, 5:10-6:10. Closer to the headliner (Steve Hillage's System 7).

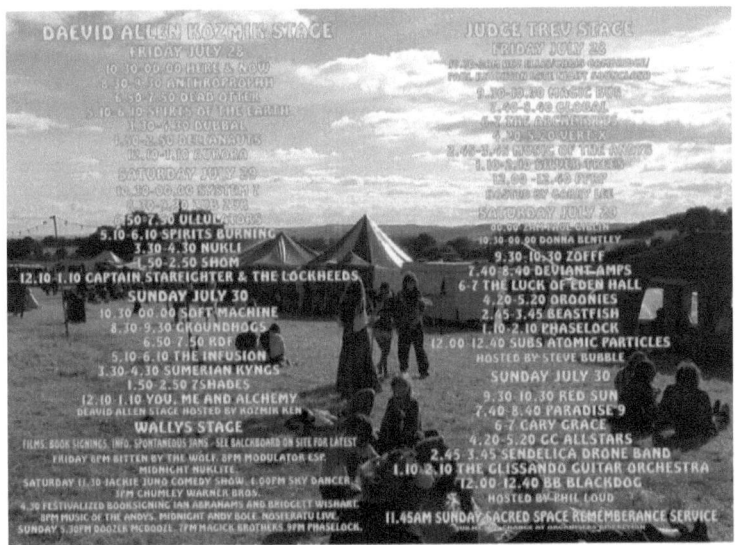

I communicate to everyone:

> *The quick story behind the switch, fwiw, is that Paul needed to place SB (with Bridget), CWB (with Bridget) and Festivalized book signing (wBridget) at different times. When Paul did his original schedule, he didn't take that into consideration. At some point he figured that out, and out of the blue, he told me that he moved SB.*

July 2017

Cary pulls out of our Kozfest line-up. The Luck of Eden set in the Judge Trev stage overlaps with our start. She is committed to that band as their guitarist is part of her band on Sunday.

Equipment & Sounds

March 2017

My choice of keyboard sounds for each song was based on the sound used in the original recording; some from physical keys, some front virtual instruments. Basically, I needed to identify the sound (or sounds) and find the same or like patches in my available Pro Tools virtual plug-ins.

Initially, I practiced with Pro Tools on my Mac tower setup, with the plan to switch to a personal Windows laptop running a newer version of Pro Tools for the gig. The first issue: I didn't have as many plug-ins on the laptop. When my Windows machine started to die a few months before the gig, I bought a new Mac laptop and immediately had more plug-ins available. Plus, I could use my work Mac laptop as a backup.

On March 18th, I began delivering mixes of practice recordings with my performance. One every few days, starting with *By Design*. During my first recording, I notice the guitar and bass are not playing the same thing, and that part of this is based off a synth part lead in the original recording, instead of my original organ. I report this to Steve to get on the same page. I also discover the band added a cool part for a lead guitar (by changing the bass note) and I develop a part for that.

Steve comments on my incoming mixes with keyboard parts when the parts do not align with the band. For example, for *Images*, I need to play the one and five of the opening chords, and not the third. That is the way!

4 April

Kev mentions that Shom's bass player uses an Ashdown, the same bass amp as Colin's, along with a 6' speaker cab. The bass rig belongs to Alan of Dubbal—yes, another band that Kev is in. Colin gets the ok to use it. The combo will be onstage, ready for him to plug into.

8 April

As I continue delivering mixes with keys in place, I make new patch decisions, often layering sounds to create more interesting textures.

> *Hi. I've posted a new version of Live Forever. Now layering the organ and piano with a whirly string ensemble and distorting the trio in the middle section. Note that I've added a little melody riff during the chorus. At the end of the song, I added the intro on top of the chorus (at least I think it's still the chorus chords).*
>
> *Also posting Alien Injection with keys. For the 'tron' parts and rhythm bass, I'm currently using a choir sound. I'll be buying a mellotron plug-in in the near future and will layer that in. Again, a little distortion. I've also worked in a mono synth to capture the original distorted bass lead.*

7 June 2017

Steve and I discuss my setup. I plan to place the laptop running Pro Tools on a nearby crate, instrument case, or unused speaker. While I will use my Venom synth to trigger MIDI notes of the virtual synths in Pro Tools, I eventually make the decision to not use any sounds from the Venom itself, as I ran out of time testing its patches. I decide not to carry an iPad and use its sounds for the same reason.

Steve has a 44-inch Casio keyboard stand. He sends a photo. The height is doable for me. I'm concerned about weight issues, especially when Steve writes "The stand is not SUPER stable, it works best with more weight on it, but I've done lots of gigs with it, I gaffer the legs, fine as long as you're not Keith Emerson!"

I respond:

> Hm… The Venom is 49 keys, and not that weighty. Would it make sense to have a second larger key on a layer below it, just for the weight? If you have an extra key hanging around…first thought. (For the computer, if I had to bend down, etc., I could adjust, I think. Maybe even put another box or something on top of a crate to give it more height.)

10 July 2017

There will be a drum kit (probably from the band Deviant Amps), onstage and available for Richard. It's a small (one tom) jazz kit.

We send our specs (stage layout and equipment) to Snake of the Kozfest crew.

I ask Steve:

> If there is a way that onstage I can get the delay effect I have here in the studio, I think it will help my voice. Does anyone have something that we could hook to the board?

Steve responds:

> I do an fx sheet/setlist for the PA man. I think it's Dave Lowe's last year at Koz, he'll be more than happy to oblige with that slap back repeat delay, I'm sure. And knows his stuff… I'm pretty sure the effect can be put

through the monitors, but even by chance not, both gigs are not that big, and you'll be able to hear the PA onstage I think.

14 July 2017

Tonight, I'm building my master Pro Tools session with about 25 virtual instruments. Had to buy a laptop recently as old one died, and then three plug-ins this week to match what I've been doing from the studio. Was kind of a big thrill tonight when the Mellotron sound played out of the laptop.

Tomorrow, I should be able to play the whole set using the new laptop, as opposed to my studio workstation.

16 July 2017

I discover that my Mbox I/O doesn't work with the new OS. I quickly purchase an inexpensive Behringer I/O.

In a few days, with Cary no longer in the band, we send an updated tech specs to Snake (some of which we'd change the day of the show).

SPIRITS BURNING 2017 TECH SPECS

- Kev Ellis: stage far right - synth - stereo DI from mixer.
- Steve Bemand: stage middle right - guitar - 60w combo mic'd up. Vocals - boom mic stand. 1 x power outlet.
- Kev Ellis: centre front stage - vocals / harmonica - boom mic stand.
- Bridget Wishart: stage middle front right - vocals - boom stand. DI (for EWI woodwind synth - mono output) - 1 x power outlet.
- Richard Chadwick: 5-piece kit, 3 cymbals, 1 hi-hat. Vocals - boom mic stand. 2 x power outlets for click drum machine and click headphone amp. Big wedge monitor please.
- Martin: stage middle front left - DI & mic'd up guitar

combo. Vocals - boom mic stand. 1 x power outlets.

- Colin Kafka: stage middle left - bass stack – mic'd up. 2 x power outlets.
- Don Falcone: stage far left - one stereo DI (from Mbox I/O). 2 x power outlets, front center lead vocals - straight stand.

By the time of the show, most of the band has shifted their stage positions. For example, I will be stage far right (far left from the audience perspective). We provide an illustration of our new layout to the stage crew, and they adapt to our changes without any issues.

Working Out Travel and Lodging

21 Feb 2017

My initial plan:

- Arrive on Monday or Tuesday for a dress rehearsal.
- Rent a car. I tell Bridget: "I'll try to minimize use as much as possible. It's been a while since I've driven on a different side of the road, with a steering wheel on a different side."
- Stay at a hotel in Glastonbury my first few days, and then head to Kozfest grounds.

26 February 2017

- Bridget and Martin offer a spare room for Monday until Thursday AM.
- They have a spare, inexpensive Argos one-person tent available for use at Kozfest.

4 April 2017

- Kev offers to van me to the festival for day 0, following the Wednesday night gig. This would negate the need to stay in a hotel Thursday night (and at the Plumley's Wednesday night). It would also negate me driving to the fest. However, I might not have a way back to the car in Bath.

- Kev suggests renting a camper van. He reminds me that it is always good to be off the ground, especially if it rains. And, If I'm using someone else's tent, best to go during the day and put it up in the light. Steve also suggests sleeping in a van.
- Karen, acting as my travel agent on the home front, investigates a camper van for the trip (instead of a car) and cancels the two hotel reservations she previously made.
- I ask Kev about where he parks at the festival. Is it behind the stage, in the lower field? And are SUVs ok? I learn that he parks in "the upper field, as high up the site as you can get. I'll get my van up there, but it can get a bit er interesting if it's a wet one. If it's wet, you'll probably be told to camp in the lower field. Lower field camping is where most people with vans are." When I arrive months later, I'll see that the stages (various size tents with stages) are in the upper field. The lower field is like a different world. In July correspondence, Kev does ask if I have driven an RHD stick before? I respond that "I'm unfortunately an automatic-only driver. I also don't know how to swim...but I think that won't be a factor here. I believe you're telling me that the hill is a bit of a hill, and probably not a good match for the automatic vehicle in my future. Correct? I asked about SUVs as I read somewhere that they are not allowed at some fests. It's a cheaper solution, but my wife is semi-pushing for me to go with the camper van, and then owe the family money...or something like that..." Carey adds: "Don, the hill can be really treacherous if it rains (mud), and I can't imagine attempting it with an automatic. And it probably will rain at some point. This is England, after all."

15-19 April 2017

- I'm in Texas recording Michael Moorcock. Mike and Linda provide some input regarding Bath, Devon, and surrounding areas.

- Karen books an Airbnb camper van for me. The owners are even willing to pick me up and drop me off at the airport. (Note: Their van has a name, Colin. The same name as our bassist.)
- I plan to stay at Bridget's M-W. I ask about sleeping in the van Thursday night, parked in front of their house, and am talked out of it. I'm told that Bath is densely populated, rows of terraced houses, with difficult street parking.
- Kev suggests that I follow him after the Wednesday gig, to Kozfest. This would require me to drive at night. Given the right-side driving, I nix the idea quickly.
- Karen books a hotel for me to stay at Sunday night (Radstock Hotel, RelaxInnz) to wash up before my Monday flight back.

May-June 2017

- Drummer Jack Gold-Molina, who has contributed to SB studio albums, tells me he is going to attend Kozfest, and the Bath gig too.
- Meanwhile, I'm having trouble as a U.S. citizen with U.S. license getting UK car insurance for the Airbnb camper van. Our plan B is a minivan from a car rental that includes insurance. (In early July, the owners of Colin add me to their insurance policy for the duration of my stay.)

Mid July 2017 (One Week before My Arrival)

- The band briefly discuss my driving in the UK. "Be prepared for those lovely romantic English country roads...small lanes and big bends and a steep drive up to the studio." And "it'll be great practice for the roads to Kozfest. Think sidewalk width..." I should think about sleeping overnight at the studio, as I might be tired and jet-lagged and not in condition to drive the lanes to the Plumley's in the dark.
- Bridge and Martin devise a new plan. After picking up the van, drive to their house. Their place isn't far from the practice studio. I can have a quick shower and bite to eat,

and then they can drive all three of us in their car. It's big enough to fit my gear. Bridget sends directions and a photo of where to park in their neighborhood.

- My flight will arrive at 1:10. The Airbnb camper van owners will drive me back to their place (in Bristol) to meet Colin, and then I'll head to Bath.

- Bridget, who is vegetarian, and I discuss coffee and food. "Some people consider me picky, albeit not as picky as when I was younger. For example, I now love Thai, Indian, Ethiopian, Japanese, and Chinese, whereas I didn't know what they were in college days and would steer clear of them. There are certain veggies I don't like…you might want to sit down…Things like mushrooms, avocados, artichokes, and for some reason I like tomato sauce but not tomatoes or a chunky sauce. Actually, I will eat a very fresh cherry tomato. That said, I love English peas, and can snack on things like peas, celery, carrots and cucumbers, lettuces, and onions all the time. As implied above with the ethnic foods, I do like lentils, beans, etc. Bread is good. Always. No allergies. Except sinus ones! I'll pack lots of sinus medicine. No issues with spicy food either."

- Martin, who had been to a Richard Thompson retreat in the Catskills a few days earlier, adds that my phone should work OK in the UK. His worked in the states. They obviously have WIFI at home. Tuesday would be my vacation day, and they put together plans for local places of interest: Mendip Hills, Cheddar, Priddy. And Bridget wants to do Stanton Drew stone circle. She notes that the weather for Tuesday is looking nice.

- Wednesday before my Sunday to Monday flight, I have most of my gear and clothes packed. During a nighttime dream, I realize I need to find a way to keep things powered over the fest days (and I suddenly suspect that I can't rev up the van to power things, or that it might not be the neighborly thing to do). I add USB power sticks to my luggage.

- I decide I will leave the festival before it ends on Sunday. I need to check in at my Sunday night hotel before then. Plus, I should drive in sunlight. I'm bummed that I'll miss two bands that have SB connections. (The Groundhogs with Ken Pustelnik and Soft Machine with Theo Travis.)
- Somebody sends me a list of what to bring to the festival. It includes a reusable water bottle (to fill up from the free taps onsite), wellies or sturdy boots, toilet paper, a flashlight, and patience.

I'm gaining new respect for musicians who perform live regularly.

Doing a Dress Rehearsal

24 July 2017

I was never concerned about jet lag. I had ample time to rest on the long flight. I knew I would be excited to meet everyone and run through the tunes. Plus, there would be that moment of setting up my gear and getting the first sounds in the PA, which I hadn't done in decades. I was good at staying level, keeping calm in the face of any challenges—even when the energy level was high. I knew it would be easy to stay focused. Stay professional. And be supportive of this band that had come together to support an idea, a dream. I would simply give each person the space and respect they each deserved, and in turn, earn theirs. I may have been overthinking the last bit. They already liked the songs and what SB had accomplished on albums.

If needed, I could always take a deep breath.

There was one area of early concern. Getting to the Plumley house. That thing about driving on the different side of the road, with a steering wheel on the different side of the car.

If needed, I could always take deeper breaths...and did.

It was a trip. I remember brushing the camper van left side against some shrubbery. I remember pulling into a gas station and asking a truck driver if I was going in the right direction. I remember pulling into another gas station to get gas and a truck driver yelling at me. I evidently went into the exit and stopped on the wrong side of the pump, and maybe in the wrong direction. The father of the station owner came out and confirmed my mis-directions. He offered to pump my gas (as done in a previous century). It turned out he used to own the station and gave the station to his son. He was at ease providing service to a potentially lost traveler. As I moved through country sides and small towns, with no definitive sign for Bath, I again questioned my route. This time, I turned off the main road and went a few blocks into an area that reminded me of an American suburb. Looking for signs of life. I finally found a family outside their home, talking in their front yard to friends or family about to get into their car. I pulled up slowly, rolled down the window, and explained who (or what) I was. They assured me that I had been on the right path and got me back on it. When I arrived at the Plumley's neighborhood, I was happy to see Bridget's face...and happy that I wouldn't have to drive again until Thursday morning (and knowing that Jack would be my navigator).

Our dress rehearsal was Monday evening. Bridget, Martin, and I arrived around 5:00. It would be my only rehearsal with everyone...except Kev, who couldn't make it that night.

I wrote prior that "I would love to play each song once or twice in a relaxed way, checking how my volumes are and adjusting afterwards, seeing if we need to review any sections, and then doing the full set, in real time." I believe that's what we did.

Playing an Optional First Gig

In January of 2017, Kev suggested we do one gig prior to Kozfest (somewhere like the King Arthur at Glastonbury). On February 1, Bridget mentioned the Love Lounge. Perhaps a Thursday night before the Saturday Kozfest show. Kev mentioned he would already be at Kozfest on Thursday. Wednesday night would be better.

26 February 2017

Colin gets us a Wednesday show at the Widcombe Social Club in Bath. Everyone in the band is onboard for the show. We can begin to broadcast the gig; except we need to keep the drummer's name a secret. It must remain a surprise.

May-July 2017

Colin sorts out a sound guy and PA. Colin Callan (The Laughing Gnome) was the first choice. After joining our Facebook Messenger chats, he pulls out. He thought our show was "mostly acoustic stuff" and doesn't have the desk channels and monitors to support a rock band. Next up, Marick, who probably has done the club before. On 20 July, Marick informs us that he can't make Widcombe. However, his buddy Jake can use his rig and handle sound. Disaster avoided.

We need to decide whether we're hiring the place and doing ticket pay at the door. The venue cost is low (£105); this covers a 4 PM soundcheck to 11 PM end. We keep it simple. Free entry and collect donations. (I offer to pay for the venue cost; we'll split anything made above that.)

We also decide to have tables and chairs for the audience, with a dance floor in between the audience and stage.

For promotions, we need a poster for the club, a local record store, and online. Colin asks Bridget if she could do one. Bridget wrote "I usually would love to but I'm really busy...@Don Falcone Is Karen busy? would she like to do the poster? FYI Karen is Don's partner in crime and an excellent graphic artist."

I respond: "Karen has already done one!"

The first draft has Don Falcone's Spirits Burning. I don't like this for various reasons. We also have some band member names listed (featuring Bridget, Steve, and Kev's full names.) As we start to add in missing info (time, city), and other performances, we remove the names.

We develop an evening of music!

Widcombe Social Club

- 16:00 Load/soundcheck (SB soundcheck, CWB, if needed).
- 19:00 Doors and DJ Kev.
- 19:30 Don ambient set—I had decided to do one.
- 20:00 DJ Kev—A chill set. I supplied Kev with .wavs of ambient songs (projects like Deeper Than Space, and a couple I was in, like the Spice Barons).
- 20:30 Chumley Warner Bros. (Bridget and Martin).
- 21:00 DJ Kev—A space rock set.
- 21:30 Spirits Burning.
- 24:00 Close.

Poster for Bath Show, Created by Karen Anderson

16 July 2017

Ten days before the Bath show, I write to Steve: "I've been waiting for the proper moment…would you be interested in playing gliss guitar during my ambient set?" Steve responds in the affirmative.

I ask him to play "All the way through, with some ebbs and flows, as you feel it out."

I provide Steve a map of my sounds and plans. For example, for part 1 of a 3-part set:

> *For guitar, start with lower gliss notes, and eventually get to full gliss palette, and then kind of repeat. I'm going to play around with samples (water, German music machine—birds, tapping on a sub hatch door that is part of a winery on Treasure Island here, rainwater, and eventually play a protest chant of "Water is sacred, water is life"). During all of that, I'll work in piano and strings after the sample-only ambient beginning.*
>
> *I'll start with Am. After some key silence, move to pretty piano thing over Bm (actually playing roots of Bm, C#, G, and then E). Then, during chant, do an F#m motif (F#, F#m D, E). Then repeat the whole thing, except after Am, replace the Bm thing with Am, F G Dm sweet wind of change like thing). As I type this, it looks more complicated than it is…*

Part 2 would be more industrial, including rhythms. Part 3 had me playing off Steve guitar loops.

Our set would go well. Sadly, the performance not recorded.

Live at the Widcombe Social Club

26 July 2017

Kev had van issues getting to the gig and made it in time. (Steve would have car issues after the gig. Jake gave him a lift home with his gear in the PA truck. Steve returned the next day, avoiding a ticket.)

One of the Spirits Burning

We arrived at the club and loaded our gear and got everything set up. We had a few hours before the doors would open for attendees. It was dinner time.

As we left the club, we split into two. Almost everyone (which included all the vegetarians) went in one direction (maybe uphill, or was it downhill and then left or right?) And Richard Chadwick and I went downhill, directly to a place that had food. I had presumed Richard was a vegetarian and was surprised when he ordered a burger. I think I ordered the same. We had a great, extended talk.

When we returned to the club, and the doors opened, some of Bridget's band mates of the past made it. My two biggest surprises were Judge Smith (Van der Graaf) and Ken Pustelnik (The Groundhogs).

It was great to talk to them before the show and after.

Judge had emailed me a week earlier and mentioned that he lived nearby. After the show, he noted that he could have sung some of the songs we did. He was a background singer on the studio version of *Our Crash*. I hadn't considered the possibility of that with one week to go before the show.

Ken asked me after the show if I would consider joining The Groundhogs as a keyboardist. That was an impossibility given my home and day job in the states. However, I'll never forget the offer.

Jack made it to the gig and took photos of the band during setup, soundcheck, and our performance. Also in the audience were three fans I knew from Facebook. Quintin Drake, Paul C. Gray, and Kevin Humphries. I was able to sell CDs to them.

I remember bartering with Kevin to sell a bundle of albums and him giving me a jovial hard time. And, I had to inform Quintin that we weren't performing his favorite Spirits Burning & Bridget Wishart song, *Lady Jane*.

He let me know after the gig that he thought we had a great selection of songs and hoped that our upcoming Kozfest gig would be released on CD someday.

Setting Up, Widcombe Social Club, in Bath, 2017
Pictured from left, Don, Richard, Kev, Steve in the Shadows, Colin
(photo by Jack Gold-Molina)

The sets before SB went well. When it was time for SB, we performed each song as a separate, almost detached entity, instead of doing a song-by-song, no chatter between song performance. That was fine, as it gave us some time to relax, and consider what went well or not. Richard did an unexpected amount of talking between numbers, kind of taking charge to let people know about the band members, my roles, and the song titles.

One illuminating thing for me was my keyboard setup. What worked at home, with a sturdy K & M keyboard stand was challenged—and dangerous—with Steve's Casio stand. Even if I was just using my Venom keyboard for triggering only, any sense of energy and hard playing could result in the stand tipping. (Historically, I was an aggressive keyboard player, courtesy of my bass guitar days.) My custom-made setup made it worse. I needed to have access to a computer qwerty keyboard to do dot-number-dot keyboard shortcuts to navigate in Pro Tools to session markers for each song and their keyboard sounds. Ideally, I wanted the qwerty keyboard accessible on top of the Venom. However, it didn't sit well anywhere on the instrument panel. So, I stacked two I/O devices on the top right-side of the keyboard—one of the I/Os, the Behringer, served as my Pro Tools I/O and MIDI router, the other non-used Mbox provided height for the qwerty keyboard to sit comfortably. Each piece was connected via Velcro, including the lowest I/O to the Venom. While the idea seemed…sound, and worked at home, it now looked silly, ready to topple. Especially if I put my hand with any extra pressure to the qwerty keyboard or right side of the Venom. Somehow, I got through the gig. For Kozfest, I detached everything except the Behringer I/O, and had the qwerty next to my laptop on an unused speaker cab to my side.

We played the entire planned set of 13 songs.

After the gig, Bridget messaged the venue 'to say thanks' and shared with the band their response… "Glad to hear it! The Club did well on the Bar and feedback for the event has been very positive. Thank you and hope to have you here again." Bridget added:

> *Talking to Don last night we made the decision to cut Crafted for the Koz Fest gig… Brings the set to an hour. Feedback from audience and band members… the sound got louder as the set went on and the dynamics got lost… The bass guitar got way louder from around Live Forever? Is there a pedal u kick in then @Colin Kafka? Well done everyone! Don didn't stop talking about it. We've made him a v happy man with all the work we've put in. @Steve Bemand Pls let Rich know.*

> *One thing we never organised was collecting donations… Lucky I went round when I did… We didn't collect nearly enough to pay the PA though. However, after discussions Marick gave us an easier target and Don made up the amount needed to reach it.*

Getting to the Festival (and at the Festival)

27 July 2017

Jack and I rendezvous at Bridget's Thursday morning and set forth to Kozfest. We listen to final mixes of the Spirits Burning & Michael Moorcock *An Alien Heat* album along the way. Jack using his phone for GPS directions…when available. The trip with Colin—my campervan—goes well overall. There is a moment where we are told to take a left at a street name. We are deep into the country and pass what looks like a path in a cornfield that has a sign saying, "Golf course." At least, I think that was what it said. Going past it for a mile, we're informed that we missed our turn-off. We turn back and take the "Golf course" road. It eventually gets us to Uffculme's town square, a place that Jack recognizes, close to the Bobbie Watts Farm where Kozfest is being held.

We are relatively early, so spend time in Uffculme. I have the greatest sandwich wrap I have ever tasted. (When I return to the states, David Gould, a Dolby coworker originally from England, said that these places were like the McDonalds of England, and were where he and classmates would go for a late-night quick meal after a gig or sports match. He is surprised that I liked it so much.) Jack and I hang at a local pub…their outside patio area, next to the quiet street. The locals inside seem uncomfortable with our presence. After I buy a drink, to go with my wrap, they lighten, and we briefly talk.

When we leave for the farm, and arrive at the Kozfest entrance, I get my first look at the lower field—yes, lots of vans—and I drive slowly up the hill to the upper area. I'm able to park directly across the front entrance of the Daevid Allen Kozmik Stage. A large blue and white carnival tent; just not as high as say a circus tent. There will be no trampoline performers. Next to my parking spot is a bus that I will learn is famous for its presence at festivals. Behind me, many tents are being erected, and beyond that, a field, and then trees, and the sky that stretches back to my spot and onward to the other direction. There are no tents or enough land for tents behind the

Daevid Allen Kozmik Stage. Between Colin (my van) and the stage tent is a wide pathway that stretches to another end of the site, and another large tent, red and yellow stripes; this is the Judge Trev Stage. In between are multiple smaller tents. One is for acoustic acts. Another for a bar. I would spend most evenings and some of Saturday walking back and forth between these four tents.

Jack and I went our separate ways for most of the day, and then reconnected at night—he would be sleeping in the front seat of the van Thursday night. His tent wouldn't be ready until the next day; actually, it wouldn't be ready until Saturday, so he would be my roommate for two nights.

I spend Thursday evening (and early-to-midday Friday) walking around the site, lower and upper, meeting with people, introducing myself. Getting tastes of cider, usually homemade and occasionally the bottled variety. I meet some of the musicians performing. Andy Bole. Kev. The Gong family contingent: Steve Hillage, Graham Clark, Johnny from Gas. I briefly talk to Steve about Dolby Atmos, which catches his interest. There are at least two vendors selling food. Kumbites Kitchen is my favorite. One dish is "Jerk Chicken, Rice, & Peas." I purchase a couple of bottles of their sauces to take back home. On Saturday, I meet Ian Abrahams, who had reviewed some SB albums over the years. He was there for the book signing with Bridget, promoting their *Festivalized* book.

Thursday night, as I prepare to sleep in the back of the camper van, I realize that I haven't considered my claustrophobia. The back of the van isn't that large. It is dark outside, some campfires barely visible. It is dark inside. Especially when lying on the van bed, distanced from the side windows above. Perhaps, I would have been ok sitting in the front seat facing out the large front window. However, Jack is there. I try to sleep, and it isn't working. My solution: Open the back of the van a little, so that there is space for air, and the sense that I'm not enclosed. It works. Yes, it makes it slightly colder. Still, it works. I can't remember if or how I explain this to Jack.

Selling Merchandise

I wanted to sell some CDs at the shows. How many? For what price? And how should I transport them?

Jack suggested a price of £10, which was what I was thinking. Both Jack and Bridget said not to expect many sales. Based on my experience at stalls for two NearFest shows, I knew that I could probably sell more than they would expect. I was a good niche at the right niche festival, and the CDs were not readily available at brick-and-mortar stores. When I got to the show, I found the main tent had a place to sell merchandise and the attendant there would handle sales. I put together a box and attached a folded 8 1/2 x 11 sheet to the front with the words "Spirits Burning family (tenner each)."

How did I bring CDs? Jack gave me good advice. Customs could go through your bag and deny you entry into the UK if they believe you were selling them without a visa. It was already too late to consider mailing CDs to Bridget. Instead, Jack suggested getting 3-4 bubble envelopes, putting a copy of each CD that I wanted to sell in each envelope, then sealing the envelopes and putting people's names and addresses on them, along with my return address. That is what I did, although many, many more envelopes than Jack recommended. And I didn't limit CDs to my carry-on only, which he also recommended so that I could directly discuss what they found. I think I had dozens of envelopes in my keyboard case, in my carry on, in my suitcase. Plus, I placed 2 or more different CDs in each envelope.

Jack also said to not tell them that I was playing professionally. When asked, I told them I was going to the UK to jam with friends, which was true, at least for the dress rehearsal.

When I was asked in Amsterdam... During my stopover between San Francisco and Bristol, while the plane was on the tarmac, I began talking to the person in the seat next to me.

A good, friendly chat.

Where we're from, where we're going. Our day jobs. Our interests. While we're waiting, a flight attendant approached me and asked, while pointing to my keyboard case on the tarmac, "Is that your case, and can you tell me if you are carrying any weapons?"

I could feel the change in body vibes of my seated neighbor, I could feel the eyes of everyone else on the plane. I quickly realized that the maker of my sturdy, strong-looking keyboard case—which I had recently purchased for this trip—also made cases for other uses…yes, a gun, a rifle, and so on.

I explained that I was a sometimes musician, visiting England to jam with friends. I probably started in on details, like, "there is an I/O Box that you connect between the keyboard and a laptop, and…"

They asked me to go down and open the case for them, which I did. When I returned to the plane and my seat, I told my neighbor everything was good now.

We didn't really talk the rest of the trip.

Performing

29 July 2017

Before Steve took off for Kozfest, he reported that his amp was broken. And he had no time to go into Bath and print lyric sheets for Kev.

In our still operational Facebook chat, Kev responded: He would be able to read the hand-written ones. Plus, he managed to borrow a rare and great sounding Marshall combo valve amp for Steve from Grant McNaughton (Grunty).

Soon after, Bridget reported that the Chumleys were onsite, and the band would soon all be on the same farm.

We're mostly set up when Kozmik Ken came onstage and introduced us (pronouncing my name "don fal-co-nee").

> *This is going to be a historic performance, that people will be talking about for years to come. For many reasons, yeah! The main man in this next band has come all the way from America. If that's not good enough, you'll recognize quite a few of the musicians here onstage, and that means Kev Ellis. Although you recognize him as well*

obviously. You're going to enjoy this. I want to hear you enjoy this. Put your hands together please and welcome... Spirits Burning!

Spirit Song

Richard was still working on the drum kit and wouldn't be available to start *Earth Born* for a few minutes. Bridget sprung a rubber band into the crowd and said:

Let your frogs fly...

We instinctively started a spacey, unplanned improv of synths, electric guitar gliss, acoustic guitar and EWI, in the same key as *Earth Born*.

As the lights gently flickered over my head, and a little smoke rose, Bridget picked up a tambourine with her free hand, still holding her EWI in her right. She did some circular shakes and set the tambourine down. She took to her mic and recited a poem she had once done with Hawkwind.

In your throat is the spirit song, a living spirit song, his name is Long Life Maker. Yes, I'm here to heal. With the healing ways, of the magic of the ground, and the magic of the earth. So, go on my friend, and sing with the healing spirit, with the magic of the ground, and the magic of the earth.

It was the moment that Bridget said the last "spirit," that her words were answered with two cymbal rolls by Richard.

He was ready.

And, as Bridget finished her last words, Martin began the acoustic guitar intro of *Earth Born*, and the band followed.

Almost as if planned.

Live at Kozfest, 2017. Pictured from left, Kev, Bridget, Don, Colin, Martin, Steve, Richard (photo by Michal Skwarek)

Tip: Selecting What to Wear Onstage

We had never talked about it. I guess it fit into my sense of freedom and each person feeling comfortable being their self. Plus, I trusted everyone. And to be honest, they had all been on a stage here before or nearby. I was the unknown quantity.

Looking at the Kozfest video and the moment we made our first sounds as a group... I had removed my glasses, my bifocals. I didn't need them to operate and play a keyboard. I also didn't want them when I took center stage and sang two songs. I had a layer look, three shirts. The top shirt was a white Silent Records shirt with a large, centered alien wearing headphones. Like the song *Alien Injection* said, I did really have two Silent t-shirts, and this was one of them. On the back of the shirt were band names, including two I had been in (Thessalonians and Spice Barons). The long-ago ended Silent website was on the sleeve. I had blue jeans. And hiking boots that Karen recommended I bring, in case of rain and mud (as had occurred the night before).

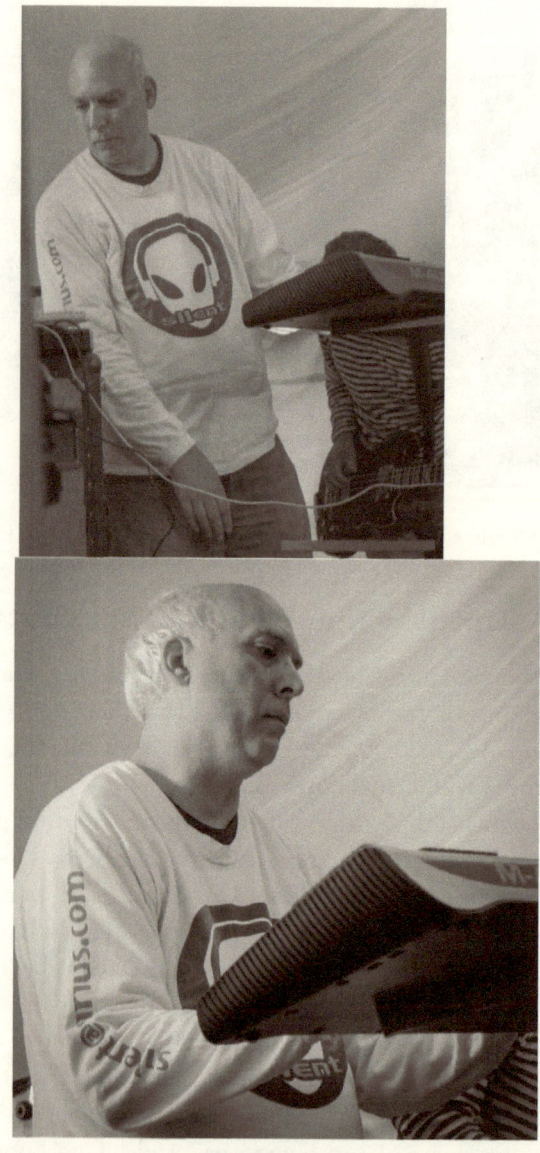

Don Playing Keys at Kozfest, 2017 (photos by Harry Collision)

Kev had a black shirt with a star and the words STAR LABORATORIES to the right of it. Colin had a striped shirt, momentarily making me think of *The Prisoner*. He was sometimes obscured by Kev in front of him. Bridget had her hair tied back, braided. A weave that stretched back, slightly tilted. She had a third eye image on her forehead and sparkles on her face, with dark blotches running below her eyes. The facial look reminded me of Kaecilius and his occult followers in the first Dr. Strange movie. She wore a cool dark t-shirt with an image on it, and a gilet vest with cut sleeves over it. Each hand had a rainbow glove, with fingers exposed. Bridget's look was the perfect mix of psychedelic, steampunk, and magic that we needed.

Bridget at Kozfest, 2017 (photo by Michal Skwarek)

Richard was relatively hidden, behind a small drum kit. Other than Kev's bushman beard look, Richard provided the classic long hair of the group. He would also provide the most movement and motion as he drove each song when needed. Martin had a pair of glasses on his head, a long, oversized shirt over a t-shirt with a jagged design. The outer shirt almost touched the sides of his knees and lower thighs. Steve was the lone band member with a cap. He also had a t-shirt, with a small image where some shirts have a pocket.

As we finished the suite of songs with Bridget, and I prepared to go to center stage to sing the first of two songs, I took off my Silent shirt. I now displayed a darker gray shirt with a hawk on it. Yes. This was planned. I figured…if I had photos wearing different shirts, it might look like I did multiple concerts. It couldn't hurt. (I had a third shirt, a dark one with light stripes. For some reason, I forgot to expose that one.)

Earth Born and Journey to The Stars

The two songs with Bridget singing and playing EWI and Martin on a sparkly-sounding acoustic guitar and backing vocals segued into each other. Both songs had a wonderful mix of sounds and dynamics, as they built from an ambient start into heavier sections.

For most of both songs, Steve played gliss with a large knife over his guitar strings, creating a variety of spacey sounds. It would be in the middle of *Journey* that he suddenly unleashed an electric guitar solo. (Bridget's EWI produced the solo in *Earth Born* and the first one in *Journey*.) Our arrangements for these two songs were noticeably special.

Kev had his Kaoss Pad sometimes on a little table, sometimes in his hand. He was situated in front of Colin and me. For the Bath gig, I think he had a seat and was on a lower level than me. While we made do on the Kozfest stage, it was a little tight, and probably looked better in Bath. However, the sound onstage for Kozfest was better. Louder. Bath was indoors. Kozfest was in a tent, and virtually outdoors.

For *Earth Born*, I could hear myself better than any performance in my life. And it made for a better, easier performance with touch sensitive keys. Unfortunately, Bridget and Martin had switched places from our planned stage layout, and with Bridget closer to Colin and me, the bass guitar and keys in the monitors were too loud for her. As we moved into *Journey*, she asked the board mixer to lower the instruments. I could barely hear myself the next song. I started to play a little harder…

The Unknown and The Hawk

We took almost two minutes to restart. Bridget and Martin exited stage right and I took my place behind a mic far stage left and announced the song title. Steve did some retuning and the rhythm section behind me discussed a chorus part. Kev made some fun synth sounds in the background. I took the opportunity to go center stage—near another mic—and asked the sound person "Is it ok if I switch mics?" With a distant thumbs up and the band ready, we proceeded.

There is nothing like being the lead singer in front of a loud band, with an audience in front of you, people at stage front dancing or swaying. It's all very moving. Especially with slap delay on the vocals. It teases a power that one doesn't get when standing behind a keyboard. It's also a lot of fun.

Plus, I had choreographed my approach to *The Unknown* and some of *The Hawk*.

Don singing The Unknown at Kozfest 2017 (photo by Pete Stanley)

Verse one and the chorus:

"I choose my place."

"Outline of flesh"—I raise my arms up high, like a preacher, and bring them down to my sides while sweeping my hands in the air, as if shaping the outline of a body.

"Remember my name"—I point my index fingers to either side of the top of my head.

"And the purpose of fame"—My arms extend further out, with each hand in an open 'stop' position.

"To dance around the spin... of birth"—I return to my outline of flesh movements, with my hands shaking more, and then settling at 'birth' with my arms in front of my chest, the top one face down, the lower one facing up, creating a virtual container of space, for an invisible womb.

"Comes the flash"—I mirror the coming of the flash by raising my hands again and exposing the palms of my hands. My left hand slightly higher than the right one.

"New lease on life"—I bring my hands down, chest-level, and close each hand and make a calm fist, as I move the hands outward, almost like I'm pulling a rope.

"We stir to wake"—I open the fists, and my hands do a new slow shaking.

"We pause to love"—I repeat the 'womb' move of 'birth'.

"I like the feel for what it's worth"—I now rub my hands together, as if to make a fire.

"I like the feel for what it's worth"—I continue rubbing my hands, right to left, left to right, and right to left.

"We take from the hand"—I make a fist of solidarity with my left hand. Next to my shoulder.

"And give to the world the unknown"—I raise my left hand and extend it sideways out to the audience. As I sing 'the unknown', I bring a closed hand back by my side and uncoil it. As I get to the third repeat of the line, I extend my right arm and use my left hand to point to my hand and pluck an invisible entity from it. And then raise my hands up again.

For *The Hawk*, I pull a nut shaker from my back pocket after the opening vocal lines and use it to accentuate the instrumental parts and incorporate it into my choreographed moves. As I sing "Go to bed boy and we will dream, go to bed boy over and out," I put my hands together as if praying (nut shaker still in one hand) and place my hands to the side of my head, a pre-Steph Curry "night night." Into the chorus, and "The hawk in my room, won't leave me alone, he's here on the wall"—my left hand and shaker seem to write on a hidden wall—and "he's here in my soul"—my right arm extends out and then I return my hand to my belly. And, as I sing "he's the worst thing I've ever owned, he cuts to the bone," I hold out my right hand, almost like it is ready to have blood drawn, and tap the shaker held by my left hand across my right arm. It all seems to make sense on stage.

I did make a small mistake in both songs. In *The Unknown*, I sang one line after the second chorus early. (I would fix that in the live album recording.) Live, the band adjusted quickly, and the rest of the song went fine. With *The Hawk*, I sang some wrong words in the second verse. However, I did sing them in time, and they did rhyme. (Well, I rhymed fire with fire. I did not fix this in the live album.)

We spent almost a minute between the two songs as Steve did some retuning. Our lost time bucket was piling up. I chimed in onstage that "We're going to do a couple of seconds of forever." A Hawkwind joke. This might have confused the band, so I followed up with "The next song is called *The Hawk*, and it's from an early Spirits Burning album, fourth album, called *Alien Injection*." That confused the band more, as we'd later perform the song *Alien Injection*.

Our set list placement of these two heavier rock pieces probably helped loosen up the band for the two instrumentals that came next. The simpler *Unknown* probably helped the more complicated *Hawk* after it.

And, as much as I enjoyed singing, I was content to return to my safe place, behind my keys for the rest of the show.

By Design and Snakebite Serum

After another minute between songs, we launched into *By Design*. (We would also take a minute after *Snakebite Serum*.)

Years earlier, I had seen Magma twice. Their leader, drummer Christian Vander was phenomenal, as advertised by those who prepared me. While I'm not comparing SB to Magma, I can say the intensity and dexterity provided by Richard on drums was phenomenal. The entire rhythm section responded in kind. The instrumentals were Colin's best moments on bass. My bass organ felt at one with his bass and Richard's kick drum. Steve got to shine on rhythm and lead guitar in multiple parts, as the smoke machine began to immerse him, and my right-hand organ chords growled throughout. (This really was my first experience onstage with smoke.) And, all the while, Kev's synth sounds provided spice to the proceedings.

Snakebite was the first song that I chose the wrong marker number in Pro Tools. I started the song with a sound I had targeted for *Second Degree Soul Sparks*, which we had dropped from the set. I didn't notice it during the tribal intro and the ensuing frantic riff runs. Once I deciphered my mistake, I had to find a good moment in the song to momentarily stop playing, turn back to my qwerty keyboard and change to the right sound. The unintended sound was a wild, spacey, sound and worked along with Kev's chosen sound and the rhythm section. For the live recording, I kept it, plus re-recorded my missing sound (which I had played at Bath).

Alien Injection

It was Kev's turn to sing. We of course took a minute before starting.

Kev had a music stand and the lyrics in front of him, and there were a couple of places where he took us on a different route. We adjusted. As Kev sang "help is on the way," a stagehand could be seen running behind the stage. Richard's vocal mic hadn't been working; his cool background vocals for the songs I sang sadly not present. The stagehand would have a working mic in place before *Alien Injection* ended, in time for the next song.

Images

Bridget and Martin returned to the stage. Bridget no longer had her vest on. The bespeckled skull on her shirt now fully in view. Her and Martin would stay onstage for the rest of the set.

Steve began the opening guitar notes of this Hawkwind song, and smoke began to emerge below him and Martin. And, then Bridget sang "Memories surround her…"

When we got to the spacey break—after the second chorus, after the band plays "da-da" chords followed by silent beats—Richard began to fix his vocal mic stand, which had started to slide down. With the stand and mic secure, he did something he didn't do at Bath or practice. He spoke! Increasing his volume with each question to the crowd. "Is there anybody there? Is there anybody there? Is there anybody there? Is there anybody there? Are you there?" The crowd responded with a cheer! Richard emoted "You are there! Welcome!"

Then Bridget entered with her refrain "It's gone now…" As Bridget finished her lines with "the fear and the anger of the lost and alone," Richard did an "Aarghh," a four-beat count off, and we're back into the song and Steve's solo.

Live Forever and Stand and Deliver

Another two songs with Kev on vocals. Plus, Bridget. And Martin, and Richard. And Steve.

Before we started. I got a message from the side that we needed to wrap it up. Technically, we didn't have time to do the remaining two songs. Let's say we ignored that and made a quick decision to dive into *Live Forever* and do both songs.

Each song has catchy instrumental intros, a good bounce, and anthemic choruses, as we had felt when we developed the set. The band had lots of smiles throughout the pieces, including after the third chorus: Richard's drum stool slid off the back of the stage and he somehow continued to play in the same stance. He then took a moment to retrieve it as Steve's guitar covered the sound, and then Richard rolled us all back into the next verse.

Ironically, we played both songs longer than usual, as we ended up vamping on the endings endlessly. There was a moment where it felt like we were singing "Live, live, live, live, live... forever" into eternity. As I couldn't hear myself well in the monitors, I overplayed. Playing harder, my touch sensitive settings produced more volume, at the expense of the intended sound. It became more difficult to do my original nuances. Deep into the song, I tried pounding eighth note or quarter note chords to get the band's attention to stop... to no avail.

We of course took over a minute to start *Stand and Deliver*.

As Kev sang the first lines, we now had more smoke onstage than previously. In the same way I say lasers are cool (for a Tangerine Dream gig), well, smoke is cool when you're onstage. Kev and Bridget alternated singing the words *Stand and Deliver*, sharing the same mic, and buoyed by her emphatic hand motions and facial expressions. It was memorably energetic.

When Bridget returned to the "What is it now..." section, leading to "Give him what you want" line, Kev suddenly made this into a secondary anthem. They now alternated singing "Give him what you want," and eventually got back to "Stand and deliver." And we brought the sound to a close, Bridget adding the tag line "Before it's too late."

Kozmik Ken:

> *Well, I promised you something special and I think you'll agree that was. Don Falcone and Spirits Burning! And including the drummer who wasn't actually here. I think he fell off the back of the stage a couple of times nearly. A wonderful set. I think you'll agree...*

In the beer tent, I sat down with Richard and a woman in a fur gilet. Later identified as Melody Oakley. I was now wearing a baseball cap. While Richard was getting a drink, I asked her what she thought of the band he played with. She said she really liked the singer. I asked, "which one?" She said the one that did all the hand movements. I took off my cap and said, "that was me." And thanked her.

Completing Post-Performance Steps

We got paid! I split the money with everyone in the band, excluding me. I was happy with what I made from CD sales.

We did a band photo. Outside the tent. Early Sunday. Both Jack and Colin's guest (future Ozric Tentacles member Saskia Maxwell) took photos. And it was starting to drizzle again. Saturday night was the night of rain and mud, very noticeable when walking to a porta potty in the middle of the night.

Band Photo, 2017. Pictured in front row, Martin;
middle row, from left, Bridget, Richard, Steve, Colin;
back row, from left, Kev, Don (photo by Jack Gold-Molina)

There were lots of great photos taken during our performance and shared online, by: Ray Baldwin, Harry Collison, Karl Frandang. Jack Gold-Molina, H-Pinkness (Pam), Michal Skwarek, and Pete Stanley.

I remember watching the Chumleys perform in the small tent and taking a picture of Michal taking a picture of me. He, his partner, and their son were everywhere. In 2020, Michal's heart stopped beating. Soon after, I got permission from his son, Tyson, to use some of his father's SB Kozfest photos in the *Hawkwindia Encyclopaedia* by Dave Thompson. Tyson died in 2022. When it came time for a live album, I asked Karen to incorporate one of Michal's SB photos into the cover design. We'd dedicate the live album to Michal and Tyson. And to Kozmik Ken, who also was no longer with us.

o o o o o o

I left Kozfest early Sunday, before any shows. I emailed Jack, as I didn't see him on my way out.

Jack wrote:

> *I saw you outside of the Kozmik Ken tent, and I popped in there briefly. When I came out a couple of minutes later, you had left. The Ullulators had an unannounced reunion jam at noon on Sunday. The Magick Brothers were amazing in Wally Hope's tent. Groundhogs were absolutely burning, and Soft Machine was in incredible form.*

I responded:

> *Didn't get a chance to thank you for your navigation role in getting to the fest. It really made the trip successful. Plus, I appreciated your SB support Wednesday and at the fest. Definitely looking forward to your photos too.*
>
> *It was great hanging out together at the fest, through music and food and the soft terrain. Actually, also great meeting you, as historically that doesn't happen with many in the SB crew. Lots of great memories. Still sorting them out, as I start to float back into Bay Area and U.S. happenings, and plan for going back to work tomorrow.*

My Message to Bridget (Last Night in UK)

Might take me longer to do a proper thank you in words to Martin and you!

Or maybe this is it...

You two are beyond special! You made a dream (and maybe dreams that I didn't even know that I have) come true.

You already know that I enjoyed the gigs and fest experiences. Eating and drinking with Richard (twice) in relaxed atmospheres was a nice, unexpected experience too.

I really enjoyed my time at the house. That was equally important and integral to the week. Great talks, meals, support, help, and my first bunny interaction in years. Everything I could hope for. Perhaps my biggest surprise...was how easy it was to talk and interact with Martin. He's a keeper!

Still floating back to the Bay Area world...peeked at work emails, did a bit of work on the next cd liner notes, and weaving in and out of fb and Kozfest comments and photos (some of which mention us).

love to you and Martin, always!

p.s.: It will be weird tomorrow...when I drive...and should mention I didn't hit any curbs on my way to the hotel, or to Bristol.

Bridget wrote:

Lovely words, thoughts and feelings Maestro. And v much reciprocal on our parts. It was a great week and we both felt very at ease with you. Time flew by with many special moments to remember. Splooshing, skidding and sliding down the muddy track leaving the festival! Toast in the garden. Snow ice in the Gelateria. Very glad to hear no curbs got crunched. Best wishes to you and the K's, Always. Yayyy we did it!

Martin wrote:

Hi Don. Thanks very much for the lovely words. I really enjoyed your visit and spending time and chatting and ended up feeling like we had a lot in common. You never know how these things are going to work out, but I don't think we could have hit it off any better. So that's about as good as it gets. I guess it goes to show to some extent how much doesn't come across in emails and messages. It's a shame that we didn't get to meet Karen but hopefully one day this'll happen. I don't have any photos of you in our road, but I have some of our day out in the Mendips, so I'll upload them somewhere and let you know where. Lots of love and good wishes, Martin.

My Message to the Band from California

Words can only begin to describe expressing the last week...I'm eternally grateful to have played music and spent time with everyone. Together, we created a special once-in-a-lifetime moment for those that saw and heard us, and for ourselves too.

Besides the musical journeys at practice and onstage, there were also moments to be a music fan and experience the fest itself. This was something that we also got to share together, from food and beer at night, to searching for each other through soft terrain, to sharing coffee in the morn...all the while, talking about music, life, and the experiences that make us who we are.

Again, my eternal gratitude. Smile and hugs x infinity.

Releasing a Live Album

This took seven years.

September–October 2017

Pete Wibrew sends me the live tracks. It's a huge zip file vs. lots of audio files. He opts to burn discs, package them, and mail to me.

I report to the band:

> *My initial goal is to get a version of the event for us, and then we can decide if we'll share some or all of it anywhere (for example, the Hawkwind bootleg emporium, who expressed an interest).*
>
> *I listened to and touched every piece. That said, I'll concentrate on the simpler pieces first, to make sure that I've got a fine enough rhythm section going.*

Besides doing some small cleanup of the tracks, Steve, Bridget, and I make decisions on where to start and end each song. We remove Ken's introduction and any of the band chatter in between songs. We eventually consider the early songs with Bridget as a single suite, a single song (instead of separate files, two of which would stop abruptly when played back out of context).

Richard Standrin, who recorded video of our performance (via three cameras), does a video mix of our version of *Images*. With our permission, he posts it to YouTube. His main camera, at the back of the marquee: a Sony HXR MC2500e. The two stage side cameras: Canon HF G30s. All the cameras recorded in AVCHD.

December 2017

I'm starting to feel swamped. I'm finishing up the first Moorcock album, working on the second, and beginning to re-release and stream previous Spirits Burning albums for Noh Poetry.

January 2018

Richard (Standrin) sends me a USB stick with the video files (including the camera two-track audio). I learn that there are blocks of video for each camera; for example, cam1 (1), cam1 (2), cam1 (3), and that I need to align these sequentially in Pro Tools to watch the video.

I align the video and its audio to the multi-track from Pete and I now can mix while watching us perform. However, Pro Tools only supports 1 video track; I'm limited to watching a single camera at a time.

February 2018 to 2023

Given the number of in-progress albums on my plate, I decide to do something different.

Before the end of February, I give the live tracks to a friend to mix. For free. Some good initial processing work is done, and we get initial mixes of the early songs. The mixes aren't necessarily what the band expected, and the number of suggestions and requested changes starts to grow. Plus, as work and home life for everyone intercedes—pushing out discussions, replies, and actions—the project eventually goes into a black hole of no movement.

Gonzo was willing to release a live CD with a bonus DVD. This will never happen. By the time the music is ready, I'm no longer on Gonzo. (In March of 2020, they offer a digital release only contract, which I decide not to accept.)

While the live audio tracks are in limbo, I combine the practice session video of *Second Degree Soul Sparks* and my home synth parts and voice samples, and then post the video to YouTube.

February 2023

I communicate a plan to Bridget and Steve: Retrieve the in-progress tracks, get them into my workstation, and I'll do the final mixes. This includes reviewing mixes with Steve and Bridget and acting upon any of their suggestions. One of the biggest changes I make is to not have the keys and guitar panned so much left and right, respectively.

30 April 2023

I send the final mixes to Robert Rich for mastering. As mastering is being completed, the first label I contact agrees to release the album by Christmas, 2024.

14 September 2023

While waiting for CD specifications and release information, the label informs me that they will no longer do physical releases. I decline the offer for a digital only release.

16 September 2023

I was in contact with Deko Entertainment regarding a re-release of the first Weird Biscuit Teatime album. While awaiting word on that contract, I tell them that I unexpectedly have a Spirits Burning *Live at Kozfest* album for them. We work out a deal within the week; to release the album by Christmas, 2024

(Optional) Release Videos

I have a coworker at Dolby interested in working on the video files. We meet a few times and work on syncing the cameras and audio on his system. However, we really must wait for the audio to be completed. By the time the songs are mixed and mastered, neither of us work at Dolby.

When Richard Standrin hears about the upcoming CD release, he expresses an interest in doing multiple videos. To be continued…

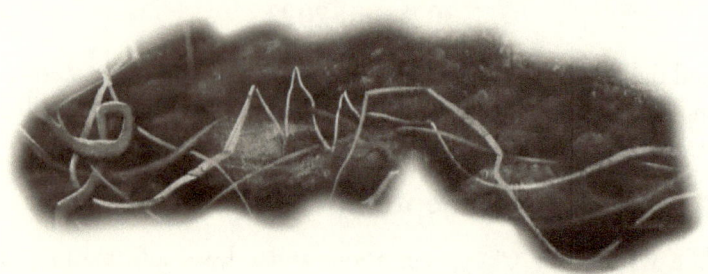

So, You Have Chosen a Band Name

DO YOU EVER play the game of coming up with a band name?

Are there words or word combinations that you love? That energize you, make you feel at one with the world, or make you feel special like a god or goddess in a mythological tale?

Like others around you, you are the center of the world, of your world. You join a band. (Or an organization—Remember the Graham Bond Organization? Or a cult—Think Blue Öyster Cult!) Now, you are affixed with others in a common cause. Can you agree on a word or combination of words to describe this new you, this group you?

What about those before you? Do you like their choice? Did the name they chose deepen your understanding and appreciation of their art, or hinder your perception of it?

Does your birth name give rise to a word? For example, I once had a girlfriend, Anita Acquistapace. Her last name would make a great band name. Or, if you were born with the name Falcone, do you have a natural affinity with birds, and a band with a name like Hawkwind?

Some bands include a color. Black Sabbath, Deep Purple, Godspeed You! Black Emperor. There was a moment in my youth where all the professional sports teams I rooted for had the same uniform color: Detroit Lions, Los Angeles Dodgers, St. Louis Blues.

Some bands make a plural choice. From there, a member of the band can be said to be a Beatle, a Beach Boy, a Pink Fairy.

Are there bands that you never listen to because of their name?

Could a historical song be used for your name? How about a song? For example, Deep Purple is a song. So is Don Falcone (a short opera).

Ah, an artist name. A stage name. Is that something to consider? Whether solo or in a band. How might that age? For every Prince or Twink, there is a DFM (not me) and Zero—both members of Melting Euphoria after me. Do you decipher their names by looking at the writing credits? Purjah = (John) Purves, who contributed to Spirits Burning and our ambient project Quiet Celebration.

Are you prepared to live with your choice until the end of time? My friend Sam Herzberg was listed as Sam Floyd on the Mrs. Green album. Any regrets?

Bishop McDevitt High School Marching Band (1973-76)

My first band. I didn't have a hand in naming the school. Our mascot was a Crusader. Maybe we were the Bishop McDevitt Crusader Marching Band. Also, we were two bands in one.

During football season, we marched. At other times, we were an orchestra. I liked playing pieces with a modern energy or mystery; in high school or college I became fond of *Malagueña*. I suffered through slower numbers like *Feelings*, arrangements of popular songs (like a Chicago medley) that ripped the guts out of the original material, or the showy pomp of a Sousa number, force-fed into every football game and orchestra program.

My freshman year, the band had one trombone player, Billy Smith. He was also a starting linebacker on the football team. Money was available for the band director (Mr. Frey) to buy trombones and teach some students how to play. My high school friends (and former grade school classmates) Patty Bowen and Ed Smith suggested I sign up. Months later, as a sophomore, I was a member of the band. One of the other newly taught trombone players was Vikkie Fricchione, my first girlfriend.

A notable spinoff was an ensemble that played at my graduation. The class of 76 ceremony was in the Hersheypark arena, home of the

Hershey Bears hockey team. Where I saw Black Sabbath, Blue Öyster Cult, Deep Purple. Also, the setting of the once-in-a-lifetime event where a girl I didn't know hopped up on my shoulders for a better view during the sweat and heat of a Golden Earring set as my friend Scott Baer and I swayed on the arena floor.

This was the place where my dad introduced me to Billy Cox, the Brooklyn Dodgers third baseman who played with Jackie Robinson; you can see Billy's slumped shoulders as Bobby Thompson rounds third base and the Giants celebrate baseball's "Shot Heard 'Round the World." We were at a Bears' game, and they saw each other. My dad initially knew Billy in the army. Then, when Billy was with the Dodgers, my dad was sometimes tasked to ensure Billy showed up to spring training and games. Another story… Some fans approached Billy and my dad as they were leaving the stadium in a car. The fans thought my dad was outfielder Carl Furillo, another Italian American. My dad said nothing, letting them think that they had just met two Dodgers.

For graduation, I wore a blue cap and gown. High above my classmates, seated on the arena floor. I was behind the organ used during hockey games to entertain and entice fans, closer to family and friends in attendance, except for a handful of classmates. Ed Smith played the organ (and trumpet). For brass songs, we had one of my best high school friends, Linda Layton, on trumpet, Pat Keating (the only non-senior in this group) and me on trombones, and maybe another brass player. A nun handed me my diploma at the appropriate moment, when we were not playing, while I was standing behind the organ. It was a bit surreal, like I hadn't officially received my diploma and graduated, like I was no longer a part of this class.

Another hurrah. Ed, Linda, Pat, and I were part of a summer oom-pah-pah 5-piece with an older German fellow who played trumpet. We were required to dress in white: shirt, pants, shoes. I remember one performance in particular, a paint store grand opening, near Colonial Park. Probably the only time in Pennsylvania I was paid to play.

Lotus (1976)

My first rock band, a sextet with two lead singers and two guitarists. Origin of band name unknown.

I played a Segovia bass guitar, empowered with a large Sunn amp and speaker cabinet. We were a cover band with a wide range: *Colour My World* (a great song to learn as a bassist), *That's The Way I Like It*, *Proud Mary*, and songs I liked (America's *Sandman*, Deep Purple's *Smoke on The Water*).

We practiced at the drummer's house in Chambers Hill, close to Steelton. A great turnout for every practice: The drummer's family and kids from the neighborhood. I liked one of the girls there and we spent some time together. One time after I arrived everyone was waiting for me to react: It turned out she thought she was pregnant, by someone else. It turned out to be a false alarm.

We did a performance broadcast on Hershey public TV enriched with swirling psychedelic colors. We played an outdoor concert on a truck bed in front of a Pomeroy's store.

Don on Bass with Lotus, 1976

Soon after I quit (probably due to going to college), guitarist Tony Seay's brother and a female singer were added, and the electric-acoustic guitarist was out. They renamed themselves The New Disco Band. A few years later, our fraternity had a version of a prom. Everyone disliked the band we had, and loved the one in the next hall, The New Disco Band. We booked them the following year. Unfortunately, disco was on the way out, and the party suffered.

Mr. Gabel, living a block from my parents, stopped me whenever he saw me in town. "When is Lotus going to get back together?"

Shippensburg State College Marching Band (1976-80)

I played bass trombone for the next four years, the length of my time at Shippensburg (where they now say "Ship Happens"). Immediate cool thing: You arrive on campus early, checking into your dorm room a week or two before everyone else.

That first year, we performed at a campaign event in Harrisburg for Jimmy Carter. When he was elected as the 39th President of the United States, Rosalyn Carter invited us to perform at the inauguration in Washington, DC. We accepted. Marching on a sunny January Thursday. Temperature ~28 °F (-2 °C), wind chill factor in the teens. (I had a frustrating early voting history. I voted for Ford; Carter won. Voted for Carter; Reagan won. Voted for Mondale and Reagan won again.)

The 1979 marching band travelled to the University of Michigan in Ann Arbor. 447 miles away. Our football team was playing rival Slippery Rock. In front of 61,000 fans, the largest single-game crowd for a Division II football game. During halftime, the entire field was dotted with band members from around the country, the event part of a marching band celebration.

My first two albums were with the Shippensburg State College Concert Band, conducted by Dr. Bennie S. Truax. We recorded two Winters Pops Concerts, and then sold the LPs to raise money. 1977's setlist included four medleys (Chicago, Stevie Wonder, Isaac Hayes,

Duke Ellington), along with *Vaquero, Feelings, River Jordan, March Grandiose*. Let's say that I loved playing *Shaft*. 1978's recording included two medleys (*Star Wars, A Star is Born*), and a collection of big band, jazz, and orchestral standards.

One band offshoot affected my bass guitar journey. Early on at Ship, Lenny Tepsich was the bassist for college musicals. Lenny was from my hometown. I knew him from little league. (Is this the place to mention that our town called it the Steelton Midget League?) I don't remember interacting with Lenny on campus. We probably were in different dorms, different sides of campus. When Lenny decided to stop, someone suggested me. It was an interesting proposition. I had never received formal training for bass guitar (other than a few introductory lessons and toying with Mel Bay books). Most of my experience was jamming in my basement in Steelton, or in a campus dorm room.

Now, I experienced the musical notations for *Anything Goes, You're A Good Man Charlie Brown*, and *Pippin*. My chops got better, as did my understanding of how to get a good, clear, strong, bass sound. The combination of a brief E-F-D-E passage in Pippin and the long sustains of notes in Wire's *A Touching Display* inspired a piece I wrote called *Alchemy*. This song would breathe life in many future bands, including one with Daevid Allen.

Unnamed Band (1980)

My last summer in Pennsylvania. We never had a name to my knowledge.

I used to drive across the Susquehanna River to a record store called Black Bart's Treasure Hunter, owned by a guy named Bart. They were the first local store to cater to ordering imports or hard-to-find albums. I remember ordering singles by Hawkwind and Peter Hammill.

My hometown friends and I still did the 100-mile trek to Philadelphia and Third Street Jazz a few times a year. Third Street had a large jazz selection on its first floor. In their basement was the largest selection of rock and synth albums that I had ever seen. They had almost all the Hawkwind and Tangerine Dream releases. 100 miles from home, or 150 miles, when my college friends and I did the trek from Shippensburg.

Back home, the nearby Harrisburg East Mall record store sold imports of European bands. From distributors like Gem Records. Regardless of the band's European record label, there was always a Gem sticker on the extra plastic cover encasing the album; sometimes on the album cover itself.

I learned that Bart played guitar and had a band. He invited me to play his Arp synthesizer. This was my first band as a synth player.

Before I joined, they were a mod tribute band, playing songs by The Who and others. At early practices, I learned *Substitute* and *I Can't Explain*. The focus of the band didn't make sense to me. The band members were interested in so many other genres and were quite knowledgeable about lesser-known bands. From punk to Deep Purple to Renaissance to Van der Graaf Generator. Soon after I joined, we replaced the mod material. We added a song by String Driven Thing and *Sail Away* by the *Burn* era Deep Purple. When I made plans to move to San Francisco for graduate school, I quit the band. The band soon dissolved. An example of how to destroy a band in a few months.

Wump (1980)

My first rock band in San Francisco, and the first to have a record. I just wasn't on it.

The bandleader had pressed a four-song, 12-inch EP. According to discogs.com, "Wump were a short-lived band from San Francisco. The record was pressed in an edition of 5000 copies. As a result of R. Fouchaux's move to Canada, 90% of the pressing was left behind in the San Francisco studio."

We were a trio, led by guitarist/singer Richard Fouchaux. When asked for the name of the band, Richard pounded the fist of one hand into the other and said "Wump!" I learned to do the same.

Richard wrote complicated, twisting, well-paced rock numbers. I'm amazed that I learned all the bass parts quickly and we were playing live so soon.

Richard remembers "a mad rush gig (probably Rock City, near China Town). Bands loaded in from one side of the stage and out the other, while the next band started playing if you weren't fast enough."

We practiced in a long rectangular basement on the corner of 22nd & Tennessee Avenue (the "T" of the alphabetical avenues that lined 3rd Street). San Francisco's Dogpatch neighborhood. This was years before a wave of shops and restaurants (like Happy Cow Creamery & Tea), years before my wife and I went to a restaurant called Serpentine, where we were served by Tara, an engineer and coworker of mine from my Digidesign days. Months later, when walking to my cubicle on the 11th floor at Dolby, there was Tara. She was back in the tech industry, doing testing.

Richard says, "the band started falling apart when water from the Bay started coming into the basement, destroying the sound treatment."

The drummer in the band was Bruce Smith. Bruce went on to play with a local Blondie-style band called The Dimes. One of the first local bands that I saw in the city, at a small club on Polk Street, with a visiting John Capozzi (who was a fraternity brother at Ship, later serving as Shadow U.S. Representative for the District of Columbia between 1995 and 1997).

Bruce and I stayed in touch, and reconnected in my next band, Kameleon.

Kameleon (1981-85)

There were two Kameleons: one with guitarist Jerry Jeter; one with guitarist Joe Diehl.

I met Jerry in a jam band, led by a creative writing classmate, John High, and featuring another classmate, Jonathan Merritt, on trumpet. They did the Five Fingers Poetry magazine that published my In A Church poem.

Kameleon began as Chameleon. We changed our name when we learned of the English band The Chameleons. While I doubt they were aware of us, they eventually used the name The Chameleons UK in North America. It's a common word. I envision a world dotted with Chameleon bands.

Inspired by the punctuated fist of Wump, we went with Kameleon—K for kick ass.

For the first years, I was primarily on bass. By the last year, I was on keys only: Roland Juno-60 and Sequential Circuits Six-Trak.

Kameleon; Pictured from left: Jerry Jeter, Bruce Smith, Don Falcone
(photo by Robin Burns)

Jerry's thoughts to Don:

> *During my time at SFSU I worked at the Student Service Center. Students would come for various things. John (High) came to the counter on a few occasions. Being the easy going, fun guy to talk to, music came up. He invited me to a jam. You were at that jam. I even remember the tune John presented...a little blues...country shuffle. It was fun! John was a good front man. From that jam and a few others, I met you. After that, for some reason the*

jams stopped but we continued, and you introduced Bruce. That, I believe is how it was born.

What went well: 'Chemistry'...what I lacked in confidence and experience was diminished by the comfort I felt playing with Don and Bruce!

The Civic Center Gig... First and foremost having my Mother there was something I will never forget! It was so much fun playing outdoors! While musically we needed to grow, we had a look that was kool! That is important too!

What didn't: Staying together. I will always think we had 'something' that could have been appealing to folks. I would rather grow musically with people I like versus a 'virtuoso' with a shitty personality!

Sam Herzberg, the drummer for the Employees, also on the Civic Center bill, reminds me that "The gig was a protest of both the Reagan administration and against the disastrous environmental policies of James Watt, former leader of the environmental protection agency." In that spirit, Sam went on to become the Senior Planner for the San Mateo County Parks Department and received a Planning Emeritus Network Award from the California American Planning Association in 2022 and won the Sustainability Award from Sustainable San Mateo County in 2024.

o o o o o o

In 1983, Joe Diehl replaced Jerry who left San Francisco for a while. Joe writes:

I remember being a bit taken aback by the fact that there was no bassist ...... or rather, the bassist (Don) chose to play keys. LOL!!! At first, I wasn't convinced, but our "sound" grew on me, and I learned to love it and appreciate that it was different.

I was hungry for something different...original,

creative. I had been playing covers for a living since 1976 and I was burnt out on top 40 crap...although it had been a great experience and a good teacher.

I really learned to appreciate the way we (you and I) seemed to understand each other on a deep level, despite our differences... which actually made us stronger... imo. Kameleon was, to me, a dream come true. It gave me the platform to reinvent myself and try things I heard in my head but had no outlet for. I almost ruined the band by bringing in my friend Adam to play bass. Fortunately, that didn't last long.

Bruce was an incredible drummer. A bit of Phil Collins in him—in style and as a prankster. And a great friend who I lost touch with and forever miss. I loved playing to his kick. It was Bruce who suggested that I become a tech writer.

Kameleon ended in 1985. In December 1986, Joe and I played the songs of Kameleon and the first Spirits Burning at a birthday party gig at the Fab Mab, and then reconnected in a 1987 version of Spirits Burning.

Years later, I played with Cyrille Verdeaux of Clearlight. He briefly was in a band called Delired Cameleon Family.

No Poetry (1982)

The first live band where I played a keyboard, a Crumar String Ensemble with a Big Muff distortion pedal and Phase 90 pedal. Meg Chin O'Leary (Crunch, Pigface) was the lead singer.

When I joined, the band was also auditioning singers and needed a new name. I suggested Noh Poetry. The other band members chopped off the h. A local paper reported soon after that:

Three former (male) members of the now all-girl group BOY TROUBLE have reassembled themselves under a new band to be called NO POETRY.

One of the Spirits Burning

Steve Sherma, the bass player, used to live in my new home out on the avenues. I suspect I met the band through Rob Burns, who also used to live there. The drummer named himself Eddy Larkin; he woke up after a night of drinking at the corner of Eddy and Larkin.

We had another singer briefly (who later went on to start Goth band Shadow Image). The other three members then met Meg on Haight Street and invited her.

We did seven gigs between October 8 and November 14, 1982. Four at Sound of Music, three at Heaven's Gate (later renamed Nightbreak). One gig with the Vktims, another band I saw on Polk Street my first year in the city. We even did a gig with Boy Trouble.

After I quit the band (to pursue my own band), I went to the next No Poetry gig at Heaven's Gate.

No Poetry were setting up their gear. I noticed the lone bartender head to the bathroom. The phone behind the bar rang. I reached over the bar, picked up the phone, and took the call. I told the caller that the bartender was unavailable, and I could take a message. As I set the phone down, starting to spring back into place on a barstool, the bartender returned. He ran towards me and grabbed me with two hands. Threw me against the bar. Yelling! "What do think you are doing?" Everyone saw this scene. Former bandmates, their sound person (Karen, my future wife, who I hadn't met yet), and the three people I was with (Karen West and two others). The bartender was hot! Extremely hot! I had intruded upon his territory—close to the till, and whatever else was there.

Karen West told him that I didn't mean any harm. That I was trying to help, however misguided. When the air cleared, he apologized to me and offered us a free beer. One I had never seen before. EKU 28. From Germany. A dark amber color. 11% ABV. It has been described as "one of the strongest beers in the world." I took a small sip. That was enough. I had never had a beer so strong. Hollie and Tracy took the next two sips. They couldn't handle it either. Karen West was the only one of our quartet that could drink an ample amount. The band's time to play approached.

Third Floor (Early 80s)

I met Scott Brazieal when he was the keyboardist for a Phoenix-based trio called Cartoon. The other two members were still in Phoenix. Scott attended the Conservatory of Music in San Francisco, and had three roommates, also from Phoenix. They lived in a third-floor apartment a few blocks from Haight-Ashbury.

We shared musical interests, especially the more experimental Rock In Opposition (RIO) bands and progressive bands. Art Zoyd. Art Bears. (I don't remember us discussing Magma, who I would see numerous times decades later.)

Four of us jammed in the apartment. Scott and his drummer/percussionist/roommate Randy Sanders. Add wind/reed player Herb Diamant and me on bass/occasional keys. Improv only!

We did at least one gig. At a laundromat. Using the name of their apartment floor.

When the rest of the Cartoon trio fully relocated to SF, Herb joined, as did violinist Craig Fry. I don't know if I ever vocalized my interest in joining Cartoon, given that they didn't have a bass guitarist. They were my favorite local band, and I would have loved to have made them a sextet.

Within a few years, Scott and Randy broke up with their third-floor girlfriends and moved; we lost touch.

Spirits Burning (1986-90)

I wrote a song called *Spirits Burning* (originally *One Spirit Burning*) and we decided to use it for the name of the new post-Kameleon band.

There were multiple versions of the band in 1986: Jerry Jeter returned, and brought in a coworker from SF State, drummer Rick Gauvreau. Paul "Griffo" Reynolds (from The Employees) joined as a second keyboardist. After Jerry departed, we picked up guitarist Walt Metts and did a three-song demo recording at SF State.

In 1987, the band went through a major change, producing the most dynamic Spirits Burning of the 80s era. Rick and I were joined by a returning Joe Diehl and two women: guitarist/vocalist Tracy

Williams (former Pizza Boat co-worker, with whom I would co-write many songs), and singer Jane Bryan (a friend of John High).

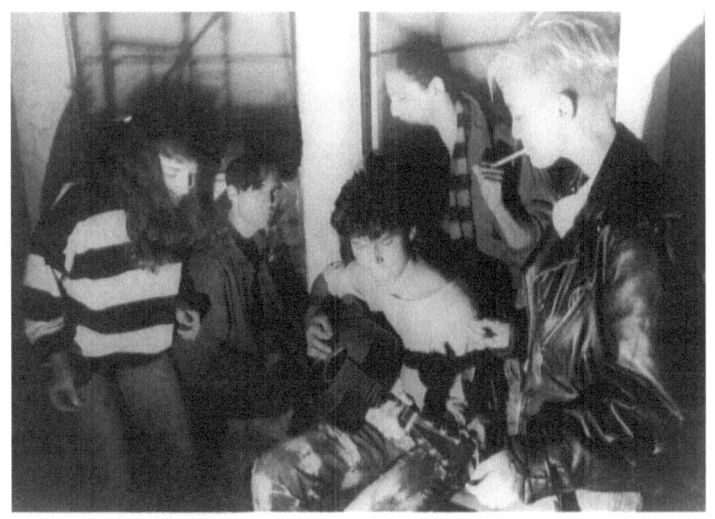

Spirits Burning 1987; Pictured from left: Jane, Don, Joe, Rick, Tracy

Joe's thoughts to Don:

> *When you first reconfigured the band with Rick, Jane, and Tracy, I was a little disappointed to lose the guitar heavy rock vibe. But I quickly got past that as I heard the potential for something truly original. I felt like we had HUGE potential...but I was struggling with personal stuff that prevented me from fully understanding, appreciating and focusing on what was right in front of me. Hindsight vs. foresight. I don't know what we could have done differently to grow it into a recording and touring act with a nice record deal, but it's a darn shame that didn't happen. I would do it all again in a heartbeat and I would savor every moment. And thank you for providing the opportunity. I appreciate you, my friend.*

I purchased a Roland D-50 digital keyboard at this time. The presets greatly changed how I wrote and accompanied songs.

This was my first keyboard with touch sensitivity—where you change the level or shape of a sound by how hard you press a key. First keyboard with sample-based sounds (orchestral, organ, piano), as well as analog synths. First keyboard with built-in effects like delay and reverb.

All of this helped us sound more modern.

(One financial lesson: Struggling musicians shouldn't purchase gear when the interest rate is 22%.)

On February 17, 1988, we opened for Yo La Tengo at Berkeley Square. Unfortunately, by April, the two-singer format had run its course. Jane was out, Joe quit, and Tracy, Rick, and I did a few remaining scheduled gigs.

Soon after, a new version of the band emerged with singer Catherine Foreman, me, and some rotating members. After our first gig, we got two new members: drummer Lee Thompson and bassist Julia Allstadt (on loan from the Gargoyles). Wire Train's Anders Rundblad was the guitarist for our third gig. (He was known as a bassist in those days. In the 90s, he would play guitar on albums by Sheryl Crow and Susanna Hoffs.) Guitarist Doug Krainman replaced Anders to help stabilize the line-up, which soon included our final drummer, Denis Murphy.

Recording Session at SF State and the Loma Prieta Earthquake

(Catherine Remembers)

It was the afternoon of October 17th, 1989, and our version of Spirits Burning was in the studio recording at San Francisco State. We had been invited to record for free in exchange for the students using the recording for instruction during the semester.

One of the Spirits Burning

Spirits Burning 1988; Pictured from left: Lee Thompson, Don Falcone,
Catherine Foremen, Julia Allstadt; Not Pictured: Doug Krainman
(photo by Karen Anderson)

*We were back for a second session, a week after laying
down the basic tracks on a couple of songs, doing some
vocals, guitar, and backup vocals. After recording a few
overdubs, we were excited to pack into the sound booth
with the other students to listen to what we had recorded.
By now it was almost 5:00 PM and I remember thinking
"Oh boy, we are definitely exceeding the fire code in this
tiny room!" We began listening to the recording,
concentrating on every little nuance and then suddenly
it hit. A 6.9 magnitude earthquake that lasted 15
seconds.*

*At first, we all froze, but when it became clear that it
was intensifying, the tightly packed crowd started
moving towards the door. Dust began sifting down from*

the acoustic tiles covering the ceiling, making it feel like we were about to be buried alive. I saw two pieces of equipment jump out of their racks and realized we must get out of here! Some of the students were braced in the door jamb, but they were blocking the rest of us inside! I grabbed our bass player Julia by the waist, and I used her as a battering ram, pushing her through the crowd and out the door, unceremoniously displacing the students who had blocked the doorway.

We were underground and there was a stairway just outside the door to the surface, yet no one had gone up it yet. The building was shaking violently now. Julia and I ran up the stairs yelling to the others, "This is the way outside!" They followed us as we leapt up the stairs two at a time and opened the door at the top, letting light shaft down the stairs. As the shaking began to subside, we all found ourselves outside squinting in the hot sun, dazed and in shock, standing in a courtyard area. Ironically, it was an incredibly beautiful day, but now all we could think about was that our instruments were still downstairs, trapped inside of a dark and possibly unsafe building. We were in our early 20s, and they were the most valuable things we owned!

As we and the other students milling about all looked at each other stunned, wondering what kind of magnitude could have caused such shaking, the aftershocks began. Every ten minutes or so another violent shaking would happen. I remember looking at my hands and they were trembling. Then, in a surreal and unforgettable moment, I heard Don and our guitar player Doug talking next to me. Don exclaimed "Something bad happened," and Doug replied "I know! We just had a huge earthquake!" and Don deadpanned "No... I sat in gum." We looked at each other and then at Don's pants and sure enough he had sat in gum. It was bad, and it was a hot day and there was no getting it out. Poor Don. We did giggle a little. It was a bit of comic relief in the middle of pure panic.

Then someone pulled their car up to the nearby sidewalk and turned the radio on full volume and we heard the announcer saying that the Bay Bridge had collapsed. We all gasped audibly. It just couldn't be possible. It was then that it began to sink in what we had just experienced. We knew that it had felt huge but if the Bay Bridge had collapsed, what had happened to our homes? The rest of the Bay Area?

We had to wait what seemed eons to be allowed to enter the building again to get our gear. We were given five minutes to get in and get out. We had no idea whether it might collapse on us. The electricity was out, and it was pitch black. We were not allowed to use our lighters to see, due to the potential for gas leaks. We felt our way through the dark like the blind leading the blind, stumbling and grabbing what we could and then packing our car, heading home soooo slowly, stopping at every intersection along the way because all the streetlights were out. The radio broadcast was saying that a gas main in the Marina district had ruptured and a whole block was on fire.

As we moved across town, there was the smell of smoke in the air and eventually we could see the fire in the distance, a massive black plume rising into the darkening blue sky. I looked out the window of the car at all the good Samaritans directing traffic, feeling so grateful to be safe, sharing this experience with my fellow San Franciscans.

I remember thinking how striking it was that Spirits Burning had just recorded our music in the middle of a catastrophic earthquake...our name eerily and precisely echoing the trial by fire that our young spirits were suddenly undergoing.

It was in that moment that the name that Don had given to his project, one that, at the time, we had no idea would endure and flourish for decades, finally resonated deeply with me.

Creative Element (1988-89) / Red Rain (1990)

After Tracy left Spirits Burning, we continued to play together. I would be in Spirits Burning plus Tracy's bands. She named her first outfit Creative Element. After that band ended, three of us (Tracy, bassist Kiersten Walter, and me) got together with a different drummer and guitarist and went with the name Red Rain. I suspect that was influenced by the Peter Gabriel song *Red Rain*.

Red Rain; Pictured from left: Kiersten Walter, Rob Craig, Don Falcone, Pete Krawiec, Tracy Williams (photo by Karen Anderson)

In 2024, I compiled a digital album of the demos from both Tracy bands and included the live set from Creative Element's gig in the

Haight district at Nightbreak. The digital package includes a 36-page pdf of photos and song info. Available on Bandcamp.com for $1: *Spirits Burning - Friends & Relations Demos with Tracy Williams & Don Falcone*.

I am planning future *Friends & Relations* albums to cover demos and studio recordings by Kameleon and early Spirits Burning.

One song that Tracy penned was *One World, One People*. We had a banner with those words behind us during our Nightbreak set. Some 30+ years later, episode six of Marvel's "The Falcon and the Winter Soldier" was titled *One World, One People*: the mantra of the Flag Smashers, an anti-nationalist group.

Thessalonians (1990-96)

My introduction to the Silent Records roster. Perhaps the most important band I was in during the 90s. An intriguing mix of ambient, industrial, ethnic music. Perhaps nothing else like it in the history of ambient music. Being in this band really pushed me to think about every aspect of sound, from its seeds to its landscapes to its groove. This was the beginning of understanding the sense of cool that can exist within a song.

In a silentrecords.net interview, tabla player Larry Thrasher said, "Kim suggested the name...I liked the fact that Thessalonians were early Christians that partied more than St. Paul could handle."

At a time when I was losing interest in "making it" locally, and the future of being in a rock band was unclear, I met Kim Cascone at Orban, Inc. Kim was a tester, and I was a technical writer. Add to that an engineer there named Paul Neyrinck.

Paul and I were invited to participate in a new version of an existing band named Thessalonians. The main line-up included Larry Thrasher (who later worked with Psychic TV and was later the main musical component of the DJ Cheb i Sabbah album; Larry played in Nik Turner's band when I saw them at Great American Music Hall, and Larry was there when the fire happened at producer Rick Rubin's house in Malibu; Larry even worked at Digidesign when I was there). Also in Thessalonians, David James, who later played with a live version of Michael Franti's Spearhead and went on to work at Amoeba Records on Haight, which replaced the Rock & Bowl bowling alley and nearby Nightbreak. Thessalonians did the *Soulcraft* album and played one live concert.

Poster for Thessalonians Benefit Gig, with Zakir Hussain and Others, 1991

Larry and David would appear on future Spirits Burning songs.

While Kim was preparing to sell Silent, Kim, Paul, and I continued work on the next Thessalonians album. With Larry providing tabla, we finished the album. It was too late. Kim no longer ran Silent. I released the album on Noh Poetry nine years later.

Red Gypsy Rain (1991-92)

This began a string of bands with bassist Anthony Budziszewski, a mix of highs and lows.

First prog space rock band. The songs really stretched me. Plus, we did a variation of the song *Spirits Burning*, with me singing.

My friends from college were no longer attending my gigs. While Karen did a couple of band photos for us, she attended a few gigs only.

The practice space was dicey, in the heart of the Tenderloin. We shared a space with Ginger Coyote and her band. They were a garage punk band. Their drummer, Lulu, had been in the all-female Boy Trouble. They had a Hare Krishna person playing hand cymbals. It felt very San Francisco.

It was hard to park. It felt dangerous outside the studio, maybe inside. My leather jacket was stolen after one practice.

Red Gypsy Rain; Pictured from left, Carter Lott, Matt Hart, Anthony Budziszewski, Don Falcone (photo by Karen Anderson)

By Design (1992) / Melting Euphoria (1993-94)

When Red Gypsy Rain ended, Anthony and I started a new band. North of San Francisco, we found drummer Michael Merrill and guitarist Dan Miller, both from a band called Myrth. (The Gonzo re-release of the first Melting Euphoria album includes three bonus songs: one by Myrth, and two by Red Gypsy Rain, including *One Spirit Burning*.)

By Design was named after a song I co-wrote with drummer Bruce Smith when we were in Kameleon. In our Hudson Street practice space, Bruce was practicing drums, playing 5/8 parts from a drum book. I looked at the book and began to play the drum notes as a bass pattern. We worked out additional parts, and then presented it to Jerry, our guitarist. The song continued to be part of Kameleon's set when Joe replaced Jerry.

A version of *By Design* made the first Spirits Burning album, with Joe doing the guitar and Michael Merrill doing the drums. The Kozfest 2017 rendition of Spirits Burning did an intense version of the song showcasing guitarist Steve Bemand, and the vicious drumming of Hawkwind's Richard Chadwick.

With the band called By Design, the song sounded quite different. Less driving. Dan had a lighter, acoustic-style electric guitar sound. I don't have any demos or live tapes of this band.

By Design morphed into Melting Euphoria, minus Dan. There was a band in-between called Galactic Warlords of Venus. Anthony then came up with Melting Euphoria. A great band name. He also dubbed himself Anthony Who.

The Melting Euphoria trio was a space rock band first and foremost. The closest I ever came to being in an ELP or Refugee type band. Although Anthony had bass pedals to add spice to our sound, the band was keyboard focused—no guitar! Besides playing keys, I was the poet for some pieces and singer for others. Playing live was tough. Lots to navigate. I appreciated the chance to perform poetry in a rock setting and sing sound poems. Practicing in another city—

San Rafael—north of the Golden Gate Bridge, a toll charge to return home, and carrying equipment to a show did wear on me.

By the time the debut CD was pressed, early 1995, I was gone. I quit in December of 94.

Our breakup was not amicable, and Anthony and I no longer talked. A couple of times I saw him at shows where a band was playing loudly, and he simply pointed at me and seemed to laugh. (Years later, he gave me the ok to re-release our debut.)

The subsequent version of Melting Euphoria did give me some consolation. For starters, they replaced me with three people: A guitarist (Dan again), a female ooh/aah singer in the style of Gong's Gilli Smyth, and a keyboardist named Zero.

Next, was my first and only use of a music lawyer in the 20th century. I met with Barry Simon (who was representing Silent Records at the time, and I learned later was Mrs. Green's lawyer). I wanted to ensure that I had writing credits for the songs I had primarily written, in case I ever wanted to use them again; plus, I wanted some copies of the CD.

I suspect I scared the hell out of Anthony and the band. They were just signed to Cleopatra Records and didn't want to upset that cart. They were reusing Anthony and Michael's parts on almost all the songs I had been on, minus my parts. On listening to their album, I didn't recognize the penultimate number. Otherwise, they fully or partially renamed the songs I was originally on, and sometimes added new intros or outros. I found it amusing when a reviewer wrote about the two albums in the same review and didn't notice that it was the same bass and drum parts on both albums.

I ended up getting 50 copies of the album, way more than expected. And, I got the writing credits I wanted, except for one song that was really a solo piece of mine with added percussion. For some reason, Michael was credited in the final legal language. I could live with it. In the end, I never revisited any of this material.

I did get to see the newly signed, quintet version of the band. A moment of small envy. They opened for my favorite band, Hawkwind, Tuesday, 24 April 1995 at Slim's in San Francisco.

Before the show or between sets, I was near the center of the club. Standing next to me was Doug Pearson (who later played violin on an early Spirits Burning album), Ron Tree (Hawkwind's lead singer), and Richard Chadwick (who I officially met and played with decades later). A shorter individual, with dreads crowning his head, if I remember correctly, was slinking through the club, going to each attendee, and giving them a copy of a CD. It was quite a novel idea, given the audience. When he reached me, he offered a copy of Melting Euphoria, *Through the Strands of Time*. The album by the trio version of the band, with me on keys and vocals. I said "No thank you. I already have copies. I'm on it." Zero did tell me that he really liked what I did. I wished him the best.

I once heard that Melting Euphoria was offered to be the backing band for label mate Nik Turner's tour and refused (and Pressurehed said yes.) I was told that Melting Euphoria wanted to do a tour as the backing band of Michael Moorcock instead. Who knew that decades later I would be the one from the Melting Euphoria family to work with him on multiple albums.

Spice Barons and Silent Trios (1993-96)

Satellite IV / Spice Barons / Patternclear / Astral Fish / Hydrosphere

The ambient 90s was a fluid time for band and project names. Many artists had multiple alternate names. The trio of Kim Cascone, Paul Neyrinck, and me took this to a new level.

I suspect Kim named all these projects by our trio. Over a three-year period, we spread our ambient message across two studio albums and various Silent compilations (like the wonderful *From Here to Tranquility* series).

Our first effort landed on the *Fifty Years of Sunshine* compilation. We called ourselves Satellite IV. The album included a dedication by Timothy Leary. Plus, I contacted Hawkwind and procured a Hawkwind track (via Alan Davey) and a solo piece by their keyboardist, Harvey Bainbridge.

For our second effort, U.F.A. (Unidentified Floating Ambiance), we took a weird turn. We decided to use different names for songs with different approaches. We didn't foresee that different names would lead listeners, reviewers, and sellers to think it was a compilation. One of our names was Spice Barons. Next time out, we clarified our identity. We released a full album under the name Spice Barons.

(Spice Barons also did a song with John C. Lilly, the M.D. who worked with dolphins and whales, and invented and promoted the use of an isolation tank as a means of sensory deprivation. Silent released the John C. Lilly E.C.C.O album.)

Kim Cascone on Spice Barons "Future Perfect State"

(September 2024, Pacifica CA)

San Francisco 1994. My label, Silent Records, was becoming known as the pre-eminent ambient music record label on the West Coast and the SF Rave scene was at its peak. The atmosphere and music scene in SF had turned experimental once again. I was fortunate to have experienced a prior wave of experimentation in the early 1980s Industrial music scene, but the Rave scene was laced with psychedelics rather than machine noise.

The demand for ambient music by chill room DJs was great, but quality ambient music was becoming increasingly difficult to find in the flood of bedroom synth tracks arriving in Silent's mailbox. Having DJed in chill-rooms, I had a sense of what the writhing pits of ecstasy-addled bodies wanted to hear and having worked on Heavenly Music Corporation albums, I had a satchel of ideas that required collaborative forces. I made plans with two musician friends, Don Falcone and Paul Neyrinck, who I had worked with at an audio company, to work on an ambient project specifically for chill rooms.

Don had extensive experience as a multi-instrumentalist in bands, and Paul had been working with samplers and honing his music production skills.

We named ourselves Spice Barons as an homage to the David Lynch film & Frank Herbert book Dune and of course spice was known to be a psychedelic substance which was au currant with the Rave scene.

For the better part of a year, the Spice Barons met each week in Paul's bedroom-studio; armed with synthesizers, drum machines, samplers and computers, we conjured a collection of lush dreamscapes, little sonic worlds a listener could lose themselves in, i.e., perfect atmospheres for chemically altered chill rooms.

We christened our album Future Perfect State in the hope that the sonic material would bring about a state of profound peace in the listener.

Trap (1995-96)

Gary Parra was Cartoon's drummer. I don't remember talking to him in the 80s. He put out an ad in a local paper, I saw it…suddenly, I was back in touch with the Cartoon family and their improv offshoot PFS (Pure Fucking Space).

The timing was perfect! With my Orban Audicy workstation, I could record and mix multiple tracks and co-produce his debut solo album. And I was happy to co-write songs, and add keyboards, bass, and even trombone. The anything goes approach we took to composition and sound influenced what came next for me—the experimental drum 'n' bass of Spaceship Eyes. (Gary contributed to the first Spaceship Eyes album, and later joined the Spaceship Eyes live ensemble.)

Gary subsequently redid Trap with two other musicians, added his name to the band name, and took this trio in a new direction: more difficult-to-play prog, less experimental to me.

They did one album, followed by a gig that Karen and I attended.

Spaceship Eyes (1995-2000)

Spaceship Eyes was my solo project. I based the name on an image of a spaceship and the two front windows that look outward to space, or into the ship.

Over time, I presented a confusing musical focus... The debut self-released album was ambient, and I did one ambient track for a Cleopatra compilation. When I got signed to Cleopatra's Hypnotic label—their electronica label—I was asked to do drum 'n' bass. In turn, I did an experimental version of drum 'n' bass for the first album on their label, and then an experimental mix of space rock and dance for the third one.

Concurrently, I put together a live ensemble locally—an ethno-ambient space band. Edward Huson's tabla was the ethno. The synths were the space (and ambient). Gary Parra's drums, Karen's percussion, the guitar/bass duo of John/Carol were the in between.

One of the later line-ups went a different route. It featured guitarist Joe Diehl, Karen on percussion, and me on synths and samples. For most of the set, we improvised sound and fury over jagged, erratic drum 'n' bass parts that I had on my Audicy workstation. Lots of fun, quite amazing, and very original.

Years later, I came upon a YouTube video for a song mis-titled *Spaceship Eyes*. (Its correct title: *Spaceship*, I think) The song is by Alisa & The Palominos, with the cool line "Is that a spaceship in your eyes?" I connected with Alisa Wood on Facebook in the 2020s, and we sang together on the Spirits Burning & Michael Moorcock *Part 2* song *On Her Island*.

Spirits Burning vs. Spaceship Eyes (1998)

A one-time group. When the offer to open for Present for an Exposé Exposure show occurred, I was doing multiple projects. This was an opportunity to meld them together. There was the Spaceship Eyes live ensemble, the Spaceship Eyes solo studio project, and part of the ensemble was now doing covers for tribute albums as Spirits Burning.

In the electronica 90s, it was common to use the "vs." title, setting one project against another. I just didn't expect it to be loser takes all. By the end of this experiment—one live show—the ensemble dissolved. I continued the Spaceship Eyes studio project for one album, and then closed that project. And I decided to take the name Spirits Burning in a different direction, as a collective.

Alien Heat (1998, 1999)

An experimental sample-based project. I suggested using part of the title of the Michael Moorcock book *An Alien Heat*.

The Marty Acuff/Don Falcone duo debuted with *Click Launch, Launch Click* on *Free Speech for Sale*, built exclusively from commercials.

I did two solo pieces for the second *Extracted Celluloid* compilation. *Shootout at Best Western*, and *Illegal Space Kids*. Both using samples from films only. *Shootout* included samples from my favorite spaghetti western (*Once Upon a Time in The West*, with music by Ennio Morricone). Years later, at Dolby, I attended an in-house event about the history of sound design; it featured Morricone's sound choices for the long opening scene. No music. Just the sounds of a train station solely occupied by a quiet gang of outlaws.

Spirits Burning (1998 to Present)

The band name Spirits Burning re-emerged when I was invited to do covers of King Crimson and Genesis songs for Cleopatra's Purple Pyramid sublabel. This didn't feel like a job for electronica-based Spaceship Eyes. Ensemble members John and Carol suggested I resurrect the name Spirits Burning.

When I started the collective, the name felt even more appropriate. I appreciate things that age well. The guitar sounds of Jimi Hendrix's *Electric Ladyland* still feel fresh to me. As do the synths on Can's *Landed*. They have aged better than some synth passages from prog greats. Moorcock's *Dancers* trilogy retains its freshness in the same manner. It's why I chose to adapt it to music. I believe the name Spirits Burning has aged well too.

At the time of this writing…almost 300 musicians have

contributed to Spirits Burning…17 studio albums, one live album, one EP, four "best of" compilations (one under the name daevid allen & don falcone).

As some of the releases were collaborations with a single artist, who appeared on all or most tracks, I started to use an ampersand in the band name, when warranted: Spirits Burning & Bridget Wishart, Spirits Burning & Clearlight, Spirits Burning & Daevid Allen, Spirits Burning & Michael Moorcock Spirits Burning & Thom the World Poet.

A band named Seven Spirits Burning appeared around 2017. An irritant when doing Google searches to find new articles and posts related to Spirits Burning. I was more upset when their debut album cover—an alien undergoing surgery—appeared on AllMusic.com as the cover for the Spirits Burning's album *Alien Injection*. This also meant that their semi-disturbing image displayed for some Spirits Burning searches. I contacted AllMusic. Eventually, the correct cover displayed.

Quiet Celebration (1999, 2000-07)

I wanted to celebrate ambient (and expand ideas started at Silent by adding melody). I named the project Quiet Celebration.

I invited three musicians: Contrabassist Ashley Adams, who worked at Orban, and used to room with Carla Kihlstedt (Sleepytime Gorilla Museum); Edward Huson on tabla and bayan (the husband of my boss at Orban), and John Purves on winds/reeds (also an Orbanian).

The keyboards were my follow up to the *Kamarupa* album. Dreamy synths with bits of electronic percussion. When Cleopatra signed me to do drum 'n' bass, I now had an album of music available. I envisioned a quartet focused on celebrating ambient in an ambient-ethno-jazz way. The tabla and bayan the ethnic ingredient. The wind/reed/contrabass informing the jazz.

Some of the music was used in film and TV, including *Beyond The da Vinci Code, Conspiracy Files: Mystery of Roswell, The Secret Life of Vampires*. And *The Pamela Anderson Story* on MTV. These sync usages happened after I signed up with Pump Audio (now Getty Music). I had no control in the usage once it was provided to their library.

Grindlestone (2000-11)

I was talking to Exposé writer Jeff Melton outside a record store in San Lorenzo.

He suggested I connect with a guitarist named Doug Erickson. He envisioned a local Fripp/Eno duo. Doug and I hit it off. He became a regular contributor to Spirits Burning. And we started a dark ambient project.

To name the project, we started with words like stone and metal. We looked at Doug's rhyming dictionary and saw "grindstone." We added the "le" when we discovered that was a word.

Fireclan (2002-04)

Drummer Michael Merrill (Melting Euphoria) previously used the word Fireclan for drum circles. Michael and Luis Davila (keyboardist Zero of Melting Euphoria) were now regular contributors to Spirits Burning, and we decided to start a trio with me on bass guitar.

Falcone & Palmer (2006)

An ambient, instrumental space project featuring musician/novelist Steve Palmer and me. We decided to name the project using our last names.

Weird Biscuit Teatime / Daevid Allen Weird Quartet (2007-15)

I briefly called us ACF for Allen Clare Falcone. At least labeling CD-Rs and folders with that name. This was before drummer Trey Sabatelli was onboard. Daevid and Michael ignored me.

¾ of Weird Biscuit Teatime; Pictured from left, Daevid, Don, Michael
(photo by Karen Anderson)

Daevid called us Weird. Hawk Alfredson even did some logo designs. Then one day, Daevid emailed Michael and used the name Weird Biscuit Teatime. With the album title *DJDDAY*. Unfortunately, some sellers and online sites thought the band name was DJDDAY.

For our second album, we turned to Cleopatra Records, who wanted Daevid's name in the band name. We had avoided calling the first release Daevid Allen's Weird Biscuit Teatime to emphasize it was a band and not a solo project. We eventually settled on the amalgamation of Daevid's name, the legacy of the word Weird, and the idea to call it a quartet, given that we were a four-piece.

Changing the name caused confusion for those paying attention.

Astralfish (2008)

Bridget Wishart and I decided to do an instrumental album showcasing her on EWI (Electronic Wind Instrument). We wanted a band name with a space feel.

I suggested resurrecting Astralfish (one of the Silent era ambient band names). I asked the other 2/3 of that project—Kim and Paul—

for their ok and got it.

Meanwhile, another artist began using the project name Astral Fish. He was not happy with our Astralfish release. He was surprised when I informed him that Astralfish existed in the 90s and I was in that project. (He clearly had not done a search online.) When I suggested he consider changing his project name, he went quiet.

Clearlight (2014)

The name originated with Cyrille Verdeaux and his 70s progressive rock band on Richard Branson's Virgin Records. Not to be confused with the 2000's American band of the same name, or the 60s psychedelic band Clear Light.

I produced 2014's *Impressionist Symphony* album and played on one song—keyboard tubular bells, a nod to Virgin's first artist, Michael Oldfield.

Michael Moorcock & The Deep Fix (2019)

This band name goes back to the 1975 album *New Worlds Fair*, and before. There was *The Deep Fix*, the title of a story in a 1966 collection of short stories with the same name. Written by James Colvin (a Moorcock pseudonym). The Deep Fix was also the name of the band led by Jerry Cornelius, the central character in Moorcock's *The Final Programme* (first a book, then a film).

I produced the *Live At The Terminal Café* album. I also played keys on four songs, co-wrote one song, and arranged a few.

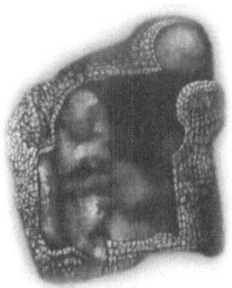

Reincarnation in the Time of Spirits Burning

IN THE FIRST half of the 80s, I was writing more than ever before. Poems that would inhabit my thesis, songs that my bands would perform on demo tapes or live. And then it started to change. I wrote fewer poems. I still had something to say, just not as often. Or, in the format of a poem. Plus, most of the words in my head were now accompanied by music and felt meant to be sung. So, that is what I focused on.

The 80s were fruitful for me as a songwriter. I wrote or co-wrote over 100 songs, most with vocals. The 90s, an inverse, mostly instrumentals. Maybe there were now less words in my head (or most were reserved for my technical writing day job). The 21st century brought a sense of balance. Two of every three Spirits Burning albums were vocal based; other project releases usually showcased instrumentals. I was now better at balancing my day job and music. The desire to voice words again was matched by the enjoyment in doing so.

My 80s compositions had a small audience. Friends, some family, musicians in our bands, musicians nearby. Live gigs and demos made tiny marks. None of my 80s bands released a single or album.

While my 90s music journey moved me to ambient, drum 'n' bass, prog, and then space rock, I never forgot the songs I wrote previously. Those songs, and how different bands interpreted them, became part of my DNA. Each song etched memories.

When SB regrouped, I comfortably looked backwards, to consider the best of my songwriting. Yes, some songs didn't age well or weren't good to start with—my reassessment. Many did retain sparks worthwhile to recreate. Some riffs, some chord patterns were intriguing while the song that housed them maybe wasn't. Lyrically, there might be a line a more mature writer could rethink. There might be a good title, deserving better supporting lyrics.

In a grade school play (with many rehearsals), I was a gym instructor who got kicked by a bad student, and then fell to the ground, the stage hardwood. I embraced falling and getting back up.

To perform another day.

Exchanging Gifts with Daevid Allen

In 2004, Daevid Allen developed the Bananamoon Obscura series—17 CDs from his archives. I was pleasantly surprised when Daevid asked me to collect our best SB work. *daevid allen & don falcone*—a rare album bearing my name on the cover. Titled *Glissando Grooves*, although some tracks didn't have his gliss sound.

I planned a return surprise! I had previously produced the *Where Stalks the Sandman* compilation; each track built from a single sound source. The highlight: Porcupine Tree's Steven Wilson donated a Bass Communion track that reworked recordings he did of King Crimson guitarist Robert Fripp. I had recorded lots of Daevid's gliss work, and I decided to apply Fripp/Eno-Bass Communion-Don Falcone techniques. The latter refers to *An Isolated Craft*, my *Sandman* contribution. A reworked a 1 kHz tone into...new pitches, lengths, and chords, delayed or reverbed, forward or reversed. I even played back parts and recorded me "DJ"-style scratching or varispeeding them. For the Daevid compilation, I began reconstructing his performance into new sound designs. Playing an instrument, this was not. Or maybe it was. The instrument: the Orban Audicy DAW and its editing controls. I did two pieces. *Lionization*, a nod to my Digidesign day job and translations of documentation. The industry term: localization, or L10N. You can see how I took L10N+ization to get *Lionization*. I named the other piece after a college poem, *In Search of Silver*. I posted the results to Daevid. He loved them. We agreed to add the songs to *Glissando Grooves* as bookend songs. Like gift wrapping.

Don at the Audicy, San Leandro Home Studio, 2002 (photo by Karen Anderson)

Pat Thomas Essay for Don

I'm the drummer, bandleader, and producer of the instrumental psychedelic band Mushroom (based in the San Francisco Bay Area)—actually, we're more of a collective than a band at times, having had countless different members play on nearly 20 albums that we've released since the late 1990s. That said, we do tend to have some core line-ups that have lasted and performed live for years at a time.

Our studio recordings are generally a lot like our live performances—lots of improvisation—when we do a studio album, we generally record nonstop for about 6 to 8 hours, for 2 days in a row. Which means we have a lot of material in the can! Obviously, it's not all good—so I generally boil all those recordings down to about 2 good hours—enough for a really solid album or so. It's those bits and bobs that I'm on the fence about, that seem slightly unfinished, that I'm always glad to hand over to Don to finish off.

It's fun to let him "have his way with us" and I make no rules about how/what he decides to do with these recordings—which he adds to and what subtracts from—adding other players, remixing or whatever. When he sends me a finished CD, I'm hearing it for the first time—just like the rest of the fans.

Other times, he's invited me into his home studio with a pile of percussion gear and I'm one of the guests contributing to Don's original vision or someone else's.

At one time, I was part of Daevid Allen's University of Errors band—I recorded two albums with them—and did some West Coast touring. I left to concentrate on Mushroom, but occasionally, I wound up (via Don's overdubbing process) reuniting with my former UofE band members that way.

I have to be honest, that I'd slightly forgotten about some of this wonderful expansive space-rock material that Don invited me into—so it's been a real joy hearing it again after all these years. I can't believe we're into our third decade of doing this music.

With love,
Pat Thomas

About Pat: As noted at the simonandschuster.com/authors site, Pat "is a counterculture historian and archival music producer (and liner-note writer) whose expertise and interests have helped him author such books as *Listen, Whitey! The Sights & Sounds of Black Power 1965-1975* and *Did It! Jerry Rubin: An American Revolutionary*."

Revisiting Our Reincarnations

For the debut SB album, *New Worlds By Design*, I dug deep into the 80s catalog.

I started with what I considered the best instrumental I was part of. The Falcone, Bruce Smith *By Design*. Next, was another 80s Kameleon song called *Heroes*, which had rather teenage lyrics. My bass part, though, was killer, suggesting other possibilities. Anthony, the Melting Euphoria bassist once complimented me on the opening bass line. I never forgot. With that backdrop, I turned *Heroes* into an intense instrumental titled *Snakebite Serum*. Coupled with *By Design*, they were two of the strongest songs for the 2017 Kozfest gig and resultant live album. There, Hawkwind's Richard Chadwick took Bruce's original forceful, tasty drums to new heights. I'm sure Bruce would have approved.

I included one vocal song from Kameleon's history, *The Unknown*. A straight-ahead no-nonsense rock piece with room for spacey sounds. I redid the simple bass part—too close to a U2 line. The new one solidified with a multi-note Lemmy drive. Karen sang this studio version. I retook the vocals two decades later, singing the song at Kozfest.

I reworked another vocal song from the mid-80s SB, *I Speak to The Wind*. Originally a heavier rock song. While I kept my use of bass guitar chords, I aimed the new production toward a mysterious, earthy spiritual direction. Knut Gerwers' talk section helped achieve that goal.

In the middle of *The Ticking of Science*, with it shifting motifs— deep experiments in rhythm and space sounds with Steven Wilson on guitar—I wanted a short melodic tease. I inserted keyboard lines from Kameleon's *Hesitate*. (Note: *Ticking* appears on the original album, but not the NPR re-release because it was licensed to Cleopatra for a best of). I previously did an ambient version of *Hesitate* for Spaceship Eyes' *Kamarupa* album. I tried to get a Cajun version on Michael Moorcock's *Terminal Café* album. After missing that project, I prepped an almost Tangerine Dream version, momentarily queued as a *Dancers* track, then shifted for use to an in-development album with David Jackson.

o o o o o o

The second SB album (*Reflections In A Radio Shower*) approached reuse in different ways. The song *Drive-By Poetry*, gathering Robert Calvert, Daevid Allen, and Thom the World Poet, began with the Kameleon demo recording of Falcone/Smith number *Akasha*. Using the demo tape gave the song an otherworldly edge. Plus, it was an opportunity to get Bruce Smith on an SB song, his whereabouts still unknown. I had gotten good at finding musicians and inviting them. Except Bruce.

Some 80s songs, like *The Cat*, didn't lyrically seem like space rock songs. I was fond of the bass line and chord changes, and reworked *Cat* into *Walking Shadow*, using a poem from another lyricist. I even got original Kameleon *Cat* singer Jerry Jeter to do the new vocals. Jerry was "rediscovered" when Rob Burns saw him during an event at SF State: the demolition of a campus dorm, Verducci Hall, where Rob (as well as my wife Karen) had briefly lived.

This album also resurrected a song I recorded with Rob at Wrong Element Studio. A two-instrument multi-section piece with me on piano and proggy bass guitar, titled *Chameleon*. I renamed the piece *Clear Audient*, an homage to the Clearlight *Symphony* album. I did exclude one part of my duet—an Am F G, Em melancholy section that had a 1-5-8-5 left hand bass, plus right-hand lead influenced by Deep Purple's *Child in Time*. By 2000, the chords had already reappeared in the Spaceship Eyes instrumental *Chameleon Sighting*. There was another version of the melancholy section in 1986 on a Tracy Lee Williams demo. This time, the song had lyrics by Tracy and was retitled *Who's Fooling Who*. With an opening line of "There Used to Be a Time," it felt at home in 2025's *The End of All Songs - Part 2*. Tracy's 80s lyrics worked for the book's Jherek and Amelia relationship and their doubts. Karen did the new vocals. There was a funny moment when Al Bouchard was critiquing the vocals, not realizing that my wife was the singer.

o o o o o o

The third SB album, *Found In Nature*, reused music from the song *Undercover*. Renamed *The Ancient Structure*, it provided an opportunity for me to play bass, including a quick stylistic flurry I sometimes do, quivering my right index finger.

I typically play bass strings with my right index fingernail, instead of a pick, or multiple fingers (which I might do for a dub part), or even a thumb (if I'm tapping higher register notes with the thumb and lower notes with a left-hand finger—as done in the intro of the *Part 2* song *As If Possessed*). Because of my index finger style, I (a) keep my index fingernail a little longer and (b) wonder if it inspired my Shippensburg State College nickname, "Spoon"—my fingernail suggesting a coke spoon. More likely, I was in the wrong place at the wrong time. A student vomited, I bent down to offer help, someone yelled "Spoon"...to clean it up?...and one of my "friends" remembered the moment. The nickname stuck for a select group of Ship students.

o o o o o o

Earth Born celebrated Bridget Wishart's vocals, the band name expanding to Spirits Burning & Bridget Wishart. In the late 80s, I mostly wrote songs for female vocalists. It seemed natural to suggest some of these to Bridget.

One 80s song making the cut was *Two Friends*. From a demo with singer Susan Hrvatin of The Employees, the band that had the Wrong Element recording space and were on the Civic Center bill with my Kameleon. *Two Friends* recalls the time my friend Stacey Newstead and I went to a film, followed by a restaurant in the Castro called Patio Cafe. It was raining and it was magical to be outside, in their darkly lit covered patio, rain sizzling around us. The Bridget version introduced some experimentation, as opposed to the original Michael Oldfield with Maggie Reilly style. The new version with Daevid Allen's gliss guitar and Richard Chadwick's electronic percussion helped recreate the sense of rain.

There were three resurrected songs whose titles started with C. First, *Candles*. No word changes and the music true to its 80s origin, except that Alan Davey's "double bass" provided more depth. Next, *Child Growing*: A slightly different arrangement, and Bridget changed a couple of words. Third, *Crafted From Wood*.

More than any song I have written, or later co-written—I'll explain in a moment—*Crafted* has more, let's say opinions…and lives. In its first life, my *Crafted* composition used a D-50 harpsichord patch, channeling The Stranglers' *Golden Brown*. Essentially a companion piece to *Candles*. One piece about two lovers configured as bookend candles, wax, with a flickering love. The other piece about two lovers, configured as wooden images, whose love can be "left to burn," as "anger can drift in a stream of air, where we say that no one cares." The second demo of *Crafted*, with Catherine Foreman singing, approached Heart meets pre-Evanescence territory. The song started slowly, then exploded into a rocker. To this day, I'm unsure if the recording's over-exuberant tempo jump was due to band members or tape reel damage when we were listening to the mix and 1989's earthquake hit.

For *Earth Born*, Bridget created a new message. She kept my main line "Maybe we're crafted from wood" spinning new words for the rest: a fairy tale with "Maybe we're moulded from tin, or possibly spun out of hay, Big Bad Wolf can blow us to heavens, And Angels rebuild us from clay." As a producer, I treated this version in a more tribal way—percussion from me, no keys—led by a wonderful earthy, playful vocal duet by Bridget and Daevid. And Richard Wileman (Karda Estra) on bouzouki.

The story continued…Bridget and her husband began performing as Chumley Warner Brothers. *Crafted* part of their set. That was cool. The song lived on. Next, as a surprise, Karen suggested my brother David learn the song for his weekly "Friday at Noon" Facebook shows. Karen gave him the version she liked best. The original, with my lyrics. My brother did a wonderful performance, returning to the song a handful of times.

End of story? Not quite. Richard Wileman decided to add *Crafted* to his live set and later an album. For reference, I gave him all the versions of the song. He chose the Bridget version. At one gig he thanked Bridget for the lyrics. I began to wonder...yes, but the title, the main line in the song...was the song abandoning me?

Let's back up. I wrote the lyrics and music for the original. When we got to the *Earth Born* version, I was now giving credit to everyone on the song. And, in this case, it was mostly new lyrics, and I supported this change.

SB with Bridget as lead singer played a version of *Crafted* in Bath. We didn't have time to repeat it at Kozfest. As the live album was coming together, I suggested including *Crafted* as a bonus track. We could "get the band back together." Bridget, Martin, and Richard first. They had been working on a version for a Chumley release. I was next, recreating the parts I did in Bath. I asked Kev to do harmonica parts he did during a practice session. I liked its Hawkwind first album flavor. Plus, I wanted to go with a pseudo-acoustic feel, light on any processing; that ruled out Kaoss pad synth parts he did in Bath. Guitarist Steve Bemand followed, doing more on this version than he did live. Adding a Lynyrd Skynyrd southern rock flavor. While unexpected, it fit the folk country vibe the song had taken since its new wave origins. Colin Kafka was unavailable, disappearing in Facebook ethers at times, so Steve agreed to do the bass. The result captured a possible band rendition of *Crafted*.

It felt foreign to Bridget. I suspect that some of the things we did in Bath—like my keys—she had never really noticed. Now, highlighted, it sounded nothing like the song she knew, played regularly, loved—not one somewhere between the *Earth Born* tribal one and the Chumleys. Whereas I knew the song as somewhere between the new wave to power rock version to a tribal version, along with folk and country versions, all variants in a multiverse where I had limited control. We agreed to let the bonus track survive as a snapshot, the live album moving onward.

o o o o o o

The title track for *Alien Injection* began with a phrase from my college poetry and a song from late 80s SB, *Dig a Thee Earth*. These jelled well with the vocals of Kev Ellis, first in the studio and then live. Another resurrected song, one also to be performed live, was the Kameleon song *The Hawk*. With an Arthur Brown flair, I proclaimed "The Hawk in my room won't leave me alone..."

The cover of *Future Memories* by ST 37 landed in the *Alien Injection* album. A new feather in my cap. A striking version! It supported my belief that titles (they even reused it for one of their album titles) and the song itself could age effectively in another century.

Not all resurrections worked out well though. The song *Imported Serpents* didn't capture the groove and mystery of its parent (*In the Movies*). The new song I started for invites to play to sounded ragged, rushed, dynamically disappointing. I should have reworked it more, or simply removed it from the album. One positive...A nudge to try again. For the first *Dancers* album (*An Alien Heat*), I re-resurrected the song as *In the Future*. With a better landscape from me and the talents of BÖC's Richie Castellano and others, it was immediately one of the better tracks in its new home.

The next album, Spirits Burning & Thom the World Poet, reused no compositions.

o o o o o o

The *Bloodlines* album with Bridget features the song *Goldmine*, a mainstay in mid-to-late 80s SB. The original lyrics I wrote were kept intact. The new version tracks had an origin in another place. The "Us" band. A brief ensemble with University of Errors bassist Michael Clare, Jerry Jeter (guitar), Karen (guitar, lead vocals), and me on keys. We met a half dozen times; some sessions recorded. Over time, I took these recordings, picked the best parts, and used them for a "new" rendition. For *Goldmine*, Michael's bass and Karen's rhythm guitar survived. Bridget replaced Karen's vocals. I did new keys. Gitta Mackay added vocals, Frank Hensel added lead guitar.

○ ○ ○ ○ ○ ○

Crazy Fluid had two reclamation projects. The album opener included an 80s instrumental romp called *The Fraction*. Of more note, was the inclusion of an emphatic song of mine called *The Preacher*. While memorable in a campy way for a previous audience familiar with my or Jerry Jeter's impassioned "You can call me the preacher..." this was the least likely song I ever thought about redoing. However, when planning lyrics about Luana Borgia, I discovered part of her life centered around a preacher. Daevid Allen was happy to do an Arthur Brown impression and give this section of the multi-suite *Luana* even more passion than Jerry or I had done. Our dog Kiara, in the room during recording, looked up questioningly as a towering Daevid sang and stomped his foot onto the floor.

○ ○ ○ ○ ○ ○

Multiple 80s songs were ripe for inclusion in the noir-infused space rock of *Behold the Action Man*. Two in my vocal sweet spot. *The Real Time* felt like a return to the past with me on organ and singing, and original guitarist Joe Diehl onboard. *Strafed By A UFO* took a piece I had written during an 80s visit back to Pennsylvania. This time, though, the former *What's Going on In That House (Over There)* became "What's going on with this case, when it fits?"

Three other songs from the later 80s stayed true to their original arrangements and lyrics. First, *This Mark You Make*: This song featured the Weird Biscuit Teatime quartet—Daevid, Don, Michael, and Trey—plus the Spirit Burning debut of singer Jsun Atoms (The Upsidedown). The other two songs came with a twist: *The Train*, originally sung by Catherine Foreman (with lyrics I wrote capturing one of her life experiences) was sung by Tracy Williams. Inversely, the song *Every Opera* that I wrote during Tracy's band tenure was now sung by Catherine (who did sing the song during her stretch in the band). I'm unsure why I did these turnabouts. The latter song was retitled to *Every Space Opera* because...I previously resurrected the song on a Spaceship Eyes album, with Jerry singing it, and I wanted to avoid any BMI registration collisions.

○ ○ ○ ○ ○ ○

The two Spirits Burning & Clearlight albums had no songs rooted in the 80s. However, the *Healthy Music* album did have two songs previously considered for Michael Moorcock's Cajun-leaning *Terminal Café* album. *Cool Can of Cola on The Forehead* (which got a bit of Americana via Dave Willey's accordion and Cyndee Lee Rule's violin) and *In Search of Friends on The Day of Masks*, the latter referring to Mardi Gras. The album also incorporated a cassette recording I did in my cousin Ernie's basement, members of Mars Everywhere playing synth, guitar, and pinball. Ernie and Deb Byrd our audience.

2014's third Bridget album took the concept of reuse into a different direction. The bonus second disk included alternate mixes of four songs, plus a cover of Pink Floyd's *Take Up Thy Stethoscope*, previously on a tribute album. One of the remixes, *No One Cries in Space*, reworked disc one's *Journey Past the Stars*; both songs including tambourine by Twink.

○ ○ ○ ○ ○ ○

For 2015's *Starhawk* album, I found eleven compositions that could easily support the *Starhawk* narrative. This gave the album a consistent 80s blueprint, imbued with new musicians and their sounds.

The opening track, *Our Crash* reworked a song I wrote called *Lifeline*. It had some good lines but lacked the focus and improved lyrics revealed when describing the first chapter of Mack Maloney's *Starhawk* book. The *Lifeline* open of "got a joke about a commie spy...." could have been at home with the *Action Man* album. Here, though it became "I've got a take on an incoming ship, a two-man crew and they're going to die."

I Have Two Names was taken from a song called *No Name*. *Live Forever* was resurrected with aural changes only. *My Life of Voices* combined two Falcone/Williams rockers, *My Life* and *Voices*. *We Move You* rebuilt from a multi-tiered life. Originally, a song from a brief

80s SB with two keyboardists, me singing "I'll never leave this country." When Catherine Foreman joined SB, I rewrote the song; now about an ex that pushed her too far..."stick my cat in a drawer, and I'll kill you" and "when you do these things, you move me." (This version made our "earthquake" demo.) For *Starhawk*, I rewrote the lyrics to cover a futuristic race around the world, with Nik Turner on sax and Robert Berry singing "run the race we run, and we'll know you" and "when you do these things, we move you, it is not prepared, it's an experiment." During the subsequent celebration of Hawk Hunter's victory and *Tripping with the Royal Family*, the music and vocal melodies hail from an 80s song called *Caught in A Flash*.

Rolling Out was based on an instrumental titled *No Mystery*. The Tracy Williams SB lineup provided *Angel Full of Pity*, *Right on The Mark*, and the *So Strong Is Desire* finale (a duet with Karen and Daevid). Karen was a natural to sing some resurrected songs. She had been the sound person for the later 80s band and knew the songs well.

The penultimate song—*This Time, This Space*, combined two elements from my 80s. First, *Right Here, Right Now* and its chorus "I didn't expect to see you right here, right now." Given the overuse of the phrase, I changed the lyrics to "I didn't expect to see you in this time, this space." Next, *This Time* took lines from a song called *Trapped in Time*, which sounded ripe for a Moorcock *Dancers* album. However, Mack's album occurred first and won out. The end phrase rewritten for *Starhawk*: "You are trapped in the time, where you are born, so strapped in the time, where you are reborn."

o o o o o o

With the Spirits Burning & Michael Moorcock albums, I continued mining my 80s songwriting. 2018's *In the Future* included the same arrangement as its parent *In the Movies*. Lyrics changed for the *Dancers* story.

Book two, *The Hollow Lands*, presented two slices of the past. The opening track *To Hollow Lands*, has Buck Dharma on lead vocals and guitar, Al doing drums, bass, additional guitars and vocals, and Jonathan Segel (Camper Van Beethoven) on violin. The song started life as a hard rock song called *Sodom & Gomorrah*. My lyrics were...fun, almost pirate rock: "Sodom...and Gomorrah...In the back seat...of my car," sung as "car-ar." Yes, I made car two syllables. (I suddenly recall Hawkwind's *Hassan I Sahba* and Calvert singing "Hashish Hashin-in" and "Black September-er.") Sodom's music originated as a cowrite in Pennsylvania with Randy Orris, who jammed endlessly with me in my Steelton basement.

Hollow Lands needed a great opener and this music had it. The poem by Ernest Downs, preceding the book's chapter 1, surprisingly fit. Al made a major suggestion: Open the song with a slower part, before turning it on with a fuller throttle. The other change...for me: I co-wrote the original as a bassist, and now approached it as an organ and piano player.

Also on *Hollow Lands*, a rework of a peppy, almost funky Kameleon piece, *The Blade*. In the *Hollow Lands* here and now, it became *Dance Through Time*. I retained many of the original "some of us are" light/dark/cool/warm/good/bad lines, given those motifs run throughout the book.

Building A Bad Scene was the lone 80s song woven into the third *Dancers* release. On multiple levels. The initial verses use music and vocal melodies from another Falcone/Orris song (titled *Flight*). Next in *Bad Scene* is an almost *Brick in The Wall* bass with music and vocal lines that hail from *Athens*, a Jerry era Kameleon song. No longer "where we watch, all the young men living in Athens," we're now "building a bad scene, before we build a good one." For added ghostliness, I inserted samples of Jerry's guitar stabs from his 1983 *Athens* guitar performance at the Civic Center.

Wrong Element Studio (1982-1986)

by Robin Burns

From Wikipedia: "'Hard rock' bands like the Beach Boys attracted the 'wrong element'—drug-using, boozing youngsters." This quote is from James Watt, Ronald

Reagan's Interior Secretary in 1983, turning down the Beach Boys' application to play on the Washington DC Mall for Independence Day.

The name for *Wrong Element Studio* was born out of this quote. A local SF band, The Employees, ran the studio with kind of a clubhouse feel to it. The space had a tremendous record collection and memorabilia hanging from the ceiling. In 1986, the studio was blown up in an explosion from an illegal fireworks factory on a lower floor.

I was the sound guy for the studio. I helped compile enough audio equipment into the space so we could do low-level recordings. It was a demo studio. We existed in a warehouse compound and would often hear band saws through the walls as we were mixing music. The Record Plant it was not, but for $10 per hour, it was a great place to go and experiment with music…which brings us to Don.

Don and I also did sessions in my recording class at SF State with John Barsotti. Don would complete 3 songs with me in 2-5-hour class sessions, while the other student mixers would rarely do more than 1 song. His song *Loralyn* was the favorite of that class. *Trapped in Time* was also part of this session.

One weekend at *Wrong Element*, Don came in to do probably about 8 songs by himself. It was early in the day and winter, so you could see our breaths hanging in the air of the studio. I recall him having trouble getting his fingers limber enough to play his bass. My favorite of this session was *Purse*, a song that lives on to this day [*Flipside Freaks Purple* compilation, on Flicknife Records]. He was using the studio to help in his composition of these songs. He was cobbling things together bit by bit, in the cold of the day. I liked the session. It was really the best usage of the studio.

Another song I recall vividly was Wood Alcohol? or Would Alcohol? I always considered this a questionable subject for a song. I never knew what it was really about, but I think this was Don using words to tease more than 1 meaning. He's a poet too.

Don was in a lot of groups. I'm not sure how he found his way into "Junior Birdmen." JB was kind of a 'tastes great but less filling' version of "The Police" with the ever-ambitious Sam Herzberg. I remember Sam would always make a sort of mask by making a circle with his fingers every time we would say the name Junior Birdmen. I thought Don would join bands like this for the experience, not necessarily because he was passionate about their music.

I remember Don playing experimental music for the "Robin Burns Birthday Orchestra" doing lots of keyboards and coordinating with Tom Nunn playing the Earwig. I can hardly describe what this Earwig did, but it looked like sculpted sheet metal with an electrical plug coming out of it. Lots of musicians from the experimental set were there. This was in the mid 80s, and it was the first time I recall MIDI being done in the studio, or anywhere else really. It was more eclectic than we thought. I wish we had done more with it.

Don was born to have a studio for himself. He gets to create and fiddle with his creations in a quiet space.

Two Weird & Other New Spells with Daevid Allen

My Road to Daevid...

...TRAVERSED IN EVERY space rock direction except toward Daevid. While I bought Gong's *You* album and their *Live Etc.* double LP, I spent more repeated listening time with Hawkwind, Peter Hammill, Michael Oldfield, Van der Graaf, Vangelis. After the Gong *You* line-up disbanded, I followed their guitarist and synth player, buying every Steve Hillage and Tim Blake album; and then Tim magically joined Hawkwind for their *Levitation* album. I dipped into some of Gilli's Mother Gong albums and the jazz fusion of Pierre Moerlen's Gong albums. The Gong family music I wasn't touching: albums with Daevid.

Except one: Planet Gong's *Live Floating Anarchy 1977*. I briefly thought this band was Gong with Hillage and Blake. My ears thought so. On closer inspection (and an article I read), I discovered my ears were wrong. This was Daevid and Gilli and the Here & Now band. This was the place, the moment the music of Daevid Allen connected with me. And then I continued to buy Hawkwind, Hammill, and other artists for a couple of decades.

Two members of Here & Now (Prof. Steffy Sharpstrings and

Keith da Missile Bass) would someday contribute to SB: Steffe to the *Starhawk* album, and Keith to *Make Believe It Real*.

In 2009, SB covered *Opium for the People*, the song that opened side two of *Floating Anarchy*. A bonus track on the SB compilation *Our Best Trips: 1998 to 2008*. Bridget Wishart sang lead vocals. Three musicians on the track—Michael Clare (bass), Trey Sabatelli (drums), and myself (keyboards)—were 3/4s of a band that assembled in 2001 with Daevid...Weird Biscuit Teatime.

Before that?

As the SB collective to celebrate space rock prepared for takeoff, I somehow set my sights on Daevid. Someone told me that Michael Clare in San Francisco could connect me with Daevid. And Michael made it so. I was introduced to this Daevid with an e in his first name, this Daevid of an incredible history...founding member of Soft Machine who performed with William Burroughs, explored tape loops with Terry Riley, developed a gliss guitar style after Syd Barrett introduced it to him, was in Gong when signed to Richard Branson's newborn Virgin Records, formed N.Y. Gong that included Bill Laswell, and so on...this Daevid that would become the most important musical seed for SB's early growth...connecting seamlessly with my openness to experiment with in-progress SB songs. I had no idea of the voice, gliss, lead, and rhythm guitar to come.

Daevid contributed to 13 of the first 14 SB studio albums, one EP, and three best of compilations. He also guested on my Astralfish, Fireclan, and Quiet Celebration projects.

Summer, 1998 (San Leandro, CA)
7 Songs for SB "New Worlds By Design"

My first session with Daevid was in our San Leandro cul-de-sac home, in a far end-of-house corner room, facing our small rectangular back yard. With windows open, I can only imagine what the neighboring houses thought. I had picked Daevid up in San Francisco, where he was staying at Pierce and Sunita's place, at Market and Valencia.

Daevid played lead guitar on the opening track *Solar Campfires/CellularPhonics*, an intense mix of space rock and tribal electronica. A song ripe for his Frippy *Baby's on Fire* crunches and squeals. There is tabla and djembe, and a second guitar (by former Thessalonians David James)—I was taking the experimental flavor of ethnic ambient into space rock territory.

Delicious Marsupials included Daevid's rhythm guitar. This song featured a recording of my dog Indy playing spoons encased with peanut butter in a ceramic bowl. Strangely enough, three of the four SB songs with Indy over the years included Daevid.

It was on *Arc - A Real Creeper*, though, that we really connected. Daevid improvised a gliss part for this otherworldly, pulsating piece that I had written with wild keys and samples, and Karen's space whispers. Here, in San Leandro, I experienced the glory of gliss in person. Heavenly! Rising! Higher and higher.

Gliss (or glissando) involves stroking the strings with a hard object (like a detached tremolo bar, which is what I saw Daevid use) while moving from one pitch to another. Someone on a blog says they saw Daevid once use a #2 pencil with electrical tape wrapped over it. And I saw Steve Bemand use a knife. Unlike a bottleneck, you stroke the strings on the neck; this interacts with the guitar's harmonics, producing a mysterious and heavenly sound.

The sustain part of gliss can be comparable to what is produced with the Gizmotron (invented by 10cc's Godley and Creme) or an Ebow.

Daevid suggested adding vocals. He asked if I had something in the room to read. I pointed to my hardbound thesis, sitting in a bookcase. He opened the book and began to randomly read parts of various poems, reacting to the keyboards and other sounds, interjecting various moods, mystery, laughter.

I took a moment to explain how I recited "Dig a thee, dig a thee, dig a thee earth." He took to its rhythm and enlivened it. When we finished, we knew we had created something like nothing before, or after.

1999 Full Moon Party

In 1999, I saw Daevid perform multiple times and continued making connections with musicians that played with him or Gilli.

March 17 was University of Errors (UofE), the band that included Daevid and Michael (Clare). Also on the bill: Malcolm Mooney (of Can) with his 10th Planet Band. Malcolm donated a completed track to the first SB album. The next gig was billed as a Full Moon Party. The line-up: University of Errors, Azigza, and Rockin' Teenage Combo. The date: July 27. The venue: San Francisco's Bottom of the Hill.

Pierce McDowell (of Azigza) says:

> *I'm not sure who set up the Goddess procession...I think it was Daevid who was hanging with Kitty Kaos a lot at that time. They had broken into Anton LaVey's house and done a seance. Her nom de plume was appropriate. A lot of things were not attributable to a single individual. A lot of it was just brainstorming while Daevid was staying at my house but, as you know, Daevid was the one who ran the show, whether he actually did or not. A factor of his charisma. At the club, there was a 'Goddess' booth set up where anyone could sit and be a goddess for a bit. There was a drum circle after Azigza played as I recall and which I contributed to.*

Before the show, I went upstairs, behind the stage. I said hi to Daevid, Michael, and Pierce. I saw Sunita before she had her costume on. I momentarily didn't recognize her; she was wearing a blonde wig.

I learned years later from Sunita (who Daevid and Michael called Pinky Psycho), that Daevid and she planned the event. Sunita said there was a "kissing booth with a transexual inside. Kitty Kaos was biting people."

I was in the audience. Near the sound engineers, closer to the club entrance than the stage front…where the procession started.

A violin player in dreadlocks, shirtless and wearing a loin cloth began the ritual with music. He was Thoth (New York based "prayformance" artist, ever-present in San Francisco parks and BART and MUNI stations in 1999, later the subject of 2002's Academy Award winning documentary *Thoth*).

Sunita was the central figure of the procession. Seated in a carrier chair and lifted high by four men. She describes her attire as "a headdress made from feathers. With a bird's nest on top. I had a round mirror in my third eye to signify the full moon. I was wearing a white gown. And carrying a bowl full of moon water to be blessed." She threw rose petals with water on those she passed. Deeper in the profession was a pregnant woman in an Egyptian pose, belly exposed; in my memory, carried by two men.

Many procession participants had percussives. As they created plural rhythms, Daevid took to the front of the procession. I watched. A snakelike quality to the group's motions. They ebbed. They flowed. Getting closer. I smiled. Taking it in. So real. So different. Closer and closer to where I stood tall. Daevid was now slinking the group in my direction. I smiled again. Content to be a witness to this once in a lifetime moment. As Daevid closed in, I could feel he wanted to say something to me. He was now in earshot. I bent down. Turned my ear to his face, and he spoke. "Get out of the fuckin' way!"

o o o o o o

In October of 1999, I gave Michael (Clare) a proper invite. "When are you free? I really would like to get you to my place…to lay down a bass line for the next SB CD. Have you put any thought into what would be the greatest space bass line ever?" Michael responded that he was "happy to come over anytime for bass playing" and "----- hmmmm, greatest space-bass ever might not come out of me, will try though." Little did we know…he would do wonderful space-bass over the next decade plus, first for SB, and then two Weird bands.

In November, I contacted Michael to see if Daevid was still in town; I had a copy of the SB *New Worlds* CD for him. (I also gave one to Michael, even though he wasn't on it.)

Michael replied "Daevideo been and gone" back to Australia, following the completion of the second UofE album. I sent the CD to Michael; he forwarded it to Australia.

September 2000 to March 2001 (San Leandro, CA)
7 Songs for SB "Reflections In A Radio Shower,"
1 Song for Quiet Celebration "Sequel,"
7 Songs for Allen/Clare/Falcone

On the second SB album, four songs with Daevid included Michael on bass and me on keys. A hint of weird things to come. Daevid was amused to be on the opening track with the voice of that Jimi guy, who Daevid had met during Soft Machine days. They briefly shared the same manager (Chas Chandler) and recording studio.

Daevid, Michael, and me, along with Teed Rockwell (Chapman stick) started the end track *Elliptical Orbits (Over and Out)*. The use of "over and out" harkens back to when I used to sign my emails "over and out." Like other songs on the album, there is a sense of telling a story through music and sound, while a monster lurks nearby. In this song, Daevid's guitar is the talkative monster (Godzilla? The other guy, the flying one?). Well, up until 5:30. Then, as the music fades, I manually play with a recording of Thom the World Poet I did one late evening at Strange Daze 99. From 5:30 to 11:07, we get Thom's philosophizing about language…sound, speech, rhythm…"adapting and dancing can be done verbally." I remember asking Thom if he was ok that I used the Audicy scrubwheel to perform speed changes throughout the playback of his outdoor dissertation. Literally, disorienting it.

It was an internal track—*New Spell*—which spoke most about weird possibilities. Against a combined percussive beat and sample drum pattern—likely from a free sample CD included with an issue of *Future Music*—grooved by Michael's slow, smooth bass…like we had entered a mysterious island…fog lifting, revealing a musical haven of synth pads and Daevid's gliss, occasionally shattered by my improv across my K2000 keys.

One of the Spirits Burning

For Michael's intro into SB, I gave him a cassette of current mixes. To listen to while gigging in Europe. When he returned, he recorded at my studio.

Don with Michael, Outside Don's Home in San Leandro, 2001
(photo by Karen Anderson)

Michael remembers:

We did the tracks New Spell and Second Degree Soul Sparks for SB and I was listening to it and thought the chemistry of you, me, and daevid was well worth an entire album so I suggested that to you, why don't we have a trio album and maybe find a drummer? and you took it from there providing the raw material that we shaped into DJDDAY.

In July, before Daevid's arrival to SF, Michael emailed Daevid:

> *Don Falcone, a very prolific fellow—as I very much like*
> *the stuff on Spirits Burning II that you and I play on, I*
> *suggested to him that we make an album like that with*
> *just the 3 of us and maybe Graham guesting as he will*
> *be here in September—he gave me a CD-R of about 20*
> *minutes' worth of cool rhythm tracks already—I am*
> *going over there tomorrow with bass to see what I can*
> *come up with, hopefully there'll be time between 7:20*
> *AM on August 7 and 11:00 AM on August 12 for you to*
> *put guitars and words if you like.*

Most of our new project songs started with my keyboards, samples, and percussion.

I recorded parts to an Orban Audicy, which had no bar and beat meters. This led to some odd time changes or jumps from one tempo to another (as I had done with Spaceship Eyes). Daevid and Michael had to react to all of this and did so with aplomb.

A couple of songs were built from a drum machine; those played more nicely.

Daevid's parts were improvised. He often did his parts in one or two takes, quickly deciphering whether to do gliss, leads, rhythms, or a combination. When it came to vocals, he pulled out a notebook with lyrics, or turned to his scat singing mode, creating human/inhuman sounds appropriate to the music.

Wikipedia describes scat, or scatting, as "vocal improvisation with wordless vocables, nonsense syllables or without words at all." (I always saw Michael and our future drummer as the sanity part of the music high wire that Daevid and I performed on.)

I initially used our last name initials (ACF) to label our band. In emails. In shared CD-Rs. Meanwhile, Daevid and Michael ignored my attempts at song titles. There was *Anterior Cat Flight* (ACF, I see), which I believe Daevid christened *Beezlebabble Slush*. *DJ Morning Extract*, which almost survived, changing to *DJ Herbal Extract*. *Pallino* (the target ball in bocce)—after my friends and I played bocce ball at Campo di Bocce in Los Gatos. *Torpedo,* *Journey into Mystery* (the Marvel Comic book that featured early Thor), and *Pieces of Zodiac.* These got renamed as they got lyrics, or the music solidified.

(I remember playing a cassette of two early mixes for Pat Thomas of Mushroom, who was over for an SB percussion session, and he was gobsmacked by what he heard. I was too!)

By October 2001, I had mixed seven songs, most with official names courtesy of Daevid.

We were closing in on a finished album.

One song, *Lavender,* was named by me, as the song co-existed on a Quiet Celebration album. Daevid guested on that album. We took his gliss and my keyboard tracks and added Michael for our album.

Late 2001 (San Leandro, CA)
7 Songs for SB "Found in Nature,"
Songs for Compilations,
2 Songs for Allen/Clare/Falcone

The third SB album included two tracks with Daevid, Michael, me, and drummer Trey Sabatelli.

Another hint at the future.

One of those tracks—*Wilder Beams of Moon*—also featured Mychael Merrill (percussion) and Tom Dambly (Electronic Valve Instrument). Those latter two eventually guested on separate tracks on our to-be-named later project album.

A few months earlier, Michael brought violinist Graham Clark over for a session. We never followed up on Michael's idea to start a band with him. Instead, Graham's parts graced four different SB albums, from 2006 to 2010. Sometimes, it takes a long time for a song to complete. Or find a home.

Surprisingly, I played bass on five of the SB songs with Graham, two of which included Daevid.

December 2002 (San Leandro, CA)
7 Songs for SB "Found in Nature,"
9 Songs for Allen/Clare/Falcone/Sabatelli

In September, our trio project grew into a quartet and migrated to a different Digital Audio Workstation (DAW).

When Daevid heard my mixes, he suggested we needed a drummer. I invited Trey Sabatelli, who I worked with at Digidesign, and who often subbed for Prairie Prince in Jefferson Starship and The Tubes. By November 17, 2002, Trey's parts were in.

The timing for this material and the *Found in Nature* album was concurrent with my change at work. I was becoming more serious about learning Pro Tools software and began to assemble a system at home.

The original ACF recordings were tracked in the Audicy. I exported its multitrack source files for each song to a disc. For most songs, I did source files minus fx, and a disc with source files w/fx. From there, I then imported the source files into Pro Tools.

(Actually, there was a weird moment where I was using the 10-track Audicy, and a greater-than-64 track Pro Tools HD system together; it was a bit gnarly. Yes, more tracks, more effects. Just too many hardware pieces to turn on, connect, and sync. I really needed to retire the Audicy as a DAW and did. My initial Pro Tools work for the quartet project was on a laptop and using a Digi 002 interface. Eventually, my Pro Tools system grew: a computer tower, Pro Tools HD interfaces, multiple external hard drives. All in place for songs with 64 audio tracks, plus tracks for virtual MIDI instruments and busses with plug-in effects.)

With Trey now onboard, and nine songs recorded and mixed, Daevid and Michael visited my home studio. Together, we did real-time mix changes in Pro Tools. I remember Daevid suggesting lessening the density. He also made three slightly invasive suggestions. I implemented each of them, enhancing the album. Add a trumpet to *Trans Human Future*—I invited Tom Dambly, another coworker at Digi; varispeed (slightly re-pitch with a slight speed change) *Oh Dear*; re-pitch the *Technicolor Tongue* bass guitar by an octave. On Dec 10, I labelled a disc The Project. A week later, I went with Inner Demons (or ID). Michael and Daevid still ignoring my naming attempts.

13 April 2003 (San Leandro, California) 3 Songs for SB "Alien Injection," 2 Songs for Fireclan "Sunrise to Sunset," 6 songs for SB "Crazy Fluid"

I was working on the *Alien Injection* and *Crazy Fluid* albums while Daevid was in the Bay Area for a gig with Makoto & Cotton of Acid Mothers Temple. Before the gig, Daevid introduced us. This was after Makoto provided a version of *Pink Lady Lemonade* for SB to rework; eventually released as part of 2006's *Found in Nature* album.

At our April recording session, one of Daevid's guitar performances was for *New Religion*. A new version of *Religion*, an 80s song I co-wrote with Tracy Williams. The opening lines of her lyrics forever memorable: "Religion pretends to be your friend, well, it's gonna get you in the end." I renamed it to credit everyone on the song; I checked with Tracy first, to ensure she was ok with this move. With Tracy now no longer nearby, I asked my wife Karen to do the vocals. In the late 80s, she was the engineer for our band and knew the song inside out.

For the *Crazy Fluid* album, I matched the music's experimental nature—approaching the Rock in Opposition genre—with a sense of play in titles. Maybe influenced by the *Gong Etc.* album I bought decades prior, and the song titled *Ooby-Scooby Doomsday or The D-Day DJ's Got the D.D.T. Blues*.

- *My Caspian See Monster*
- *Slicing Through the Unknown Plantagenets*: Remembering the *Last of The Plantagenets* book we read in high school. We had a combined history and English course. Two teachers!
- *I Don't Want to Grow Up and Be a Scent Dealer Like You*
- *Liquid Clocks*: A song by Daevid/Don/Michael/Trey that

didn't make it to our future nine-song album.
- *Fondue Fuels*: Karen now making fondue bimonthly.

The *Crazy Fluid* album wouldn't be released until 2010. It took longer for assigned parts to arrive and be incorporated. Plus, it needed at least one more song, not written yet.

○ ○ ○ ○ ○ ○

In the first half of 2003, we—the ACF/ID project—were called Weird by Daevid. Michael now shared images with the word Weird on it; plus, he had Hawk Alfredson design hand-drawn Weird logos. And we had the album title *DJDDAY*. Years later, I noticed the *Ooby-Scooby* title contained the phrase "D-Day DJ."

Michael remembers: "If I recall, Daevid came up with Weird while still in Australia, then UofE were on tour in England when he said to me—I think it should be called Weird Biscuit Teatime."

In August, I announced publicly: "The new and weird quartet of Daevid Allen, Don Falcone, Michael Clare, and Trey Sabatelli have a new name: Weird Biscuit Teatime. Cover artwork will be courtesy of painter Hawk Alfredson."

Michael Clare, Bass Player

I was always working with music in one way or another. Began as a bass player in bands in 1965 and did that for 10 years until the summer of 1976 when I was in the most popular band on Martha's Vineyard (Skyland Band). During that time, I had also begun to do radio shows on college radio stations which I continued for another 10 years until I moved to California.

After the band on Martha's Vineyard, I realized that I wasn't a good enough musician to make a career of it, so I retired and ended up in the record business working in distribution and owned a small record store from 1980 to 1985. I did play bass with friends occasionally but not professionally, although one of the bands (Anglion Audio

Theater) did open for the Zu tour in Hartford in 1978 (NY Gong, Mother Gong, Y'ochko Seffer, etc.).

My bass playing career revived in 1998 when in a slightly drunken stupor I asked Daevid Allen if he wanted to record a song on his last night in San Francisco. He said sure and I was quite nervous not having played in many years. The octave doctors must have been watching because it ended up being a series of jams instead of a song and became the first album by Daevid Allen's University of Errors.

After that success, UofE lasted for 15 years and recorded 3 more albums.

I also played in many bands after that, including Spirits Burning, Weird Biscuit Teatime, Transcender, The Zonkers (60s cover band), Loud Milk (blues power trio) and Men in Grey Suits (classic instrumental surf rock band).

2004-2005: "DJDDAY" by Weird Biscuit Teatime

Rick Wilson (who mastered the first two SB albums, and albums by Sonya Hunter, Matmos, University of Errors, Mushroom) had already mastered six of nine tracks.

After completing the changes Daevid suggested, we switched to a different mastering engineer because Rick moved to the East Coast. The only time a studio album I produced had multiple mastering engineers. We went with Mark Pappakostas, a Digidesign coworker who now mastered SB releases.

In 2005, Daevid presented the finished album to Rob Ayling at Voiceprint.

The response was positive.

They set an October 2005 release date.

19 November 2006 (San Bruno, CA, and Digidesign Studio, Daly City, CA) 4 Songs for SB & Bridget Wishart "Earth Born," 11 Songs for Weird Biscuit Teatime II

Daevid was in SF for a UofE show at the Hemlock Tavern on Polk Street. I talked to Daevid and some of his fans pre-show. Comfortably listening.

I was always comfortable around Daevid. Always felt he treated my music with respect.

He was maybe the first notable musician who I met and never commented on their history and notoriety. With our sessions, we had a casual way of getting down to business during our recording sessions—the fun of experimenting with music.

My praise for him was never about the past. It was about the present, and the future; what he did in my studio in this decade (and from his home in the next).

Daevid enjoyed singing duets, especially with a female vocalist. I had no idea. I experienced it with *Crafted for Wood* for the first SB & Bridget album. I suspect I asked him to play guitar and he suggested singing with her instead.

Bridget later told me she was totally overwhelmed and amazed when she heard the results.

Earlier in 2006, Trey floated the idea of a WBT live gig in November.

After considering live ramifications, we decided on a band recording session instead.

In an interview for All About Jazz by Jack Gold-Molina, I described the session and new songs as "more band oriented, whether due to songs with verses and choruses, jam-based songs, or even keeping some instrumentals to a shorter length."

Daevid at Digidesign Studio, Daly City, 2006 (photo by Michael Clare)

There were a couple of songs that I started with keyboards and brought to the Digidesign studio for Daevid, Michael, and Trey to basically learn on the spot and play to. This included Secretary of Lore—I had a boss at Digi that used to call old ways of doing things 'lore'—as well as a piece we later named Under the Yum Yum Tree Cafe. I also taught Michael the bass line for Alchemy the night of the session, and Daevid and Trey jammed to it. Alchemy was a piece I used to perform when I played bass for Kameleon, which morphed into the first SB, back in the 80s.

There were two songs that the studio trio created via jamming: The Latest Curfew Craze and Banana Construction. The latter piece was part of a longer improv jam, and Michael and I decided on the best parts to use. For these improvs, as well as Alchemy, I wrote keyboard parts afterwards, at home.

The rest of the album was constructed in my home studio. For example, I started two songs on my Pro Tools system that became vocal pieces—Imagicknation and Kick That Habit Man. Next, Daevid came over to my home studio, listened to the pieces, pulled out his notebook of lyrics, and worked out his vocal parts. He also did guitar takes for Kick That Habit Man. There were some shorter keyboard-based pieces too; Michael worked out bass lines for these and uploaded his parts to the cloud for me to import into the working sessions.

For some reason, the album then rested in digital limbo in my Pro Tools system external hard drives. I had signed a multi-album licensing deal with Voiceprint and my attention was elsewhere. Daevid's and Michael's too. For the songs that needed drums, Trey and I scheduled and cancelled recording sessions at his home. Trey, now busy with Big Bang Beat and other paying jobs, and like me, his day job at Digidesign.

April 2007 (San Bruno, CA)
3 songs for SB & Bridget Wishart "Bloodlines,"
11 songs for SB "Behold the Action Man"

Daevid's work on the *Behold* album represented his largest presence—most songs—on an SB album. I suspect we did two sessions to get through 11 songs. I even got our Weird quartet as 4/8 of the opening track, *Rendezvous at Lava Lounge*, which featured the James Bond-esque vocals of Silver Convention's Gitta MacKay.

The session included Daevid's guitar for *Stand and Deliver*, a song SB would perform live in 2017. And it brought Daevid onto my first effort with Albert Bouchard. Al provided drum and instrumental tracks for *Internal Detective*. I kept his drums and acoustic guitar, replacing his other parts with Daevid (electric guitar), Michael (bass), Hawkwind family member Alan Davey (synths), and me on mellotron and a bell sample I had recorded during a Mediterranean vacation with Karen.

2008

I think this was the year Michael, Karen, Jerry (Jeter), and I got together and toyed with starting a band. We met a half dozen times over three months; practicing songs I wrote (or co-wrote with Tracy Williams). I called us the Us band. Karen called us the No Name band. I recorded six songs. Years later, I used the best parts on SB albums.

Michael did some work on the second Weird album. This included a keyboard song that I dubbed *Untitled Monster*. At the 2006 Digidesign session only Daevid and Trey recorded parts.

Michael later noted:

> *I'm well dug into Untitled Monster and now realize why I probably didn't play on it in the first place. It's probably the hardest piece you've ever sent me to play on, weird time signatures, lots of changes and parts, but I've got some good ideas for some of it and working on the rest it will come with a few days of visiting it, listening, playing along, listening, taking notes, etc. until it is good to record.*

3 June 2009 (San Bruno, CA)
"The Book of Luana" for SB "Crazy Fluid,"
1 Song for Astralfish "Far Corners"

This was the last session that Daevid did at my studio.

When Daevid arrived at the house, he presented me with a gift: Robert Calvert's *Centigrade 232* book/CD, which had been released on Voiceprint, the label we shared. Daevid knew I was a big fan of Calvert's poetry and music. I was blown away. Interestingly, I had brought Daevid and Robert together on two pieces a few years earlier on the *Reflections* album.

We spent most of the session working on *Luana*, a four-part, 10 minute+ piece.

Daevid did guitar in two sections, and I presented him with lyrics and vocal lines for three sections. This included Daevid's spirited singing of the *Preacher* part of the song.

2010 to 2013 (Remote, from Australia)
1 Song for Hawklords "Friends and Relations,"
2 Songs for SB & Bridget Wishart "Make Believe,"
1 Song for SB & Clearlight "Healthy Music,"
1 Song for SB "Starhawk,"
2 Songs for SB & Clearlight "Roadmaps"

Daevid no longer visited San Francisco. Our new workflow: I posted in-progress songs to the cloud for him to download and import into Pro Tools; he recorded his parts, exported them, and saved them to a CD-R that he mailed to me.

I previously helped Daevid set up a Digidesign Pro Tools system, using an M-Audio Fast Track Ultra interface and Solaris mic. He used this setup for some Gong albums and other projects. (Avid purchased M-Audio in 2004, and the Tech Pubs team I managed created guides for both Digidesign and M-Audio products.)

In 2010, the Digidesign brand name was phased out, the company logo removed from the top of our Daly City office building.

We got new business cards saying Avid, and then I was laid off.)

On April 1, 2010, I asked Daevid about his computer's health, his thoughts regarding the in-progress mixes of Weird Biscuit Teatime II (which Michael and I were continuing to work on) and told him that I had some new SB songs coming soon.

Daevid responded:

> *Well it has been a long process ironing out the HP wrinkles (wish I had got the Apple!) but the pro tools and fast track ultra are exactly what I wanted to thank you. I have begun recording a poetry album and have contributed some voice parts to a hu hopper benefit cd. But the SOLARIS microphone is no longer usable...it now cuts out 50-60% of the time and since it is sealed, I can't really get inside to see if it needs cleaning or what...I am currently just and only just getting away with a basic voice sound using a borrowed SM58 Shure which has nowhere near the quality of the SOLARIS which was excellent while it was working. Not quite sure what to do next.*
>
> *But very happy with protools and fast track ultra. Send me whatever you need me to add to. I have WBT disks from Michael but have not had time to listen to them yet.*

I ordered a new Solaris for Daevid and sent it to him. Daevid continued to have mic issues. He sang quite close to the microphone. He suspected his moist breath was getting through on the diaphragm, or inside the mic itself; he temporarily used a loose knit scarf over the mic, which unfortunately muffled his voice.

I believe I got Daevid an M-Audio Sputnik mic, and that solved things.

○ ○ ○ ○ ○ ○

Daevid now had less time available for SB. He felt pressured, catching up on the backlog of drawing commissions he was doing, and that had been paid for two years earlier. Plus, his housing was potentially changing.

University of Errors had an upcoming May tour, and he was doing the bookings, which he didn't enjoy. He wrote "I find it the worst kind of focus for doing anything creative at all. In fact, AAAGGGGHHHHH!!!!"

I told Daevid I was going to start posting Space Rock Recipes. "They'll be everything from food to music tips, etc. So, if you have a recipe you'd like to share, I can post that someday too." Daevid responded "OK. But I really am no kinda cook..."

I eventually dropped this idea.

Daevid did provide parts for various albums from 2010 to 2013. For *So Strong Is Desire*, a song where he and Karen sang together, Daevid commented that he really liked the piece. He was surprised I wrote the music and its words.

It was an 80s song of mine, with the new intent to capture the psychedelic feel of a mid-70s Hawkwind number (like their *D-Rider*), with Nik Turner and other Hawks harmonizing. One cohort said it was the poppiest song he ever heard Daevid sing.

For the reggae infused *Bring It Down*, he used his voice for multiple parts. He supplemented his lead and backing lyric-based vocals with vocal rhythm parts: a vocal bass, vocal cymbal, vocal kick.

The *Roadmap* album bookend tracks were originally from a song I composed in an Ableton Live class a few years earlier. When California paid for employees taking courses relevant to their line of work.

I titled my class-created song *Yet Skylarks Perch*.

I presented it to Doug in Grindlestone and Bridget for Astralfish or SB and neither was interested.

I sent it to Daevid, and he took to it.

CD-Rs of Parts from Daevid

Daevid's initial guitar parts followed my structure. This became the opening instrumental. A few months later, he added guitar and vocals (about a female friend of his ending up at a hospital) and called it *Roadmaps*. This included his digital cutting and pasting of my two-track, forming an entirely different arrangement. I was able to recreate his structure in a copy of my Pro Tools instrumental session.

> *Hi Don,*
>
> *I have worked a bit more on ROADMAPS so the former files i sent you probably won't line up with these anymore. I made wav file mixes of:*
> *A TOTAL MIX*
> *FOUR VOCAL TRACKS MIX*
> *MAINBACKING MIX*
> *MAGICK BITS MIX*
> *54236 EXTRAS MIX*
> *so, i guess if you import them into protools in parallel they will all replay perfectly together. This method is*

*easier for me because vocal tracks are usually composites
of four separate tracks. I can also create and demonstrate
the sound/tonal properties i like to get with my voice.*

Daevid suggested the *Roadmaps (Beatrice)* piece for WBT II. Michael
saw it as more of a Daevid solo album track. For me, as it was built
on top of my *Skylarks* piece...I brought it back to SB and an album
with Cyrille (Clearlight). There, it became the album's final song.
Combined with the instrumental version, it inspired the album title:
The Roadmap in Your Head. (I was momentarily concerned when the
track listing for the first Gong album after Daevid's death—*Rejoice!
I'm Dead!*—had a song called *Beatrix.* It turned out to be a different
song.)

∘ ∘ ∘ ∘ ∘

I presented an idea to Daevid:

*I have a Spirits Burning concept...seven songs (a.k.a.
interpretations) using the same lyrics. Each song would
have a songwriter starting their interpretation, then
having me fill in the blanks with SB invites...or, having
the songwriter starter take it onward to completion if they
prefer.*

The lyrics were a poem I wrote about my father's time in San
Francisco when Karen and I got married. He and my mom stayed at
a hotel next to the McDonald's that used to be at the end of Haight
Street, across the street from the east end of Golden Gate Park.

I See Poets Simmer on the Corner

i see poets simmer on the corner
sipping whiskey from a paper bag
with their backs to the store
they mumble 'neath the flicker
paint chipping in the weight
of a tempting night

One of the Spirits Burning

my father
my father from a small town
investigates my city
he's staying in a hotel
one block from poetry

and when the sun gets its turn
he unwraps the dream stares
the voices wake for money
and the stomachs wake for food

i see poets stand with schoolbook hands
tinted with treasure, they can barely touch
i see poets, eyes slide in their sockets
searching for a home
in the feet that pass

so much good lip to go around
you can hear the skin and bone

my father
my father from a small town
puts on socks, his history
he's heading for the talk
— (at) the heart of poetry

"let me not be condescending"
he says so from the start,
and he goes into his pocket
and he pulls out what he knows

i see poets simmer on the corner
sipping whiskey from a paper bag
sleight of hand drawing

one crouches, one leans
and for my father, now gone
they still reek of poetry

Daevid responded:

> *Hey it's a really nice poem but no music flickers into my*
> *brains on first sight…I will see what i can do with that*
> *poem of yrs. leave it with me for a bit.*

Daevid never did get back to this. Neither did I.

I also asked Daevid for help in contacting Robert Wyatt. To invite him.

This was my second attempt; I previously tried through Jeff Melton and one of his Exposé magazine contacts. Daevid didn't have Robert's email, and said "it's complicated to ring him…" His lady answers, and she "really disapproves of me bigtime."

2014-2015: Weird Biscuit Teatime II

Michael and I dove back into the second quartet album. Michael recording missing bass parts from Hawaii, me doing new mixes and experiments. For the pieces needing drums or percussion, we invited Paul Sears, now regularly contributing to SB. By the end of September, 2014, Paul had finished recording drums at his home base in Arizona.

Michael and I continued to discuss and implement changes to improve some of the songs. And I continued experimenting. For example, *Imagicknation*: In November of 2014, I told Michael that I recorded a 1/4-inch jack one-thumb performance (with distortion and reverb); a short phrase in three places—"I think the 'flying' part twice, and then after the start of the instrumental section." This was my studio pre-step to get my Eleven Rack guitar rack input (for *Alchemy* distorted bass) feeding digitally into Pro Tools. For some reason, I didn't have the front connector previously set up. I had more news for Michael: I "added a sine wave synth to play off of your bass line. (I think it's during the 'I think' part, after 'flying'." And I "added a cello in the instrumental section. Karen made a suggestion to add cello, so I gave it a go." By November, Michael had procured the album cover from Hawk, as well as his *Razbad* piece for the inside or tray. And he came up with an album title: *Elevenses*.

On the home front, I replaced my tower's local drive with an SSD. Backups and performance improved.

In early 2015, Michael introduced me in email to Udi Koomran. We planned to have him do the mastering. Michael described me as "the producer, engineer, chief cook and bottle washer on the album. so, you two should communicate…" Udi was known for recording, mixing, and mastering Gong, Soft Machine, Present, 5UUs, and other bands. Udi verified that he could take our 88.2/24-bit files. I had to check. Higher sample rates still felt new for me.

Two days later, Daevid asked to hear the premasters before we send them off to Udi. I included a number in front of each song (1_, 2_, etc.), so that Daevid would hear them in our preferred, positive order.

Two Emails Daevid Sent to Michael

…and then Michael Shared with Me

(Preface: Daevid had been diagnosed with cancer in early 2014. He underwent treatment that had been deemed successful and was now planning tours with Gong and University of Errors. I had uploaded the current quartet mixes for Daevid, and Michael asked him "did you get the files from Don OK? Any thoughts?" The subject line was "last chance to turn around."

On 23 January 2015, Daevid responded.

> *Dear Friends,*
> *My apologies for the noreply and subseq silence.*
> *I finally listened thoroughly to WBT tonight.*
> *Well Don you have done a fascinating job of mixing this up for me and I find myself both moved and nicely*

surprised.

I can hear vocals, poetry, some glisss…what a garden you have created!

The thing is, I hate to have projects hangover but this is a severe case of physical tho not artistic or spiritual energylack at this end.

All I can say is I love it and would hate to see it go out without what I can still offer it.

It is on the top of my list to work on once the recording wing is set up on my desk here.

I will get it back to you as soon as I possibly can.

Love to you all and thanks for your patience, your cards and your sweet caring!

Huge hug

Daevidxxxx

In February of 2015, Daevid's cancer returned, and he was given a few months to live. On 4 February, Daevid contacted Michael and included a status report regarding touring and recording.

So clearly, any further touring is highly unlikely in fact.

I am attempting to record on the wbt tracks but keep falling asleep mid take and waking up several hours later. So far not so good but I will persist.

Daevid was unable to do any recording and passed away 13 March 2015.

○ ○ ○ ○ ○

Michael went to Daevid's memorial in Australia. I attended a small gathering in San Francisco to toast Daevid a final time; some unexpected things came out of this. Warren Huegel (UofE's drummer) was interested in contributing to SB. Jay (Radford) was back onboard. And Ninah and Das (Big City Orchestra) scheduled an online jam in Alameda with Karen and I for one of their radio shows. For the live broadcast, Melissa Margolis joined, making it a quintet.

Michael and I continued onward to bring our album to a close. Michael had Daevid's computer checked for any trace of recordings for the album. None could be found. We were ready to finish the mixes, do mastering, and find a label.

When we delivered the premasters to Daevid, we excluded the song, *Killer Honey*. The bass guitar and mix weren't quite ready. *Killer* was originally a finished SB track that I didn't have room for on *Crazy Fluid* and sent to a compilation (where it got a rare rejection). During *Elevenses* development, I removed parts by non-Weird musicians (guitarist Richard Wileman and Scott and Herb from Cartoon), kept Daevid and my parts, and then brought in Michael and Paul.

Michael asked about the title's meaning. I answered "I read something, somewhere, about honey being used for killing something, or honey being used to lure in a prey. Can't remember. Plus, the two words felt like a play on many, many levels, from good-tasting honey to a femme fatale… Just found this online: 4. Remove Parasites. Hopefully you'll never have to use this trick, but if you do, combine equal parts honey, vinegar and water and drink. The combination of these three ingredients is the perfect parasite killer." Online source: naturalmebeauty.com.

Our original *Dim Sum* recording was twice as long as the finished version. When we previously trimmed the song in half, we made available over four minutes of Daevid gliss for another song. I built a new piece around this with keys and percussion, and Michael and Paul added their parts. Titled *Grasshopping*. I also weaved in mechanical birds I recorded at a museum in Germany.

God's New Deal was the last addition; we felt the album needed one more vocal piece. We used a live recording of Daevid singing a shanty. I added a keyboard accordion patch for a folk feel and Michael added bass. With my electronic percussion in place, we invited Jay Radford to play bouzouki and guitars, making the piece a quartet.

Before re-completing the pre-masters, I noticed some songs were missing the Avid HEAT plug-in, which had become standard for my mixes. I highlighted for Michael the "improved tone and definition"; the mix now "appreciably richer and warmer."

Mid-2015: Cleopatra Records Contract and Robert Rich Mastering

One label said, "it's going to be too 'out there'." Another label thought we wanted vinyl only. Another label email silent. We decided to avoid Gonzo (formerly Voiceprint) for various reasons.

On Jun 14, I contacted Brian Perera at Cleopatra; he immediately expressed interest in the album. He suggested a different band name, Daevid Allen & Weird Biscuit Teatime. Brian wanted Daevid in the name, to help sales, to justify the release. We eventually said OK to his later suggestion of The Daevid Allen Quartet. Michael had last minute second thoughts and came up with the name we adopted—"Daevid Allen Weird Quartet."

The contract included CD/vinyl/digital, with marketing/pr (via Glass Onyon), and an advance.

On Purple Pyramid, a sub label of Cleopatra. They approved an 8-page booklet with color interior; photos could retain their original color. We would have to rearrange our initial song order to achieve under 25 minutes on each LP side.

(While researching vinyl length and streaming considerations, I learned that services like iTunes didn't allow people to buy a single track that was 10 minutes or longer. Instead, songs of this length were only available with the purchase of the album. Our album didn't have any songs over 10 minutes. So, more of a lesson for future Bandcamp uploads.)

I wrote to Michael:

> Reading about vinyl the last few days and have learned (or gleaned) a bit of info that has me concerned with us going over 24 minutes, let alone 18 or 20. Concerned, but not freaked out yet or anything like that.
>
> I didn't realize that the more music on a disc, the lower the volume (partially to deal with vinyl noise). I read that bass heavy music results in shorter disc time. There are even recommendations that heavier, denser

*(brighter?) tracks should be towards the beginning of the
record, if I got that right. It's not clear to me if a record
with lots of dynamics (like orchestra music) allows you to
have more time or not.*

*So...I'll be very interested to talk to Robert [Rich]
about this. He tends to be very savvy, and all-knowing
about the world of audio, so it'll be interesting to see
what he knows about vinyl and what he recommends.*

All the above did turn out to be pertinent.

There is a reason that many album sides end with a softer song.
And, yes, the first song or two have the best dynamic range and
ability to deal with bass. (I suddenly envision a world where Deep
Purple's *Made in Japan* is re-released with each of their greater-than-
six-minute songs on a respective, single side, which means seven
sides, four discs, to ensure each song sounds the best it can. And the
almost 20-minute *Space Truckin'*, already a single side, not improving
its sound.)

We asked for these changes in the contract:

- Update the delivery time from within 30 days to 45, to
  provide some breathing room.
- Add a line that we (Licensor) were delivering the artwork.
  The contract already noted we were handling mastering and
  delivering ready-to-manufacture audio.
- Exclude from our delivered items "multi-track elements,
  master Pro-Tools files," with the understanding we could
  consider providing the tracks for future remixes on a case-
  by-case basis.

When we delivered the artwork for vinyl and CD, the label had one
suggestion: Everyone in their office loved the back of the vinyl album
(Hawk's artwork) and wanted the CD tray to be relatively the same.
Their graphics person used the word "awesome!"

o o o o o

We had put Udi on hold after Daevid's passing. When it came time for mastering in July, we switched to Robert Rich. Perhaps, it was because he was local to me, and provided an opportunity to have another set of ears listen to the premasters and provide in-person input. Michael wrote "I'll pay for it, you did at least 10 times more work on it."

Jay accompanied me to Robert's studio. I reported back to Michael: "No issues with the length or frequency content in terms of vinyl reproduction. As mentioned before, he will pull back the limiting for vinyl." Robert did provide some suggestions to improve the premasters. I took notes.

Side 1

1. *TransLoopThisMessage*: No changes.
2. *Imagicknation*: Vocals (especially during verses) are in a cloud, due to verb and bass. Lessen verb on Daevid (and/or add pre-echo). Dip bass at 80 Hz, boost at 1 kHz.
3. *The Latest Curfew Craze*: 70s-style flat mix. Very compressed. Not bad. Make drums louder, to help drive. Specifically: Boost the kick and snare. Remove compression on guitar and keys, if present.
4. *Kick That Habit Man*: Good drums. Two suggestions. Lessen the verb on the voice a little. (This will also help Robert when he deals with 600 Hz honk during mastering— probably from vocals...could be in other parts too). Guitar solo: Take a smidge of verb (2 dB) off, so the guitar is more present.
5. *Secretary of Lore*: Nice mix. No suggestions.
6. *Alchemy*: During mastering, Robert will notch 800 kHz to 1 kHz, as there is a bit of nasal energy. One suggestion: Add a little gain to kick and snare to take the mix from a garage sound to a recording one.
7. *The Cold Stuffings of November*: Nice ending to side 1. For vinyl master, Robert will slice off lo freqs (starting at 100 Hz).

Side 2

1. *Grasshopping*: No suggestions. Robert impressed (intrigued) that it sounded about the same in stereo vs. mono. Mastering will deal with 60 Hz.

2. *God's New Deal*: Definition issues with 'double time' kick (the one that plays with and in-between bass guitar) as well as Daevid vocals. Kick is a pillow over the piece. Needs more definition. Lessen kick compression, cut kick eq at 100 Hz. Give Daevid a little more definition and bring him out of the soup: Lessen reverb. (Robert understands that I can't boost the high end, due to origin of the vocal material.)

3. *Dim Sum in Alphabetical Order*: No suggestions. Mastering will take care of subsonics (<50 Hz).

4. *Killer Honey*: Add 2 dB to snare @ 4 kHz. Note: compression of kick and snare are fine.

5. *Under the Yum Yum Tree Cafe* (formerly *Untitled Monster*): Good mix overall. "Piece sounds like a practice by Caravan or other Canterbury band after a gig. In a good way. Shame to bury the piece at the end of the album." Maybe Robert's favorite. He really liked Daevid's guitar picking too. Would also make a great side two second song…after hearing *Banana C*, Robert said: "Last two pieces segue really nice." Dip bass 2 dB. Dip first synth solo a bit.

6. *Banana Construction*: Voice sounds good. Mix feels right, as crazy as it should be.

We took a moment to listen to the first Weird Biscuit Teatime. It's the one album that I've produced that sounds brittle in places, especially at higher levels. I foresee a day where we re-release it with new mastering; maybe consider me doing remixes that include the Avid HEAT elixir.

I told Michael that Robert "heard what I meant by tinny, brittle." Robert expressed that it didn't sound anything like the mixes I'd brought him over the years. I mentioned the results were a combo of my mix (interpretations of how to deal with Daevid's preference of <500 Hz vocals and less mid-range stuff that I usually keep) and the mastering engineers. He said that it sounded like the 200 Hz area was sliced out of almost each song. When I mentioned that some (or all?) mixing went through the Digi 002, he said that it was a box that unfortunately added jitter.

o o o o o

Back to *Elevenses*, Robert wrote:

> *I am treating this album with great respect, knowing Daevid and feeling some importance to it. I am treating it like a vintage 'record' and hoping we can make something that sounds good and similar in all formats.*

Robert reminded me that the vinyl-cutting engineer might add different EQ and gain curves; Robert would try to predict what those needs might be. Also, the song spacing would need to be adjusted if the vinyl cutter used the mastered 24/88 files (which they would). The CD master included short gaps added between songs for timing flow.

Robert dropped low frequency and overall levels a bit toward the end of each side, and made sure low cuts were clean throughout. He noted that even on CD this will sound more like a 70s album. Michael and I ok'd the CD being louder, +2-3 dB. And Robert reduced the subsonic cut, as he had used for the CD.

o o o o o

Michael and I had a conversation about a WBT Mach II. Maybe a weird bass army of Michael, Mike Howlett, Keith the Bass, and me. It would have been an interesting quartet.

Daevid Allen Weird Quartet "Elevenses"

12 February 2016: For Immediate Release...

A sticker on the CD and vinyl packages reads "THE FINAL RECORDINGS FROM GONG SOFT MACHINE CO-FOUNDER DAEVID ALLEN." Online promotion says the same. So, was it? The simple answers: It was the last album he was working on when he passed away. The final mixes of the songs have his parts from years before and were completed without any new additions from him.

Both Michael and I were surprised at the sticker. In my original dialogue with the label, I said "It was one of the last albums that Daevid was working on before he passed away this year." (I wasn't sure if there were others.) I never said that it was his last recording. When Michael and I saw the last recording statement in the one-sheet, we should have spoken up.

In retrospect, I guess we could have presented the release as songs we did with Daevid and considered finished (two to four that Daevid then considered adding to and was working on before he passed away).

We did address it publicly.

A Message from Michael on Release Day

> One of my bands has a new album released today with a new name. It is the follow up to one we released in 2005 as "Weird Biscuit Teatime." The band name has been changed to "Daevid Allen Weird Quartet." It is the last album that I worked on with Daevid and although it is being promoted as Daevid's last album, I think that phrase is more correctly applied to the final album by Gong—I See You from 2014 or his final solo album Soundbites 4 tha reVelation from 2012. This one is the last band album that he contributed to and was doing some work on a year ago when he was fading and losing necessary strength and finally died with some ideas still in his head and recording software.

> *It is an album we started years back and recorded most of the basic tracks together at Digidesign Studios in Daly City, south of San Francisco. Overdubs were done at home studios and occasional visits to the Bay Area and all of it edited and mixed by Don Falcone and me in 2014 and 2015 (mostly Don).*
>
> *I am grateful to Don and Paul and Trey and Jay who play on it and Hawk Alfredson for the artwork and Karen Anderson for the design, Robert Rich for great mastering optimal sound quality and to Cleopatra / Purple Pyramid Records for believing in it and releasing it worldwide today on CD and Vinyl LP. And I am grateful to Daevid Allen.*

Mysteriously Floating into Another World
Summer 2015 to Summer 2016

2015 or so is the year that many bands and artists saw their music suddenly appear on YouTube. To my knowledge, labels did this in the background. What was strange for me (and Michael too) was seeing some of our "ancient" Voiceprint releases—Five Spirits Burning, the daevid and don *Glissando Grooves* album, two UofE releases, and Weird Biscuit Teatime. Also strange: Digital versions were on sale at places like iTunes and Amazon. The Voiceprint label no longer existed. So, who was controlling this and who was collecting money for streaming or sales? We had presumed that the digital rights reverted to us when Rob sold Voiceprint.

We contacted the streaming aggregator—Orchard Enterprises, and their department named "The Orchard Disputes Team." They informed us that Floating World claimed to have the contracts for these releases and gave us their email address.

Floating World was surprised to hear from me. Surprised that I wasn't aware of the deal with Voiceprint. I deciphered that as Voiceprint went into liquidation, they sold their stock to Floating World in July 2010. The deal included the rights to the Voiceprint catalog and physical stock. It was the former, the digital rights, that we had the right to ask for back after the term of the initial contract.

I communicated on "May 15, 2016, that I am officially terminating my licensing deals with Voiceprint (and Floating Word). To this end, I need you to close your digital streaming accounts and download sales (via Orchard and any other companies that you are working with) in a timely manner (within 60 days)."

I also had to prove that I was the owner of the Weird album.

(Another oddity: the YouTube page listed it as a Daevid Allen album, instead of Weird Biscuit Teatime. Perhaps this was because the original Voiceprint contract was with Daevid (even though the cover obviously had the band name).

At some point, Daevid instructed Voiceprint to transfer control to me, and I began to receive the royalty checks. I sent another email to Floating World, with heavier legal language.

> *The licensing deals with Floating World (via the original Voiceprint contracts) have expired. The original contracts had a term of 5 years plus 6 months. These contracts were done over 6 years ago, and there were no extensions.*
>
> *Consider this email a 90-day notice to end the licensing deals for the releases noted below. This would mean having Orchard or any other distributor of digital audio that you use remove download sales and streaming from the web. As we previously discussed, this includes multiple sales sites (such as Amazon U.S. and U.K. and iTunes), as well as streaming services (such as YouTube.com). Also note that some of the titles have been marketed with different names (some of which I may not be aware of).*

Floating World accepted all this. They contacted Orchard and had them take down the streaming of the respective titles. Surprisingly, I even got a little money.

One title had generated some revenue.

Spirits Burning & Daevid Allen—The Roadmap In Your Heart

22, April 2017

In March of 2016, I told Rob at Gonzo (formerly Voiceprint) about the *Roadmap* bookend pieces and asked if he'd consider releasing them as a single under the name "Spirits Burning & Daevid Allen."

Gonzo typically didn't do vinyl, so this would be a different venture for them. In early July, he gave the ok with the caveat to release it for Record Store Day 2017. This was fine. It provided time to do alternate mixes, plus add a new track using one of my recordings of Daevid's gliss guitar.

For the new *Roadmap* vocal piece, I replaced certain parts, for example bringing Michael in for bass guitar, and I looked to Daevid's old emails. He said to add drums; in came Warren from University of Errors (who was teaching drums a quarter of a mile from my home). Daevid also mentioned muted trumpet. In came my former coworker, Tom Dambly, who had also guested on a *DJDDAY* song.

The two Spirits Burning & Clearlight albums had covers by Hawk, as would this EP, and given that the albums had *Health* and *Head* in their titles, respectively, I stuck with the "Hea" of things and called the EP *The Roadmap In Your Heart*.

The new song with Daevid, Bridget, Michael and me: *An Ambient Heat*.

When the single test pressing came in, I went to Robert's house. He had done the mastering, and I didn't have a turntable at the time. We were amazed with the bass energy. The label had gone with 45 RPM. Maybe that helped. The sound of the vocal piece was a little darker than the digital version, still sounding good.

The single was released on Record Store Day, in the UK only. This concluded my experience with Daevid.

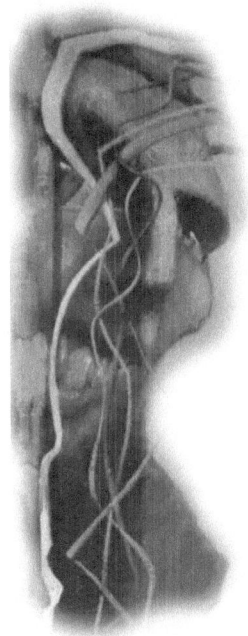

The Incident

IN THIS CHAPTER, I refer to myself in the third person.

○ ○ ○ ○ ○ ○

He deduced the date of the incident, 1975, September 26 or October 3. A Friday following a category 3 hurricane that caused the second major flood of the decade in his hometown, Steelton, Pennsylvania.

Memories intertwine the two floods. Both caused the town's main street and steel mill to close. Both resulted in people uniting to help one another.

Three years earlier, Agnes flooded the town's west side district. By Eloise, the west side no longer existed. The government had completed demolishing houses and buildings. Some Front Street business owners had moved out. Many residents had relocated to surrounding communities.

Hurricane Eloise: Enough damage across the east coast that the name was retired from the Atlantic tropical cyclone naming list.

He lived on Cottage Hill, safe from the waters that covered the town flatlands, a half dozen or so blocks below. Safe from Front Street, the Bethlehem Steel Plant, out to the Susquehanna River, and Three Mile Island ten miles to the south.

He stood on 2nd Street. Dirty brown water encroached about halfway up to 2nd Street, and then stopped. He saw his dad's office window, half under water, the Steelton Coal & Oil letters still visible. An occasional two-person boat passed by, perhaps the National Guard. He would someday title an instrumental *Raised on Coal & Oil*.

Throughout the week, they would gather clothes and other items from Front Street businesses. They laid them out in his backyard and other backyards, wherever the sun could reach them to dry and recover.

He had done it a few days before. He was now perfecting his method. Technique. Follow through. He took piano lessons when he was younger. His sister preceded him, his first lessons overlapping with hers. He hated having to sit up straight. The songs didn't resonate. He navigated the motions, and it affected his tempo.

Trombone was different. A social aspect. Other classmates learning at the same time. They practiced and grew together. He didn't own a trombone. The school provided one. Years later, they lent him a bass trombone; he suddenly hit lower notes with greater confidence. Still, he didn't like practicing at home, except to blurt strange sounds from his 2nd floor bedroom, his mother wondering why his music adventure led to this sound. He wondered too. The buzz of creating tones left his lips blistered and red. Perhaps he wasn't practicing enough.

He didn't think of himself as a show-off. A friend reminded him that he grew more competitive when a girl walked near the tennis court.

He was a teenage umpire. The little league field a block away from his home. He enjoyed making calls at an infield base, ripping off the umpire mask, his bushy hair expanding…he ran towards the play, made the call with arms and hands extended, while exposing his gray

Hawkwind t-shirt to players and people in the stands.

In San Francisco, he would play softball in Golden Gate Park. He and his friends merged with The Theatre of The Deranged—local comedians like Will and Debi Durst who used the same field. And Robin Williams played there at least once. From his center field position, he could see the famous comic hanging to the side talking to people forever. It was like everyone was in the on-deck circle...even though there wasn't really an on-deck circle or a bench. Theresa gave him the nickname "vacuum" because he caught anything in his vicinity. This was decades before he had arthroscopic surgery on both knees. He sometimes moved in the opposite direction from the ball's destination, so he could dive back sideways and slide to make the catch. He learned how to catch fly balls with a closed mitt, using the back of the glove, so that he could "catch" the ball and throw it home in one motion. He stopped doing this after one attempt resulted in catching the ball barehanded with his throwing hand, causing unwanted swelling.

He usually didn't regret his actions. There was a moment of hesitation; that might have been the difference. He did regret when he and two other kids playacted a scene from a prison camp. In his memory, they bullied the younger kid. And, even if that kid didn't think of it as bullying, it wasn't an action or attitude he ever wanted to display again. He also regretted not going to see Kate Bush during her 22-show *Before the Dawn* residency in London in 2014. He wondered why he didn't ask Jill Calvert for use of an album's worth of her late husband's poetry readings. While the two songs on the Spirits Burning *Reflections* album preceded the Brock/Calvert project by a few years, he knew he could have done more. Spirits Burning & Robert Calvert. Maybe he wasn't ready. He later vowed to never work with performances that weren't provided directly from the musician. It felt more ethical. The day his graduation photo was taken, he parked his yellow Valiant across the street from the photography studio. While waiting, he worried about the legality of where he parked. He decided to move the car. As he drove the car into the alley to the side of the studio, the alley entrance revealed something he had never seen before. Wooden poles on both sides of the street. He stopped the car, considered his options. He proceeded onward. The entire left door ripped off from the car.

He knew he could deal with an injury. After a future arthroscopic surgery, he returned to the softball field within a week, getting a hit while hopping to first base—then having a pinch runner take his place. More years later, he simply picked himself up. While playing for the Digidesign softball team, he made the call for a pop-fly heading his way. The left fielder was Kevin Smith, son of Olympian track star Tommie Smith, famous for his courageous black power salute. Kevin was built strong. He was not. Kevin leveled him like a defensive back leveling a receiver. The ball dropped harmlessly.

In the late 60s, his family travelled to a baseball game between the Braves and Phils at Connie Mack Stadium. The seats about 20 rows behind home plate. His oldest brother Rich was a Braves fan, Hank Aaron fan. His favorite team, the Dodgers, his favorite player, Jim Lefebvre. He also idolized fellow lefty Sandy Koufax. They arrived in time to watch batting practice. To his right was a woman. He listened. Soon, he was talking to her. It became clear: She was the sister of Hank Aaron. She said: "Would you like to get Hank's autograph?" He answered affirmatively. She stood up, yelled Hank's name, made a writing motion, and pointed to the boy. From the field, Hank eyed her and did a dismissive wave. She adjusted. They could get Hank's teammate, her other brother, Tommy Aaron. The boy smiled. She got Tommy's attention, and he motioned for the boy to come down towards the field. He took four or five steps down the aisle...suddenly men in suits pounced on him. Secret Service! Seated a few rows in front of him was David Eisenhower and President Nixon's daughter, Julie. It was probably Tommy Aaron who secured their attention and told them to let him through. No harm. No foul.

He didn't know his friend Scott had stopped by that night, asking about his health. His first twenty years of life had a shifting set of friends. Attending Catholic grade school uphill, instead of the public school, downhill, on Fourth Street, created one pool of friends, nurturing a potential disconnect with the neighborhood kids who were not

Catholic. Sunday church did bring together the kids with an Italian heritage. During the summer, he was friends with ballplayers on the same little league team, until he was too old; or the teener team, until quitting. The Cottage Hill Blackhawks street hockey teams, a revolving door of players besides Scott Baer, Bart Devore, and himself eventually ended. Spending more time in his basement, listening to music or playing music removed him from neighborhood happenings. Perhaps others of his age were going through the same changes.

Before the basement, there was the porch. Surrounding 3/4 of the house. The long side perfect to create a war zone. He inherited from his cousin Billy a large toy howitzer, maybe 2 feet long, 2 feet high, and its plastic shells. He and a current friend took turns picking shelter pieces and then toy soldiers. Log cabin logs, Lego pieces, Hot Wheels or Johnny Lightning cars, tanks, airplane models, Major Matt Mason space station accessories, anything that provided cover for the soldiers. Next, army men that could stand, that had a base. Different sizes, even different nationalities. His favorite had a flame thrower molded onto his back. After the sheltering and soldiers were strategically set up, each kid took a shot with the cannon and missile shell from behind their army lines. When a soldier was knocked over, they were removed from the playing area. You then carried the cannon to the other player, for their shot. This went on until one person no longer had any soldiers standing.

He never knew why he chose to play Hawkwind's Space Ritual while he lay in bed that night. It was the most tribal, barbaric, acidic, dark album he owned. Vangelis would have been more soothing. Better able to address the intense scene playing back in his head. The choice became all the stranger when an uncle stopped by. Turning on the light. Invading his world. There was nothing of value to see here. Next, came a doctor friend of the family. The doctor once lived on the west side. Its remnants recently covered with water again. He brought a title, a degree, experience. And an assessment that was incorrect.

He didn't wear a tie to school for weeks. He was exempted from that requirement. He had a history of being treated differently. He was younger than other classmates. Born in November, his parents had a choice: Wait until he turned six and have him start first grade the next year or have him begin as a five-year-old. They chose the latter. Walking a block uphill to St. Anne's with his older sister began his schooling.

His first-year report card spoke volumes. No grades for the first two quarters. He was in the hospital three times. First, the infinite runny nose; second, the momentary inability (or struggle) to move his legs. The family doctor had no answers. A new doctor, Dr. Martz, did. After traversing tests and fears, the diagnosis was rheumatic fever. Removing his tonsils and adenoids brought him back to health.

At school, the first-grade nun gave him a small milk carton while other students looked on. Students usually purchased milk for lunch. He would get free milk each morning. He was exceptionally thin. He thought about it, especially when a nickname like "stick" in grade school or "spoon" in college started. His favorite nickname was "shadow." Two people in college called him that, until they dropped out of school. By his teens, when the home basement became his area, his parents supported him trying to gain weight. The basement refrigerator, a few yards from his record player and album collection, was filled with loaves of bread and beer. He ate the bread, sometimes a loaf at a time, and occasionally drank. No weight was gained.

He returned to school about a week later. That first day, a nun approached him in the hallway. As she got closer, and looked at him, her face and hands took an Edvard Munch *Scream* position. She bent over, turning away with her hands now covering her eyes. He kept his composure. This would be his last year of Catholic schooling. College would find him no longer attending church. In his next life, by the time he moved to California, he wondered what would have happened if Constantine had chosen a different religion during his Constantinople heyday. Would the world, guided by the leaders of the chosen religion have fed a multi-god palette? Or a goddess religion?

During the next semester, he took a marriage class, which he considered quite liberal for a Catholic school. Each student couple worked out budgets, prepared a dinner so their parents could meet, and pretended to have a child. The class was led by Father Blood, the only teacher to later sign his yearbook. "May you always be open to others, may your silence lead you to another land, let your music fill your future with the best." When considering a wife, the obvious choice was his best friend, Linda Layton. Nuns and other adults expressed concern. Linda was black. He was white. One teacher told him directly to make a different choice. He never did talk to Linda about getting married. Instead, he asked another girl, a white girl. Sherrill. They would take the class together and learn from the experience. After high school, she became a nun.

He was impressed with how his dad handled the situation. His dad had been in the army. Didn't talk about it much. There was a story about being in Italy, and the next day coming over the hill and seeing Mussolini's body. His dad was one of the adults who helped St. Anne's break new ground, moving from 2nd Street to above Cottage Hill in the early 60s. The location supported a long, flat church and classrooms. The dream: a real church on the land just below the new buildings. Instead, the parish, its flat church and school would be phased out, combined with others in the area. The spiraling church never built. The plot empty. The dreamers passed away.

When he wanted to go to see a production of Jesus Christ Superstar in Hershey, his dad said "yes"—if they went together. In the last act, as the Christ actor was on the cross, the wooden beams began to slowly tilt backwards until it was fully flat, and the actor...remained suspended in air. His dad found it quite moving. A shared memory never forgotten.

When the incident happened, he described the accident to his dad with clarity. He usually confronted the truth, even as a kid. This single moment where he lost control. The weather, the randomness. He didn't like being wrong. Years later, he worked towards presuming, instead of assuming, and being honest whenever he simply didn't know.

He never subscribed to the evils of comic books or rock 'n' roll. He avoided the latter term, as it implied a sound from the 50s, before he was born. He did later help name a song *Space Rock 'n' Roll*. A moment of play.

He was skeptical when people tried to pinpoint a belief or non-belief, or event on culture. They were ignoring personal influences, other reasons. He looked for the root cause even before he knew of the phrase. While he wasn't a fan of Kiss, he didn't think their flame-breathing bass player was responsible for anyone mimicking an aspect of it. In his role advocating hard and space rock, he was more invested as a listener in Arthur Brown and his Kingdom Come. Aware of Brown's past, The Crazy World of Arthur Brown, where Brown wore a headpiece that danced flames above his head. When he mentioned Brown's hit, *Fire*, most people said they never heard of it. When he mimicked the opening, "I am the God of Hellfire, and I bring you...Fire...I'll take you to burn," they might say, "oh yeah, I remember that." Years later, Andy Dalby, from Brown's Kingdom Come, contributed guitar and background vocals to his Spirits Burning.

He remembered where it happened. Near Schmidt's Sausage Shop, next door to the Jorichs, a short driveway in-between. Up above Schmidt's, was a cage for the Jorichs' dog. A series of German shepherds named Major. He got bit by one when he was younger...he stuck his hand in the cage...The grandfather was Mr. Schmidt. He and his wife ran the original shop. That was how Mrs. Jorich eventually worked there, and her sons inherited the business.

For the incident, someone supplied a newspaper. A few years earlier, sitting on his front porch, where friends played games like Risk and Stratego, they did their version of smoking pot. They got some line paper, white paper, not golden rod, grabbed a few leaves from the large bush in front of, and reachable from the porch. They rolled the leaves into the paper, lit one end, and each took a hit. They each coughed. They brought the flame to a close, and never did it again.

For the incident, someone supplied lighter fluid.

One of the Spirits Burning

The children gathered...across the street...Mrs. M. watched. She could have stopped it; maybe she was slow to realize what was happening. His memory: Everyone knew what he was going to do and gathered to see it. She said something like "you're going to hurt yourself."

He put some lighter fluid in his mouth, as he had done before. He spit the fluid towards the flame at the end of a twizzled and lit newspaper, held and extended out with his left hand. This time...the wind was blowing. There were more people gathered than usual, many much younger than him, like newborn birds chirping and jumping to be fed. The first spit didn't create the expected result, the single extension of flame that occurred a week before. Without thinking, two things happened. Perhaps to correct or enhance the initial moment. He instinctively decided to spit again any lighter fluid still in his mouth, and he brought his arm inward, such that the remaining flame was closer than ever before. Some of the fluid dripping down to his neck.

His face and neck were now on fire. He jumped around and patted his face to bring the fire to a close. The neighbor was still at the door, watching. He couldn't account for the kids' reactions. Did some disperse? Did some check on him? Had he scarred them forever? He did go to the one adult present. For some reason, Mrs. M. decided to give him Vaseline to put on his face. He later learned that was a mistake.

Bill Jordan remembers "us being in awe after the first successful spit, but the second blow being the one where the lighter fluid blew against his face and ignited. I recall yelling 'take off your shirt' when I saw flames coming up from under his t-shirt collar and him then patting his face to get the flames out while we all watched in horror. A neighbor came out and took him inside, and everyone scattered."

Before he returned home, Mrs. Jorich appeared. Her middle child had informed her of the accident. She checked on him, talked to him. She then called his dad to tell him he was heading home.

His dad was alone. His dad didn't yell at him. He wanted to

make sure his son wasn't in shock. He had him do basic actions and watched: wash off the Vaseline, go to the refrigerator and get ice, create an ice pack with a towel, and then go to bed.

That night, or throughout the coming days, when he looked at his face, he saw a long stretch of distorted skin past the side of his nose. His neck also had damage. There were blisters, bubbles. Black. Clear. Stretches of skin. Red and yellow. Memories.

He was in bed, lights out, listening to Hawkwind's *Space Ritual*. An uncle stopped by. The last thing he needed was exposure to more people. He felt embarrassed, vulnerable.

A visiting doctor friend looked at the burns. Told his parents not to worry. The burns would heal on their own.

As Saturday morning arrived, his sister expressed concern about the burns, and the previous night's assessment. She reached out to Dr. Stephen Graf, a doctor she worked with at the hospital. After a mid-day appointment, there was a new 'assessment': second degree burns. He thought he heard "with some light third-degree burns."

The burns were initially kept covered, and then treatment began: He probably earned more respect from his mom than ever before. She heard him in the upstairs bathroom stomping his foot on the floor, shaking some of the house, as he scraped a section of the post-fire dead skin with a washcloth. This was a multi-times a day ritual, and he kept at it religiously. Supplemented with A&D ointment, which provided cooling.

Months later, his face displayed no sign of the incident. If he looked closely, especially after being out in the sun, he could imagine it. His neck had light remnants, almost like a hidden art piece. Nothing that ever made him feel disfigured or hindered in future lives. He resumed wearing a tie.

Perhaps the incident made him better understand the birth marks and scars that others carried in their lives. The incident made him thankful for the care he received, and his resolve to follow that care.

Tips—Sharing an Event

NEARfest 2007

JEFF MELTON OF Exposé remembers:

NEARfest 2007 was my last of four treks to Rob and Chad's ode to progressive rock. The niche happening was held in a rundown industrial college town: Bethlehem, P.A. (not the easiest travel destination from the Pacific Northwest). I had come out again to support my editor, Peter Thelen and my main writing gig with Exposé Newsletter (published in the SF Bay Area). Don not-so-surprisingly appeared at our strategically placed vendor table across from the dreaded Progression magazine. He was an interviewee in our current issue on sale and we happily re-kindled our friendship during those diverse and inspiring days.

Although it was Magma's second time headlining a day at the festival, they were certainly no easy pill to swallow for the average prog fan raised on Yes, ELP, and Genesis. Founder Christian Vander's diverse ensemble was always an impenetrable wall to pass through any conduit into their vast catalogue. However, my editor was a tried-and-true acolyte of the group as he made many earnest attempts to convert me to the dark side so to speak. Each attendee had the privilege of seeing that legacy French ensemble perform in their absolute prime on the live stage. I must admit that after the penultimate performance, that somehow it all was starting to make sense. That's what happens when you open the festival with a French fusion outfit, One Shot, where each member also played in Magma on Sunday night. Smart promoters and happy attendees!

o o o o o o

I was positioned at the Exposé table before and after each performance. I disappeared during the performances. I didn't get in line early for shows, as Jeff and Peter did for better seating. I was sometimes at the table alone. I looked forward to Hawkwind, PFM, and for the first time, Robert Rich, and perhaps the best live band of them all—Magma. Seated one row from the back of the performance hall. I told the guy next to me that Magma's drummer was special, unforgettable. Early into their set, he yelled to me: "He's an animal."

Exposé provided an area on their table for multiple stacks of my CDs. I was there as much as possible. Selling CDs, doing signings. I wasn't going to lose any moments...except...I was spending my Saturday night at home, in Steelton (81 miles away)—driving back to NEARfest Sunday. (I skipped Friday's pre-show.)

The entrance to the Zoellner Arts Center, where NEARfest was held on the Lehigh University campus, has large, oversized glass windows and doors. On Saturday morning, after finding the vendor hall where the Exposé table was located, I gingerly headed back toward the entrance to retrieve CDs from my car...and walked into a window. Hard! I drew blood on my forehead.

Momentarily stunned. I looked at my forehead in the bathroom, wiped away the blood, retrieved CDs, and returned to the table.

I enjoyed the rest of the weekend.

NEARfest, 2009

Voiceprint gave me their table, as they couldn't make it to the states. I invited my cousin Ernie (Mars Everywhere), and encouraged him to bring albums, which he ended up selling and signing. This time, I'd be in Bethlehem overnight. This included attending the bar scene at the hotel where the bands stayed. Ernie and I talked to other attendees, like Cyndee Lee Rule and her husband (Jeff Nutkowitz). Paul Sears was there. I met Johnny of GAS (Gong Appreciation Society) sitting in the back corner in a sea of smoke. Gong had played on Saturday. Unfortunately, Daevid was feeling ill, didn't attend the post-show band meet & greet, or the hotel conversations afterwards. I wouldn't see Daevid this weekend. (At the meet & greet, I introduced myself to Steve Hillage, and then moved on.)

○ ○ ○ ○ ○ ○

Ernie Falcone Remembers NEARfest 2009

NEARfest 2009 was a wonderful event. Along with seeing excellent bands and having opportunity to socialize with the band members, which was always one thing good about NEARfest, it was an also opportunity to have a shared experience with my cousin Donnie. Both Donnie and I have a love for similar types of music, and we have been involved in bands going back to the early 70s. Donnie moved out to San Francisco while I stayed in the Washington DC area, each of us pursuing our own musical endeavors. For me, I was the founder of a band Mars Everywhere and one of the original founders of Random Radar Records. When we attended NEARfest, I took copies of the Mars Everywhere album Industrial Sabotage to sell. I enjoyed the many conversations I had while selling albums with both old and new fans 30 years after the album's release. It also gave me a chance to experience Donnie's extensive network of musical

*connections firsthand. The drive back was an excellent
opportunity to share our memories of an event where a
good time was had by all.*

Some San Francisco Events

November 1984: I organize a Kameleon & Friends concert at SF's
Fab Mab, gathering former band members and other musicians. The
night includes the live debut of roommate Ed Kazala singing the
words he penned for our *Bourgeoisie*. The setlist has three covers.
Surprisingly, I usually avoid covers; they result in less time for our
originals. We play Gabriel's *I Don't Remember*, The Yardbirds' *Heart
Full of Soul*, and Zappa's *Black Napkin* (featuring Cartoon guitarist
Mark Innocenti).

December 1986: Paul Reynolds (who performed at the '84
Friends show) puts together a like event at the Mab—gathering 14
musician friends to perform at his birthday party. Guests during the
first half include Ed Tywoniak and Tom Nunn. The second half
showcases different bands and projects of mine (including Kameleon
and Spirits Burning). Paul had briefly been a second keyboardist in
SB. Five musicians onstage this night regroup in 1987, forming a new
Spirits Burning: Joe Diehl, Rick Gauvreau, Tracy Williams, Jane
Bryan, and me.

January 1999: I put together a show for Café Du Nord's
"Downhear Series." I secure The Grassy Knoll to headline. Next to
last, Spaceship Eyes—an experimental drum 'n' bass jam built from
my keys and Audicy tracks, with improv guitar by Joe Diehl and
percussion by Edward Huson and Karen. Before that, a rare Quiet
Celebration ethno-ambient-jazz performance with the original CD
line-up: Ashley (Adams), John (Purves), Edward, and me. Opening
and spinning between acts—DJ Sep. Three sets of dub to glue the
evening music together.

In a Deep Fix with Michael Moorcock

In the Beginning...

...THERE WAS ROBERT E. HOWARD and Conan. My entry points. I purchased all of Marvel's sword and sorcery efforts. Conan, King Kull, Red Sonja, and their magazine-format, more explicit Epic Illustrated.

In Conan issues 14 and 15 (March, May 1972), a new character appeared. His name: Elric. The front page plastered expected credits, including Stan Lee, editor, Roy Thomas, writer, Barry Windsor-Smith, artist. Each issue noted Conan was the "hero created by Robert E. Howard." For these two issues, two names new to me appeared. "Plotted by Michael Moorcock, creator of Elric, and J. Cawthorn."

I adored Windsor-Smith's artwork in the series, and anytime he guested on my favorite book, The Avengers (favorite character: Hawkeye). I was sympathetic when an issue's deadline was missed, presumably due to his intricate style. I could be patient. In 1972, I had no notion that some Moorcock readers didn't like Windsor-Smith's rendition of Elric—for example, the pointed hat on his head (probably influenced by cover artwork of an Elric paperback).

Soon after my introduction to Howard, my cousin Bill LaVia, about five years older, showed me his bedroom; a wall-high library filled with fiction. I began to borrow books. Howard, L. Sprague de Camp, John Brunner, Ursula K. Le Guin, and the Elric author— Moorcock. (I later discovered that Cawthorn was an artist; his artwork would grace *The End of All Songs - Part 2* album.)

My first Moorcock reads were not Elric. Instead, I began with *The Eternal Champion*, the Corum novels, and seemingly standalone stories, *The Black Corridor* and *Behold the Man*. I wasn't privy to the multiverse yet. I read Elric's *Stormbringer* soon after.

In 1974, I bought a live album by a British band: Hawkwind. The setlist included two songs co-written by a Moorcock, one titled *The Black Corridor*. No connection made. It would be a year later, probably after Hawkwind's *Hall of The Mountain Grill* release, me now following the band, that I returned to the live album, amazed to connect the dots. This band growing into my favorite band worked with one of the writers embedded in my cousin's library, one becoming my favorite writer.

I was a fan of Blue Öyster Cult. The *Black Blade* piece with Moorcock lyrics that opened their 1980 *Cultösaurus Erectus* album was the highlight of the album for me. I never saw the *Heavy Metal* film that included the Eric Bloom/Moorcock song *Veteran of the Psychic Wars*.

I was part of the BOC-L[3] online discussion group in the 90s. With the Moorcock connection as a jumping-off point, it provided harbor for fans of BÖC and Hawkwind. It always seemed to have more Hawkwind discussions. Maybe I just paid more attention to those. It was difficult to find Hawkwind fans in the real world. My North American world.

○ ○ ○ ○ ○ ○

SB's first albums did well mixing known and lesser-known musicians from the space rock community. Daevid Allen (Gong) and Steven Wilson (Porcupine Tree) the first two major crew members. The first Hawkwind family member: Robert Calvert (posthumously). I then started inviting other Hawks, including Michael Moorcock. Full

---

[3] Archived at https://www.glaver.org/boc-l/

disclosure: Mike is on the opening song for the *Reflections* album; I used a sample from an interview I recorded off the radio. The 90's wild west days of sampling wasn't fully out of my system yet.

First Contact

I attended Mike's November 27, 2005, reading at Dark Carnival, a Berkley bookstore specializing in sci-fi and fantasy. It's sometimes hard for me to get out of the house for concerts and readings. It helps to have a companion. That didn't stop me this time. I flew alone. Intent on making contact and discussing possibilities.

After the reading, fans lined up for Mike's autograph. Some fans carrying their collection of Moorcock books, some buying a book. I made a couple of decisions. First, I purchased a hardbound copy of his *Dancers at The End of Time* book, which combined three books that I owned individually. And yes, I might as well get his signature. I'm not a collector of them, and at times find them distracting (especially on a cover). In line, I could see that this wasn't the time or place to discuss a music venture. I decided to tell him that I'd talk to his wife, Linda, standing nearby, and give her my contact. That's what I did. I mentioned a shared friend to her, to break the ice, and kept it simple. We exchanged contact information.

I tend to notice acronyms. Perhaps a victim of technical writing and associated industries. They exist everywhere. Even when they don't. Like a game. I notice the *Dancers* acronym is DATEOT. I see DATE - OT. Old Testament? Overtime? I wonder: Do others, outside the tech world, do the same?

Deep Fix Demos with Pete Pavli

The demo recordings were first revealed in Hawkfan 12 (1986). They covered two Moorcock books (*Gloriana*, and *The Entropy Tango*). These were primarily sessions with Mike and Pete Pavli (High Tide). They were low-quality, live practice performances with a bit of tape hiss and background noises. They hinted at two future albums, and what might be revealed with a full band. Some songs were fragments or ideas not fully developed. None of the songs sounded like Mike's previous UA album or Hawkwind. I understood how his 1980 label was not interested.

Brian Tawn, who publishes Hawkfan adds:

> *The Entropy Tango, by Michael Moorcock and Pete Pavli, was planned as an album to tie in with Michael's book, The Condition of Muzak. There was also interest in it being a stage show and/or a video and work on it began in 1976, as it did with work on an album called Gloriana, to tie in with Michael's book of the same name.*
>
> *It turned out to be slow going on the business side of things and a lot of the music was lost when an engineer failed to save several songs. Then in 1977, the BBC showed an interest in Gloriana being broadcast on Radio Three, so The Entropy Tango was set aside.*
>
> *Unfortunately, the BBC interest fell through, but Michael had a fresh plan for The Entropy Tango. It was for it to be an album, sold with a large format, illustrated book, entitled The Entropy Tango and published by Pierrot. That deal fell through when Pierrot went out of business and Michael returned to his 'proper job' of writing. The Entropy Tango was published as a normal hardback book by New English Library in 1981. The music might have never seen the light of day, had Michael not sent a copy of the rough demos to me, who was keen to see at least some of the music preserved on vinyl.*
>
> *This dream was realised when I decided to make issue 12 of Hawkfan fanzine special by having it recorded and released as an LP, instead of being on paper. With Michael's approval, I selected the best parts of the demos to slot in with me telling the story of the album and it appeared as the lead track on side two of Hawkfan 12.*

After I got a copy years later, I suggested to Mike that I clean up and re-release the sessions on my label, Noh Poetry Records. As a historical archive. The release would include the songs, minus the track where Brian Tawn talked about the sessions. In return for my monetary input (over a grand to have it cleaned up and mastered by Tom Dimuzio, plus the cost of the manufacturing), I worked out a deal with Mike. Let me take 4-5 of the songs and rework them on the next SB album with additional musicians. And, I would keep any income, to pay off my investment.

I didn't know until years later that Pete (Pavli) wasn't aware of this plan.

In 2024, Pete noted:

> *I did talk to Mike when we met last year about the Gloriana/Entropy Tango release, which I wasn't very happy about, for a couple of reasons; I wasn't asked or consulted about the release, it just appeared, and also, I didn't feel some fragments should have been released because they were just that, short ideas and experiments that needed more work. I would have liked a hand in the editing and selection. Too late, so it doesn't matter now, but I don't have anything positive to say about it. I did say all this to Mike, and he did understand, and apologised. As a musician, you want control of music that you produce.*

For the CD re-release, I procured a captivating cover from Jilaen Sherwood, and the liner notes included my interview with Mike; a chance for Mike to talk about these lost, uncompleted works.

This was the first NPR release without me as a musician. I did some research and decided that I was the executive producer; a title that can refer to the person who finances a project. The release became the most successful NPR release, the only one to sell out. When Bandcamp came to be, I added it there as a digital album. (One label tried to pry the processed master from me to re-release it. I declined. There was no real offer of money for Mike or I.)

Don Falcone

Alien Injection, 2008

The late John Purves (often credited as Purjah) worked with me at Orban and then Digidesign.

The first half of the 90s, we rarely talked. Then one day, I learned he played sax and flute. I soon invited him to play in a quartet I dubbed Quiet Celebration.

John became the key musician on the Moorcock songs on the SB *Alien Injection* album. He also played guitar, other string instruments, anything that made sound.

When John passed away in 2015, it made me less inclined to build a full album from the demo sessions. He would have been perfect for such an endeavor. Although Mike and I talked about doing a full album, I tended to move the idea to a back burner. I never told Mike that not having John affected my interest.

By 2024, it was clear: If Mike, Pete, and I were going to do something, it should be something new, as opposed to resurrecting this past.

I had lost touch with Pete. It took a few years to procure his new contact info. When I gave him a link to *AI* songs with him, he wrote "I've never heard some of the Moorcock song treatments on the *Alien Injection* album...quite a revelation."

There was one more demo session element weaved into the *Alien Injection* album. *Logger's Revenge (Brian Tawn Speaks!)*. I included snippets of Brian Tawn's unused demo narrative. Done in a way that took Brian's words and short phrases to tell a different message.

Brian remembers:

> *I recorded The Tale of The Entropy Tango in our bedroom, using the twin cassette part of my music centre and a microphone. I would play a piece from the demo tape onto my blank cassette, then stop both cassettes. Then I would use the microphone to add my words to the new cassette before adding another piece of music and so on.*

The hardest part was getting the timing right when stopping or starting the cassettes and I spent a lot of time recording the same things over and over until I got the gaps pretty much right. Another problem was that I kept stumbling over my words or getting the timing wrong. It didn't help that I thought I could do it without reading from written notes. Big mistake! As a carpenter would say, measure twice and cut once. Well, I skipped the measure completely and had to cut many times.

And, in turn, I cut and pasted these lines into *Logger's Revenge (Brian Tawn Speaks!)*.

Songs, demos, project
  The lyrics to this novel
  Songs, demos, project
  The only opportunity
The only opportunity
  The clips heard here
The only opportunity

A Next Michael Moorcock & The Deep Fix

As 2010 started, I went into research mode to contribute to Mike's idea for a Cajun-infused MM & The DF album.

I told Mike that I was "educating myself with Cajun and other southern U.S. music via HBO these days, as we're now watching both *True Blood* and *Treme*."

I started to get others, like Cyrille Verdeaux, interested. I asked my brother to write a Cajun piece, and he composed a song titled *Doneque* (although I can't remember if that was a Cajun piece or Greek one…another ask).

By mid-year, I touched base with guitarist Martin Stone for the first time. Martin was Mike's primarily musician for the project.

I wrote:

Mike probably filled you in that our starting point (thematically), is the 'house band' of his Terminal Café (from the Multiverse comic published by DC Comics). The cafe is in Biloxi, Mississippi, and they play Cajun, Zydeco, etc. So, musically, we've got a starting point, with possibilities of mixing in rock, space rock, etc. and see where it takes us. (The actual story mixes 3 timelines, including an Elric one, so Mike has lots of lyric possibilities...and maybe we can even mix in a 'Viking' horn in a piece as it's part of the climax that affects all 3 timelines...maybe :)

I know you play guitar. Mike said that you and he can rehearse and record a bit while he's in Paris this June. He also mentioned that you can maybe provide some other instruments (musicians?).

I have 2-4 pieces started here as well, which I can send soon (I'm hoping to have guitar parts by Daevid Allen of Gong, and a local accordion player in place sometime in June.)

My role is a mixed one...producer, mixer, engineer on this side of the pond, some keys/bass/etc. You can think of me as bringing together whatever you two do, and others who contribute from across the world.

My other role is to gather the other musicians and instruments we need (I'm currently working on getting a collection of accordion players and fiddle players, as I have other instruments available, including a couple of Hawkwind alumni probabilities). I have another project (called Spirits Burning) and it's the same process, sometimes bringing together 40 people (although, I think we can keep this one under 20).

On the equipment side, I have a Pro Tools | HD system (my day job is at Avid; mgr of tech writer group that writes the Pro Tools guides, etc.). For Pro Tools sessions, I typically work in 88.2/24-bit. So, I can accept higher rate (or lower rate) .wavs or .aiffs. When we get to you sending me individual tracks, you have other choices (dry tracks, wet tracks, or even a Pro Tools session if you are using Pro Tools).

I think that's it for now. If you have any quests/thoughts, let me know. I have some other tips for long distance projects, and I'll mention those down the line when we're closer to sending files.

I also have some notes about typical Cajun and Zydeco keys, etc. I can send those if you are interested. (All deciphered via online research.)

cheers, and looking forward.

Over the next months...Daevid Allen felt that Cajun wasn't his "cup of tea" and declined...My brother David (the acoustic guitarist in the family) did his piece...additional musicians expressed interest in being involved (Mack Maloney, Steve Taylor, and Deb O'Nair from the Fuzztones—she briefly went to the same high school as me).

In August 2010, the early sessions for the Cajun-infused MM & The DF album had commenced. Mike had come up with the album title *Live at The Terminal Café*. The initial plan had Martin Stone on dobro and guitar, Simeon Gall on guitar, and Mike on vocals, triangle, and maybe guitar. The latter wouldn't occur, as Mike's health issues prevented him from playing guitar).

By the end of July, Mike and Martin put together an actual Cajun band for the whole album. This was always a possibility. They set up practice and recording sessions in France; the plan to provide session tapes to me to mix and treat. Pete Pavli was invited to the sessions and was unable to attend.

Mike and Martin initially had trouble receiving recordings of songs that I started. I used Digidelivery and sendspace in those days. They wanted to try playing them loud and rough as a band, as opposed to playing on top of the provided two-track. I suspect they had trouble deciphering the songs. Unfortunately, I hadn't included notation (which Pro Tools could export) or even a basic outline of the chords (which I sometimes do).

None of the songs I provided, including my brother's piece, would be used.

(I told Mike that if any of the songs I started weren't used, I'd probably use them for other SB albums.)

Many of Mike's early song titles changed or didn't make the recordings. Some discarded titles: *Cartes D'Identities* (renamed *Terminal Café*), *The Dead Heron, Joli Colinda, Joli Ma Coeur, Colour Sang the Blood She Pour* (some lyrics used for *Blood*), *Waltz De Beast Paul, Jack En Route a Le 'Trip'*.

○ ○ ○ ○ ○ ○

The 2015 final sessions for *Terminal Café* were delayed due to health problems with Mike's foot and Martin's sinus cancer. Martin needed to do remaining backing and lead guitars, and Mike remaining vocals. For fiddle, Mike identified "one of the best fiddle players around in Bastrop"—Sean Orr. Plus, we agreed to plan for extras like harmonica and accordion.

Mike questioned my interest a few times. He thought the album wouldn't be to my taste. I told him that I still wanted to mix the album, reserving judgement until I heard the songs. They decided to send what Mike felt were two rockers. Martin chose *Dream of Eden*, Mike *Mississippi Turn Round (Waltz)*. I liked both pieces. However, it was an earlier song Mike sent, *Lou*, that I (and Karen) fell in love with. I suspect Mike didn't know that I liked English folk; it was easy for me to connect to the Americana and Cajun stylings of their songs. Mike's vocals on *Lou* had a bit of Johnny Cash. The tune was up-tempo and catchy. One of my fave pieces on Mike's *World's Fair* album was *Come to the Fair*, which had the same combo. It made you want to get up and swing around.

I was in mix mode when hearing *Mississippi* and *Dream* the first time. "*Mississippi* vocals are nicely placed in the mix. *Dream* might need a little boost. All the vocals will sound even better, more present, with a little eq (rolling off the low end), and where needed, either limiting or basic gain automation (to raise the ends of certain phrases where the vocals sometimes start to disappear in the mix)."

Mike thought I wanted to release the album on Noh Poetry and Martin wondered about a joint release with his company (a book-based company, I think). I wasn't convinced that NPR was worthwhile. Another record company could give it the distribution, exposure it deserved.

From my vantage point, this project went quiet for a few years.

I did notice…every time I shortcut the name of the band, MM & the DF, I saw my initials.

A Different Alien Starts to Heat Up

In December of 2014, while awaiting news of the *Terminal Café* status, I was ready to ask Mike's permission for something new. I had spent the previous year completing a double album with Bridget Wishart, was close to finishing the *Weird Quartet* album with Daevid, and was deep into the *Starhawk* album, an adaptation of Mack Maloney's Hawk Hunter novel. I was used to multi-tasking. Adding another didn't scare me.

I wrote:

> *I'm starting to think about future Spirits Burning CDs, and the recent work on the Mack Maloney novel has highlighted how much it helps me to have something that provides focus.*
>
> *So…my questions:*
>
> - *Would you be ok if I did an adaptation of An Alien Heat (with the possibility of the second and third books if all goes well with the first)?*
> - *Would you want to be involved in any way (other than me using/crediting any text from the books)? E.g., any suggestions on the musical direction? Would you be interested in being on any pieces? I could have someone come to your*

place down the road and record any vocals or
harmonica.

• *Would you be ok if I released it as Spirits*
Burning & Michael Moorcock?

Let me know your thoughts on the above. I probably
wouldn't start anything until early next year, and I
suspect it wouldn't be completed until 2016, as these
things can take some time.

My early Christmas present: Mike said, "The idea sounds interesting
and I'm happy to pursue it!"

○ ○ ○ ○ ○ ○

By August of 2015, I had songs started and was beginning to do
invites.

For example, I invited Monty Oxymoron (The Damned's
keyboardist) and surprisingly—probably for both of us—invited him
to play percussion (as I had seen he did percussion for an event in the
UK). The target: *Geronimo*, initially the opening song on the album as
it covered chapter 1. "The version posted has my keys and a
temporary percussion loop. I'd like to replace the loop with
percussion and or drums that help emulate a train and provide
changes between some of the parts."

And *Soirée of Fire*…"based around a dark/gloomy-based soirée
in the future. On one hand, it's technically not ready for you, as the
guitarist will be redoing full parts in a couple of weeks. However,
you could record percussion to the rhythm loops. So, I posted a
couple snippets for you to hear where the guitar is headed. Note that
I had him play over some Greek beats' loops, which will be replaced.
I've also posted the loops, which you can perform over. Ironically,
what I'm looking for is African rhythms, as mentioned in Mike's
book." I never did remove the Greek Beats (from a sampler CD that
Karen gifted years earlier).

Another early invite was Andy Dalby (Arthur Brown's
Kingdom Come). When I sent him a couple of songs, he asked, "what

are the tempos?" Since then, I now always include the tempo in the song name. For example, "<song title> <number of musicians and mix letter> <BPMs>.")

He also asked for a full list of chords, which I provided. For a future song for him, I exported the notated sheet version from Pro Tools. Andy asked if the songs had vocals. I said there would be when the lyrics were written and sung. Both songs had temporary titles. *New Owners* eventually became *Thank You for The Fog*. *Twilight* became *Seven Finger Solution*.

Andy delivered two versions of each guitar part: dry (clean feed, no effects) and wet (guitar with effects). Many instrumentalists do this, giving me the option of which to use (or combine on rare occasions). When using the dry version, I add effects from Pro Tools plug-ins.

I provided Mike my full plan:

> *An Alien Heat has 14 chapters. I envision 14 songs using the chapter titles, or parts of them. For example, chapter 1 is A Conversation with the Iron Orchid, and I could see an opening track being The Iron Orchid or Geronimo / The Iron Orchid. A couple of chapters have some lyrics within them. My last notes say chapters 1, 4, 12, 13, so that's a lyrical starting point. I'm about to read the book again, to confirm my notes about lyrics, sounds, and instruments that pop up.*
>
> *I'd also like to experiment with some songs, using the book's context as an influence. Basically, the 'dancers' put together period piece celebrations, bringing together music, lyrics, poetry, sound, and so on, but...ultimately doing it wrong. That is, there is so much past, that they aren't aware that what they think is one time period is an amalgamation of many. So...I'd like to try applying that to some of the music: Unexpected mixings of styles, or sounds, or instruments. (Kind of like the unexpected groupings of musicians on a typical SB song.) We may*

get a cacophony moment or two along the way (which the book does mention), and we may also get some wonderful, or intriguing colors.

In terms of moving forward...

I'd like to run with the opening track, as I have some music ideas to mix with the train, Iron Orchid, and your variation of the Woody Guthrie piece. I'm in contact with Steeleye Span's new violinist and would love to have her on the opening piece. Cyrille Verdeaux (Clearlight) might be available to start a very Victorian piano/symphony piece. Plus, I have a local organ player who teaches classical music and runs a San Fran new music show, who might be an interesting fit to start a piece.

What I need to know before I dig in and start any songs: Which songs (chapters) would you want to do lyrics for? Of those, which would you want to write the vocal melody? Plus, would you want to be the vocalist or not? Did you want to try to start any songs with harmonica? Or do you want to do this more loosely on your end, where I suggest places for you to contribute?

One other thought, even if I'm starting most pieces: Would you want to come up with titles, based on the chapter titles? See the list of chapters at the end of this email.

Let me know your thoughts. I'm fine to start all the music on this end if needed. I'm also fine with writing lyrics as needed too (and bringing in other writers as well).

My ideal would be to have all the songs and lyrics started this year, and then me working hard with invites around the world to get this done mid-next year. Kind of aggressive for me (and probably for you), but that's my hope.

All the best, Don

With Mike's time on his books his main priority and his health status fluctuating, it became clear he was unavailable to do lyrics to the workflow speed I was establishing. For now, I would transcribe his text into lyrics and create new ones too. I didn't know that another collaborator would arrive in a few months, and help with this task, propelling the project to new heights.

Enter Albert Bouchard

In January of 2016, a year after starting *An Alien Heat*, I contacted Albert Bouchard to tell him the SB home for our *Coffee for Coltrane* piece (*The Roadmap in Your Head* album) was taking longer than expected.

I mentioned the adaptation of Mike Moorcock's *Dancers* trilogy.

> *If you have something started that might work for a vocal piece, let me know as I'm putting together the starter material this month.*

At this point, I had seven songs started of a planned 14 (which would grow to 16). Five of the seven weren't aligned to a specific chapter yet.

After Al expressed interest, I sent a follow-up email, clarifying that we were starting with book one—an album titled *Dancers at The End of Time* since I had already done an album called *Alien Injection*. I added: "14 songs for 14 chapters. Probably all vocal pieces. Songs for chapters 1 and 7 have already started. Any other chapters are available for songs. If you want an overview of the other chapters, I can provide that. Musically, it'll be bits of space, rock, prog, folk...kind of the usual. However #1: The tale eventually moves to 19th century England, so there might be a bit of that injected somewhere, somehow, deeper into the album. However #2: I'd like to consider playing with some odd music combos, or missing instruments (for example, some 'rock' pieces with percussion, instead of drums)... Long-story short, the dancers (gods/goddesses) give theme parties/events to celebrate their recreations of the past.

They are so far into the future that they often get things wrong, or mix things up in odd, incorrect ways. So, on a certain level, maybe the music could play with that too."

Al wasn't familiar with the book, and within a few weeks ordered a copy. One of the first songs he presented became *Fall in Love*. The acoustic guitar of the demo revealing an early David Bowie feel.

The first Moorcock track he contributed to was probably *Old Friends with New Faces*. He provided guitar takes, wet and dry. I used the wet ones. I started a shared folder in Dropbox—"Songs that need a vocalist"—and placed a scratch vocal version and an instrumental version there. Al responded with new lead vocals.

This became a song that mixed lyrics by Mike and me. It took a while for me to come up with the lines Jherek sings from his jail cell after a priest visits him.

> I've got another man
>   Also in black,
> It must be a fad
>   When things go bad.

> And he says...
> I've got a new dead friend
>   And one invisible one
> So sad, it turns out
>   He's the dead friend's dad

I felt the album needed to start with something more driving than the semi whimsical *Geronimo* piece (about Carrie Joan, instead of Casey Jones). And, I had finally decided to use the Wratislaw poem that Mike placed before the start of chapter 1. I composed music, verses, chorus, and transitions for *Hothouse Flowers*. Al suggested an addition where the drum break occurred. A ringing guitar part that leads into a halftime jam like already present, except in halftime, sort of like the end of *Starship Trooper* by Yes. I lined up Ryan Avery, a coworker at Dolby (and Digidesign before) to do violin and had him wait until we finished the new arrangement.

This was also the moment where Al said he could contribute drum tracks to any songs that needed them.

A few days later, Al delivered drums, acoustic guitar, four tracks of percussion, and a lead and harmony vocal. I agreed with his assessment. His parts "fit perfectly with the music and sum up the whole thing pretty well."

(The music with vocalist Jsun Atoms was briefly considered the opening song too, as it had several fun "era" lines, like the "rope girl era" that set the landscape. I ended up dividing that song into two songs. The music and sung vocal lines of *In The Future* were from an 80's song I had written called *In The Movies*. It was easy to change the lyrics to fit the *Dancers* world.)

Al now offered transcribing lyrics for the songs that needed them. Mike gave his approval. This took some pressure off me as well.

Mike was still having health issues, dealing with medication, and juggling priorities (like finishing a novel, polishing a Cornelius novella, two French comics, and a new Kabul book). And, for the *Terminal Café* album...Martin Stone had died, and it probably took more out of Mike than he expected.

We were now calling the *Dancers* album *An Alien Heat*, with 12 songs needing vocals. I thought 3-4 songs might be fine as instrumentals; Al convinced me otherwise. Al sang on some in-progress pieces, and then proceeded with invites. These included *Soirée of Fire* and *Quest for Bromley*, both of which got some of the best vocals on the album via Ann Marie Nacchio.

I had written most of the lyrics for *Thank You for The Fog* and had doubts about my vocals. I accepted Al as an official collaborator at this point and asked for his thoughts. I implemented Al's suggestions, which included some level changes to instill "drama in the music," some reworked vocal lines, and a basic drum kit to add some oomph to the djembe sample I had in place. The song was now ready for Al's drums to replace the basic drum kit. My vocals would survive. Al comparing them to David Bowie.

All this work with Al was in January, with both of us dedicating many days and nights (excluding my Dolby day job hours). Al was now involved on every song in one way or another. He even sent me mixes of new parts or lyrics daily during a two-week cruise Karen and I did from Singapore to Thailand and Vietnam and back.

We had started most of the songs, approaching 75 minutes, close to the limit for a CD. The rest of the year was spent completing the instrumentation for the songs and bringing in vocalists.

There was a short line in an email where I wrote "I like when songs from a concept album work well on their own (outside of the full album)." It's probably the one area that the Moorcock albums didn't adhere to as much as I wished.

Invite Thoughts & Examples

As Al was now part of this SB collaboration, I brought him up to speed on how I created a crew for each song, including the ones he started.

> *To answer your quest about the musicians for the pieces you started: The songs will be the usual mix of different line-ups. Typically, this includes some musicians who regularly contribute, plus some new faces / sounds.*
>
> *If you have any cohorts / connections who might be interested in being on a piece or two whether for your starter pieces or others—especially if they are fans of Mike's—let me know.*

Al brought in Donald 'Buck Dharma' Roeser to sing the new opener (*Hothouse*), his brother Joe, Andy Shernoff, Don Fleming, Richie Castellano, Ann Marie Nacchio, and others.

I consciously try to bring in some new blood each album. And re-invite those that I know like the project and have done well with past material. For *Alien Heat*, the mix included Hawkwind family members Harvey Bainbridge, Mick Slattery, and Bridget Wishart,

Groundhogs' drummer Ken Pustelnik, guitarist Igor Abuladze (via Doug Erickson and their experience in Fripp's Guitar Circle classes), violinist Ryan Avery, Steve York, Andy Dalby, Jack Gold-Molina, Lux Vibratus, and others.

There were some interesting attempts that didn't work out. Hawkwind dancer Stacia. Bob Weir (who I knew Mike liked a lot); I contacted his manager on LinkedIn. Al reached out to Eric Bloom (who had introduced Al to Mike's works many years before). Eric would end up on the second *Dancers* album.

○ ○ ○ ○ ○ ○

In late 2017, Al wrote:

> *I must apologize for kind of hijacking the project, and if you never thought that great. But it was an idea that piqued my interest to almost an obsessive degree for a few months there. I must say I had a good time working with you on this project and I hope you will consider me for the next one.*

I responded:

> *It was a really good hijacking!*
>
> *I always looked at it as you simply had a true, passionate interest, and I welcomed it. You consistently provided inspiration and a sounding board, and I was happy and honored to have you onboard as a musician, songwriter, lyricist, and virtual talent scout.*
>
> *Over the years, I suspect that you've had some special, emotional moments with a few songs during their growth. I had more than a few of those moments when Karen and I were in Asia on the cruise, and you were posting updated songs. When I heard Learning the Art...I almost cried... :-)*
>
> *> I hope you will consider me for the next one.*

Absolutely.

Technically, I'd like to do things in the same manner as AAH. The challenge will be to do as well starting closer to scratch.

As we get into November, I'm reviewing the book II outline I did a few months ago—thinking about potential styles for some songs—and reviewing a few unused songs that I've started. I should be able to share what I have after Thanksgiving. That's my current goal.

I also typically try to create a list of possible crew members / instruments early on. I've got a list of a few musicians who would like to contribute, or that I'd like to reach out to. If you want to add to that some possible musicians, that would help me at this point. Potentials are fine. I'm used to having some people on the list who decline at some point.

Cheers, Don

Example Guidance to an Invite, Richie Castellano

For some invites, I provide guidance, especially when asked. For Richie Castellano and his guitar parts for *Any Particular Interest* and *In The Future* (which were combined when initially presented to him), I wrote: "think of it as…if we were in a band, in the same room, and you were working out guitar parts, what would you do based on my first thoughts? Basically, I'm open to other possibilities."

My first thoughts included: For the *Any Particular Interest* intro:

Anything that helps keep it mysterious, maybe even dark. For the 'electronica' section, consider a guitar-rhythm to go with the turtle violin and e-percussion, maybe non-pitched (or barely pitched, like Bowie's Modern Love?), maybe with a wah.

For the *In The Future* song:

> ...*rhythm guitar throughout, and lots of soloing in the section that has no vocals.*
>
> *Here is an example of my shorthand chord info, which covers the solo section:*
>
> *2 x [Am (bass line = AGA, GA, GAGAG) x 2*
>
> *C (bass line = CBC, BC, BCBCB)*
>
> *Am (bass line = AGA, GA, GAGAG)*
>
> *(Em Em Em, Em Em Em, D D D, C C C) x 2]*
>
> *I might have a violin solo in this part too, responding to what you do (kind of like a band of old called High Tide). Since you're first, he'll have to respond to what you do.*

For *Hothouse Flowers*:

> *Mainly rhythm, plus harmonizing with the little transition motifs. Feel free to add a melodic line in the intro, or where you think it makes sense. No real solos, as I'll probably have violin or sax do a solo in this one.*

Live At the Terminal Café—Act 2 of 2

Martin Stone died of cancer 9 November 2016 in Versailles, France.

Mike considered Martin his musical director, and with him gone, asked if I could take over at an earlier state.

Mike knew he was essentially asking me to work on two records at once, probably unaware that I generally worked on four or five at once.

Mike noted real issues, though, which felt beyond my current reach. The album was unfinished. Some songs had rough guitar takes. A nine-minute track had "some nice guitar" maybe "better if used as a linking piece between more conventional songs."

Mike was concerned that his harmonica playing "might be too rusty to play on a lot of stuff."

Mike suggested we consider writing any new material and getting other new stuff worked out when I travel to his Texas home.

A Trip to Texas!

In March of 2017, I informed Al of the recording session with Mike.

> Hi Al,
>
> Some good news!
>
> I'm going to be doing a session with Mike in late April, in Austin. It'll be a short session, so I'm going to try to limit it to background vocals, maybe some soft-spoken parts, and two or so harmonica experiments.
>
> I'd like to see if you have any other recommendations other than my first thoughts (for example, backing vocals on at least one of the songs that you started).
>
> Background vocals:
> - In The Future chorus
> - Geronimo chorus
> - Hothouse Flowers chorus and end (even though we don't have final vocals for this)
>
> Harmonica:
> - Geronimo
> - Soirée of Fire background
> - Any Particular Interest, maybe…
>
> Spoken parts:
> - Mike is going to listen to the current mixes and see if there are places ripe for spoken parts. If yes, he'll write lyrics.
> - While I don't know if there will be time to record, I suggested he consider writing some parts for Hollow Lands.

My flight was Wednesday, April 19. Mike, with Linda driving, picked me up at the airport. I had emailed a photo of me, so they knew what I looked like. We planned an afternoon session, and then getting me back to the airport.

Our rendezvous was months in the making.

We briefly talked of me paying for a session at a nearby recording studio or even Mike recording in the Bay Area (if he was here, visiting Harlan Ellison). The studio idea with or without me, possibly with a former Digidesign coworker of mine, Nick Pellicciotto. Linda pointed out legitimate concerns with the wear and tear of Mike traveling or being in a studio for any length of time.

If we were to record at their home, she had concerns about lots of equipment being lugged in the house.

I responded:

> *In terms of equipment, it's not as much as you'd think:*
> - *a laptop*
> - *a little box that connects to the laptop*
> - *one mic stand, and one mic*
> - *two headphones*
>
> *That should be it.*

I added a tiny headphone amp. The little I/O box that connected to my laptop didn't have two headphone jacks.

Once we got to the house, Linda showed me the dining room where we would record. I set up the equipment quickly (as practiced at home). As Mike got comfortable in a chair near the table and mic, I introduced him to the mic, mic stand, and his headphones.

One of his cats jumped onto the table and curled around the mic.

The session concentrated primarily on *An Alien Heat*. I recorded Mike's vocals first (backing or choir vocals, now a total of 12 songs), and then harmonica (three songs). We also did a couple of early songs for the subsequent album (*The Hollow Lands*).

Mike reading a passage from The Hollow Lands, 2017 (photo by Don Falcone)

Before and during the session, I kept my workflow notes nearby:

1. Put on the headphones and do a quick test of levels to ensure Mike can hear the audio and his vocals comfortably.
2. (For vocal songs): Have Mike locate the lyrics that I had Mike and Linda print out.
3. In Pro Tools, navigate to the two-track snippet of the song. I use song markers to locate the song snippet. The location is typically 4-8 beats prior to the vocal start. This gives Mike a virtual count off, and ensures any pickup note is recorded.
4. Tell Mike what you'd like him to do. If necessary, play back the snippet and demonstrate what you want.
5. Record the performance 2-3 times (Make sure that Mike

sings or voices each word well at least once, even if they are spread across multiple takes.)

6. (Optional) Listen back. Do this if necessary to highlight something.
7. Repeat steps 2-6.

For each song, we followed the same procedure.

Behold The Box Set!

The record label decided that the release could support a standard CD release, plus a boxed version. Using PledgeMusic, a direct-to-fan music platform.

• CD: Spirits Burning & Michael Moorcock *An Alien Heat*.

- Lyric book: *Michael Moorcock with Spirits Burning — The Lyrics of An Alien Heat*.
- Signed certificate (signed by Mike, Al, and me). The label head became even more excited when Mike agreed to sign 250. That really solidified doing a boxed edition.
- Small poster.
- Four postcards.
- Sticker.
- Second CD (*Instrumentals for An Alien Heat*). I told Rob at Gonzo I had instrumental versions available, which I did for all vocal albums, starting with *Starhawk*—primarily for possible sync usage in film or TV. I suggested a bonus download. Rob countered with adding a bonus disc. While I was concerned about anything that would push out the release date, it was a nice touch.

The Certificate Story…

The color certificates featured three illustrations: CD cover, lyric book cover, disc artwork. There was a light block to denote the sheet number (limited edition of 250 units). And three blocks for each primary collaborator to provide their signature from their respective locale. The workflow: Get the certificates from the English factory to Mike (currently in France), to Al (New York), to me (California), and then back to the label in the U.K. The sheets completed their full trip in just over a month.

During Al's leg of the medley relay, he noted:

> *I signed them non-stop in about 20 or 30 minutes so I might have missed one or two, but I really got my sig down by the end. I've been studying the one I got from Obama, and I think I'm moving in that direction.*

Al was honored at the White House by the former president for being an outstanding educator and member of NAfME (National Association for Music Education) for over 25 years.

After I completed signing the sheets, I sent some extra completed certificates to Al and Mike.

Bound to the Lyrics

Designing a lyric book was new territory for Karen and me. We had numerous questions and issues to work through with the label, the manufacturer, and the book itself.

1. Concern with pastel-based artwork and how it would print. I was amused they said to go back and talk to my designer. I looked across the room and said, "hon…" (since my wife, Karen, was the designer). This was probably one of the first manufacturers that required pdf proofs, instead of direct-from-Photoshop tifs (which felt easier and now seems a thing of the past). We let the design play out with risk. It turned out fine.

2. The number of ads at the end of the book. At one point, 20% of the book was ads, the book ballooning from 24 pages to 30. I was concerned about the increase in cost (to fans, and to Gonzo). The final reworked book: 24 pages.

3. The inclusion of ads for the Frank Zappa *Porn Wars* book. I advocated for Gonzo books with a Hawkwind connection (such as *Festivalized*, by Bridget Wishart and Hawkwind scribe Ian Abraham). Plus, I didn't really want cartoon nudes in the context of the "dancers" artwork by Jilaen. We had put together a certain steampunk/serious approach to the package and music, and the *Porn Wars* seemed inappropriate. Surprisingly, all ads were removed.

4. A mistake found by Jonathan Downes, the label person managing the lyric book. The lyrics for *Quest for Bromley* read "As Eva sped to Hitler, as Oscar sped to Boise," with the vocals also "sped to Boise." In real life, Oscar's lover was Bosie. I contacted Mike and we rewrote the lyrics: "As Oscar sped to Bosie ('boysie')." My research revealed that Bosie's sister gave him the nickname Bosie, based on the term

'boysie'. Jonathan less convinced with our solution.

5. 666.25 x 10.25, the size specifications for the saddle stitch book. Maybe the presence of 666 should have concerned us. Then again, I believe the number spells Nero and not the devil... Anyways, work on the box package and book had now stretched into 2018. This gave us time to update the CD booklet—we had discovered two missing crew members. I was able to contact them and tell them the good news. Meanwhile, the release wasn't in the PledgeMusic queue yet. It was...approaching. On April 19, we were informed that the lyric book design was too large for the box. We had been given incorrect specs. We needed to adjust to "royal octavo."

In mid-May, PledgeMusic requested access to the Spirits Burning Facebook band site, to start an advertising campaign (paid for by the label). Our release was live in May (for pre-orders), shipping in June. Then they pushed it out a month again to get more orders. The post-box, CD only version released Sept. 11, 2018. (Almost four years since I first conceived of the album.)

The good news: The second SB & Michael Moorcock album was now well under way.

Otherwise: What was the status of *Live at The Terminal Café?*

Mistakes Are Made

I PICKED UP Nik Turner on a 2012 morning. Noon closing in, as was the wind from the Pacific Ocean. Nik was staying at a place north of Golden Gate Park (the Richmond district). A short 22-minute, 12-mile car ride from our home in San Bruno.

Northwest San Francisco could be cool at night, cool during the day. When my Shippensburg college roommate Ken Schmidt visited us, he, his wife, and daughter met us at The Cliff House, a nearby restaurant overlooking the Pacific Ocean. Underdressed. Short sleeve shirt and light jacket, short dresses. They quickly discovered: San Francisco is the city of layers.

I was too punctual, nailing the time we had set. Nik wasn't ready. Nicky Garratt answered the door in a robe. Nicky had been in the U.K. Subs and now fronted Hedersleben. They were opening for Nik's tour and were his backing band.

Nik packed two saxes and a flute. We headed to my home studio. I asked Nik if he still played oboe. He said "no." (His oboe on the Hawkwind song *D-Rider* swirled in my head.)

Don and Nik, San Bruno Home Studio, 2012 (photo by Karen Anderson)

For these one-day sessions, I prepared my studio software ahead of time. A single Pro Tools session with stereo versions of every song we might touch. Having everything in one file eliminates the time it takes to open and close multiple sessions. I'd import his parts to the source multi-track sessions later. I had the individual sessions ready too, in case Nik wanted to hear more or less of any instruments or the vocals while recording.

I created a few empty mono tracks for him to record to. I rarely use the loop record feature that creates a playlist of takes. It feels more natural to manually start again, even with the extra hand moves. (When I first started recording, I sometimes used the pre-roll feature too close to where I wanted the recording to start, and the first note of the performance, or an unexpected pickup note, would be rudely cut. I really needed to pick a record start time well before the instrument entrance, whether using pre-roll or not.)

One of the Spirits Burning

Nik Turner, Hawkwind's wind and reed player, the wind of the Hawk, the member that inserted a carnival look to their Space Ritual show. The frog outfit...How often do you see a frog play saxophone?

Nik Turner, the guy that Jim Hendrix described as 'the cat 'in' the silver face' or was it "the cat 'with' the silver face?" Double quotes with the words appeared in multiple articles and books about Hawkwind.

Around the century's turn, I wanted to open SB's second album with a song that included a sample of the "silver cat" moment. If it existed. If true.

One of my coworkers at Orban was Marty Acuff. (As Alien Heat, we released a sample-based collage piece on the *Free Speech for Sale* compilation. Marty also lent me his trombone for Gary Parra's *Trap* record. First time buzzing a trombone in years left my lips blistered.) Marty knew my new goal. He was friends with a big fan of Hendrix who had bootlegs of all his gigs. This friend was well-known local DJ Big Rick Stewart. I supplied straight-forward puzzle pieces. The moment happened during Hendrix's set at the Isle of Wight Festival, August 31, 1970, three weeks before his death. He was addressing people playing for free on the other side of the fence. This included members of Hawkwind and The Pink Fairies (together dubbed Pinkwind) The story always said that Jimi dedicated the song to a face-painted Nik.

Rick listened to the gig and brought life to the myth. He gave me a CD-R with the new truth. Right before Jimi's guitar teases *Purple Haze*...

> *This is dedicated to Linda. To the cat right there with the silver face. Dedicated to Kirsten, Karen and that little four-year-old girl over there with the yellow panties on. And I'd like to say thank you for the last three years. One of these days we'll get it together again. Thanks for showing up and you're outtasight.*

I had my sample! In subsequent years, I shared this truth to various

Hawkwind book scribes: Ian Abrahams, Dan Thompson, Joe Banks.

Back to 2012: The session with Nik went well. Songs for the in-progress *Starhawk* album, one song for a future instrumental album, and a piece without a home (*Purse*).

I took Nik to Thai Nakorn, my favorite Thai place in San Bruno. Nik required soft food, his teeth no longer a match for other food. We ordered a salad with larb, instead of beef strips, my favorite curry, this time with pineapple, instead of chicken, plus steamed rice. And, for my first time: Palm Fruit Juice.

We discussed the heavy topic—clubs and articles listing the Nik Turner tour as a Hawkwind tour. Hawkwind had been running as a unit for decades under Dave Brock. I felt Nik and his label (Cleopatra) using the Hawkwind name in the states created a schism in the fan base. Again. (This previously occurred in the 90s.) It created a strain on the Hawkwind family too. Some past members aligned with Dave. Some aligned with Nik. I was inviting all of them to SB; I appreciated each family member's history and what they might contribute. The online battles between current and past members could be harsh, topsy turvy. When a current member became a past member, they switched allegiances.

I suggested Nik avoid this and make it right by considering a different approach. "Nik Turner plays the music of Hawkwind." "Nik Turner, the Spirit of Hawkwind." (He later did a book with that name.) I don't remember if I told him that I added my name and thoughts to the online legal proceedings. Hawkwind, with Brock in the lead, had been playing live and recording albums for decades. Nik hadn't been in the band for decades. Hawkwind having not done a full U.S. tour since I saw them in 1995 didn't justify a second Hawkwind. Even if the poster for the show at Slim's reads *Hawkwind Feat. Dave Brock*.

At our dinner, Nik kept a comfortable face with a hint of a smile. He accepted that he could be considered the spirit of Hawkwind. He disagreed with my assessment on the usage of the name. Our discussion moved to tales of Hawkwind past.

My time with Nik confirmed his sweetness. He still had peace and love to give. His fans adored him for it.

He expressed support when the *Starhawk* album was released, and he got his copy. I saw him at a subsequent tour. He seemed distant. I said hello and got no response. He looked tired; I decided against mixing with the fans that surrounded him. This was the night I finally met Brian Perera, the head of Cleopatra. (I had been on Cleopatra in the 90s with my Spaceship Eyes project and they were now releasing our Daevid Allen Weird Quartet album.) We briefly discussed the Hawkwind trademark. I told him I thought the situation could have been avoided. Our conversation moved to other topics.

When Nik and I finished our Thai dinner, I took him home. It was dark now. I missed the freeway exit and drove much deeper into the city than intended. The 22-minute ride became a 44-minute ride, maybe an hour. Did Nik notice? I decided not to address the giant U-turn. I got him home safe and sound. The final goal.

o o o o o o

I use the conga line approach to mixing. After I do my part, or a new part comes in (via Dropbox, WeTransfer, or other), I invite the next instrument. Occasionally, I'll do two invites for a song concurrently if I feel confident the parts won't affect each other (for example, a vocalist replacing my temp vocals and a bassist laying down bass notes).

One time, I mistakenly invited two bassists to a song (*Skyline Signal*); my digital notes and white board had an incorrect status for the song. I considered uninviting one of them. I decided to let it go and "fix it in the mix" or pick one. (There had been some rare cases where I excluded a part provided, so I was prepared for that.) Miraculously, one bassist went high, the other low. I used both!

Another mix-up...

- Jack Gold-Molina (who played with Nik in Flame Tree) provided drums as starter material for a song. Some parts in a non-standard (non-4/4) time signature: 7/4. I restructured it (cut and paste) to create a working song with an intro, verses, chorus, and transitions.

- I recorded my keyboard parts.
- I invited other instrumentalists, one-by-one.
- When the guitar parts arrived (by Andy Dalby, once of Arthur Brown's Kingdom Come), they were accompanied by a temporary drum track. He did the drums to help him understand the time signature changes better when recording his rhythm parts.
- When all the parts were in place, I produced a final mix…unfortunately, using the temp drums, instead of Jack's.
- The song was mastered, temp drums in place, the liner notes completed with Jack being credited for the drum part, and the album released.
- Jack noticed that the drum part was not what he had done. I went back to the mix history and was stunned.
- To make it up to Jack, I used his original drums to create an entirely new song (different chords and feel). For the next album.

Jack adds:

> I actually had two guys from Exposé magazine approach me at a festival I was playing at. They were both like, 'Jack, what's up with that 7/4 Spirits Burning track? That doesn't sound like you at all!' I had to explain, diplomatically I might add, that there was a production error and somehow the wrong mix wound up on the album. I was pretty impressed that they had the ears to catch that.

o o o o o o

Walking from the Judge Trev Stage tent to the Daevid Allen Kozmik Stage tent at Kozfest 2017, I was stopped by two people. One was Lee Pugster. The other asked: "Do you know who I am?" I tried a few guesses. He said, "you know, I'm on a Spirits Burning album." He was short, looked like Andy Ortenzio, a guitarist that I had jammed with in Steelton, who had the same features as Steve Palmer; we had collaborated in each other's bands, and for a Falcone & Palmer album. No, this wasn't Steve. I tried more names, musicians that I didn't have a corresponding face. He said he was listed in the credits as Alan, and his name was not Alan. The mouse trap game continued. I was sweating. Our witness suggested mercy, and it was granted. I had mis-credited him. I had apologized too, long ago, and since forgotten. He was Andy Bole. Musician and friend of the family Gong.

○ ○ ○ ○ ○ ○

When I was in Spice Barons, I was the secretary of the group. I kept track of song titles, synth and fx settings, and the samples we used. Kim also included me in editing liner notes.

Our recording sessions at Paul Neyrinck's apartment were more than just sessions to compose, record, and archive. We listened to songs by artists that Kim felt were musically inspirational— African Head Charge, Miles Davis, The Orb, to name a few—and we talked about other interests; *Twin Peaks*, *X-Files*, *Star Trek*. Kim had worked as an assistant music editor for director David Lynch's *Twin Peaks* and *Wild at Heart*. I remember reviewing the list of songs:

1. *Future Perfect State (Persian Songbird Mix)*
2. *Bioluminous*
3. *Cheebah*
4. ...

Song 8 was *Voyager*.

As we had been talking about the new generation of Star Trek, I added a note with my review: "(And What Did You Think of The First Episode?)"

When the CD was pressed and I got my copy, the title for track 8 read:

8. *Voyager (And What Did You Think of The First Episode?)*

o o o o o o

Before moving westward, a five-piece band that included jam friends Randy Orris, Tim Griesemer, and Andy Ortenzio played a wedding reception at the Liberty Fire House in Middletown. They were Mist, named by mixing the first two letters of their hometowns: Middletown and Steelton. They had colored lights, effects, and dry ice for fog. During the show, Andy left the stage to do a floor-level lead to a Van Halen song. (He had a guitar made up to look like Eddie Van Halen's guitar, and Tim had customized it with powder and flash pot paper to have smoke come out of the body and flame come out of the top of the neck as Andy slid down the neck and hit a button.) Andy slipped on the water from the dry ice and fell on his back. There were flash pots on the floor too. During the finale, they didn't go off. After the lights came on, and the guests were gone, the pots were tested. Boom! Boom! And Boom!

I was the light person (and sometimes sound person). They had a makeshift board with simple switches to toggle lights of different colors. To create different color combinations. During their firehouse set, I decided to try an extra color. At one point, I turned the last two remaining lights off, to reveal the new color: black. After a few seconds, I returned to a non-black color scheme. The band were not happy with this new color.

o o o o o o

The Spaceship Eyes live ensemble was the only live band I led that my wife was in. Originally, a six-piece: Gary Parra of Cartoon and Trap (drums), Edward Huson (tabla), John Pluth (guitar), Carol Weeks (bass), Karen (percussion), and me (keyboards).

We mostly performed songs from the *Kamarupa* album.

After Gary left the band, I realized that he was the glue, the adult in the room, ensuring I could steer a proper ship. Warning signs appeared when preparing for the next gig—Spaceship Eyes vs. Spirits Burning, opening for Belgium band Present.

I was a big fan of Eno's *Oblique Strategies* deck of cards. Just never purchased it. (Years later, when I worked at Dolby, one of walls on the 11th floor, where I sat, had the complete set, with each strategy card attached to a hook.) Each card has a different phrase. A band could have each member pick a card, and then play as "directed" by the card. I used a poor man's version for many years. (We probably did this in a Kim project too.) Each band member wrote a word or phrase on a piece of paper, crumpled the paper, and threw it into a hat. We did this multiple times. Each of us then picked one piece of paper and used the phrase to inform our performance.

For the Spaceship Eyes vs. Spirits Burning band, we had an automated song via my Kurzweil K2000 keyboard that the band played to. At a specified time, I stopped the sequence, and we would begin improvising, inspired by our chosen phrase. At the cue, John and Carol immediately went into a rock boogie. I asked them if that was really what their phrase inspired. We picked again. We resumed playing. I stopped the sequence. A boogie began.

The new set included SB covers of King Crimson's *Red* and Genesis' *Return of The Giant Hogweed*, as had been recorded with guitar, bass, drums, and keyboards for Cleopatra tribute albums. With the addition of heavier songs, and with the absence of Gary, it was harder to temper the guitar/bass levels. The ensemble had always been a mix of ambient, space, ethnic, rock, jazz. This new ensemble with a different drummer was loud from set start to set end. Karen and Edward soon quit.

We were now a rock band, with two twists. Besides my two-tiered keyboard setup, my third keyboard was on the ground. I used my foot to play wind or synth sounds where pitch didn't matter. I also brought my Orban Audicy out from my studio. It was an expensive piece of gear—a $40,000 hardware/software DAW, which I had because I wrote the manuals and did testing at home. Live, I used it for real-time audio scratching and varispeeding, and playback of samples. It's possible this setup never occurred elsewhere in the history of music.

The night of the gig, the club was packed, and our drummer was still learning the songs. We started, stopped, and restarted one number. For most of the gig, our guitarist and bassist faced the drummer, or stood sideways, ready to turn to him, to help him. It was videotaped. It wasn't a good look.

This was my last performance with these musicians. However, the seeds of the next SB were now planted.

○ ○ ○ ○ ○ ○

Trev Thoms (also known as Judge Trev) played in Nik Turner's Inner City Unit. I really like the crazy, anything goes space rock of ICU— they were the perfect antidote for the changing music landscape of 1980. At least in the UK. I also liked Trev's solo acoustic album.

I first invited Trev to play guitar on four tracks of the second SB album (*Reflections in A Radio Shower*). When it came time to send me the parts, which he had recorded to cassette, the tape was eaten. His package soon arrived—a cassette with most of the tape no longer in the shell, tape wrapped around the cassette. There was a rip in the tape too. After I carefully unwrapped the tape, spliced the tear, and then used a pencil to slowly wind the tape back into its shell, I figured I had one playback at most.

Trev's parts when transferred had a bit of a mellotron tape quality, an occasional stretched warble, and maybe a sense of reel-to-reel warmth. His parts had survived. An unraveled cassette is better than no cassette.

○ ○ ○ ○ ○ ○

At Kozfest, I sang two lines wrong for the song *The Hawk*. When it came time for the live album, I left them in. To capture the event, be true to the event. For the preceding song, *The Unknown*, I had jumped in early for one line, and after a somersault on the timing, eventually stuck the landing on a subsequent line. I had done the same thing at our practice. It's strange. I wrote the song, music, lyrics, vocal lines. Know the song inside out. Why was I trying to outdo the 4/4 and its beats? When it came time for the live album, I took the Hawkwind *Silver Machine* approach. Well, I didn't replace Calvert vocals with Lemmy. Instead, I selected the mistimed words, cut them, and then pasted them in the correct spot. End of story!

○ ○ ○ ○ ○ ○

When Meg joined No Poetry, she had to weave her lyrics to the music the band had in place. She was adept at this. Very catchy lyrics that gave new life to our punk/new wave sounds.

I had written one of the songs. *Alchemy*. It previously had a Wetton-era King Crimson crunch, perhaps a nod to Crimson's *21st Century Schizoid Man* (which early Kameleon used to jam to, with the garage door of my Sunset home open). There is even a version of *Alchemy* recorded in PA during a visit there. Years later, I introduced it to Daevid Allen and Michael Clare for a Weird adventure.

No Poetry's *Alchemy* was simpler, a snippet of my original song. This version required words, and Meg complied. At a 1982 Sound of Music show, she forgot the words. And, in Meg style, recovered. She sang "I forgot the wordsssss," and proceeded to make up new ones... "Four score and seven years ago..." It was also on this night that she pulled off the impossible, although maybe it showed the simplicity and sameness of our songs. She forgot the words to another song and sang the same words to two different songs. Kind of amazing.

○ ○ ○ ○ ○ ○

Spirits Burning & Bridget Wishart *Make Believe It Real* had a costlier mistake. Gonzo, our label, had approved a double CD. The first disk all new songs, the second a bonus disc of remixes and extra songs. A great plan. I did want to avoid an issue I saw with Hawkwind, where they inserted a live version of an old song or two inside the sequence of new material. It came across as if they didn't have enough new material. I would have placed all the live songs at the end. Keep the initial flow of new stuff, and then add bonuses. While we had no live songs, we had the single non-rock exposed piano piece close disc 1, followed by a disc of all the bonus tracks.

Jakko Jakszyk did the mastering. As he finished our project, quite likely his last mastering job for a while, Jakko got the call, the invite to join King Crimson. He was ecstatic. He delivered the master songs to the label, who routed it to the manufacturer.

I was disappointed with the initial online price—the cost of 1

1/2 discs. Not quite the one-disc cost with a bonus CD I expected.

The bigger issue: Did I notice it when I got my copy? Did someone complain online first, or express confusion? A song listed in the liner notes was missing. I checked my final delivery to Jakko and approval of the masters. All songs present. Jakko checked his delivery to the label: One song missing. The label recalled the album and did a new run. I was never sure how thorough the recall was. Add to that: Online sellers began selling it bundled with another SB album. You had to purchase two CDs instead of one, or in this case, three disks, instead of two.

o o o o o o

Some magazine writers thought I played on the first Melting Euphoria albums on Cleopatra. Probably because the credits included a musician named DeFM. This was guitarist Dan Miller. We were in a pre-Melting Euphoria band called By Design. Were writers confused by my DF initials in the name? Wasn't the credit for guitar a clue?

After my Spaceship Eyes solo project signed to Cleopatra, Brian (the label head) called me. He asked if Melting Euphoria were Nazis. Thoughts running through my head. Why? And why ask me? This was a band that I had quit a few years earlier.

I'm not sure if Brian knew about the finality of when I quit, or the use of lawyers while the first Cleopatra album was moving forward; me wanting to ensure I got writing credit and received copies of the pre-Cleopatra album.

The band had sent a letter to Brian and wrote it on the back of a band flyer. The flyer had some Nazi symbols. I presume it was for a punk or metal show. I told Brian that no, Anthony and Michael were not Nazis. I didn't know the other band members. I was sure the use was simply a bad choice of flyers.

o o o o o o

I reviewed some albums for Exposé magazine (as I had done in high school). I stopped when I didn't like an album. Plus, it felt strange reviewing albums in a zine that reviewed my albums and interviewed me. In 1999, Exposé #19, I documented the Strange Daze festival;

some musicians there would contribute to SB.

I wrote an article about Hawkwind in college, and then an article about Robert Calvert for Knut Gerwers' website devoted to him. Years later, I would bring together many of the Hawkwind family members in SB.

Robert Calvert, Art Hero and Inventor appeared November 15th, 1997. Originally written for the Robert Calvert "spirit of the p/age" website, produced by Knut, now housed on the Aural Innovations site; also republished in Progression magazine, issue 36, Summer/Fall 2000.

Hawkwind by Don Falcone, published in the 1978-79 *Reflector*, a student magazine funded by the Student Association of Shippensburg State College. Advisor: John Taggart. The article included a *Discography of Hawkwind*, and *Hawkwind Roots and Offshoots*. Martin Wheatley assisted in collecting the data. (Article available online: https://issuu.com/nohpoetryrecs/docs/hawkwind_article__reflec tor_magazine_)

Re-reading the Hawkwind article is a trip. At the time I wrote it, I didn't know David Brock's *Assault* lyrics were lines by William Butler Yeats. I didn't know the nude centerpiece of the 1973 *Space Ritual* album was not Stacia. (In 2024, I saw the female image at a San Francisco Museum of Modern Art exhibit. Victor Moscoso used the photo in his 1967 poster for a Feb 16th free Fillmore show by The Blues Project. The seated woman is from the silent screen era.) I didn't know Hawkwind's *Opa-Loka* is a clone of a Neu song. I didn't know that the band name Hawklords was used for legal reasons. I didn't have the full story about Lemmy's Canadian drug bust; the border officers thought his amphetamine was cocaine. I didn't know Simon House did the initial shows for Hawkwind's 1978 U.S. tour, before joining David Bowie.)

As an American, I experienced the band through their albums (audio and LP jackets), a 1977 live show, and critiques and behind-the-scenes details via Melody Maker and other zines.

Rereading the article, I find a voice sometimes overly optimistic, naive, or prophetic (given my later music experiences).

It's An Alien Injection...

John Capozzi, a fraternity brother at Shippensburg, was friends with Dave Penn, a staff member of the American Beauty magazine. An 8 1/2 x 11 zine, nine single-sided pages held together by one staple on the upper left. The banner below the zine title: "The Newspaper of the STUDENTS FOR THE LIBERATION OF MARIJUANA."

John and I hit it off. We were both fans of Blue Öyster Cult; we knew what was later thought to be a Ronnie James Dio hand sign was used by BÖC fans. John also used to teach me about all the different types of pot, even though I never smoked.

John suggested I send a poem to the magazine and my poem "Incubus" appeared in a 1979 issue, page 3, tucked to the side of an article titled "NO NUKES!"

On page 9, an article titled "random radar" starts with "The Muffins are coming," along with an ad for FREE CONCERT by THE MUFFiNS at the AU [American University] s.u.b. coffeehouse. The same Random Radar Records label of my cousin Ernie's band, Mars Everywhere. The same Muffins whose line-up included future SB contributors, saxophonist Dave Newhouse and drummer Paul Sears.

One future song with Dave would be the song *Black Squirrel at The Root of The Staircase*. Dave had walked up that staircase in my childhood home (when he was dating my cousin Diane). The staircase had a porcelain squirrel that you could grab onto for support. The squirrel's small night light was no longer present, leaving a hole and a few extended wires.

A fellow classmate, a female poet, had planted the word incubus and its meaning during a casual discussion about poetry and subject matter. My follow-up poem turned to the other word, succubus. In a dream, one of her roommates who I knew morphed into a cat. I woke up after she was on top of me. Of course. As I wrote the poem, I focused to another girl on campus that I liked from afar. I was in a fraternity called Phi Sig, which had an interesting mix of people, just not necessarily the popular people; and I was in the marching band. She was in a sorority called Delta Rho, either on the band front or the cheerleader squad. She dated a guy from the TKE fraternity who was on the football team. We were never going to connect.

The second poem, the succubus one, was a personal codec, which I suspect no one ever noticed during my college days or when its lines weaved into an SB song called *Alien Injection*. Remember the societies I mentioned? Delta Rho. TKE.

Alien Injection includes the lines:

And the boat that she rows,
On the delta narrow,
Is an antique ship
That salt water will rip

When I shopped the fourth album by SB, Italy's Black Widow Records expressed interest. They were one of the few labels I've worked with that suggested adding and deleting songs. They strongly encouraged me to do more songs with mellotron—there would be seven—and more with Michael Moorcock; he ended up on four. They also said that I should remove a song titled *Alien Injection*, which had music started by Finnish band Dark Sun and lyrics and vocals by me. They felt it was not spacey, and not as good as other songs on the album. I said I would continue working on it.

The follow up version included:

- The debut SB lead vocals by Kev Ellis (who reminded me of Ian Gillan meets Ian Anderson; he later played in the Spirits Burning Kozfest live ensemble).
- My Lemmy-style backing vocals, distorted rhythm bass chords, and mellotron.

When I sent the results to Massimo at Black Widow, he said it was the best track on the album and should be the title track. So was born the album *Alien Injection*.

There were some surprises on the way to this birth. Black Widow decided to manufacture the CD version, plus a double LP.

Vinyl at last! They also redid the internal artwork and some of the back cover. Without telling me. I saw the changes for the first time when I received my artist copies. In the CD booklet and LP sleeves, the songs and lyrics were presented out of order. The editor in me not happy. Luckily, the cover was as intended by artist James Lascko and me. (I had met James at the Strange Daze space rock convention, and we had kept in touch.) Karen's internal graphics artwork was replaced. The new artwork included an alien with a giant needle. Sure, my use of injection implies needles, drugs. I'm sure many fans thoughts it was rather cool. However, I was not romanticizing the symbolism or doing a sci-fi fantasy horror of aliens subjecting humans. I suspect that was their interpretation. It missed the mark.

The title track was a mix of source material from various parts of my life: the succubus poem from college, lines from a sound poem that I had also used in a late 90's song titled *Dig A Thee Earth*, an unpublished poem about a woman whose body was found in Golden Gate Park, the word peacekeepers, which was in the news, an alien ball (I had this little white plastic ball with two aluminum tabs that you pressed, and the ball made an alien sound).

There was even a play on dialogue from the *Psych-Out* movie.

Dave (played by Dean Stockwell): *You see this little beam of light. Well, that's all there is. The rest is in your head.*

Stoney (played by Jack Nicholson): *Yeah, but, except we're in a box, on a roof, in San Francisco, in America.*

One of the Silent projects had previously used a sample from that scene during the wild west time of sampling in the 90s. Here, I would rephrase Jack's words with where I kept my alien ball in my studio: *in a closet in a room in a house, in a country in a world in a planet.*

The song also mentioned owning two shirts. Indeed, I had two Silent Records shirts. Front: Large alien logo. Back: Silent artist roster, including two I was in (Thessalonians and Spice Barons). I wore one of these shirts at Kozfest.

Alien Injection

Dig a the, Dig a the, Dig a the earth . . .
Dig a the, Dig a the, Dig a the earth . . .

It's an alien injection, that's what she needs
An alien injection for all our infections
One little boost to see the up and the coming
A solution we pray: Help is on the way

Saw her today, she looked dead
It could be, I heard she died
Scan the paper, touch the ink
She finally got her name in print

That's all I see, that's all I need
I don't know time, I don't know space
Lots of creatures just like her
They dance with rhythm, then they pull away

Rattle and reach — I come apart
Rattle and reach — to put together again
Rattle and reach — make images
Rattle and reach — to dig out . . .

Send her flowers she can't wear
Send a card that she can't read
This happens when the children stay
Out too late and really start to play

And the boat that she rows on the delta narrow
  is an antique ship that salt water will rip
And the scarf-covered course
  that once bridled a horse
Soon tames a black cat
  and makes others grow fat

Don Falcone

Rattle and reach — I come apart
Rattle and reach — to put together again
Rattle and reach — make images
Rattle and reach — to dig out . . .

Dig a the, Dig a the, Dig a the earth . . .
Dig a the, Dig a the, Dig a the earth . . .

It's an alien injection, that's what she needs
An alien injection for all our infections
One little boost to see the up and the coming
A solution we pray, and help is on the way

Rattle and reach — I come apart
Rattle and reach — to put together again
Rattle and reach — make images
Rattle and reach — to dig out and dig in

(Just give it a day, help is on its way)

I like to wear my alien close to my heart
It's such a cool t-shirt,
I bought two right from the start
I guess you could say I treat it
  like a piece of art
This alien that I wear so close to my heart

I've got a round alien ball to boot
She comes to life when I squeeze her roots
I keep it in a box, in a closet, in a room,
  in a house, in a country, in a world,
  in a planet, and I hope she'll live forever
Mmm . . . I hope she'll live forever . . .

One review of *Alien Injection* shocked me. Disappointed me. I couldn't believe it.

They criticized it as a song about rape. They had entirely missed my intent. This was a song about earth (mother earth) needing a change, a panacea from somewhere different (somewhere alien). Whether that was green creatures from another world, or new thinking from earth, that was left open to interpretation.

SB performed *Alien Injection* live in the UK two times in 2017. No distorted rhythm bass or my Lemmy style backing vocals. I was on keys, didn't have a mic, and no longer had the vocal range to mimic Lemmy.

The song sounded good overall.

As we continued to vamp on the final chorus, we just needed to work out when to stop.

Don Falcone

Things that Start with S

I'VE ONLY LIVED in towns that start with S. In California, the three S towns start with San. Spirits Burning starts with S. As does Spaceship Eyes. Maybe there is something to this.

Don Playing a Sears Organ, Basement of Spruce Street Home, Steelton, PA, 1970s

Steelton

There was a baseball player named Bruce Brubaker. He had reached that moment of notability where he was expected to make his major league team, the Dodgers. Topps Baseball Cards gave him his own card. The back of his card listed his hometown: Camp Hill.

The John Harris Memorial (South) bridge spanning across the Susquehanna River, separates Camp Hill from Harrisburg, and Harrisburg leads directly to Steelton, my hometown.

Once upon a time, everyone was fingertips away with a push button telephone. Or an index finger away with a rotary phone. A friend and I pulled out my parent's phone book, navigated to the Br names. There it was: Bruce Brubaker, with a Camp Hill address. We did what we were born to do. We dialed. A woman answered.

I did the talking from our kitchen phone. My friend on another phone, most likely the basement phone as kids rarely used the one in the front room.

"Is Bruce there?"

She answered: "No. He's out playing ball."

That sounded about right. It was springtime. He probably was at their spring training camp.

I said: "thank you," "good-bye," and hung up. This was the last time I did a call like this.

It wasn't the last time that I searched for and contacted someone I didn't know.

My Experience After Watching the Original Version of The Fly

When I awoke during the night, I heard sounds coming up the stairs, my bedroom door started to open, and I saw a creature with a disfigured face standing there. I started to reach out and went unconscious (or back to sleep). In the morning, I vowed to reach out and touch the creature the next time this occurred, to confirm if the creature was real or not. I never had the experience again.

Don Falcone

A Letter from Marv Wolfman
(Editor, DC Comics)

(John and I collected Marvel comic books. John was a big fan of Spider-Man. I loved The Avengers and Daredevil. When we were 12 years old, we created two superheroes and sent our idea to both Marvel and DC Comics. We got a reply from DC only.

Our idea: Two brothers, with the family name Queensley. They were named Jeffrey and Elvis. They were English, children of a good witch. I created Jeffrey and John created Elvis.

Jeffrey Queensley was the Black Raider. He had a costume that looked a little too much like Marvel's Black Knight. Like the knight, he had a blade. He had some vague magical powers too.

Elvis Queensley was the superhero named King Arthur. He had a crown. He also was a hairy ape.)

National Periodicals
PUBLICATIONS INC.

909 THIRD AVENUE
NEW YORK, N. Y. 10022
(212) 758-6100

Aug. 10, 1971

Don and John;

Thanks for letting us see your work, but all our stories are staffed assigned, or written after a close discussion with our artists or writers.

Besides, most of our work is produced by professionals who have done work besides comics, such as television, movies, magazines, and books.

Best of luck, and keep pluggin away. Perhaps someday you will be able to join our staff of happy workers.

Best

(Marv's signature)

M. Wolfman

Editorial

Music In the House (by My Brother David)

What I remember most is that there was always music in our house but in a nuanced kind of way. We were all given the opportunity to play an instrument. So, growing up there was a guitar (Rich), and an accordion (David) and a piano (Cindi). Don, you were born in 58, so by the time you were ready to pick up an instrument and play, I was more-or-less gone. I do remember you played the bass guitar in high school (is that true?)...but as mentioned, I would have been gone by then. So, I don't really remember much about your musical beginnings.

About the "nuance" mentioned above...while we all were playing instruments, there was not much of a musical presence otherwise. As best I remember, other than a 45 player for which we had almost no records, there was no stereo to play records on until 1964 when we needed something to play our first album on. Something New, by The Beatles. Of course, I may be wrong about this, but this is what I remember. We bought the album and then said, "Dad, we need something to play this on." It was then that we got the stereo console that you remember so well.

What followed? I started buying folk albums: Peter, Paul and Mary, and Simon and Garfunkel for sure. Rich was getting Motown Soul, and Mom was buying Andy Williams, Engelbert Humperdinck, and Tom Jones. There were also some movie soundtracks: The Sound of Music, and Dr. Zhivago come to mind.

Don Falcone

We did get a menu of music from TV as well: Hootenanny, Lawrence Welk, and musical guest acts from a number of comedy shows (e.g., The Smothers Brothers, and Dean Martin).

That is what I remember from home. The interesting combination of having instruments to play but not so much music to specifically accompany playing them.

(Worth mentioning: by the time I started playing guitar by ear and playing folk music—I was 17 years old by then—the folk albums did provide a model and inspiration...an exception to the above).

Brothers David and Don, Spruce Street Home, Steelton, PA, 1970s

Shippensburg State College (Four Years of Fall, Winter, Spring)

I had classmates at college who previously went to my high school. One time, they were spotted by the dean of Mowrey Hall (our dorm), traversing the back entrance of the dorm with a large suitcase. Dragging the suitcase up and down the side stairwell, stopping off somewhere between the 2nd and 5th floors. Then repeating the action. It wasn't uncommon for students to look for ways to get beer or illegal substances into their rooms. It was uncommon to do this in broad daylight. When they were caught, the dean asked them to open the suitcase. They slowly complied. Out popped a large music speaker, surrounded by underwear.

Once, I was directly privy to one of their schemes and confess to getting caught up in their web. While I regret the intent of their and my actions, there were some "music qualities" of note.

In the same dorm as us, were two very quiet students with glasses, who looked like future scientists. My friends nicknamed one of them R2D2. They usually kept to themselves in their shared dorm room, in the lunch hall, and elsewhere. I never really knew them or talked to them. My friends had identified their dorm room, and had a friend located in a room directly above them. They devised a plan to lower a string with a small tape recorder attached to it towards their window to, well, irritate them during their studies or quiet time.

I don't remember how many times they did this, except that at some point I suggested they consider some of the more interesting music I could provide, as opposed to Boston and other radio friendly bands. My first contribution: White Noise's *An Electric Storm*. I immediately went with side 2. This includes the slow, devil churn of a chant that starts *Black Mass: An Electric Storm in Hell*, which then rolls into tribal drums, spiked randomly by what sounds like a sci-fi laser and a scream. I also included one of the most eerie, heart-wrenching songs ever recorded, *The Visitation*. Following a car crash, the weeping of a woman fills the air and cannot be ignored. Surprisingly, little reaction below, except for what sounded like a window closing.

I now provided a new recording for this venture. Steve Reich's *It's Gonna Rain*: a 1964 tape recording of a Pentecostal preacher, made in San Francisco's Union Square—a place I would someday visit. After the preacher speaks of the end of the world, the line "It's gonna rain" loops over and over. This time, we raised the playback level. Then lowered the recorder again to outside their window. The two students were in their room, and this audio was irritating them. They were now trying to grab the recorder. One of my friends momentarily swung the recorder away from them a few times. Each time the recorder swung back, close to their outstretched hands, it looked like the recorder was about to be grabbed. It was only a matter of time... He quickly pulled the recorder back up; into the room we occupied.

We revised our setup: Surround the recorder with pointed objects (like tacks and nails) facing outward, held on to the recorder by putty. Mission accomplished, we pressed the play button and lowered the recorder downward again. It worked. Each time someone below reached for the recorder, their hands recoiled back.

I will never forget what happened next. As the preacher continued voicing... "It's gonna rain, it's gonna rain, it's gonna rain...," hands appeared again from their window. This time...with some scissors. Slice! And we heard the tape changing speed with "it'sss gonnnna raaaaaaiinnnnn" until there was a splat! The recorder smashed on the ground.

Perhaps, we had new respect for our two quiet classmates. I don't remember my friends (or me) ever doing something like this again.

Cafeteria Food

I found the cafeteria food compromised. Friday pizza was ok. During the week, I found myself eating potato chip sandwiches as chips and bread felt fresher than most of the served hot food.

I could do a sad trick where I would place Jello on a spoon, turn the spoon upside down, and the Jello would not fall. The Jello, like the chips and bread, was edible.

(I did like eating a personal pizza and a meatball sandwich downtown at least once a week. And I was proud to represent our fraternity in a hot dog eating contest at the local burger place. I came in second.)

Two Short Stories

I was on the staff of the college's literary magazine, The Reflector, from 1977 to1979, co-editor-in-chief in 1980. Besides having poems and a Hawkwind article published during that time, I had short stories published in two issues of the Reflector. They can be found here: http://www.donfalcone.com/words.html#.

The Fraud In Your Mind (Published 1977): I was 18. I had switched my major, from Journalism to English. Dr. John Taggart, the Reflector's advisor, would soon be my personal advisor.

Under his guidance, I primarily focused on poetry—and did have two poems in the 1977 issue. The *Fraud* story originated in a short story class. My *Ghost* poem in this issue would be one of the poems later admonished in graduate school.

The opening lines:

> *I believe in ghosts, the kind that you could touch, like the first girl that you kissed, who's been gone for seven years.*

Panacea (Published 1980): I was 21, a senior in college. Co-editor-in-chief of the Reflector. The *Panacea* story opens with a poem, which starts with "Balance is alive, and sensitive to touch...," a motif influenced by the poem in Michael Moorcock's *Black Corridor* that begins "Space is infinite, it is dark, Space is neutral, it is cold..."

The Moorcock poem was featured in the Hawkwind song *Black Corridor*, which was part of their *Space Ritual* live set. My intro poem became the lyrics for *Balance... (Panacea Brew)* which is on the Melting Euphoria album *Through The Strands Of Time*—rereleased as *From The Madness We Began.*)

Steelton to Shippensburg to SF to San Leandro to San Bruno

A Recipe for White Spaghetti with Anchovies

Let's cut to the chase: Anchovies are a good food choice to ward off people who you eat pizza with, and you don't like their topping choices. In my experience, nine out of ten times suggesting anchovies gets them to back off.

I first had spaghetti with anchovies in Steelton, prepared by my mom. Probably not on a Thursday.

Every Thursday my father expected spaghetti and red sauce. He would dejectedly accept a rare change to raviolis, manicotti, lasagna, or gnocchis. Those were better for a special Sunday lunch, or another dinner. For Thursday's dinner, he was disappointed with any alternative. Throughout the day, he would think about (and legend has it, smell) the sauce from his downtown office, anticipating my mom's spaghetti.

In those days, when she made spaghetti with red sauce, she usually prepared a main bowl for the family—covered in spaghetti sauce; and a separate bowl of plain, naked spaghetti, along with a separate bowl of red sauce for me. This let me control my percentage of sauce to pasta. Yes, I was spoiled. Given my appreciation of plain spaghetti, it wasn't that far of a reach to someday serve me cooked spaghetti and a plate of anchovies. Eventually, that happened.

When I went to Shippensburg, and lived off campus, and had to cook, there were only so many things that I could make consistently. White spaghetti with anchovies was one of them. By the time I got to San Francisco, I was a pro.

When I got married, I taught Karen of the existence of this dish. She sometimes makes it for me. She has never tasted it.

White Spaghetti Recipe

- Cook the spaghetti to taste, and then separate from water.
- Serve spaghetti on a plate.

- Top with anchovies.
- Use flat fillet anchovies in olive oil from a tin. Do not use rolled anchovies with capers or white anchovies (which sometimes are marinated in vinegar).
- (Optional) Sprinkle cheese.
- Serve and enjoy.

A Letter I Sent to My Parents (June 1998)

This was just after Orban had been sold to CRL. I would leave Orban in December 2000 and start working for Digidesign/Avid.

I'm also including this to remind Karen that I used some music money for our home. At least once. When we started the second account mentioned in the letter, it became my music account, for any future music earnings. We would move from the rented 'ship shape' house when mold began to develop. I decided: I would never live in a ground floor home again.

The theatre where we saw the film mentioned was on Polk Street, the street of my first job in San Francisco.)

Hi Mom and Dad,

I figured it was a good time to write, as Orban was officially sold last week. Over the next two months, we'll learn more about the merger between us and the parent company, CRL. Already, we're mixing product brochures in mailings and sharing booth space at trade shows. We got our final pay checks from previous owner (Harman), as well as a check to cash out vacation time. I had 200 hours of time, so it was a big check. We're going to start a second savings account. I'll probably buy some new clothes and I'm thinking about a bass guitar. There's a couple of computer peripherals both Karen and I want— like a CD burner. But that's about it. Should have plenty left over to stay on top of bills, etc.

Over the last few months, I've gotten some good size

payments from BMI (music publishers), and I've used those to better our living space. We finally bought a kitchen table and chairs (nice wood) to replace Loralyn's old one. And we bought an inexpensive bench for the front, next to the front door.

Speaking of house, we finally got the landlord over to fix the sink. It's all fixed now. Next, he's sending over someone to check on a leak in the shower/tub. Otherwise, the house is in ship shape.

I sent a few emails to Dave, Rich, and their family last week. Had big music news. Three of my songs were used in a movie that just came out. It's an independent film, currently only showing in about 15 major U.S. cities. It's a documentary about the U.S. rave scene, entitled Better Living Through Circuitry. One of my pieces is actually used for the film's intro. Karen and I went into San Francisco last weekend to see it and stayed to see the credits as well.

I'm busy working on several recording projects as usual. Just redid the music studio, so that it looks roomier, more inviting. I have a new Spaceship Eyes CD coming out in August. The label is finishing up cover art this week. Jerry, who sang Loralyn years ago sings a piece on it—but not Loralyn. It's another electronica/dance CD.

I've been in touch with Randy a lot of late, via e-mail. He's buying a new guitar, and I have a number of friends here who offered advice, etc.

Karen is looking at a pamphlet that came in the mail today. Thinking of taking a class/course like candle making.

Cat and Dog are in the living room here with me. Birds chirping. We're waiting for the Giants game to come on TV. K and I going to another game in mid-July, a few days after the All-Star game.

Both Karen and I went to the eye doctor this week.
New glasses for both. I'm getting bifocals. Dr. said my
right eye is 20/60 and old glasses were worthless.

Well, we're probably going out to eat tonight,
celebrating all the good things of late, except the eyes—
either Greek in town, or Thai, or Indian.

Take Care. All our love. Talk soon. Don + K

A Moment of Sausalito

In 2024, When Hoshiko Yamane (Tangerine Dream) was in the Bay Area for her residency at the Headlands Center for the Arts, I offered to take her out to lunch. (We also took pictures and recorded some sounds below the Golden Gate Bridge, near Fort Baker.)

Our lunch destination: from the Headlands, to a single-lane tunnel, past the northern end of the bridge, and then downwards into the town of Sausalito that touches the Bay and looks to San Francisco.

We went to Sandrino Pizza & Vino, one of our favorites. Karen and I are part of a group of former Pizza Boat employees and friends who do a pizza crawl every now and then, where we go to three pizza places in one day or night. This was how we discovered Sandrino.

A Letter I Wrote to My Friend Bill Jordan (2023)

Bill was present for various moments in my life when I lived in Steelton: when I got into a fight during a little league practice, when he and I began umping little league games, and then when the incident happened.

I wrote this in late 2023, after I was notified that the Northern California technical writing team at Dolby was being laid off, and before my last day, 31 January 2024. And after Bill told me about his divorce.

> *I started thinking about 'bubbles.' As in, we live in a*
> *collection of bubbles. And, maybe in some cases,*
> *cults/sects (e.g., if I went to church; and maybe some*
> *work scenarios can be thought of as a cult of sorts).*

Anyways... There is the bubble of the house you live in. The bubble of your neighborhood. The bubble of family near, and family far. There can be bubbles of friends, like hometown, high school, college, etc. And, of course, work bubbles—the company, the teams you work on, potentially multiple bubbles. And, for me, there is a music bubble, people I've practiced and played with in years past, and then the collaborators for Spirits Burning and other projects. Lots and lots of bubbles.

After I got laid off...and thinking about my dad and his last years... He changed when he retired for the final time. He slept in more. And, seemed to have little interest in each day (unless someone was visiting, or stopped by for his insight). I can simplify, and say, well, he simply had no hobbies or other interests, and I've got music, so I'll be ok. I know it's not as simple as that. With the layoff in mind, I've begun to reconsider the bubbles idea and connect the bubbles to moving forward, and maybe looking for more than my simplification...

What I've come up with (as I'm running on typing empty, and the Lions game has ended, badly): In each of the bubbles of our life, we can have purpose, and feel of import. It's potentially hyped at work, which makes the loss of that bubble all the harder. Especially when we consider the hours devoted to, invested in that bubble. And I can see where a divorce, no matter how healthy and needed, can also be the nail in the coffin of a bubble and what you brought to it. Again, the hours devoted to, invested in. Nonetheless, there are other bubbles where we have a purpose and importance, regardless of the level of purpose and import. The house (and maybe time for a pet again?), family, friends, and...

This might be the main thing...understanding that you are important to yourself. Maybe that means I missed a bubble above. The bubble of oneself.

Bridges to the Plumley House & Extended Hawkwind Family

Martin Plumley's "Spirits Burning Papers"

In the Early 2000s, Bridget and I had settled in a small mining town in the foothills of the Mendip Hills, near Bath in the UK. We were both recovering from significant life upheavals prior to meeting, and falling in love, in 1998. We were parents to a baby girl, and I was working full time. Bridget was being approached to perform; often this was with no rehearsal, payments, or expenses. Frequently, the gigs would be on the other side of our, albeit small, island.

I don't remember when or how, but Don contacted Bridget. He had briefly met her years before when she was in *San Francisco with Hawkwind. I think he emailed and asked her to contribute to a recording. I remember peering into our old CRT monitor in the corner of our sitting room at his space themed Earthlink website. We downloaded a short, low quality, clip over our dial up connection. I think I thought the music was weird and confusing. However, we were intrigued! Bridget got involved.*

For their first project, Bridget sent vocal tracks she had previously recorded for a song called Salome and one other. Don added all the instrumental tracks and did the whole production. When we heard the track, we were very impressed. I still really like that song. She had recently collaborated with somebody locally and neither of us really liked the result. So, this was a great start.

Subsequently, Bridget and Don planned their first album collaboration: Earthborn. Bridget and I had started rehearsing and arranging songs to play in a live set. Earthborn was a song she had played in the band, Star Nation, written with Rich Chadwick, Alan Davey and Steve Bemand. We had written our own arrangement. It would be the title track of the album.

I bought a little mixer and mic and got hold of some very unstable recording software and we started our home recording journey. There was a lot to figure out. However, my engineering background did help speed things along. At the time of recording, I had a cheap acoustic. I thought the least I could do was restring it. So, went to a local, old fashioned, village store. The place sold just about everything. You could buy fresh cooked bacon rolls, tobacco, sweets, Lego, an inflatable dinghy, and they had an acoustic guitar in the window. I went in and asked if they sold guitar strings. The shopkeeper said we could have a look. He ushered me behind the counter and through a door into a sitting room where someone was sat in front of a television.

There were shelves piled with all sorts of ephemera; he searched them and eventually found a pack of Martin guitar strings. I don't know what type; I had no idea there were different types back then.

With the guitar restrung we set about recording the acoustic guitar in the most unsuitable way possible. Remember that I knew nothing back then, other than how to record a sound and end up with a file to send to Don. I was renovating our old cottage, so, by now, the sitting room was stripped to bare stone walls and a concrete floor. I set up in the corner and started recording the finger picked guitar part for Earthborn…and generating all sorts of unsympathetic reverberations. The part recorded was the take used on the album. Given that it was a poorly recorded, cheap guitar, played by an amateur in an unsuitable recording environment, Don made it sound remarkably OK in the mix. Earthborn is still one of my favourite Spirits Burning tracks.

The album project proceeded, and I became increasingly dissatisfied with my acoustic recordings. One attempt at a solution was a Line 6 Variax modelling guitar that pretends to sound like all kinds of classic guitars by digital wizardry; one of these being acoustics. The acoustic sounds, it turns out, are unconvincing and terrible! Still, I persisted, recording the accompaniment to the song Storm Shelter. This song always makes me think of a sort of novelty, but catchy, Christmas record for some reason. I still cringe when I hear the guitar on this track. However, again Don made it sound a lot less bad in the mix than it really was.

Don is so easy to work with in a lot of ways. I still marvel that he didn't throw back my early efforts and tell me to "Try harder!" I also used the Variax to record electric guitar for Always which, again, I was very pleased with when I heard Don's mix. The Earthborn project also meant that I needed to learn to become recording 'engineer' for other contributors. I recorded Jasper Pattison's bass on a couple of tracks and Rich Chadwick's hand drum for Crafted From Wood. The latter track turned out to be a stripped-down duet with Daevid Allen and minimal instrumentation. Rich and I had to figure out how to clock Rich's Korg Electribe drum machine to be in sync with the audio we were recording against. When I hear these tracks, I still think of the recording sessions very fondly. Overall, I love Earthborn; it's eclectic, interesting, full of surprises and really well mixed and produced.

I bought an Earthborn domain in support of the Earthborn album and wrote a website, with loads of information about the album, the artists, recording and the history of the project. Don being a technical editor by trade had lots of suggestions and there were 'discussions' regarding American versus English grammar rules. The domain has long since fallen out of my control, but the site may be archived somewhere on the web.

Bridget went on to collaborate with Don on numerous projects and became quite self-sufficient in terms of recording. I contributed to some of the songs on Bloodlines and Make Believe It Real and was pleased with the tracks. However, life was becoming busier and more complicated in the background. I always marvelled at how egoless and democratic Don was in handling the material he assembled from around the globe and at how creative he was in crafting them into finished songs. Having said that, I struggled when I wasn't so pleased with the result. Being more reserved and British about such things than Bridget I would never have addressed this directly with Don. I also accepted that it was really inevitable. You can't please all the people…and so on.

I decided to step back and didn't really record for other Spirits Burning songs for a number of years.

Don was invited to contribute to a Pink Floyd tribute CD. We were one of the last groups to be allocated a song. We were given Take Up Thy Stethoscope and Walk. It was a song I wasn't at all familiar with and the first time I heard it I had no idea how to go about it. Don had asked me to start the ball rolling with acoustic guitar. Late one night I sat down and started recording some arpeggios. Bridget added suggestions for the break, and we recorded her vocals. When I heard the final mix, I absolutely loved what Don had done with it.

Writing this, and putting this into the context of passing time, I realise what a journey it's been and how I've developed as I've worked with Don, as an artist, performer and recording engineer. All of this has been with the support of Don, who's always happy to provide advice whenever I've needed it.

Bridget Memories of Our Journey

Hannah was now a small young child, and I was becoming more used to being a mum and had a little bit of time on my hands.

The Internet beckoned. I'd never followed Hawkwind's path since we'd parted ways but found I was curious. On searching their name, I discovered a website called The Hawkwind Museum [run by Dave Law]. I left a message saying hi on one of their pages which resulted on them messaging me back. I did an interview by email for them and that's how Don managed to get in touch with me. He saw the interview and messaged the museum. Our first communication was through Dave Law. I was nervous of reentering the big world of musicians, so Dave was an intermediary for quite a few of our first conversations 😵 *!*

Don invited me to contribute vocals to his next album (Alien Injection). Martin and I Googled the band and listened to a track or two. It sounded chaotic and noisy, and I wasn't too sure about it! I did have some vocal tracks that I had recorded for a band project with Mike Vesty (RIP) that had folded a few years previously. I liked both songs and decided to send them to Don to use as he wished. I thought it would all end there.

How wrong could I be! Here we are nearly 20 years later and we're working on yet another full-length collaboration!

I didn't hear what Don and his crazy crew of creatives did with my songs for a long time. However, fairly shortly afterwards I did hear from a collaborator of Don's, Stephen Palmer (my email address for a guitar solo was the deal I believe). It was an invitation to collaborate on Mooch's next CD. This was the point when I started writing songs again and recording. Martin was instrumental in enabling. He bought an experimental Italian DAW called n-Track for his computer and a Behringer mic. Also, he gave me for Christmas my best present ever. An Akai 4000s! (An Electric Wind Instrument) Alongside this, he quickly added the 50 onboard sounds written for the EWI by Matt Traum...so much better than the originals! Plus, Garritan Orchestra for MIDI work.

My next contribution for Don didn't see the light of day for many years. It was a poem called Outcast and some siren sounds made with my clarinet for a track called Stand and Deliver...hmmm was this pre EWI times?

These pieces were destined for the film noir album, Behold The Action Man, that Don did in close collaboration with Roger Neville-Neil. For whatever reasons, it wasn't released for many years.

I enjoyed working with Don and we both felt there was 'more in the bank' and we agreed to work on a full-length album together. This ended up being an all-encompassing project that took up all my spare time for years! The track listing consisting of old songs that we had in our respective catalogues and new ones that were written specifically for the project.

Martin was very supportive, and I selfishly took advantage and let him take on cooking duties many evenings when he came back from work so I could work on the songs.

I got in touch with musicians that I hadn't seen or spoken to for years to see if they wanted to get involved. Mostly, they did and that was lovely. I had left Hawkwind in a cloud of confusion that left me doubting my musical abilities and though I had continued to go on to form Daze with Danny from 2000DS that project sank as Dan struggled with personal issues. After that, I had turned to Art and dance until Don brought me out of musical retirement... I wasn't sure about it at first but by now I bloomin' loved it!

Martin and our house hosted recording sessions from many good mates: Richard (Chadwick), Claire and Sarah, Huw and Jasper.

Crafted from Wood was a track based on an old song of Don's. I rewrote all the lyrics except for his "Maybe we're crafted from wood" line. New lyrics and melodies came easily, and I recorded the vocals in one session. I hadn't tuned my voice to anything which happened a lot until I had my EWI up and running. So, they were only in tune with their self...I sent them to Don and was totally blown away when he sent me what the song had grown into. Daevid was singing on it! And it sounded PERFECT! We had to detune Richard Wileman's bouzouki until it harmonised. Richard Chadwick re-

corded the drumming one evening using a hand-painted shallow handheld Apache drum and he absolutely killed it! He always says yes to a coffee and at this time I was making him 2 or 3 double strength mugs during a session!

Some of the songs started in more traditional ways but I don't play guitar so would send my starter songs to Don with only the vocals recorded to a metronome so that they were in time. I loved hearing what people did with them. Though sometimes I wasn't happy with the results, so Don and I did have a few extremely detailed discussions via email where we argued for and against the inclusion of various instruments in particular places during the song. Though this was more a feature of our next album Bloodlines... ooh yeah... The song Cleopatra stands out in my mind. Don had added clarinet through the track. I liked it but felt there was too much... Nuff said methinks! Back to Earth Born!

Always was another track I recorded without any accurate pitching. Martin was away in Ireland, Hannah was in bed, I had the lyrics written and it was me by the window with a microphone and the melody poured through me. I knew I'd have to re-record it to get the vocals in a recognisable pitch, but I was SOOOO pleased with the results, it was all there, a song in one take! I didn't realise at the time just how many times I would have to record it in order to recapture the effortless soft voicing of that night.

There are so many memorable moments on this album. Like when Martin played electric guitar for Always, when Steve (Swindells) was playing on One Way Trip and got Jerry (Richards) to add guitar, when Don sent me Candles and I first heard Jerry Jeter's voice (I got goosebumps!), having the opportunity to design the cover knowing that Karen could effortlessly do all the

*tech/graphicky stuff that I had no knowledge of. The
moment finally came when I actually held our CD in my
hand, and it was such a feeling of achievement and joy
alongside the knowledge that the years of our hard work
had a physical, playable and long-lasting presence in the
world. I'd been on records before, with the Slags,
Hawkwind etc., but this was different. This was such
more!*

*Don and Karen had met me briefly when the Hawks
toured America but sadly, I didn't remember the
exchange. So, it was a friendship and a working
partnership born of the technology of the modern world.
The Internet made Spirits Burning the super group that
it is today. I could record in our house in England, send
the files to Don in America and then they could be going
anywhere in the world where he had links to amazing
musicians.*

*Martin put together a great website for the CD. It
had a page for every person who had played with photos
we took or found on the net and text about them and their
musical backgrounds. Eventually we lost the domain
name. I think we might have passed the html etc. to Don
but I'm not sure.*

*The release was with Voiceprint Records and made
some small but significant waves in the music press. I
enjoyed reading the reviews, which were, on the whole,
pretty complimentary.*

*It wasn't long before we started work on a second
collaboration. We discussed doing a concept album and I
had found a tiny book in a charity shop about Kings and
Queens that I was charmed by and suggested we base the
tracks on Royalty. I really enjoyed finding out about
characters and writing lyrics about them. We stretched
the concept worldwide and to its limits, so tracks include
lyrics in English, Shona and Ndebele about Chaminuka,*

the African Prince of Peace and in another song, the viewpoint of a concerned mother to be, for the destiny of her, as yet unborn child (Vlad Dracul).

I remember listening to each track, being invested in every second and having intense discussions on timings, where instruments could/should/must be put/in/louder /quieter. It got quite intense sometimes!

I think Don's general rule of thumb was to take what had been recorded and stick it all in. The more the merrier. I don't think he does that so much anymore, but even back then he was known for moving parts to different places in the song if he felt they'd work better, which surprised and disconcerted some musicians when hearing the changes to their work. I soon learned not to leave anything 'extra' on a take as Don might add it into the song. Hit the Moon (on Earth Born) has an 'Oh no' that I'd said when a take had gone astray!

Sometimes, knowing Don's ways of working, I would send him clips/sections of MIDI EWI which had no fixed place so he could have free rein as to which parts to use and where to place them.

I started calling him Maestro and created an image of him with 8 arms. He was the head of a huge, rambling, tumultuous, creative melting pot of musicians linked to him by threads of music which then tangled us all up in a web of melody and rhythm which he would comb and patternate. When we worked in collaboration, I considered that role to be partly mine too.

Photo Illustration by Bridget Wishart

After Bloodlines came out, we went on a tangent and produced an almost completely instrumental CD under the name Astralfish. Far Corners was fun to do. I jammed a lot of my parts, using rhythm as much as melody to create atmospheres and journeys. I used the samples on Garritan Orchestra to create some pretty inventive sounds.

I felt we'd pushed each other quite intensely on Bloodlines so I resolved to take a back seat on our next song project. I slightly regret that now because when I hear the songs from Make Believe it Real, I think they probably could have been better if I'd played a more active role in their internal weavings and tbh, I actually prefer the extra CD. All through these albums we didn't meet. We talked a couple of times on the phone, but our methods of communication were email and our music.

Happily, I also got to do the artwork for Bloodlines and Make Believe it Real. I was so lucky to be working with Karen. She killed it on the graphics, lettering and lyrics.

We did have plans for a fourth collaboration and even had a title...Rift. It never, never happened. But I guess, to a degree a rift-like amount of space grew between us. I continued to contribute EWI and the occasional vocal for Don's albums, but we made musical partnerships with other people. Don, with Albert Bouchard & Michael Moorcock on the Dancers at the End of Time albums and myself, working with Lee Potts and Omenopus. Then much later writing with the classical/rock bassist Gabriel J. Monticello and our Band of Doctors creating the benefit CD Ghost.

There was even a time when life was giving me grief and I wanted to try and make a better/clearer/un-cluttered/fresh space for myself, that I messaged Don to say that I didn't think I'd be working with him anymore. I felt crap about it immediately, but it took a bit of time before I got the courage to write and ask if we could forget about that idea and keep on keeping on.

That was more recently though...before that, in 2017, we actually got to meet in 3D and even play a couple of gigs together.

Spirits Burning is a conglomerate of musicians that Don has put together over the years and they live all over the world so playing gigs isn't something that's easy to accomplish but Don had set his sights on playing his music in front of an audience. His plan was to play a festival in the UK. When he wrote to me discussing his thoughts, I suggested playing Kozfest over other Festivals because I felt it would be the best fit and have the likeliest successful outcome. Sonic Rock Solstice was also a contender but was further afield and Koz had a more 'traditional' field festival set up with marquee stages.

I suggested Don's plans move forward a year to 2017 because Chumley Warner Brothers were already on the bill, and I believe in striking while the iron is hot. I'm sure Don will have lots to say about this, so I'll just get to the part where I went outside and there was Don in his van wondering where to park. We lived on a narrow road and there was little space. Luckily there was a lane ending in a car park for the flats opposite and I sat in the van with him as we drove the few yards.

It was surreal to be meeting him in real life after 10 years of working together. I had the odd thought like, what happens if we don't get on? But we all got on just fine. Don met Martin and the rabbit and settled into the spare room. We rehearsed out at the studio at Rockaway Park. Which Magnus was running at the time (Magnus from Tarantism and more recently Hawkwind). My old buddies Rich and Steve were going to be playing and they had come out to ours a couple of times to do some preliminary rehearsing. Playing music with these guys is always fun. They both really get on with Martin and have been in my life since I was 18. Steve had recruited Colin on bass who I knew from when I was living in Bath.

Don was an easy house guest and was happy to eat vegetarian food. We took him to see some of the local sites. He wasn't too keen on driving the small windy lanes of the English countryside. Having seen the roads in America I can understand why!

Martin and Don, Ebbor Gorge on the Edge of the Mendips, 2017
(photo by Bridget Wishart)

We did a warmup gig at Widcombe Social Club. I hadn't been there since the Hippy Slag reunion, and it was all different. The PA guy had a decent, modern setup with a portable mixing desk and got us a great sound. The stage wasn't big enough for all of us, so we split the boxes and put the drumkit and me and Martin in the middle. Stage left had Colin and Steve and stage right had Kev and Don. Kev was making crazy noises with his box, singing and possibly playing harmonica? A tall hairy man with a wonderful disposition and an inborn ability to make a lot of noise would be a good way to describe him I think .

Martin and I as Chumley Warner Brothers were the support band. There were people from his work in the audience as well as Hawkwind fans, old bandmates and good friends. Everyone was extremely supportive.

Martin and I got to play with Spirits Burning and be in the audience for their set as we weren't playing on every song. I remember it was very loud!

We met up with American drummer Jack Gold-Molina, who took some cracking photos at the gig. He was coming to Koz and getting a ride with Don. A serious well-meaning chap who had a lot to say about Hawkwind related stuff, which, even though I was in the band, wasn't my sphere or something I knew much about. We waved Don off and planned to drive down and get onsite later.

We only took a small tent and camped quite near the Daevid Allen Stage. This is the bigger marquee and the one Spirits Burning would be playing in. It was raining and certain parts of the site were starting to get muddy. Our tent stayed dry though and though small it meant it was warm and cosy with enough room to leave wet boots in a tiny porch.

My book signing with Ian Abrahams went well. It was in the Wally Tent, where all the wild and wayward events happen. That's where Chumleys played that year. We were sandwiched between 2 noisy bands in the main marquees, so it was impossible to hear our quieter songs. We ended up cutting the set short rather than struggle to be heard.

I was looking forward to playing with Spirits Burning. I figured the music would go down well with the crowd and most of the audience would be familiar with some of the songs on the set list. I hadn't intended to wear gloves, but my fingers were cold, and I needed to keep them warm in order to play the EWI, so they became part of my unintentional, rather raggedy look. Playing at Festivals is always a juggling act with time. The band before has to be on time, setting up has to be perfect, sound check has to be tight, all band members need to be present and ready to start when the soundman says go...! We didn't do too badly. Rich wasn't quite ready... Dazzer's drum kit had been set up very close to the back of the stage and him and the stool had toppled off. While he sorted this out, we jammed, and I recited what I could remember of a poem I'd written for part of the Hawkwind track Black Elk Speaks. The gig got going and I have flashing memories...singing Images and seeing more people come into the tent as they recognised the song. Standing next to Martin our fingers in our ears, singing into the same mic, trying to hear our harmonies! Being in the audience watching everyone enjoy the show trying to remember which track was which so that I'd be back on stage for the right songs. Looking across at the sea of faces trying not to look too closely because I didn't want to lose my concentration. The sound onstage was a sea of woven sounds with pockets of energetic insanity exploding into my ears. All too soon we were done, and it was finished, and the cycle begins again. The rush to get gear off stage, gear on stage and the next band ready.

We had done it; we had fulfilled one very special American's dream and created some mighty fine musical moments in that doing.

There were photos taken, before, during, after. Don sold all his merch at the stand. We signed a few autographs and enjoyed the afterbuzz.

Bridget and Don at Kozfest, 2017 (photo by Michal Skwarek)

I don't remember much afterwards. We obviously got home! Life continued. Don at some point sent us the recording of the gig with a plan to release a live CD of the gig. Both Martin and I thought the quality of the recording was questionable and doubted the quality was high enough. Don sent it for mixing and when we heard it again, it sounded a bit better. Then he got it worked on again and somehow out of a tangle of sound the songs were appearing, and it seemed like it could be viable. And now, in 2024, Spirits Burning Live at Kozfest 2017 has a home with Deko Entertainment. The final link in a chain that goes back in time is about to close the circle and complete the play.

So, in the last year or two Don and I have decided to have another go at that fourth collaboration. We are

271

choosing sets of songs under different themes. There is a trio started by Don on nature, an unfinished trio adopted, adapted and updated from Omenopus plus plenty more that you can find out about when you listen to the album. Hey, you know, I haven't designed the cover yet; there's always something to look forward to!

Martin Plumley Remembers Kozfest Live

In 2016, Don raised the idea of making a trip to England and playing a live Spirits Burning set at a festival. I don't know really how it all came about but I think Bridget contacted people and pulled some levers. A spot was organised at Kozfest, which took place in Uffculme in Devon in those days. We had played there several times in the past. A lovely, small festival that always has a really friendly community feel.

We started rehearsals at home with Steve Bemand (guitar) and Colin Kafka (bass). The practice sessions then moved to a studio/rehearsal space at nearby Rockaway Park. Rich Chadwick played drums at the sessions, and we had a full band setup. I hadn't really played in a full band setting before, so it was an exciting learning experience for me. Practicing continued over a couple of months and recordings were exchanged with Don. Kev Ellis got involved and came up to a couple of practice sessions.

Eventually, the week arrived, and Don turned up at our house in his rented camper van. The evening he arrived we had our first, and probably only, full band rehearsals at Rockaway Park. Don sailed through it. I have no idea how as he must have been massively jet lagged. A couple of nights later we played at a performance space in Bath. Bridget and I played a few songs as a support act and then played some songs with Spirits Burning. There was a section of instrumentals and songs where Don sang where we sat out. The band sounded good and really quite polished given how little preparation time there had been.

We had a fun time with Don, showing him some of the local area over the week and we all enjoyed each other's company. At the weekend, we headed off to Devon for the festival. Bridget and I played in the Wally Tent earlier on Saturday afternoon. Later in the afternoon, we headed up to the main stage to play with Spirits Burning. I was definitely the baby of the band, but nobody made me feel anything other than 100% part of the whole. It was an absolute blast and, while I struggled with the onstage sound and playing acoustics in a full-on electric onslaught, I absolutely loved it. We posed for a group photo after and drifted off in separate directions.

The rain really set in as the evening progressed, in age old British festival fashion. We repaired to the beer tent with Don and spent the evening drinking and chatting before closing the evening watching, and dancing to, Steve Hillage's System 7, and dashing through the rain back to our cosy little tent at the end of the night.

It was so nice to meet Don and spend time with him after many years of collaborating on music. It was a real pleasure, and we made a lot of happy memories.

Steve Bemand on Kozfest 2017

Don contacted me to suggest a live gig in the U.K. at Kozfest. He asked if I knew who could be conscripted to make up a band.

I immediately thought of Richard for drums, and although it was possible he would be busy with Hawkwind around the same time he accepted the challenge.

And of course, Bridget would be performing so the

three of us were already accustomed to playing together, had done in Demented Stoats, Hawkwind and quite a few other projects and outfits.

Don presented a long list of SB songs which were whittled down into an initial setlist.

We found Colin, who I had known for years, a great musician, to play bass, and Don brought in Kev Ellis for vocals and synth. We did get Cary Grace on synth for one rehearsal, but she wasn't able to carry on with the project.

For rehearsals we used Rockaway Park, through Magnus Martin who was engineer at the studio.

Colin and I firstly got together to go through the music, then we met up with Richard at the studio for the three of us to whip the set into shape.

Then Bridget and Martin joined the three piece and Kev came along, and we recorded all the rehearsals so the music could be sent to Don to keep him in the loop.

Truth is, some of the music Don had assembled was possibly more technically demanding than any of us had played previously, and we had to work very hard to get it polished. There was not really enough rehearsal, but we leant on our years of experience to make the music happen.

Don came over to U.K. to have a live rehearsal with the band, and we played a great warm-up gig in Bath, then Kozfest, which went off very well, and was recorded, 24 track audio and video.

The Hawks in My Room

The first Hawkwind musician to be part of SB was one no longer alive, Robert Calvert. When I became aware of Bob's *Centigrade 232* readings, I contacted his wife, Jill. She gave me permission to incorporate the readings I requested. I sometimes wish that I had asked for more…for an entire album. At other times, I'm glad I did two songs only, and let him rest in peace.

Energized by successfully incorporating Gong's Daevid Allen more fully into the band—seven songs on both the first and second albums—I continued my efforts to build a roster of space rock musicians. I invited two Hawkwind family cousins: guitarist Trev Thoms, who had played with Nik Turner's ICU, and Canada's Don Xaliman, whose Melodic Energy Commission sometimes served as a haunt for former Hawkwind synth player Del Dettmar.

Two albums later—*Alien Injection*—brought onboard two Hawkwind family musicians who planted the seeds for future collaborations and invites for years to come: Bridget Wishart and Michael Moorcock.

Bridget was the musician I didn't know I was a looking for. It had been over two decades since I had worked regularly with a female vocalist, and it was a collaboration that I found natural and rewarding. As in my past musical lives, she would write lyrics for most songs and be open to mine as well. The bonus was that she played an Electronic Wind Instrument (EWI) and had a great sense for songwriting. We would do SB albums primarily highlighting her voice. Plus, an instrumental album focused on her EWI, under the band name Astralfish. And we would eventually play live in the UK.

Mike brought a different plate to the table. He had his writing notability, his Deep Fix ensemble, and his music collaborations with Hawkwind and BÖC. He also provided something that I always looked for in space rock: Variation. Stems in different directions. These would reveal in the medieval songs of *Alien Injection*, and then in future inspired works from Cajun to the tips of post-rock. I would be able to spend years immersing myself in my favorite Moorcock trilogy—*Dancers at the End of Time*. And I would get to produce and be part of a Deep Fix album.

The fourth SB album also introduced Adrian Shaw, Capt. Black (Keith Kniveton), and Steve Taylor. Adrian was the bassist when I first saw Hawkwind in 1978, Tower Theatre, Philadelphia. Keith was briefly in Hawkwind, showing up on two 2001 live albums. Steve played bass at the Strange Daze festival in the U.S. when Ron Tree and Dave Brock couldn't get into the country because their papers weren't in order.

The first album highlighting collaboration between Bridget and me was titled *Earth Born*. We were credited, along with others, on all 13 tracks. For each track, I listed the musicians in reverse alphabetical order, so that Bridget Wishart was usually first. The CD tray noted "A song-oriented journey by a cosmically festive crew... presented by Bridget Wishart (Hawkwind) & Don Falcone." In the following list of notable contributors was the first time I included the phrase "Hawkwind family members." Here, followed by "Simon House (Bowie), Richard Chadwick (Star Nation), Alan Davey (Bedouin), Steve Swindells (Dan Mingo), and Jerry Richards (Dan Mingo)." I'm pretty sure that Bridget was responsible for connecting me to all of them (except for Jerry, who she reminded me came via Steve). In some cases, like Richard's "space drums" and "storm drums," she was even present for their recording.

The second Spirits Burning & Bridget Wishart album was the band's debut of Harvey Bainbridge. Although I had collaborated with Harvey on a Spaceship Eyes piece in 1998 and Karen and I visited him in the 90s, I believe it was Bridget that invited Harvey. Returning Hawks were Alan, Simon, and Steve. I probably now had direct access to them via email.

The more experimental *Crazy Fluid* album was more streamlined in the Hawk attendance. Just Bridget and Keith Kniveton. The return to vocal space rock with *Behold The Action Man* debuted Paul Hayles, who I had seen perform at my first Hawkwind concert and contacted on Facebook. Bridget and Alan were on the album too.

When SB, along with Cyrille Verdeaux took a turn slightly closer to jazz and other genres that could support synths, organ, and piano, Andy (Anderson) with a pedigree that included The Cure and Hawkwind provided drums for the *Healthy Music In Large Doses* opener. Bridget, whose presence on SB albums was now integral to the band, was back. As was 2/5 of the Hawkwind line-up I saw at the Tower Theatre—bassist Adrian Shaw and keyboardist Paul Hayles.

The third Spirits Burning & Bridget album—*Make Believe It Real*—produced the largest collection of Hawkwind family members. Newcomers included Dave Anderson and Twink—both of whom I contacted—and Steve Bemand and Dan Thompson—both of whom came in via Bridget. Returnees included Alan, Richard, Paul, and Simon. And of course, Bridget, which makes ten.

It was around this time that I assembled the *No One Cries In Space* promotional CD, which accompanied some orders of the *Space Ritual Live* album by Hawkwind 2014. The SB compilation was "a celebration of the last 15 years of Spirits Burning," featuring 10 musicians with ties to Hawkwind. The cover spread collage by Karen weaved the 66 musicians on the album across a cluster of stars, named NGC 602.

The next studio album—*Starhawk*—was the SB debut of Nik Turner, who I had contacted online, and then scheduled a recording session at my home studio. He was the first Hawkwind family member to record here. The *Starhawk* credits included Alan, Bridget, Jerry, Paul, and Twink.

Another new Hawkwind player at the Strange Daze festival was Steve Hayes. He made his SB debut on *The Roadmap in Your Head* album. Future SB live members Bridget and Steve (Bemand) participated. Nik was present again. (We had one remaining song from our session, *Purse*, which opened a Flicknife Flipside sampler.)

The Spirits Burning & Michael Moorcock albums continued Bridget's involvement on vocals and EWI, with lots of Mike on vocals and harmonica. Harvey provided synths which were spread across the first three albums. Adrian plays on the first two.

Mick Slattery debuted in SB with guitar on *An Alien Heat;* Dead Fred added violin on *The Hollow Lands* and lead vocals on the next album's last song—he and I also collaborated on *SF*, a song for a compilation; Crum and Paul Rudolph arrived at *The End Of All Songs - Part 1*. Mr. Dibs (vocals) and Niall Hone (bass) on *Part 2*. Various Hawkwind family members would reappear. Steve Bemand returned to the fold for *Hollow Lands*, Alan for *Part 1*. Dave Anderson and Paul Rudolph on *Part 2*.

The *Evolution Ritual* album was trickier.

I wanted acoustic or acoustic-sounding instruments only.

From the Hawkwind family, I was able to work with parts provided by Alan (sounding like an upright bass), Mick Slattery (acoustic guitar), Mike Moorcock (harmonica), Paul Hayles (keyboard bassoon), and Bridget. Over the course of six songs, Bridget's EWI triggered baroque organ, piccolo trumpet, English horn, French horn, trumpet, glass harmonica, bass flute, horn, flutes, and strings.

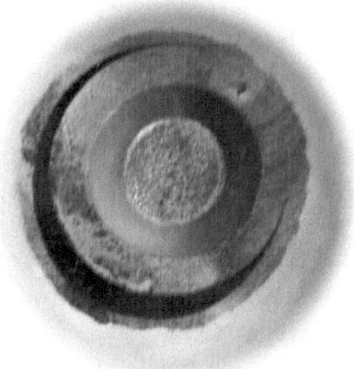

Tips—Style (& Wondering About Space Rock)

"I DON'T REALLY LIKE ARPEGGIATORS." I direct this statement to Robert Rich…I'm hand-delivering premasters for a listening session, a supplement of his mastering service, or giving him his copy of a release…I stun him. Robert's ambient music is often built from arpeggios. We both love space rock and ambient, two genres whose history embraces synthesizer arpeggiators—the feature that automatically creates musical patterns (arpeggios), so the musician doesn't have to physically play the pattern. Think Pink Floyd's *On The Run* on *The Dark Side of the Moon*, Tangerine Dream's *Love on a Real Train* in the *Risky Business* film.

I confess. My music sometimes uses arpeggiators. Via a physical keyboard, or virtual instrument plug-in inserted on a digital track. I accept automated patterns from invitees. I use the percussive variant of arpeggios too—programmed drums. A scratchpad to play over. When mixing, I sometimes combine the virtual with the real, or let the former be the lone drummer.

I'm less intrigued with pressing a key, letting the pattern repeat endlessly. Or, pressing multiple keys simultaneously so that a chordal-based arpeggio plays back. I did that with the opening two songs of Heavenly Music Corporation's *In A Garden Of Eden*, the

Melting Euphoria debut, early Spaceship Eyes. I understand: If not watching a musician live, the recipe is hidden. Seeing Tangerine Dream's Thorsten Quaeschning manually play arpeggio notes on some songs is impressive. I do like their mix of automatic and manual styles. The opening song of Spirits Burning's *Starhawk* album includes a pattern created via an arpeggiator. When we perform the song in Bath, I play the arpeggio parts by hand. It's challenging. I'm relieved when we don't have time for it three days later.

My bass guitar experience and harder rock jamming informed my early keyboard playing. My left-hand drove songs, syncing with the kick drum, and when applicable, I created two-hand riffs or patterns that avoided the tendency to play root notes or 1-5-8 (two root note) patterns—I did a lot of those too. A thin line between 8th-note riffs and arpeggios. Sometimes adding delay effects facilitated playing less notes, with inflective touches building a unique symbiosis between the initial and repeated notes. When my Roland D-50 keyboard died, the sound, its effect, and how it sounded when played in real time couldn't be recreated, even with a future D-50 plug-in.

I appreciate moderation. I might press a key to trigger the start of an arpeggio and have it play for a four-beat measure, for limited use within a song. If using an arpeggio for a longer length, I can use a free hand to adjust the sound's shape and color over time (starting with controls for modulation, envelope, cutoff). In Pro Tools, adjustments can be saved as an automation playlist. Many musicians make an art of this. I was well-schooled on this method with the Spice Barons and Thessalonians. For arpeggios and pads.

I'm concerned that space rock has stagnated. The template of synth arpeggios, reading a poem, and pounding away on root notes is too easy, becoming repetitive album to album, band to band. Is wrapping instruments (such as violin, sax, guitar) in the effects of the past or current era enough? Space rock is the place I always found newness: such as audio generators (early Hawkwind), synth arpeggiators (next-gen Hawkwind), full theremin integration (when Tim Blake returned). Are Hawkwind and their descendants otherwise trapped using the arpeggiator component and other tools relatively the same way for recent decades? Are there new ways to use these tools? New sound generators?

Long ago, my use of an Audicy workstation felt novel, while spacy. Performing effected scrubs and varispeeds of pre-recorded sounds. And then the Audicy become too hard to boot up and use.

In the here and now, I float ideas within recent Spirits Burning albums. I'm a small cog in a wheel. Part of a niche vehicle. Whether it is space rock, post rock, or something else…whether what I do is new, or influences others…remains to be seen. I remain committed to the attempt.

o o o o o o

In *True Blood*, when Dionysus-worshipping Maryann Forrester (actress Michelle Forbes) is jolted by the photo-kinetic powers of Sookie Stackhouse (played by Anna Paquin), Forrester quizzically expresses "Come on, it'll be our little secret. What are you?"

A coworker latches onto my ambient years, deducing I do instrumentals only. Older friends remember my lyrics. Tongue-in-cheek lines stick. "I want your purse, I need your purse…I want to know…what it's like to be you, for a day"—sung by a thief. My late mother's favorite song was *Loralyn*, hidden in an 80's demo, never resurrected for CD-era Spirits Burning. To many Dolby coworkers, I share the lone song released as Don Falcone: The 20-plus minute *An Isolated Craft* instrumental experiment built from a 1 kHz tone. One coworker's newborn loves it. Sleeps to it.

Spirits Burning implies space rock. What do you do when each turn challenges that definition? The acoustic-based *Evolution Ritual* is not the RIO-attempt of *Crazy Fluid*, which is not the spacier *Alien Injection* (which includes five Moorcock tracks that cross into the experimental and medieval). One reviewer says the *Ritual* album is a rip-off because it is not space rock. They vow to never review Spirits Burning again.

My brother tries to classify Spirits Burning during his weekly Friday acoustic guitar performances on Facebook. Each time he adds a new genre I provide, the description lengthens, a hyphenation feast!

In the U.S., most people are unfamiliar with space rock. They might decipher a guess with Pink Floyd. While a puzzle piece, the core sound of Spirits Burning is not a Floydian one.

Spirits Burning on Wikipedia offers space rock, progressive rock, psychedelic rock. The Don Falcone entry adds ambient. Reviews fuel the fire of confusion.

I stretch the branding, continuously reaching out to neighbor genres and beyond. And, having different musicians song to song, album to album. Mixing space rock relatives alongside distant cousins—such as musicians whose earlier music doesn't imply a space rock appreciation or influence.

I am comfortable with embracing the plurality, the collective power of many voices. Even when my answer stumbles.

∘ ∘ ∘ ∘ ∘ ∘

At heart, I am a songwriter. At heart, I am a sound designer. I value both pursuits; in my music and the music I listen to.

From P. J. Harvey to Godspeed You! Black Emperor. When not tripping to the sound aspect of a Hawkwind (the best of which I acknowledge as a welcome drug),

I advocate the songwriting interplays of the band's Calvert years, or the evocative instrumental weaves within their *Levitation* album.

I start most Spirits Burning songs with chord progressions (of a moving nature or a longer pad-based one) and notable riffs (if any). I might affect keyboard stabs or reworked samples. Even add a synth lead. What is usually missing, surprisingly, is the space rock 101 sounds: arpeggios and falling synth clusters. Sometimes, another musician provides that element—such as guitarist Steve Bemand (live and in the studio), or another synth player, like Harvey Bainbridge on *Heavens Hide*.

If not present...consider Calvert and Moorcock solo works that discard it, the definition of space rock expands. You get songs aligned with space rock themes, or by musicians associated with space rock.

The genre remains intact.

One of the Spirits Burning

○ ○ ○ ○ ○ ○

I was never one of the cool kids. Others hung out at night around the neighborhood wall; less of a wall, just flat stones behind a back yard that faced an entrance to a football field. Or kids hanging outside high school in Harrisburg, smoking before, during, and after the day's last period. Those kids did give me some street cred. I wrote album reviews for the Twin Towers school paper. Had lots of bushy hair. One Steelton student there even called me Musky, my dad's nickname.

I remember when Darlene DiSanto told me "Bass is cool." She played bass (and tuba). Her brother played bass. Her boyfriend played bass. She got me started with a couple of casual lessons. Years later, my niece Jessica, visiting the Bay Area, got to meet our dog, and said "Dogs are cool." They were both right.

Which brings us to…experiencing a piece of art and feeling…that was cool! We know our moments. Tori Amos' live at the Fox in Oakland, the middle of her *Bliss* segues into Kate Bush's *Running Up The Hill*. A slow-motion audience coming-to-realization as a quarter-note kick drum bounce returns with its count of 16 beats and the band plays another 16 beats while Tori stays silent, and then she sings "If I only could, make a deal with God…" causing a roar and chill from head to toe and a tear. For over two minutes.

Or, visiting S.F. MOMA, experiencing Ragnar Kjartannson's *The Visitors*: an hour-long art piece presented on nine huge screens, each screen focused on a room in a house and the musicians performing there…until they stop playing, reunite in the main room, and leave the house together, singing. It's magical. Creative. While it wasn't musically heavy…well—spoiler alert!—maybe the cannon explosion was…I immediately felt a post-rock essence. And it was in 3/4 like lots of Godspeed songs. I discover afterwards that Ragnar did another installation with music by Kjartan Sveinsson (former member of the Icelandic post-rock band Sigur Rós); who Al Bouchard met at an Iceland rock festival, and suggested we invite to Spirits Burning. That would be cool.

I used to think my phrase "I don't believe in absolutes" to be

283

poignant, and clever, given its use is inherently an absolute. The term lost some luster when I discovered Cornelius in "Planet of The Apes" said "Don't speak to me in absolutes."

In my teens, I saw a movie about painter Paul Gauguin. Forgettable, except for one takeaway: "Be mysterious and you will be happy." When I wrote this into Thessalonians' "E-Space," Kim coaxed me to change it to "the mystery will make you happy." Regardless, the value of mystery has stayed with me. I remember long walks on a dark, windy campus in Shippensburg. And, how silence can create mystery.

I attempt a sense of cool or mystery with every song. With potential roots from...the line-up; the sounds; the dynamics, the journey the song creates, the story it tells, the reveal of passion.

○ ○ ○ ○ ○ ○

When my mom was in the hospital in 2007, she introduced her four children to the nurses. As we stood around her bed, she said… "This is my oldest. He's a high school teacher."

That was my brother Richard. Recently retired.

She turned to my other brother, David: "He's a college professor." He teaches psychology; and carries his guitar wherever he goes.

She next looked to Cindi, my sister. "She's a vice president and a nurse." My sister was a nurse who became a VP at a risk management company working with healthcare providers.

My mom looked to me—the technical writer by day, forever thinking about music. Years later, a consultant for a job placement agency noted: "You light up every time you talk about music. Is there anything else you could do music related?" My mom started with "This is my youngest." The technical writer by day, the sometimes musician.

She added, "He's a creative writer."

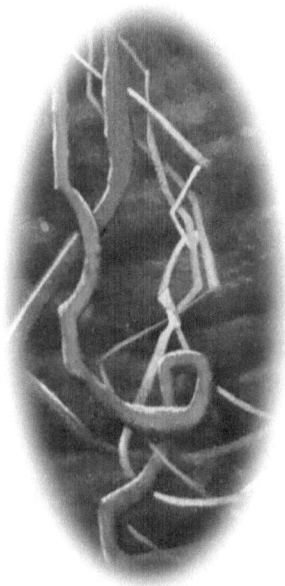

Note-Ability

ARRIVING IN SAN FRANCISCO, I didn't know anybody, and nobody knew me.

John Taggart, my Shippensburg college advisor was friends with poet Kathleen Fraser, a teacher at San Francisco State University. She probably helped with my application to their graduate program. I never took one of her classes. Perhaps I should have. She was on the panel the first time I took my Masters oral examination; the years of non-communication didn't help. She didn't know me and didn't seem to appreciate my approach. Perhaps a little too casual.

My cousin (and Mars Everywhere guitarist) Ernie knew a girl who moved here from his home base in Silver Spring, Maryland. He didn't provide contact info.

Another cousin, on my mom's side, had an in-law who lived here. From my hometown of Steelton. Quite older than me, and I didn't know him. No contact info was provided. I met with his family and my cousin when they were in town following his death.

Ernie mentioned another friend, Pat Fahey, who arrived before me and taught at a high school. We met decades later; talked about Pro Tools, recording, mixing. Pat was probably interested in Pro Tools training. I declined. As much as I like to coach and teach, I didn't want to jeopardize the balancing act between my day job and music projects.

When the last fully functioning SB band of the 80s practiced regularly at the Hudson Street Studios, the bass player was Julia of The Gargoyles. She began moonlighting in SB in 1988. In the middle of a practice about a year later, she turned to me and asked, "Are you related to Ernie Falcone?"

o o o o o o

I love the ability to play notes. The stories they can tell. I appreciate the energy of a guitar solo, the passion transferred from the guitarist to the speakers. I appreciate the sound more than the number of notes squeezed into a few bars of music. Speed or complexity can be passionate. It just doesn't guarantee it.

It is fun to play with someone who skillfully rips off a cool solo (I think of BÖC's Richie Castellano on SB's *Hothouse Flowers*), or a bass guitar run (for example, William Kopecky's lines towards the end of *Part 2* song *The Ballad of Lord Jagged of Canaria*). It's invigorating to write (or start) a song and have someone of greater skill take it to a height that could never be accomplished without them. You hope they appreciate the invitation, the journey, the result. And would want to do it again. (Some will. Some won't. Some will forget— their lives filled with other memories, other priorities.)

While I often prefer an instrument effected with hints or homage to psychedelic, progressive, or post-rock times, I also love the sound of an acoustic instrument recorded on a front porch. Our tastes can be complicated. The notation doesn't have to be.

I'm surprised when someone describes an SB song as complicated. Maybe some are...

Is it easier, or even self-preservation to accept certain simplicities in music given one's skill level? I chose not to practice regularly, such that my keyboard and bass abilities developed more slowly. Especially after being in a band that practiced multiple days a week. Moving targets? I do concentrate on the sound. On song-writing. Another target: I built my engineering skills as a mixer, as a producer. And, over time, I improved at locating people with like interests, getting them onboard for collaborating. None of this makes me notable, of course. I can make the case that it reveals that I've always been an over-achiever—working harder with less (a Sekova bass when I should have chosen the Fender Precision Jazz, juggling music with school for half a decade and then 35 years of technical writing). It might explain why I took on greater roles with Mike Moorcock and Cyrille Verdeaux as they became part of my music story, and in turn, I began to help them with their music stories.

○ ○ ○ ○ ○ ○

The inclusion of Thessalonians and Spice Barons on my music resume, along with my Spaceship Eyes solo album, led to my record contract with Cleopatra. Producing Gary Parra's *Trap* album, the first album on Musea's Gazul imprint paved the way for SB debuting on Gazul.

Notability, from personal successes or your association with others with a level of success, might lead to a record contract, a slot at a UK festival, or a favorable response when you invite another musician to your project. It might get you on Wikipedia too.

Each Wikipedia article (or page) has a View history tab. Click the tab to reveal a list of changes. The more popular the page, rather the greater the number of edits, the longer the list. Click "oldest" at the bottom of the list to reveal a list ending with the initial entry.

A friend started the *Don Falcone* Wikipedia page as a gift on December 14, 2005. They didn't necessarily consider Wiki's rules and requirements. They might not have even thought the article would survive.

Wikipedia is all about notability. Their definition of notability. In early 2006, a Wiki contributor recommended the article for deletion.

Don Falcone

The notability of Don Falcone is not clear from this article. The only contributions to this article come from anonymous IP addresses with no edits aside from this article; this leads one to believe that this is a vanity article. Combined with a lack of notability, this would make the article a candidate for deletion. If no evidence of the notability of Don Falcone is added within the next week (by February 28, 2006), I will be nominating this article for deletion.

I was privy to the article, honored to be there. While I could see that my "notability" was indeed questionable, I decided to work with others to help maintain my presence there, if warranted. My Wiki education began...

It's better if new content originates from a Wiki contributor—an established account with an actual name. Otherwise, Wiki grabs the IP address label that identifies your computer on a network, considers it anonymous, and lists it in the article history. The *Don Falcone* page was initiated by a Wiki contributor. Many subsequent edits were not.

Wiki provides an article for musician notability. https://en.wikipedia.org/wiki/Wikipedia:Notability_(music).

There are degrees of notability within Wiki. For example, you could have a platinum record, which I do not. A childhood friend of mine spoke online of their platinum records while alive and their obituary repeats this. Checking the database for platinum records, my friend is not there. He got "platinum record" awards via AirplayExpress, a video and music delivery system that creates their own charts. The services use of the term "platinum record" feels questionable, especially when AirplayExpress doesn't have a Wiki article. Neither does my friend.

The discussion for article deletion momentarily went astray given the DC comics use of the Falcone mafia boss Carmine Falcone, a.k.a. Don Falcone. That, of course, would be a different article (or a different wiki, the gotham.fandom wiki).

One of the Spirits Burning

A case was made to retain the article: It met three of the criteria. (Circa 2005, before collaborations with Bridget Wishart, Cyrille Verdeaux, Michael Moorcock, Albert Bouchard).

1. *Falcone has released two or more albums on a major label or one of the more important indie labels (i.e., an independent label with a history of more than a few years and a roster of performers, many of which are notable). Falcone released two albums on Cleopatra's Hypnotic Records (which has been in existence since the early 90s). Cleopatra's roster has included releases by Gary Numan, Yes, Motorhead, Hawkwind, Future Sound of London, and more recently Elvis Presley and The Ohio Players.*

2. *Falcone leads a number of music projects that contains at least one member who was once a part of or later joined a band that is otherwise notable. Falcone leads Spirits Burning, a musical collective that has included members of many well-known progressive and space rock bands (such as Gong's Daevid Allen, Porcupine Tree's Steve Wilson, Hawkwind's Bob Calvert, Can's Mal Mooney). Falcone is also part of Weird Biscuit Teatime (CD on Voiceprint), with Gong's Daevid Allen.*

3. *Falcone has performed music for a work of media that is notable, e.g., a theme for a network television show. Falcone's Spaceship Eyes wrote the theme for the rave film Better Living Through Circuitry. Article would be better served to have the above info in its intro. The material about Falcone's hometown, college, and early bands (pre-1990) should be removed.*

The notability discussion includes "Definitely notable, despite the fact that I've never heard of him," "I'm still not sure about the notability of this guy, but he certainly seems involved in a lot of projects that release commercial CDs (even if I've never heard of any of them). I'll give him the benefit of the doubt now" and "Has enough recording credits to indicate notability within genre."

My favorite: "apparently notable more by association than anything else, but gets just enough legit mentions (e.g., at planetgong.com) to put him over the top. May not "deserve" to be notable, but there are many, many categories of articles whose subjects fall into that category (Serial killers, people on sex tapes with Paris Hilton, fortunate sons who've been undemocratically installed as US President after losing the popular vote...)"

A final response, prior to the decision to keep the page was "membership in several notable bands (with allmusic.com entries)." This focuses on a Wiki foundation: Properly sourced data.

Wiki considers the AllMusic online music database a good online source. This can be frustrating as the info there is sometimes incorrect or incomplete. An artist or their management can join AllMusic and feed the site with correct information, or not.

A site like discogs.com often seems more current and correct. Yet, Wiki doesn't consider Discogs to be a reliable source because it is user-generated (which seems convoluted as Wiki is volunteer-generated). Wiki provides an information article discussing questionable sources (Wikipedia:Reliable sources/Perennial sources).

Quotes for interviews or reviews can be a good source...if the content is from a Wiki-vetted source. For example, I did an interview with Perfect Sound Forever. They are allowed. However, an interview in Exposé magazine does not qualify. Additionally, it helps when content is online, able to be referenced with a link. (For guidance on sourcing reviews and interviews, plus albums, see Wikipedia:WikiProject Albums/Sources.)

Piero Scaruffi's online History of Rock numbered "Don Falcone (Melting Euphoria, Thessalonians)" as one of the top 50 keyboardists of all time. In the latter half. A few years later, Piero's site reset, listing the top 21, followed by 79 bulleted ones. I became a bulleted keyboardist.

One of the Spirits Burning

Note: Wiki does not consider the Scaruffi page a reliable source.

○ ○ ○ ○ ○ ○

As an artist, we can keep telling ourselves that we have arrived. Especially if we worked towards some public acknowledgement and received it. For me, this translates to: Taking the "what have you done lately" motif to "what are you doing today to reveal something in the future?" It's an ongoing process.

Still, it's nice to reflect...One arrival was *Better Living Through Circuitry*, a 1999 film about the 90s dance scene, produced by Cleopatra Records. My Spaceship Eyes project was on Hypnotic Records, a Cleopatra sub-label. The label informed me that music from my *Truth In The Eyes Of A Spaceship* release was in the film. Karen and I went to a midday showing. The film began and...da-da-da-ch! ta' ch! It was one of my songs—launching the film! A wow moment!

The movie included interviews with Moby, The Crystal Method, Psychic TV's Genesis, Steve Hillage. It incorporated three Spaceship Eyes songs (including a Freaky Chakra remix from the album and 12-inch single). A half dozen uses sprinkled throughout. I smiled each time. I had reached another level of...well, notability.

○ ○ ○ ○ ○ ○

Mauro Moroni, the head of Mellow Records, an Italian label specializing in progressive rock, envisioned a compilation album with each song about an Italian porn star and the music using 70's progressive rock instruments.

I previously did songs for tributes for Cleopatra (King Crimson, Genesis), Black Widow (Hawkwind), and Mellow Records (Santana, Yes, Steve Hackett, Pink Floyd). It's a way to promote your band—its name and sound. And Cleopatra always paid well. However, I was tiring of covers. I regretted our almost note-for-note renditions on the Cleopatra tributes. As a fan, I prefer how Hendrix reimagined Dylan's *All Along the Watchtower* or Universal Totem Orchestra rethought Hawkwind's *Alien I Am*.

I was surprised when Mauro invited SB to this new compilation, one that wasn't a covers album. I was intrigued. I didn't know at the time that the project would not come to fruition (to my knowledge). After doing some research, I got the ok to do a song about Luana Borgia. I continued onward with the song, mixing in the idea of her notability (or notoriety) and some ideas about the value of doing art that leaves a mark, however small. This latter idea inspired by an interview with American poet John Taggart.

The Book of Luana (Part IV)

It's our carnival of time
Our carnival of space
We take it on the road
To see what we can show

It's not about — art
Or note-ability
We just want to leave a mark
On society

You can be god, you can be a man
and I will be the host
You can be the players, you can be the audience
and I will be the host

It's our carnival of time...

It's not about — art
Or note-ability...

You can be god, you can be a man
and I will be the host
You can be the start, you can be the end
And I will be the host

Luana, Luana, spirit here and now...
spirit here and now...

○ ○ ○ ○ ○ ○

I always believed that if all (or most) of the members of a band I was in were better than me, and I was doing my share, it would build a better, stronger, band.

What did I bring? In the early days: songwriting, drive (first as a bassist, and then as a keyboardist), passion, new sounds (especially when I switched to keyboards), and I think, friendship and care. The ability to listen.

I was a good bass player, getting a good sound despite the model. Sam once said he thought I was a better bassist than keyboardist. We briefly formed a tight rhythm section when I did session work for the Junior Birdmen (pre-Mrs. Green) demos. I also remember Karen being impressed with my crafty Crumar keys on the No Poetry demo with Meg and company. My potential was there, regardless of which instrument path I chose.

Rob (Burns) asked me: "Who is the most famous person you have played with?" It's tough to answer. One person's famous person isn't necessarily another's. Maybe members of BÖC, although people born in the 90s might not know them or the famous cowbell Saturday Night Live skit. I was in an elevator at Dolby one day, holding a new Spirits Burning CD. A woman in her 20s asked me "Is that...a CD?" Like it was some ancient artifact, read about in a book, or seen in a film about another time.

Prog followers might say Steven Wilson, who contributed to the debut SB album and one compilation I collated. Wikipedia notes that "his honours include six nominations for Grammy Awards: twice with Porcupine Tree, once with his collaborative band Storm Corrosion and three times as a solo artist. In 2017, The Daily Telegraph described him as 'a resolutely independent artist' and 'probably the most successful British artist you've never heard of.'"

I've worked with musicians who played with David Bowie (Simon House and Keith Christmas) and Peter Gabriel (John Ellis and David Jackson). The reality is that the average person who knows Bowie and Gabriel is unfamiliar with musicians who backed them in the studio or live.

The late Steve York was one of my favorite SB crew members. He embraced connectivity; mirrored in the tentacle reach of his music adventures. He played with Marianne Faithful (co-writing *Broken English*), Dr. John, Laura Branigan, Arthur Brown, Manfred Mann, Graham Bond. He was at the center of the *Live at the Manor* album, the third album released on Richard Branson's Virgin Records. Much like a future SB album; bringing together many musicians.

Speaking of the Manor...SB and projects with Daevid Allen and Cyrille Verdeaux place me two degrees from Branson and his early Virgin Records. Or let's stretch the connectivity in a different direction, toward The Police—multiple future SB contributors have live or recorded moments with members of The Police: Mike Howlett formed Strontium 90, which included Sting, Stewart Copeland, and Andy Summers; Daryl Way played with Copeland in Curved Air; Howlett, Nik Turner, Steve Hillage, and Harry Williamson appeared with Sting on the Radio Actors release. During research, I discovered in the PoliceWiki that Andy Colquhoun "played guitar in the Rockets and was considered as The Police's guitarist when Stewart Copeland started the band. Andy Colquhoun however wanted Stewart to join the Rockets."

That said, no, I haven't appeared on a song with Bowie or Gabriel, a Beatle or a Stone. Close? The bandtoband.com app, forever in development, missing many SB releases, does show proximity to Clapton—Ginger Baker, who played with Clapton in Cream, was in Hawkwind when Harvey Bainbridge was there (and Harvey contributed to my Spaceship Eyes project, and then played synth on SB songs). More recently, Clapton guested with Hawkwind, whose drummer Richard Chadwick has contributed to SB. Many two degrees of separation in an endless circle that doesn't really feed into what Wikipedia considers notable. It must be direct, without separation (essentially, one degree of separation).

Michael Moorcock's written works (Elric and his sword Stormbringer, the multiverse concept, and beyond) and his music contributions to Hawkwind, BÖC, and yes, SB are notable. You can spend days reading Mike's Wiki pages. Better yet, years reading his books. It's debatable as to how well Mike has seeped into the next generations. The inability of the film or episodic industry to bring him in to the 21st century can be disheartening for a fan, or someone that wants to see him refresh…his already established notability.

More recently, Rob has rephrased his question. "Who is the person you have played with who has had the greatest impact?"

Don Falcone

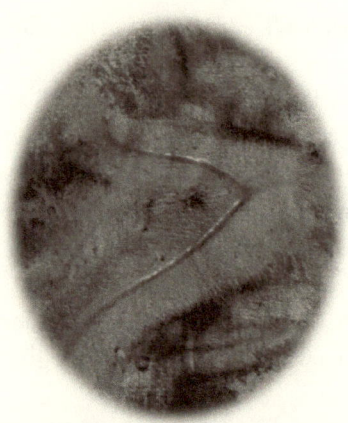

Healthy Music & Twisting Roadmaps with Cyrille Verdeaux

CYRILLE VERDEAUX = CLEARLIGHT, the French progressive rock band, and not another band with the same or like name. I originally thought the band was Clearlight Symphony, due to the album front cover fonts for each word being equivalent. Clearlight is the band; *Clearlight Symphony* the album.

My mom's name is Clara. Everyone called her Carrie. When she was in her seventies or eighties, we looked at her birth certificate; it showed the name Chiara. My mom expressed disappointment. Her life missing the opportunity to have this unique, romantic name.

On the second Spirits Burning album, released 2001, I named a piano-based piece, a new rendition of my 80's *Chameleon* solo piece: *Clear Audient*. Here, the six-piece included upfront mellotron by Kenneth Magnusson (The Moors) and Judge Trev's guitar. A version of the song with my piano more exposed and five new musicians, including Daevid Allen on guitar, was added to the third album as *Chiaro (Clear Audient v3.0)*. The 3.0 because the album release was delayed by the label and another version of the song appeared earlier, on the daevid allen & don falcone *Glissando Grooves* best-of album. This one combined all 11 musicians. Titled *Chiara Obscura (Chiaro +*

Clear Audient Mix).

In 2007, my mom passed away, followed by our dog Indy two days later. Soon after, Karen surprised me, adopting a dog from the local shelter. This two-year-old female Chow already had a name: Kiara.

Cyrille and I became Facebook friends in September 2009. We began a correspondence that escalated into two Spirits Burning & Clearlight albums, and opportunities to bring various dreams to fruition.

Clear Skies in 2009

Cyrille started our dialogue, asking about my interest in prog. I mentioned my day job—managing the team that wrote documentation for Pro Tools—and my band, Spirits Burning. I said I had...

> *...an affinity for music that originated in Europe. Can in Germany (love Landed, even though people rarely talk about it). And Nektar's Remember the Future. Gong, Hawkwind, Vangelis (especially Aphrodite's Child), Kate Bush, the Go live band. I'd say that your Clearlight was an influence for some Spirits Burning paths.*

I added:

> *I tend to be intrigued with music that is 'progressive', as opposed to music that emulates what once was progressive. I do love starting with ideas/sounds from the past, and hope that I'm not repeating it.*

I shared my web pages and invited him to contribute to the next album. Cyrille responded that he would love to collaborate, with one concern. He didn't have the music software or MIDI interface to link his keyboard to a computer.

I suggested—and yes, the hardware and versions here are of a bygone era—giving him my extra Pro Tools LE system (Mbox USB interface and Pro Tools 7.4 software). The Mbox could connect to Cyrille's computer via USB. The gear would allow him to record in Pro Tools and "work with me on…first thoughts here…cd by Spirits Burning & Clearlight, cd album name tbd (although I do have an unused title *Healthy Music In Large Doses*)."

Cyrille was unfamiliar with Pro Tools and plug-ins. I told him he had a huge advantage over people just starting with Pro Tools; he previously touched other DAWs (Cubase and Digital Performer 3). I explained that processing plug-ins (such as compressors, EQs, reverbs, delays) could be inserted on any track. And virtual instruments are plug-ins of synths or samplers that are inserted on an Instrument track. These tracks house MIDI notes that play back the plug-in's sound. Notes can be drawn in, imported (.mid files), or recorded via an external MIDI keyboard (which Cyrille did have). Unfortunately, the Mbox didn't have MIDI ins and outs; to record MIDI, Cyrille still needed a MIDI interface (between his keyboard and computer).

I offered to send Cyrille the Pro Tools system. As he learned how to use it, we could schedule time to write new material, establish instrumentation needs and musician invites, create and review mixes, do mastering, and then hunt for a label to manufacture and release our creation. I mentioned multiple labels, including Voiceprint, my then-current label. Voiceprint would go into insolvency the next year, and then rise as a "phoenix company," Gonzo Multimedia…the future home for our *Healthy Music*.

When Cyrille received the Mbox, we discovered it was not compatible with his laptop. Plus, he still needed a MIDI I/O device.

Going To California, 2010

Cyrille's daughter Laetitia lived in California. Cyrille suggested we record in my home studio when he visited her in the spring.

I took PTO (Personal Time Off) days on Thursday and Friday, the former to prep songs for his recording, and Friday for our first of at least two sessions. I told Cyrille: "We have a very sweet Chow

Chow, she will bark (no bite) when you come in and see if you're up for playing, which isn't required." He shared that he was "from the old 70's school for improvisation and appreciated the green for better results." He hoped it wouldn't be a problem. The deck overlooking our back yard would suffice for any smoke he produced.

Cyrille at Don's Home Studio in San Bruno (photo by Karen Anderson)

Over the three-day weekend, Cyrille did keyboards for the in-progress songs that I or another crew member had started. A few days later, we addressed his home recording setup. I configured a system with the Mbox, Pro Tools, and two pieces of hardware I procured for him: a used compatible Windows laptop, and a MIDI controller. I gave him a demo using a MIDI keyboard, and he was now ready to record with his keyboard when he returned to his home in Brazil.

An Album Takes Shape

Some of the new crew members included:

- Andy Anderson (The Cure, Hawkwind briefly, and Cyrille's former label mate Michael Oldfield). Andy provided drums for what became the album's opening track, *Treasures At The Dawn Of The Century*.
- Multiple Black Widow Records label mates. Spirits Burning *Alien Injection* had been released by the label a few years earlier. I asked Massimo Gasperini (the label head), for contact info to Universal Totem Orchestra (UTO) and guitarist G.C. Neri.

My UTO guidance for an in-progress song: "non-lyric ooh/aah vocals are ok (I just want to avoid any words on this as the cd will basically be all instrumental." They could start a new piece too; just "leave room for additional players. At its heart, SB is about bringing people together and creating new line-ups of musicians." Yanik from UTO asked if there were any other restrictions for the starter piece. I responded. "It's definitely not a compilation. So, definitely not looking for a finished UTO song. And I definitely want to keep it original, i.e., new songs. I tend to be pretty open to new ideas."

Meanwhile, SB alumni Daevid Allen planned to do gliss on 1-2 pieces when he returned to Australia in the fall. Upon completion, I reported to Cyrille: "In the here and now, he kind of did a Jack and The Beanstalk on us. He went ahead and added vocals (and guitar, and interesting vocal percussion) to the reggae piece. It all sounds good, and it does get you two sonically entwined. however, it doesn't fit with the other instrumental pieces, so I'm going to slide that piece over to a vocal SB CD." I later changed my mind and placed the reggae piece at our album's end.

○ ○ ○ ○ ○ ○

I regularly posted my Bay Area mixes for Cyrille to review in Brazil. In turn, he would make suggestions to improve the song. We exchanged 100s of emails and Facebook messages for this album and two future ones.

Long-distance mixing ideas were easy to try. These included level changes, effects suggestions, quantization of a MIDI per-formance, even re-pitching (or hiding) a bad pitch from an instrument.

Given Cyrille's California recording sessions were improv-isations—and sometimes rushed as we moved through each song—we agreed on cleaning up his performance. I deleted any unintended notes. I tested quantizing MIDI notes to 16th (or 32nd) notes—a process that slides the note to be more on the 16th (or 32nd) beat, in case it wasn't (and if that improved the sound). Music is a funny thing. Not every note needs to be absolutely on the beat. Sometimes, it can sound unnatural.

Cyrille suggested some musicians redo a part. Usually, this was impossible. Most crew members were a one-time recording effort. They were not full-time band members available on call.

I was used to building songs instrument by instrument, contributor by contributor. This made the contributor a composer. Plus, I usually encouraged early musicians on a piece to play less, leaving space for the next musician, next instrument. I told Cyrille: "We need to let each composition develop via incoming parts and then my edit and mix moves."

My ambient sensibilities were noticeable too. I was more at ease to have an instrument very exposed, or to play with silence for a few bars (as done in *Our Secret Cloud*).

301

Meanwhile, Back in Brasilia

By December, the list of needed instruments was clear. This included guitar.

Michael Clare put me in touch with Gong's Fabio Golfetti, who lived in Brazil, the same country as Cyrille. I had two quests. Guitar for three songs, plus help with Cyrille and his Pro Tools setup. It had been over six months since Cyrille was in Ca., and he had never gotten the setup to work. I asked Fabio if he knew anyone in Brazil willing to help Cyrille for free.

Fabio provided wonderful parts for *Italian Lake* (a place in Harrisburg, Pa that I experienced when younger), plus two songs originally written for the Moorcock Cajun project—*A Cool Can Of Cola On The Forehead* and *In Search Of Friends On The Day Of Masks*. My titles highlighting different panaceas.

Fabio found a contact in Brazil to help Cyrille with his Pro Tools system. Unfortunately, the contact didn't speak English. Cyrille never did get his Pro Tools Mbox system to work. My distant home studio remained our best solution.

The Song Started by UTO

Returning to December 2010, Yanik of UTO delivered parts for *Our Secret Cloud*. It immediately became my favorite song on the album. Yanik sent 15 tracks (three female lead vocals, five backing female vocals, four male 1 and two male 2 backing vocals, and one guitar track). Each performance was exceptional. Especially the vocal parts by Ana Torres Fraile, Francesco Festi, and Uto G. Golin.

I initially ear-marked Yanik's other delivery, a song that UTO started, for another album. Then, a year later, made the decision to add it to the album with Cyrille. Since Cyrille couldn't record keys from Brazil, I suggested we go with a spoken word performance: "...a stream of conscious or improv about one or more of your philosophies..."

We set up a Skype call for Cyrille to recite text he wrote. I recorded the call on my laptop Pro Tools, feeding into my studio Pro

Tools setup. (I had stopped connecting my main studio to the internet a few years earlier to safeguard it from viruses and dedicate processing to music only.)

Cyrille would highlight this song, *Invisible Cities*, as his personal favorite in terms of level of musicality.

Heading into 2012, we were all systems go. The best was yet to come, although a month earlier, I was laid off from Avid.

A Moment of Unhappiness

I know of two cases where a musician posted online an in-progress SB mix or did a remix incorporating the temporary mix I had provided to them to record to.

I never thought to tell people not to do that, presuming it would be obvious. You shouldn't do that.

For a *Healthy Music* song, an invite was accepted, I sent the musician the in-progress mix, they did their part and delivered it, and…made a loop from part of the song and included it in a dance mix, which they proceeded to post online. I was not happy.

In a nice voice, I wrote that the loop contained performances by one or more people that provided their parts for Spirits Burning use. From a legal standpoint, and more importantly—maintaining the trust of those involved—it would be better for me if it wasn't posted.

The remixer thought that I owned the sample…which begged the question: how would that translate to use of the sample outside of Spirits Burning without asking? They replaced the loop with one from elsewhere. I never invited them again.

April Gong

When it was announced that Daevid, Gilli, and a new Gong were prepping to tour, Cyrille asked me to contact Daevid and let him know he was available as a keyboardist. I emailed Daevid, who responded "The band is finalized…send my love to Cyrille!"

While I believe Cyrille was serious, I later noticed his request aligned with April Fools' Day.

Finalizing Healthy Music in 2012

By mid-May, the album neared completion, and by day, I was a contract writer at Dolby.

We made a late decision to add drums to *In Search Of Friends*. Local drummer Scotty Smith (Kevin Gilbert's Giraffe) provided parts quickly. The final files imported were Paul Sears' drums for *Raised on Coal & Oil* and *Hand Signals*.

With Cyrille's approval of current mixes, we began the mastering phase with Robert Rich.

I shared with Paul Sears:

> *I also met Robert at NearFest. Found out that he did mastering and he's since done some of my instrumental projects. He does a very good session with clients, where he reviews each track and suggests some final mix adjustments. I usually use Paul Cobbold in the UK for rockier material, but thought I'd do something different, since this CD is more instrumental.*

The listening session with Robert went well. I reported the results to Cyrille, with plans to update mixes in June.

Key takeaways:

- My mixing was better. On non-Spirits Burning albums Robert previously mastered, he noted excessive bass and subsonic frequencies, which can happen with headphone mixing. I had adjusted my headphone workflow and only two new songs had this issue.
- Multiple songs had drums that could be improved. First, by boosting the kick and snare. Next, reducing reverb on the whole kit or the hi hats (which were washing out).
- The piano sometimes sounded harsh at 880 Hz. Robert suggested cutting a couple of dBs at 880 Hz on piano tracks, so that he didn't have to cut everything in that frequency

when mastering.
- There were other items to address: Removing some clicks and pops, bringing down high frequency bells in *The Road To Shave Ice*, (which I told Robert upfront I was concerned about), adding gain to the female vocalist on *Our Secret Cloud*, and slightly lowering the accordion and organ volumes in a Cajun piece.
- Robert felt the *Infinite City* track with Cyrille on vocals was a strong track and suggested making it the second song. I disagreed and kept it fourth, after *Our Secret Cloud*.

Cyrille and I decided to help *Hand Signals* by getting John (Purves) to do some additional wind/reed parts. Cyrille noted:

> At 3:49 to 5:10, I hear a virtuoso dialogue electric violin-soprano sax-flute the same way it is in *Birds of Fire* of Mahavishnu. That would really bring this song to the next level. As it is, this song doesn't reach its full potential in my opinion because of the lack of lead instruments clearly put in front.

John quickly did woodwinds and sax and sent them in time for a new premaster.

I was concerned with the song's denseness, seven musicians. To highlight John's parts, I cleared out some of the other sounds that occurred during the time Cyrille identified and made the piano the sole lead in an earlier section.

We delivered finalized premasters to Robert in July.

Online, Cyrille wrote "It has been a real honour and good surprise to be able to work on this project with such a music lover called Don Falcone, ready for all the sacrifices to make his artistic dreams coming through, and all the good people from all over the World that collaborated to this Opus."

It was time to answer Cyrille's questions about what came next. Gonzo, a UK label run by Rob Ayling, would release the album. Rob used to run GAS, the Gong Appreciation Society fan club, then started Voiceprint in 1990, which turned into Gonzo. Rob's labels had released albums by Daevid, Gong, and Hawkwind. Karen and I prepared the graphics (with artwork by Hawk Alfredson). Gonzo didn't supply physical proofs for review—due to distance, money, turnaround time. Instead, they provided a pdf to verify no text dropouts or odd interpretation of color. They were probably pressing 500 CDs. Once manufactured, I would get 25. I'd buy an additional 20 at artist cost to cover getting a copy to each of the 40 people involved. I offered to buy five more for Cyrille and ask Rob in a "pretty please" email to give additional copies to Cyrille. They had good distribution, worldwide and via their website. Their releases were sometimes available digitally. Ads: Limited. Once, for *Crazy Fluid*, they included Spirits Burning in a big full page Prog Magazine ad with Gong, Hawkwind, Hillage, Man, Anthony Phillips, Renaissance, Van der Graaf Generator, Wakeman, Zappa. (I turned that one into a large, framed poster for my studio.) For promotion (reviews, interviews, and airplay), they used Billy James' Glass Onyon services. They had an online magazine (Gonzo Weekly) and interviewed me there. When mastering completed, Karen and I created a teaser video on YouTube.

New Possibilities

Cyrille announced he would be in the Bay Area late October until early December. I began to spin some ideas to him and Rob.

Cyrille performing solo. Cyrille previously mentioned he could play piano to a CD-R of his background music. My 61-note K2000 wouldn't suffice. He needed an 88-note keyboard as his parts were created on a full acoustic piano. And could his daughter sell crepes at his show? She had a catering business (Crêpe-Madame).

I pursued three possibilities for Cyrille.

- House concert (living room). Exposé contact and photographer Brad Owens was willing to host the event in his backyard. Having done at least one concert before. I wanted to see an example performance there, to know what I was signing Cyrille up for. Unfortunately, their next concert was after Cyrille's visit. I couldn't sign off on the event with confidence.

- Perform with Spirits Burning and solo at a small club that was ok with a minimum audience of 100 people. I lined up a gig at Café Du Nord in San Francisco. I retracted the application after trying to assemble a band and realizing two months wasn't enough time. Drummer Marc Weinstein (owner of Amoeba Records stores) was one of a few musicians onboard; he expressed relief in not having to rush learning songs.
- Perform solo at an already-scheduled event. Lo and behold: The NorCal Prog Festival.

Celebrating the _Healthy_ CD. Wine and cheese at the Falcone abode with the locals involved with the release? A jam at a local drummer's studio? A record release party and BBQ? We settled on a listening party at Brad's house. By the time we did it, we would celebrate something else.

SB & C II and Clearlight: When I asked Rob about Gonzo's interest in a follow up album, he said yes, and more.

- Would Cyrille be willing to do a new Clearlight album, a _Second Symphony_ or a new band/project called "Clearlight Second Symphony?" Rob offered to talk to Steve Hillage and Tim Blake (who were on Cyrille's debut _Symphony_ album). I offered to produce the album, play on each song, including a song that I would start, based on my _Clear Audient_ piece. (My song would eventually drop from the project.) Plus, I could provide access to any needed musicians. Referring to Craig Fry (Cartoon), I wrote "I do have a wonderful classical violin player who would die to play on a track with Steve H. (He used to play in Paul Drescher quartet, if you know them.) Also, I know Paul would like to play drums on something like this."

- Rob offered to re-release Cyrille's entire catalog. Cyrille was interested in seeing the catalog refreshed with physical releases, ongoing promotion.

NorCalProg Festival 11/11/2012

A few months before the festival, I contacted the promoter, a member of Quasar, one of the bands performing. The BayProg music site revealed that a band had cancelled. I suspect I was able to get Cyrille on the bill to fill that slot.

We quickly addressed the main details: Date, time, location (Z Space, a San Francisco artist space), Cyrille's share of ticket sales, and Cyrille's need for a keyboard. Quasar's keyboardist would lend his 88-key Yamaha P80.

I recruited Cyrille's daughter to cater the event. The promoter hadn't booked any food trucks yet. They ok'd her supporting breakfast for 150 or more people. Laetitia and an assistant had a simple, thorough setup near the foyer back wall, leading to the performance hall. You first chose the ingredients of your crepe; they then assembled it, cooked it, and served it. This would be my first time tasting a made-to-order crepe from Crêpe-Madame. I had a few, as did others.

I managed a merchandise table nearby—front doors to my right, crepes line in view to my left. Here, I sold Cyrille's albums and my own. We also had postcards promoting the upcoming *Healthy Music* release. I sold all the CDs I brought. These included the recently released Astralfish album showcasing Bridget Wishart's EWI, many Spirits Burning releases, and my lesser-known projects like Fireclan, Grindlestone, and Quiet Celebration. One person purchased a dozen or more CDs from my catalog for $100 or so.

Anil Prasad, music journalist and music industry commentator, and founder/editor of Innerviews—the Internet's first online music magazine—reminded me years later that we first met here.

Cyrille was scheduled to play 90 minutes. Since the CD-R lasted only 68 minutes, he began and ended with solo piano pieces. We did forget my CD player. Luckily, one was available onsite.

The LadyObscure website review:

> Then something truly unexpected and amazing came next. Cyrille Verdeaux, pianist and composer for Clearlight, came on stage to perform the Infinite Symphony album in its entirety, accompanied by a backing track of the other instruments, drums, cello, etc. He shuffled to his instrument a man coming on in years, but the moment he started to play, he turned into the accomplished master he is, and for the next hour, literally owned all present, young, old, male, and female, no one had a chance. The amassed crowd sat in stupefied wonder, being drawn more and more into the music, to a point where the individual seemed to disappear, and only the music remained. It was a moment of life I will take with me forever.

I smiled as Cyrille performed, and Laetitia watched. Multiple dreams! Each fully accomplished!

A Clearlight Impressionist Symphony

Cyrille was better prepared for this album than I imagined. Years earlier, he had recorded piano parts with another producer. Other instruments were never added, as Cyrille hadn't found the needed musicians, and the producer pulled out of the project.

Cyrille had the producer send me flash drives of the performances—a couple of times, as one plastic envelope arrived with a half-eaten standard white envelope and no USB stick. The files were 48 kHz Sound Designer II files (a format of the past that Pro Tools could still import). For future compatibility, we changed the files to .wavs. We decided to use 88.2 kHz sessions, supporting higher sample rate new parts and effects. This was before I did 96k. There were missing files too. I found previous (lower numbered, earlier recorded) files and used those.

I informed Cyrille that Rob's contracts were simple, one-page documents (different than other contracts). While I had met Rob a few times when he was in the states, the contracts were always handled in email. They were licensing deals (to sell physical CDs and downloads). Rob's label would handle manufacturing, distribution, promotion, and sales.

I initially acted as a go-between for Cyrille and Rob. I did an estimated CD budget for the project, covering mastering and 3-5 guests, plus at least 100 CDs and money for Cyrille. I also reiterated Cyrille's other desires, which included a catalog refresh and promotion.

In the meantime, Paul (Sears) offered his studio in Arizona for his drum recordings and a bass session. Paul also gave Cyrille a substantial amount of money to help with his expenses.

○ ○ ○ ○ ○ ○

Cyrille worked out the official title—*Impressionist Symphony*—eyeing the 40th anniversary of the 1973 *Clearlight Symphony* release on Virgin.

> *Each piece in my mind would represent an impressionist painter...I have Monet, Toulouse-Lautrec, Van Gogh, Renoir, Picasso...that should be enough.*

Rob's offer came in and it upped the number of CDs for Cyrille to 200. I was surprised. I typically got 25. I reminded Cyrille his advance would go against royalties, plus some of the advance was needed to cover mastering and fees for guests. I recommended Robert Rich for mastering. Cyrille decided on a less expensive option, via the label. While I believed Robert would have mastered a better sound, the lower cost let Cyrille budget more elsewhere.

Cyrille previously suggested him, me, and a third person pay for the costs, including manufacturing, and then do a distribution deal. I didn't have money available and was skeptical that we would make the investment back. Other than CD Baby, my experiences with distribution deals and co-releases had been mixed. Plus, I didn't want to do accounting for a shared venture. For those reasons, I never suggested that I release it on Noh Poetry Records, the label I ran.

There was some confusion with the word "producer." Cyrille thought that I wanted be part of the sales and resultant dollars; that was never the case. I wanted to produce, as in guide, steer, and shape the sound of the project. Like Brian Eno. And not like…Richard Branson.

I also said:

> Historically, for me, a licensing deal has been better than self-releasing. (Fwiw; We've only had one self-release approach breaking even.) Getting on labels with people I admire and have been inspired by, has helped to spread the music to places it never would have gotten to via self-release. My situation is different, of course, given our histories, and your ability to play live more. Whether you see doing a new CD as a good investment for a label interested in your catalog is your call.

I knew that Cyrille wasn't happy with most of his previous contracts.

○ ○ ○ ○ ○ ○

By mid-October, Steve Hillage and Didier Malherbe were onboard; their parts arrived in April 2013, (after the contract was finalized). Cyrille was now considering a vinyl release of the five *Impressionist Symphony* songs, while the CD could add my *Clear Audient* piece. The vinyl to be financed via an Indiegogo crowdfunding, and if successful, would need to be revealed to Gonzo. I could envision the Gonzo deal falling apart due to the presence of a separate, potentially competing vinyl version. This collision was avoided when the crowdfunding didn't provide enough money to proceed with the vinyl option.

Don Falcone: Producer, Postproduction

I momentarily dropped out of producing the Clearlight album. I switched to engineering the 2-3 local recording sessions and doing quick mixes and transfers, in return for Cyrille recording for the SB & C II album (later named *The Roadmap In Your Head*), and for me to appear on one Clearlight song.

By the end, I was credited as the producer, and for postproduction. My initial proposal of being involved as a musician on each track wasn't to be. And my producer role was very different than what I did with Gary Parra's *Trap*. There, I helped shape and guide each track. I did all the mixing too. With Cyrille, the piano parts were pre-recorded, and he had specific ideas of where to take each piece. Additionally, Cyrille did the initial mixes (usually with me outside the music room, watching sports in my living room).

My idea of taking Cyrille to a different musical area, would be left to Spirits Burning albums only.

For the *Impressionist* release, my work included:

- Collating the existing piano and other remote recordings (like Paul Sears' drums).
- Setting up Pro Tools sessions for Cyrille and teaching him how to automate mix moves.
- Helping Cyrille locate and select virtual instrument plug-ins (like the Bösendorfer piano) to perform with.
- Selecting candidate reverbs and delays.
- Suggesting violinist Craig Fry (and Paul).
- Helping dreams: Cyrille's dream to complete his *Impressionist Symphony* and have it released; Paul's dream to play with Cyrille on a Clearlight album; Craig's dream to play with Steve Hillage. Cyrille once described my participation as "the one that woke up the IS, so you become some sort of God father..." (I also told another friend that I was a traffic cop.)
- Creating a beautiful mix to close the album; my

proudest producer move. In June of 2013, the album almost done, I took the second song (*Time Is Monet*), duplicated the session, and then began to mute most of the instruments. My plan: Create a duet of Cyrille's piano and Craig's violin. With some subtle changes, Cyrille and Craig loved the results. The album now had eight songs, ending with *Monet Time Duet*. My favorite track on the album. Years later, this idea influenced my production of the Moorcock/Deep Fix album; I suggested ending that album with a stripped-down version of Mike's *Dream of Eden*.

Contracts...

In January 2013, I wrote to Cyrille...

> *In today's music world, it's my belief that most independent musicians make money from touring, selling merchandise at shows, and royalties for placements on TV, film, etc.*
>
> *Meanwhile, small labels have their hands tied for physical product because both distributors and brick 'n' mortar stores are disappearing. I wouldn't be surprised if Rob is actually concerned that if he doesn't sell over 250 copies of each, he will risk breaking even. Things are that bad. For everyone.*
>
> *It's a little late at this point, but I would have kept Impressionist Symphony separate from any re-pressings, as it's really the main thing I know you want to come to fruition.*

Cyrille decided to sign a licensing deal with Gonzo, which supported having the *Impressionist Symphony* and the original *Symphony* both in print. Plus, other albums from his catalog.

While I believe that Cyrille was happy that the dream of *IS* came to be, I know he felt like his catalog was held hostage for the length of the Gonzo contract. Especially as the royalties for *IS* and his other albums didn't cover the advance plus the manufacturing costs of the entire catalog. Within a few years, Cyrille and Rob ended their agreement.

The push and pull between Cyrille and Rob didn't affect my standing as a Gonzo artist. I still had five years and five full lengths to come.

Champagne

Near Thanksgiving, Cyrille returned to California to do sessions to complete mixing the parts from Steve and Didier. Paul flew in too, and we did a listening party of the current mixes at Brad's house.

Bassist Linda Cushma and Tim Blake's parts arrived later. (Tim, like Steve, supplied helpful input on how best to effect new parts with delay, to achieve their respective signature sounds.) Cyrille and I exchanged many emails to do the final tweaks, and Cyrille lined up Johnny Oldhitz for the mastering.

To complete our premasters, I informed Cyrille that I did three important things:

1. I added the Pro Tools HEAT plug-in to each session. This single session-wide plug-in is applied to audio tracks only, giving the mix a more analog sound. We previously used HEAT for the *Healthy Music* songs.
2. For each song, I also cut 2-4 dBs as HEAT added some volume. The HEAT control usually produces more width, spaces, sheen, and warmth. If there is too much sheen, you can adjust its Tone control. If the verbs of any songs are too distant (due to the cuts I applied), you can add gain to the send feeding the verb, or the verb itself.
3. I routed all tracks to an internal audio track. This let us mix to a track (rather than bounce to disk). Some people think this results in a better sound (that is, no loss of quality). What it also gave us, though, is a session

file that we can then export in different formats (mp3, 16/44.1. wav, or 88.2/24-bit for the premaster) without having to record the song in its entirety for each format. (Years later, Pro Tools added a bounce to disk feature that was almost instantaneous, instead of the playback length of the song, plus processing time).

4. I ensured two seconds of silence before the start of each piece. The mastering person could then trim these as needed.

As a final cherry on top, and to complete one of my initial proposals, I added to the *Pissaro* song French church bells (from Notre Dame in Cannes), which I recorded during a trip there and tubular bells from a keyboard patch. Cyrille approved the additions. I was now a part of the Clearlight musician crew. Soon after, Cyrille wrote:

> *In order to celebrate the wrap, I was picturing this: you with a flute of champagne (or any yellow liquid in the flute if you don't want to open a bottle) and my smiling face on skype on your big screen computer with also a flute of champagne (a real one, I just bought it today) and we chin chin like that...*

We made it so. Cyrille's Facebook post: "Don Falcone and myself celebrating the final mix of the final song of the Impressionist symphony, featuring the legendary GONG trio HIllage-Blake-Malherbe. Even at 7000 miles away, we could celebrate this moment with a good champagne."

I would continue to godfather the project to its end, providing dozens of edits to the CD text and press release.

The album released 24 March 2014.

The Roadmap Taken

Daevid Allen died in 2015 while the second Spirits Burning & Clearlight album was half done. I decided to dedicate the album to Daevid and gather as many of the Gong family as possible. This included Steve and Didier.

I set aside time to review the *Impressionist Symphony* tracks to decipher the amount of unused Steve and Didier and found some gems. For Steve, there was a lovely, mysterious 40 second wah-wah section that I could use to build an ambient piece. There was also a 42-second whale section that worked at the end of that piece. This song with Steve became *The Old College Try Is Where We Left It*. For Didier, there were two minute-plus sections that I could use to build a jazz piece. This resulted in *Déjà Vu*.

I ran the idea past Steve and Didier, let them hear the songs as they developed, and they each ok'd their respective pieces, as did Cyrille.

In November of 2015, Cyrille returned to San Francisco. The months prior gave me a chance to add more tracks, invite and add more Gong family members, and ensure Cyrille was on each piece. This also provided breathing room as I was finishing up the Weird Quartet album Daevid was on, and the *Starhawk* album (with Cyrille on three tracks).

○ ○ ○ ○ ○ ○

I started a song called *Fuel For The Gods*, which segued sections in 4/4 to 3/4 to 7/4 and back to 4/4, and brought onboard Harry Williamson (Mother Gong) in October for that piece and another called *Mrs. Noonness*. I provided Harry with chord charts of both songs.

In November, Bridget delivered EWI parts for *Birth Of Belief*, including some angelic choir sounds. I had spent part of day in an escape room—"team building thing at work. we escaped in a little over an hour. Lots of clues to get to keys and other items. I kind of cheated and lifted part of the cell door out of its joints to get outside my cell. Then got the keys to open the two cells in our area. Turned out, we couldn't exit out the main door. We had to find another way out..."

In mid-November, Cyrille's daughter Laetitia gave a first anniversary party at her creperie shop and Cyrille performed piano there. The day before, I gave Cyrille a tour of the Dolby building on Market Street, where I now worked full-time.

I decided not to rush completing songs, and continued with new invites into 2016, The opening song would get bass from *You* era Gong bassist Mike Howlett, plus autoharp from Judy Dyble (Fairport Convention).

Upon completion of sessions for a new Gong album, Fabio added glissando guitar to *Fuel* to complement the harmonic parts, which included Harry's 12-string guitar and charango.

During reviews, Cyrille suggested a soprano sax for a passage on *Birth Of Belief*, and I connected with Gong's Ian East. Cyrille also suggested Irish flute like the one in the Titanic song for *Fuel For The Gods*. Ian didn't do Celtic flutes and recommended Paul Booth (Steve Winwood). Paul recorded a wonderful flute part in his hotel room in the middle of a Winwood tour.

I invited Theo Travis (Gong, Soft Machine) to do saxes for the Albert Bouchard started piece *Coffee For Coltrane*. This would be one of the last songs to complete. The initial bassist never delivered. I reached out to William Kopecky, and he provided bass guitar, and an extra ebow bass part that created a new, extended ending.

The Roadmap In Your Head released on November 25, 2016.

Don and Cyrille Celebration II with Wine, Back Deck of Don's Place
(photo by Karen Anderson)

A 2024 Letter from Cyrille

I have only negative feelings about how harsh the musical world became lately especially for independent artists having no access to any medias.

My last album Impressionist Symphony couldn't exist at all without your active participation all along. I am just sad that such a good idea to link painters and this music has been wasted by Rob at Gonzo...It's never too late, but who would like to put together a DVD of the music and the painters? And have all the museums of the world for distribution? No clue...

Tips—$ense

MY MUSIC LIFE has rarely been about money or some sense of fame. Like the road to Hana in Kauai, it's about the journey, and not the destination. Composing, collaborating, mixing, completing an album. It's fun. It's interesting. It can be exhilarating. If there is a consistent end goal for me, at least up to this point, it's getting a collection of songs released as an album by a label. Alternatively, if necessary, self-releasing. And then, doing it again.

In the same way I have trouble answering the question "what kind of music do you do?"—because it's different at different times, and sometimes different concurrently—I have trouble talking about music and money. There is a reason I had day jobs. A reason I was a technical writer for so many hours of life. I was never in a position, or comfortable to take the leap, to try to make music my sole income. I was ok with that. I just needed to find a way to continuously create, to remain at heart, a musician.

I could lament experiencing record labels that didn't pay royalties or do promotion as expected, or .00xxx payouts via streaming. When it comes to the business side of music, I'd rather remember successes. That includes insights that helped me set expectations, which fed into promotion, a level of branding, one's legacy, and yes, maybe some money.

○ ○ ○ ○ ○ ○

The first record contract I got on my own was Spaceship Eyes on Cleopatra sub label Hypnotic Records. I used a self-release as part of my resume, and it worked. Credits for playing on Silent Records albums and the debut Melting Euphoria release also helped. As did Melting Euphoria getting signed to Cleopatra after I quit the band.

In those days, Cleopatra released lots of electronica albums on their Hypnotic imprint, and my solo project fit there. They were also developing a space rock/prog rock imprint, Purple Pyramid. I did some tribute songs on this sub label in the 90s—starting with a cover of King Crimson's Red—and then found a home there decades later for releases with Daevid Allen, Michael Moorcock, Spirits Burning.

○ ○ ○ ○ ○ ○

You can shop an album to a label you know or find online. I've done many online searches for ambient labels, space rock labels, and so on, and then contacted them. It doesn't make sense to send an ambient or space rock album to a label that releases death metal music only, or one that releases music associated with a single artist only, or one that doesn't accept submissions. Definitely look at the label about page or FAQ page before contacting them.

It can get tricky, of course; some labels support multiple genres. Or, if you've established a certain brand or level of notability, that can affect a label's response. When I shopped the Spirits Burning acoustic-based *Evolution Ritual*, some labels said no because it didn't have synths and wasn't space rock. Meanwhile, another label said that Spirits Burning was too established for their label. I found that interesting. I wouldn't have contacted them if I had a larger label willing to take the album. In the end, I self-released it.

Self-release considerations: Do you have the funds to pay for manufacturing, mastering, marketing, and other costs? Can you guarantee that you will make these costs back? Does that matter to you? Are you doing physical media, or digital only? Do you play live, such that you can do sales at shows? Do you have distribution to get your release into brick and mortar, as well as known online distributors? Do you want to sell on Amazon or like sellers, given the cut they take for a sale? Does it make sense to stock physical media with them? Do you consider smaller distributors that sell your type of music, even if they are on a different continent? Should you do smaller manufacturing runs? For example, 250 CDs, instead of 500 or 1000, which you could justify years earlier. If it only makes sense to press 100 CDs, do you consider CD-Rs? Or do you consider CDs (CD replication) more professional than CD-Rs (CD duplication)? If yes, can you find a CD replicator that does professional CDs at lower runs? They exist. Often in unexpected countries.

Postage becomes an issue if you are selling to another country. Or manufacturing in another country. Having a label dealing with these costs, lets you move on to the next album, or concentrate on playing live. Yes, you make more money, per sale, if you self-release. You just might not have as wide a net.

○ ○ ○ ○ ○ ○

I've been privy to the birth of two labels. Silent Records, started by Kim Cascone, a coworker of mine when I first started at Orban. And, Noh Poetry Records, a label I started.

Silent Records

In the early 90s, there was a loft in San Francisco that I could visit. To experience Silent Records. To see Kim and his wife Kat (who did their graphics). And their small band of employees. CDs and vinyl everywhere…like a roadmap of how to traverse the loft and discover the new world of ambient.

I learned a lot looking at and listening to Silent albums. Their covers were professional, magical, cool. The artwork well thought out. The sound matched those qualities. They had several compilations that you wanted to listen to—when you were relaxing on a couch at home or in a chill room, enjoying a long car trip, expanding your palette inside headphones, or turning out the lights and about to dream. I was honored to be on multiple *From Here To Tranquility* compilations, as well as the *Fifty Years Of Sunshine* compilation. They made you want to check out the full albums by each artist. Deeper Than Space, Heavenly Music Corporation, Makyo, Solitaire (featuring Steve Roach), to name a few. And I was on full albums by Thessalonians and the Spice Barons.

Each release showcased how Silent advocated for and interpreted the concept of ambient. There was experimentation. New sounds. New experiences. These are all things that one would want if you were starting your own label. I never forgot this.

Silent was the perfect mix at the perfect time. Until they weren't. Not only was the interest in ambient changing, so were the distribution channels and Tower Records of the world. It was as if everything in the industry was dying, and it was no longer the era where small independent labels got to play side by side with the majors. The journey for Silent would take a detour into obscurity when Kim sold the label. He would resurrect the label in the next century. I would write the liner notes for the first new *From Here To Tranquility* album, 2016's *Volume 6: The Renaissance*, as I had done for some releases in the 90s. Otherwise, I would not be part of the resurrected label's journey. My attention was elsewhere.

For From Here to Tranquility—Volume 6 (The Renaissance), Released 2016

We shade our ambient in sound colors light and dark.
Signals in and out of the calm and stillness of what
is left unsaid. Treasured roadmaps. Coded experiments.
We retouch the mindset of the past and turn to the
future. We 360, deeply in space. We craft, and we flow
onward. Here are new stories for each rhythm of sun
and moon to earth and back. This is where the weave
of light is one world, the weave of dark another.
Together, they form a voice of contrast. Illumination.
Connectivity. Immersion. Clarity. This is the music that
forever drifts in our soul.
This is our silent renaissance.
— Don Falcone

Noh Poetry Records

I started Noh Poetry specifically to release the first Spaceship Eyes album, essentially a resume.

To show that I was serious as a solo artist, that there was good music here, and that it was supported by reviews and possibly interviews. It would serve as a template for a live ensemble too. If I was doing the release today, I'd press fewer copies and do more research into releases in the same genre, along with their labels and magazines that cover them. Maybe find a label to release it.

Given the success I had having notable musicians with Spirits Burning, I'd try the same approach with a solo record. However, I'm aware that having notable names onboard does not guarantee label interest. In the mid 90s, I couldn't have imagined a 2024 album like *Evolution Ritual* with family members of King Crimson and other notable bands not being enough to achieve label interest.

The 1995 release of Spaceship Eyes did create a question. What would Noh Poetry do next, if anything?

Over the years, the answer included:

- A compilation for a long ambient track that I didn't have a home for. *Where Stalks The Sandman* includes the almost 26-minute *An Isolated Craft* by Don Falcone, along with tracks by Steven Wilson, Praxis, Kim Cascone, my wife Karen Anderson, and Monocaine (featuring Grindlestone's Doug Erickson).
- A co-release. The first Quiet Celebration was a Noh Poetry and Musea sub label Gazul release. This would be our only co-release. It gave us some distribution in Europe. In retrospect, it didn't seem to make sense financially, given the initial costs we covered. There was a Falcone & Palmer release, which I eventually ok'd Steve (Palmer) selling digitally at the same time as Noh Poetry.
- A home for albums no one else would take: Astralfish (an instrumental album highlighting Bridget's EWI), Falcone &

Palmer, Fireclan (featuring Melting Euphoria family members), two Grindlestone albums, a second Quiet Celebration, the first Spaceship Eyes. Looking at this list, I do wonder if Astralfish or any of these could have found another home with a little luck, or more research.

- A home for special projects: The *Where Stalks The Sandman* compilation, which invited musicians to create music from a single sound source; the Michael Moorcock & The Deep Fix *Demo Sessions*, which cleaned up Mike and Pete Pavli's demos and brought them to interested fans.

- A home for previously released albums. As I got the rights back to Spirits Burning albums, we re-released digital album versions of them.

- A home for archive material. I have cassettes of demos, practices, and live performances by bands and projects I was in prior to being on a CD. Some of this material is worthwhile to share, with the understanding—upfront honesty—they are demos. There are some real nuggets here, and some of the songs were later done or reworked by Spirits Burning. I can digitize and clean the cassettes a little by reducing some hiss, hum, and noise, and then normalize song levels so that a collection sounds more consistent from start to finish. Plus, I can gather photos, lyrics, and other information together, and with Karen's graphics skills, create an archival booklet that produces something special, memorable. In some cases, we even have videos we can share. Our first NPR venture into this territory, released on Bandcamp in 2024, *Demos with Tracy Williams & Don Falcone by Spirits Burning - Friends & Relations*. The title clearly influenced by Flicknife's Hawkwind *Friends & Relations* compilations, which I always bought, and the Hawklords' *Friends & Relations* album that includes a Spirits Burning song. And Mike's *Demo Sessions*.

Karen writes:

> *The label was Don's brainchild, I'm just along for the*
> *ride. I went from audio production to studying graphic*
> *arts at SFSU. My contributions are thus: graphic art,*
> *layout, design, photography, graphic illustrations and*
> *web construction and design.*

The label name Noh Poetry Records includes the word "Records." For some, it implies vinyl, and we have never done a vinyl release. Many record labels that no longer do vinyl have kept the word in their name. We live in a time where the definition of a record or album can be CD, digital album, or vinyl LP. Even cassette.

I was aware that NPR was our acronym, and that our catalog number would always include NPR in it.

I'm not fond of the term "vanity label."

I understand it, and I've even used it in conversation and interviews. I shouldn't. If you don't like a term, avoid it.

○ ○ ○ ○ ○ ○

I've signed contracts that were x albums released over y years. Where the label owns the sound recording rights for perpetuity. I've done licensing deals where a single album is now in the hands of a label for x years. I've seen 3 years, 5 years, 7 years. I've gotten advances, and no advances.

Some contracts are 15-20 pages, some a single page. One label simply did an email (virtual handshake).

Some contracts ask for access to the multi-track DAW mix. I've done everything from saying no and having it removed from the contract, to saying it's not necessarily available to well, ignoring it. Given the time it would take to successfully prepare or recreate them. For early Pro Tools sessions, I no longer have some of the plug-ins I used to own. Plus, I have dozens of archival hard drives in storage (although I do have text files documenting each drive's contents). I'd rather work on new music than weed out tracks for reuse by others.

Or those early Spaceship Eyes and Spirits Burning albums done on the Audicy. For me to find, let alone record out for re-use any track, I need to turn on the Audicy and get it working. There is a reason why it's in my music room closet. To use it, you must reset four pages of BIOS settings. Quite frustrating. The reason I rarely use it anymore. However, I haven't thrown it away either. Dreaming of spending a week recording digital scrubs and varispeeded audio.

Once a licensing contract has termed out, I can contact the label to get the rights back for the release. I then do digital album re-releases on NPR. Initially, on Bandcamp, which doesn't charge for the setup, and does pay more than normal streaming services. They also support including album artwork and some bonuses. Just one video though. I wish more.

I did run into a streaming issue if the music had been streaming via the former label and their digital aggregator (like The Orchard). I needed to stop the streaming, and the aggregator collecting any money for the label. In some cases, the label would contact the aggregator to stop the streaming. In others, I had to contact the streaming service directly. Sometimes, the cease and desist took multiple emails and a length of time. Perseverance is recommended.

If you're doing a song for a compilation, ideally, the contract states that you can use the song elsewhere.

There was a time where the best of the independent labels did lots of promotion. Maybe via an in-house promoter. Or they paid a promotion service (like Billy James' Glass Onyon). The label might do print ads in music zines and record store zines (like Tower used to do). They might even publish a zine or booklet promoting their recent releases or entire catalog. These are becoming rarer for smaller independents. I was happy in 2024 to see an inside front cover full-page ad of Cleopatra space rock releases for a special all-Hawkwind issue from Record Collector. The ad included four albums I was on and produced: two Spirits Burning & Michael Moorcock albums, Daevid Allen Weird Quartet, and Michael Moorcock & the Deep Fix. The tech writer in me, the musician in me, wishes I could have been an editor for the ad. Spirits Burning was spelled twice with a singular adjective—"Spirit Burning."

Both Gonzo and Cleopatra used Glass Onyon's services at times. A good working relationship where I could be involved directly. I usually started the one-sheet for promoting the release. I also supplied Billy with a list of known reviewers of past releases, in case they weren't in his database.

Billy's work was informative for me when it came time to promote a self-release. For example, I could do an internet search of every pre-release online post during his employ, and then contact those sites for an NPR release. Billy always shared reviews published in print or digitally. This also fed into my collection of contacts. Plus, this helped my morale (and when I posted it online, or shared it to any collaborators, another musician's morale). Less so when the review was less flattering.

When independent label budgets started to tighten, and they no longer used someone like Billy to do promotion, it made sense for me to step in and do some of what he used to do. Having a growing database helped.

Part of the process of doing a release is preparing a press kit. (Some kit pieces can be used as bonus items on Bandcamp.)

One-sheet: Typically, a one-page pdf or email announcement that a label or artist provides to promotion sites to announce a release, and to reviewers. You might notice some reviewers lean too much on the one-sheet, and you get redundant, data-heavy reviews.

CD artwork: A single pdf that combines the CD booklet, disc, and tray. We usually also include a separate high-resolution version of the cover. For *An Alien Heat*, which has lyrics in a separate book, we included a pdf of the book.

.wavs of songs: 44.1 24-bit, or 16-bit, unless .mp3s are specifically requested. I don't see a reason to provide inferior audio.

Photos: if any.

Videos: if any. Teaser promotion videos. We did these for the first Spirits Burning albums with Clearlight and Michael Moorcock, respectively. These had snippets of each song, some artwork, and additional photos related to the band and album.

I have never done a kickstarter for Noh Poetry. I have been part of one crowdfunding (direct-to-fan) music platform, when Gonzo used PledgeMusic, prior to the service going out of business. PledgeMusic created an online page for the release. It announced the upcoming release, provided lots of details, and took pre-orders. I could even offer teasers—like the release of a single song—to anyone that was in the order queue. The label used the page to gage how many boxed versions to manufacture, as well as the first run of CDs—all of which would be separate from the label's website and distribution of future runs. Services like Music Glue have replaced PledgeMusic.

Streaming… Well, first off, there are some realities, despite the low payout of streaming services. Many people listen to music via streaming services. Besides Amazon Music, Apple, Spotify, Tidal, and so on, I would include any streaming radio service (like Sirius). Second, if you aren't there, they may never hear you, or even take you seriously. It may feel like a no-win situation for a musician, and maybe it is. I just accept that I need to be streaming. To be there. Now. Ironically, I had complained to a friend about the bad payouts, and he decided to never sign up for a service. That wasn't my intent. He has bought CDs of some of my releases, and he did eventually sign up for Sirius, although I suspect I'm not being played there…Sirius does have a web page to submit your music for airplay.

I'm behind on streaming albums that I regained control of. I first got them re-released on Bandcamp and have since been setting up streaming a release every few months until I finish all of them. For a digital music distribution service, I'm still using CD Baby, vs. say Distrokid (which many self-releasing artists use) or The Orchard (which labels like Cleopatra use).

What I like about CD Baby…one, low price for having it streamed everywhere forever. Usually. You don't have to pay monthly or yearly. And, if for some reason you don't want to stream to say TikTok, you can just uncheck that box when you submit your initial request.

I say usually because sometimes a company changes ownership or even their underlying code. That explains why some early NPR releases are not on Amazon Music. (It doesn't explain why some are. Yes, I contacted CD Baby. I was told that I needed to resubmit the release to get it on Amazon, and yes, that means paying the fee again. Choices.)

Some things I don't like...CD Baby is 44.1 kHz. They don't support 88.2 or 96 kHz. This makes me question using them for newer releases, where I have the higher sample rate available (and have included on Bandcamp).

CD Baby has a confusing interface for dealing with multi-named bands. When I did the first Spirits Burning & Bridget Wishart album, I was careful to note the band name was Spirits Burning & Bridget Wishart (one box)—what CD Baby considers a single primary artist (their example: Simon & Garfunkel). I presumed this would show the correct band name, and an app like Amazon Music would display the album for a search of just Spirits Burning. A mistaken presumption. I should have said the band name was a "compound artist" (their example: Robert Plant & Alison Krauss)—Spirits Burning (first box) and Bridge Wishart (a second box). Due to my mistake, the album does not come up as a Spirits Burning album when you search for Spirits Burning. CD Baby does not support changing the band designation after the submission has gone public...unless you pay to resubmit.

Distrokid: I simply do not like that they are subscription-based. My understanding: If you do not renew the service, they pull the streaming. I like CD Baby's service where I can die knowing that I'll probably continue streaming to some service in Japan I've never heard of for some length after I'm gone.

○ ○ ○ ○ ○ ○

Not all labels provide quarterly or even yearly royalty (sales) statements. I had to learn by experience. Silent paid regularly when they existed, and Cleopatra provides regular statements too. Cleopatra provides digital statements, and then a physical check in the mail. This covers physical and digital sales. When Cleopatra changed their online reporting to a new agency in 2024, I got an email from an unknown service. I emailed Cleopatra to make sure the new service site was legit. It was.

I also get sales royalties from self-release sites, like Bandcamp, as they occur. And monthly statements from places like CD Baby, which used to sell physical media, and now are primarily doing digital album streaming only.

Anyone paying out royalties will typically have a minimal requirement before doing a payout. For example, you might not get your first payment until $100 in sales is achieved.

○ ○ ○ ○ ○ ○

There are other types of royalties.

Performing rights organizations (like BMI and ASCAP) collect money for songwriters and publishers when their songs are used in film and TV, played on the radio, or streamed online (for example, via Spotify, YouTube, and so on.)

BMI and ASCAP are the most popular organizations for U.S. songwriters. From what I know, PRS is the most popular for U.K. songwriters. I'm a member of BMI. I joined when they were one of the free organizations and another bandmate was a member.

When I release an album, either the label or me supplies song information to BMI. For licensing deals, it's always me. When I'm doing the task, I submit each song on BMI's site. The submission includes the names of everyone credited on the song, and their share. Most organizations require the credits to add up to 100%. BMI does 200%. All of which means, if there are two writers, with split credits, you both are 100% to add up to that 200%. It's a bit of an oddity that BMI members deal with.

I don't know if BMI and ASCAP and PRS talk to each other...such that a writer from another organization would get money via the BMI submission data. To ensure that they do, they probably need to get the data into their organization's database.

BMI does have a template and a database of prior input. I created templates for various size song credits, such as two writers, three writers, and up to eight. It saves a lot of time when doing larger song credits or ones that don't nicely add up to 200%. In some cases, I've given an extra .x% to the main writer to sum to 200%.

BMI distinguishes between author (someone who creates lyrics) and composers (someone who creates the music). A person can be both. There is no inherent difference in payouts for authors vs. composers.

For each person being credited, you include their performing rights organization, their personal id number, and their official account name used with that organization. There are some musicians who are not registered with a performing rights society. For them, you select "No affiliation." BMI's database remembers the names and info from past entries.

As a release approaches, I contact the new crew members and ask for their performing rights information, if I don't have them. I ask everyone on the release for their snail mail address, so I can send them a copy of the release, when available. (It's amazing how often some musicians move.) For Sprits Burning, I also ask them to provide a couple of digital photos because I plan photo collages of the line-up for each song, Karen does the graphics work, and I then post them on Facebook, typically one a week once the release is available.

Entering data into an organization's database is not fun. It can take a couple of days to complete an album's worth of data. I've made things more exasperating by having so many musicians involved with each album.

There isn't necessarily much money here for an individual writer of an independent song. However, any positive cents and dollars doesn't hurt. For some releases, I submitted songs to an agency that places music in film or TV. If a song, or even a snippet of a song is used, there is the possibility of a little more money (100s of dollars, instead of 10s) for each songwriter.

By law, people who use music (e.g., film, TV, radio, streaming, etc.) must report the use to the relevant agencies. They also pay a fee for the use. The agencies collect the money, and then dole it out to songwriters and publishers. (For Spirits Burning, the writers are usually the publishers too.) When I did my first record deal with Cleopatra, they took a percentage (publisher share) of the 200% performing rights. That turned out to be a good thing, as it incentivized the label to get songs used in film, which then happened with Spaceship Eyes songs in the *Better Living Through Circuitry* film. Both the writer (me) and publisher (the label) made money from the usage of songs.

There are other organizations…like SoundExchange, which collects money for the musicians on a song, as well as the owner of the master (the original recording)…and the British-based PRS for Music, which collects performance royalties plus mechanical royalties (royalties from sales of digital or physical reproductions of a song).

United States performing rights organizations like ASCAP and BMI do not collect mechanical royalties. In this country, SoundExchange collects and distributes digital performance royalties for non-interactive streaming (such as Pandora and Sirius Radio), while the Mechanical Licensing Collective (MLC) collects and pays mechanical royalties for interactive (streaming) digital audio services (such as Amazon Music and Apple Music). Both SoundExchange and MLC are free, and you can be a member of both. (As an artist, if I am on a label and they own the master recordings, they collect mechanical royalties on my behalf. These include royalties for streaming, downloads, and the physical reproductions too. Otherwise, for self-releases, where I own the master, I should sign up for SoundExchange and MLC.

I get a 1099 form from BMI and other royalty services to use for our taxes. I get forms from any source of music income. Any label that pays. Any distributors I use (such as Bandcamp and CD Baby).

o o o o o o

Collaborators…money…realities… Most people who have contributed to Spirits Burning have done so for free. They liked the project, the concept, and wanted to be a part of it. These are musicians who are used to getting paid for live and studio work. I am honored that they contribute. The greatest honor: When they continue to want to be involved. It does means there is a certain pressure for me to do my best to create a great release, one where they shine and everyone around them shines.

There have been exceptions…professional musicians who belong to a union, a handful of major artists who required a fee. If I want them to be part of Spirits Burning, I must pay them. In the end, it helps to give more name recognition to a particular album and should result in giving the song a special flavor too.

For every new studio album, I try to get a copy of the CD to everyone involved. It sometimes gets difficult when a musician disappears online, or their email address no longer works. Over the last two decades, I've also started to give credit to everyone on a song. It seemed like an additional way to say thank you. Lastly, I try to promote each Spirits Burning crew member on the SB Facebook page. I could do better. I've thought about starting at the top of the list, alphabetical order, and posting something about one musician a day. I haven't quite done that yet. We'll see.

o o o o o o

Your Alexa rank matters. Labels sometimes ask about your web imprint. Alexa rank is a global ranking system of domains and their relative recorded traffic. That ranks millions of websites in order of popularity. It's calculated by looking at the estimated average daily unique visitors and number of page views for a given site over the past three months. The lower your Alexa rank, the more popular the website is. For my to-do list, given music comes first, promotion later: Consider reading *How to Improve Your Alexa Rank (5 Quick Tips)*, as documented on the Alexa rank page from Kinsta.

○ ○ ○ ○ ○ ○

Somewhat less to do with money, more to do with how I spend my time...

Is there inherent danger concentrating on what you do best? Not necessarily. Even in areas you consider to be your strengths, there is always room for growth, room to experiment. Is it time for that secret project—an acoustic space rock album (which actualizes as Spirits Burning's *Evolution Ritual*)? Or, for each keyboard in the room, create new patches that are feathery, and see how they work together? Let's put it in a to-do plan doc, or on a daily calendar.

Is it Wednesday "W for web day," and time to work on your digital imprint? A personal site (perhaps purchased from GoDaddy and edited with BBEDIT). Do you promote your band on Facebook, Instagram, Pinterest, any newer sites? Do you still consider Reverbnation and Soundcloud? How and where are you streaming? Is your music getting to Amazon Music, Apple Music, and other streams, and is it via CD Baby, Distrokid, or another service? Bandcamp has become a stand-alone place to sell digital albums and physical ones. It also supports communicating news directly to fans via email lists.

Some people don't know Bandcamp supports CD and vinyl. Karen and I didn't know that initially; it's why we didn't list physical CDs as an option for our early NPR albums there.

○ ○ ○ ○ ○ ○

Is the data about your band and releases online current? Correct? This includes global databases like AllMusic and Discogs. It can also include sites specific to your music. Because I've done music in the progressive rock sphere, I make sure my bands and projects are covered on Prog Archive, Proggnosis, and the Exposé sites. As someone who plays mellotron, I ensure that the Planet Mellotron site knows when I release a song that includes mellotron. Bayprog/org serves musicians in the San Francisco/Bay Area. I probably should be more active on Moorcock's Miscellany. Most of these sites are responsive to input from artists and labels. Some of them have ongoing forums. (Which reminds me: Facebook is a place to promote and discuss music with your fans. For example, when I do a new release that has a Hawkwind family member, I make sure to post the news on the myriad of Hawkwind group pages, as well as pages such as Sci-Fi Proggers, Space, and SPACE ROCKERS, HIPPIES AND FREAKS.)

Are you familiar with MusicBrainz? This database captures information (about artists, their recorded works, and the relationships between them), and feeds into other professional databases. Signing up and providing missing info will require time to learn the app and enter the data for consideration.

Are your compositions registered to a performing rights society (such as BMI or ASCAP)? Does Sound Exchange know if you own a master, or are a musician on a release?

Are you familiar with Gracenote (a media database that stores album and song metadata for various apps)? I remember inserting my release into a USB CD player and the wrong band or song name displayed in iTunes (now Apple Music). The label had forgotten this part of the release workflow. As a user, you can edit the data in Apple Music and submit it to Gracenote.

○ ○ ○ ○ ○ ○

As services like Bandcamp change ownership, there can be a legitimate concern that it will change, that the best it offers will be lost, or the service itself will end. When it comes to a service that helps promote your band, I do not see a need to worry about what may or may not occur in the future.

Instead, it makes sense to make use of what the service offers— here and now. To nurture your journey wherever you can. Always.

Tips—Selecting Titles & Concepts

Song Titles and Album Titles

IS THERE AN originality meter that listeners use when scanning the name of songs on your release? Maybe internally, subconsciously. Regardless, as an artist, why wouldn't you try to be original?

When I say original, I'm not talking about being difficult or clever for the sake of it, for example coming up with song title *2wedfghjkl*, which I just created by running my finger over the keyboard.

Do you want to use a title used before—perhaps associated with other uses? Does it matter that a common or reused title will be lost in the search results?

There are other considerations:

- Sentence case (*This is the title*) vs. title case (*This is the Title*) vs. lower case (*this is the title*) vs. initial case (*This Is The Title*): Whatever you decide, be consistent for the titles throughout the album.
- Does your title have an apostrophe? It turns out performing rights society BMI does not support apostrophes. That means a title like *Logger's Revenge* is entered as *Loggers Revenge*. Surprisingly, a Logger's Revenge search leads to Loggers Revenge.
- Do you care that some style guides say to avoid contractions to simplify reading when English is a second language?

- New versions of old songs: You might run into problems if you wrote a song called *Every Opera* that you registered when you did an instrumental version and now do the vocal version. Since I wanted to give writing credit to every musician on the new version, I avoided the issue, naming the new version *Every Other Opera*. Otherwise, BMI does have a box to note an existing song used within a new song.
- Originality and timing: When I released the Spaceship Eyes album *Kamarupa*, which included a song of the same name, the phrase Kamarupa was virtually absent on the Internet. Less than a dozen search results, one of which was "Kama+Rupa." In 1998, *Kamarupa* was a very original album and song title. I presumed it was a little used word in the real world. I was wrong. It turns out that the Internet simply didn't have the data in place yet. Doing a search for Kamarupa decades later reveals over 400,000 results. And it's not because the Spaceship Eyes sold 100s of thousands of copies. (Weirdly, a search a week later totals 109,000.)

Vocal songs usually have a title that relates to the chorus or the story the song unfolds. That does place some responsibility on the lyrics, which you want to be good anyways. A simple title might be fine. An interesting phrase maybe better. Instrumental song titles have more leeway; can reach for something different.

I like titles with multiple or unexpected meanings. Two examples occurred on the mostly instrumental album *Healthy Music In Large Doses*, where each song refers to a panacea. *A Cool Can of Cola On the Forehead* literally means placing a cool can on my head. It's what I sometimes do when I have a headache. The song *Logger's Revenge* a bit more obscure. It's a ride in Santa Cruz, where you sit in a log that slowly crawls upwards to the top of the ride, and then rapidly descends and you and the log splish splash into a pool of water at the bottom. The panacea? Besides being refreshed, especially on a hot day, it's a great way to clean your glasses!

I do consider the implied acronym of a title, especially for album titles. When people identify a title in a shortcut manner, will it make sense and be easy to remember? The *Healthy Music In Large Doses* album and its HMILD acronym has a nice ring to it. A more famous example is Game of Thrones (GoT). Returning home: Every song title on the Grindlestone *One* album is a phrase that relates to a real-world acronym. *Tombola Beano Ductile*=TBD.

As we were finalizing the artwork and DDP master for the first part of the third *Dancers* album, I researched the use of the word *Part* in a title. Many films with parts (like *Harry Potter*) use a dash in their official name, as opposed to using a comma. That's what we decided to do: *The End Of All Songs - Part 1*. My mastering person confirmed that his DDP creation software supported the use of a dash.

Everything Is a Concept

In my record collecting days, I purchased lots of lesser-known concept albums (at least, from a U.S. standpoint).

These included *The Butterfly Ball & The Grasshopper Feast* (Deep Purple's Roger Glover bringing together musicians like singers Ronnie James Dio and David Coverdale, and violinist Eddie Jobson). *Peter and the Wolf* (with Brian Eno, Manfred Mann, Phil Collins, Bill Bruford, Cozy Powell). *The King Of Elfland's Daughter* (with musicians brought together by Steeleye Span's Peter Knight). All these featured musicians I followed. So did the original *Jesus Christ Superstar* studio album (with Deep Purple's Ian Gillan, and Hard Stuff's John Gustafson, whose voice I loved, and who also played bass on Roxy Music's *Love Is The Drug*).

As a musician, a producer, I see the definition of a concept album as pliable. Not required to be an adaptation of a book or film. Open to focusing on an idea, a genre, a featured musician. Most Spirits Burning albums have a focus, sometimes multiple ones concurrently.

I remember getting Phillip Glass' *Einstein on the Beach* album, an opera in four parts. One of the first boxed releases I bought. Four LPs. Expensive, at least for a 1978 college student. The package is beautiful. The vocal songs enchanting, haunting. The synth-oriented arpeggios can feel...repetitive. I was listening to the album in my corner of the basement.

I remember my mom coming down the steps to do laundry and, in one of the few times she commented on my feelings about an album, she said: "You don't like your new album, do you?"

In a Deeper Fix with Michael Moorcock

Michael Moorcock, creator of numerous legendary characters such as the definitive fantasy anti-hero Elric, the proto-cyberpunk Jerry Cornelius, and arguably the first modern steampunk protagonist Oswald Bastable, will be attending the Silicon Valley Comic Con, April 6-8, in San Jose, CA.
—Tachyon Publications website, 2018

OUR FIRST COMIC CONVENTION! Karen and I were there primarily to meet with Mike and support him (during his talk/Q&A session) and visit his table. We had breakfast with the Moorcocks at a hotel next door to the convention center, and then walked to the event with them. We sat with Linda during Mike's talk, and she occasionally whispered some insights. When a question regarding Mike's *Epic Pooh* essay came up, Linda said "not this again."

Mike and Don, at the Silicon Valley Comic Con, 2018
(photo by Karen Anderson)

Outside the halls and ballrooms, Karen and I skipped the long line for a photo with Stan Lee; from a distance, he looked frail, overworked, immobile. He would pass away eight months later. Deeper inside, Karen and I weaved through the halls, appreciating artwork and cosplay creations. I was on the lookout for anything that made sound. I decided not to talk to Marv Wolfman, who had written a letter to a young Don Falcone about his idea for a comic. Visiting Mike's table, we saw Lux Vibratus, who contributed to our *Dancers* project, and I was introduced to a fan of Mike's books and music—local fantasy writer Cliff Winnig. (I saw Cliff again, a few nights later, at Mike's reading at the American Bookbinders Museum in San Francisco. There, I quickly recognized the museum's operation manager—Madeleine Robins. Madeleine is married to Danny Caccavo, whose mellotron is in my studio. Madeleine has written books, done tech writing for audio companies, and was a Nebula Awards Commissioner. Mike won a Nebula Award for his book *Behold the Man* in 1967.)

○ ○ ○ ○ ○ ○

Songs for the second *Dancers* album (*The Hollow Lands*) were underway while the first album was being completed. An early 2018 example: I invited Steve Bemand to play guitar on *Dance Through Time*. The initial mix was my keys, temp vocals, and virtual drums. By the time Steve did his parts—four months after my invite—I had updated the mix with Al Bouchard (drums), Andy Dalby (rhythm guitar, backing vocals), and Adrian Shaw (bass).

Throughout the Spring, Al started multiple songs (music, transcribed lyrics, vocal lines): *Conflict & Illusions*, *Mr. Underwood's Soliloquy*, *Time Machine Cabriolet*. These included guitar or vocals from Al invite David Hirschberg (who later played in Al's *Imaginos* band). Both appeared on *Awful Dilemma*, a song originating from a jam by Lux, Ron Howden (Nektar), and Andrew Scott (Brainticket); and *Memorable Night At Café Royal*, started by Grindlestone's Doug Erickson. I was intent on keeping the music composition roadmap from the first album: Three songs started by Doug; the other song starts (excluding the jam) split between Al and me.

When Summer arrived, Al retired from his high school teaching job, organized lyrics for all chapters—only a handful that I had written or transcribed—and volunteered to invite vocalists where needed. I was busy with Gonzo and PledgeMusic—the *Alien Heat* campaign. Things like collecting photos of crew members and having Karen create pictorial collages for each song. We posted these to our normal sites, plus the campaign photo gallery. There, I noticed that the PledgeMusic box set photo was missing images of the posters, postcards, and sticker. When I inquired, the label discovered they had never been printed. This was quickly addressed. Complete box sets shipped in October. For some reason, copies for Mike, Al, Keith Donald (the artist), Karen (graphics), and Robert Rich (mastering) arrived after Christmas.

The next month, Al reported he talked to Richie Castellano at a BÖC gig. They would soon work on a new song. Plus, Al spoke to Danny Miranda, who said he'd love to add bass to a track. (Buck, Eric, and Jules were already on songs.) BÖC present and the Bouchards of their past would all appear on *Hollow Lands*.

Retrospective—Lessons Learned

Feedback matters. Billy from Glass Onyon shared incoming reviews of *An Alien Heat* (and I did daily internet searches). One hopes for the best and appreciates when a reviewer gets it—the attempt, the achievement. Comments can inform. What went well? What could we consider doing differently?

- **Vocals:** Some reviews criticized the lead vocals. The Rocker wrote "And there is some very good spacerock on offer here… What it's missing, though is a good vocalist." Another reviewer thought the box set included instrumental versions to mask vocal issues; actually, we included the instrumentals as a bonus since they existed and had an alternative charm. One reviewer did call the bonus "cool." Addressing the vocal criticism, Al wrote "I'm thinking for this next one we need to do a better job making the vocals more memorable, both in terms of performance and structure. Not that I think we should pander to these reviewers because as the late great Sandy Pearlman always said, "I'd rather have a small group of people become fanatical fans than have everybody like it." Still, I can see how the lack of choruses and hooks in the songs could confuse people with short attention spans and have a boatload of records to review. Somehow, I'd like the next one to tell enough of the story as to make the first one make a little more sense to the uninitiated and unfamiliar with the trilogy." When Al brought in Fabienne Shine, one thing he did was have her try different songs, and then scheduled her to return for the one that sounded best for her.

- **The Landing:** I was happy with the *Alien Heat* ending. Al felt it wasn't strong enough, and at least one reviewer considered the final two numbers to be inferior to the other songs. For the second album end, I initially had a medium-tempo proggy (multi-part, tempo-shifting) Tull-ish number, called *The Door,* waiting for a home. Following the book's lead, I worked in chords and vocal lines for *All Things Bright and Beautiful*. While the song had coolness, it felt sluggish. Plus, as other songs developed, its length pushed us over 80 minutes. We eventually replaced it with a better, shorter piece. (*The Door* found a home with a Bridget album and her vocals, where we changed its tempo from 90 to 92 BPMs; sluggish no more!)
- **Lyrics:** The first album lyrics were in a book included in the box set or purchasable separately. Some reviewers (and CD buyers) lamented "the lack of a much-needed lyric sheet." For the next album, we included the lyrics, the CD booklet growing from 8 panels to 12.
- **Story:** Some listeners unfamiliar with the trilogy struggled with the story; even with provided lyrics. With the third album, I added a short scene description for each song.
- **Credits:** Presenting all the album credits followed by all the album lyrics created an unintended codec. For the third album, I kept each song's credits and lyrics together.
- **Promotion:** Services like Glass Onyon are on-hire by a label for a limited time. Input for press releases or promotional contacts need to be presented sooner.
- **Mike's Session:** While the 2017 Texas session was well-prepared and productive, what if we planned two sessions instead of one? And wouldn't they be more relaxed, even more productive if I didn't fly in and fly out the same day?

An Alien Heat produced many positive reviews. One reviewer, so taken with the album, created a Wikipedia article of the release. This was probably never attempted for SB before. Unfortunately, they were unsuccessful; the album not considered notable.

The article was deleted.

Prog Fox called the album "a masterpiece." They noted that the opening *Hothouse Flowers* was "sung by the immortal Buck Dharma (but you couldn't even make him do a solo?)." Well, no, I couldn't. He did add guitar on the next two *Dancers* albums: one with a great solo.

Our Return to the Terminal Café

September 2018, Cleopatra asked Mike about doing the *Terminal Café* album (perhaps with music input from Alan Davey). Mike was committed to me and wondered if I would be interested in doing a co-production. I was not.

I reminded Mike where we left the project: We had stereo mixes of six songs, three with fiddle. I asked Mike to contact the studio engineer to get the original tracks, maybe even the session for each track, regardless of the software used. The latter would be simpler on their end (albeit lots of data to put on USB drives or upload to an online file sharing site). At work, I had access to all common music programs, could do track transfers there, and then take the tracks to my home system.

I verified with Mike that he didn't necessarily want to make a space rock album, and instead "wanted to keep it more in the style of a Cajun-based rock band playing in Cajun country."

∘ ∘ ∘ ∘ ∘ ∘

The first delivery from France wasn't what I requested. The package was one CD-R with the six files I previously downloaded. We asked again. This time, I got all the session mono tracks. Except for fiddle. We would have to re-record those. Linda and Mike put me in touch with Texas fiddler Sean Orr.

I soon made a major mix decision. Instead of separate Pro Tools sessions for each song (as I always did), why not create a single session with every song on the same timeline? It should simplify keeping the sound of each instrument and the general mix consistent from start to finish. The approach seemed obvious given the core band—one guitarist, bassist, drummer—and Mike's voice throughout. (The single album session method here served as a test for how I eventually mixed the Kozfest 2017 live gig.) One workflow adjustment involved markers. I normally use single (and double) digits for each song section. Here, I used them for each song, covering section parts (like verses) with three numerals (201 for song two, verse one).

Mike briefly had an unnamed San Francisco band and Alan Davey interested in contributing to the album. Mike rethought their involvement. I agreed. This should be a Mike/Martin Stone joint project—focused on songs with Martin—as it was his last album.

The album did feel short. My first suggestion: two versions of *Dream Of Eden*, the second more sparse, just vocals, fiddle, organ. I also knew that the longer *Sam Oakenhurst* piece needed to be whittled down. Mike mentioned that he could "add more narrative, if necessary," which "might involve repeating some music." This planted a seed. I could take some of *Sam*, reworking it to create a new song.

Mike mentioned adding female background vocals. I suggested the same. (He offered doing these himself; I talked him out of that.) My choice: Catherine Foreman, who sang lead for early 90s SB. She was in a country swing band at the time (Moonshine Maybelline) and seemed like a good match. I recorded her at my home studio.

I began thinking about the next recording session with Mike. We set a date. March 5-6, 2019.

Back to Texas, 2019—Where Dancers and Cafés Collide

Karen booked an Airbnb room in a home near Mike's place for me to stay overnight. Just over a hill that led directly to the Colorado River. A one block walk. A nice place to chill, see a hawk in the wide-open sky, take photos. The husband/wife owners of the house were very conservative, religious. (I can't remember how I deduced that.) I mainly interacted with them at breakfast, which they provided. I'm sure they were concerned, even leery about this guest from

California, so close to San Francisco. They seemed to warm up to me when I talked about my small hometown Steelton, and my late parents.

For The Hollow Lands...a Dance Through Time

During the session, we covered multiple songs for *Hollow Lands*. This included taking a risk and having Mike sing every word in *Dance Through Time*, a lengthy number with four different sections to learn on the spot and adapt to. Mike took to the song well. We recorded in small chunks—one intro, verse, chorus, interlude at a time.

...and a Conversation with H.G. Wells

A spoken track; with a twist. I had transposed the best parts of this countryside conversation about time machines, and then presented it to Mike to perform the voices of both speakers. On the paper printout, I think I had Jherek's parts left justified and H.G.'s parts to the right—in the same spirit I later mixed Jherek slightly to the left and H.G. slightly to the right. Mike did a splendid performance, inflecting the two voices differently. It really feels like two people conversing. Jherek begins "I am extremely grateful to you Mr. Wells. I had begun to wonder if I should ever find Bromley." H.G. responds "You have friends there, have you?" The conversation continues over a musical jaunt jelling three Hawkwind family members—Dead Fred (violin), Bridget (EWI solo), Harvey (synths)—over my keys and percussion and input from others. The conversation concludes with Jherek's hunt for a time machine expressed with "You wouldn't be prepared to build me one, would you, Mr. Wells?" To which, H.G. replies "I'm afraid I'm more of a theorist than a practical scientific person."

For Terminal Café...

We had six songs originally, with five more taking shape...

- *The Effects of Entropy*: Mike did two readings. One for the album's intro, and one to open part 2. However, the music didn't exist. When I returned to California, I took parts of *Sam Oakenhurst*, and re-arranged them while including different combinations of instruments, to build new distinct songs. Adding my keyboards (piano and organ) helped reshape the music too. I was probably under the influence of Nick Cave when I did my parts. For the intro, Mike envisioned the narrator standing outside the club where the band was playing. I located club audience sounds from the Spirits Burning vs. Spaceship Eyes show. These include Exposé writer Jeff Melton, who emceed the event—"Alright let's start this again..." and "thanks for coming out, we appreciate the turnout." The club's last call announcement and more audience sounds follow, including laughter, which I affected. Then, I weaved in Mike's first narrative.

- *St. James Infirmary*: My Texas surprise. During a break in our session, Mike suggested I record him performing a cappella. With no words in sight, he did two takes of this traditional piece. As he sang the last word, he gently picked up his harmonica and played a short coda. It was amazing. Mike suggested we ask Pete (Pavli) to add "something soulful in the background...instrument of his choice." When Pete was unable, I did an improvisational electric piano performance. Mysterious, cool, maybe...out there. I wondered what Mike (and Linda) would think. They both loved it. This became the closing number on vinyl album side 1.

- *The Heart of a New Orleans Night*: Mike's second narrative, to open vinyl side 2. This repurposing of *Sam* emphasizes the acoustic guitar and shimmering, snaky tambourine, and then bass guitar, until the song rebuilds into a melee including electric guitar and rimshot 'n' kick drum.

- *Blood*: I wanted one more song and prepared this one before the session. What if I took some moments of *Sam*, created some longer loops—including one that stayed on the same chord—and did a four-chord keyboard pattern harmonizing over that root chord? And then added a new bass line, via piano? The result: a new song. Mike provided the lyrics and haunting vocals to complete this creation.

- *Eden Revisited*: The acoustic guitar version of *Eden*, with a touch of organ and female backing vocals supporting Mike's more exposed vocals; Sean's fiddle taking the acoustic lead after the second chorus.

For Evolution Ritual...

Some months after our session, I told Mike:

> *I've completed mixing your vocals and harmonica parts... For two songs [for The Hollow Lands], the harmonica parts didn't work... Would you be OK if I used them to start songs for a future Spirits Burning instrumental album? It would be an acoustic space rock album, potentially somewhere between Third Ear Band and Dead Can Dance, depending on how other musicians interpret the songs.*

∘ ∘ ∘ ∘ ∘ ∘

On Saturday, March 30th, Mike appeared onstage as part of the North American Space Ritual 2019 two-night event.

The timing was bad.

He was in the midst of a medical procedure for ongoing health issues. He was scheduled to be part of the headlining Moonhawks ensemble—with Nik Turner and Alan Davey. Instead, he would appear earlier in the evening, performing *Standing At The Edge* and *Sonic Attack*, backed by Flame Tree and Nik.

I had inquired about the event, and decided I couldn't put a band together in time.

I had other concerns.

The location, line-up, and other details shifted over time. It was easier, safer, to sit this one out.

The final lineup included multiple musicians who contributed to SB: Friday night headliners ST 37, and then Mike, Jack of Flame Tree, Nik, Alan, and Alisa Coral.

Legal Stuffings

In April, as mastering and a label search for *Terminal Café* neared, I discussed with Linda what I called legal stuff.

Songwriting: Mike needed to register the song credits with his performing rights society. In the BMI database, Mike was listed as a PRS member, covering songs by Blue Öyster Cult, Hawkwind, and Spirits Burning. This was incorrect. Mike had no account with them; in turn, they were not collecting his royalties. I suggested Mike register with BMI. Linda submitted his registration. Confusion ensued. BMI thought he was already represented by PRS. He wasn't. Linda submitted again. The PRS info included ALCS, which Mike did belong to. They're an organization that collects royalties for literature only. BMI momentarily confused. Linda submitted again. The third time worked.

Inputting song data and credits into the BMI database is time-consuming, tedious. When we got a label, I volunteered to do it for Linda. This did require that she give me Mike's password. I also requested BMI update all of Mike's other songs so that BMI was listed as his performing rights society. They did this promptly.

Copyright: I told Linda the label gets a © for their name/logo and ℗ for the sound recording (physical reproduction). We include ©Michael Moorcock & The Deep Fix. That should suffice. I wrote: "I really can't imagine Nik going out on the road as Nik Turner's Michael Moorcock & The Deep Fix. I've also never registered my songs [for copyright]; except the first ones I wrote as a teenager…"

BMI states "Your composition is copyrighted automatically when the work is "created," which the law defines as being "fixed" in a copy or a recording for the first time. The registration of your copyright is recommended, but not required." You can register copyright with the Library of Congress (copyright.gov).

○ ○ ○ ○ ○ ○

I contacted these labels, in alphabetical order: Cleopatra—maybe an advance and maybe CD and vinyl as done for Daevid Allen Weird

Quartet; Esoteric/Cherry Red—they did Hawkwind, and presumably had the rights to Mike's *New Worlds Fair* album; Flicknife—
they released some Moorcock projects long ago; Gonzo—the label
SB was currently on (typically CD only). I didn't consider my Noh
Poetry label. While we previously released Mike's demo sessions,
we didn't have the distribution this release deserved.

The Age of Dénouement

I worked with Mike, Linda, and Cleopatra to secure a deal for CD,
vinyl, and digital. The deal included a better advance with the caveat
of Mike providing two spoken word pieces for Cleopatra and Alan
Davey. I was pleasantly surprised my name was included in the
contract; in the years to follow, I would get some of the sales and
streaming royalties.

I was incredibly proud to produce *Terminal Café* for Mike (and
Martin and his survivors). Proud of its results. Plus, I was happy to
finally be part of the Deep Fix family.

For the cover, we loved the Gustave Moreau piece that adorned
Mike's *Blood* novel. We could use it for free as it was available via
Creative Commons.

An unexpected collaboration: Karen and I worked with Walter
Simonson, who provided the artwork used inside the package. I read
his Thor work in my comic book days, remembering well his Hela,
Beta Ray Bill, Surtur, and Thor frog. And his work for DC's Michael
Moorcock's Multiverse; it was these illustrations we had access to.
Walter delivered hi-res scans, Karen was given the ok to create
cutouts from the artwork (to avoid word balloons or provide a better
focus). When Walter saw the mockups, he liked Karen's work and
suggested he color an item that needed it and complete a sword that
cut off at the comic panel margin. That's how we got a long,
complete sword.

I continued my legal discussions with Linda. Most of the
contract's text about copyright referred to the manufactured
release—the audio medium and printed materials. Typically, a
contract gives the label the right to create shirts, etc. from the

artwork. Although I don't think any label has ever used my projects for merchandise. For the *Café* album, we were using artwork copyrighted by Walter; we had the initial contract updated with "Interior artwork by Walter Simonson cannot be reused for merchandise like shirts, cups, etc. as they are (c) Walter Simonson and he donated the previously copyrighted pieces for booklet and vinyl insert use only." Because Mike's words were copyrighted, we had the contract state that he retained all copyrights for the lyrics.

When to release? The best date is the planned, expected one. Cleopatra gave us a Sept-Oct 2019 timeframe. In time for Christmas. They then changed the release to February 2020 until Linda stepped in and got them to return it to 2019. I was happier with the 2019 date for two reasons, even if the label had to split releases of two formats—the vinyl wouldn't be ready in time. Reason one: We wouldn't have to change the copyright dates on artwork. Reason two: The new date was closer to release dates for both Alan and Nik albums. People buying physical copies from the UK might be more likely to buy multiple albums at once, to deal with rising postage costs.

(There are many articles written about release dates. Surprisingly, some suggest January and February are best, because they're after the end-of-year saturation.)

When writing credits and lyrics for this album, I needed more help from Mike than usual. Many French phrases. I took Spanish in high school and that's as close as I got to French (other than using Google's translation tool when I get a French review).

There was one last item to cover with Linda and Mike: our free copies. "I should prepare you, in case it is a new experience for you: The CDs have a nasty hole punched through the case on the back. About half the labels I've worked with over the years do this. It's irritating. Long ago, one label rep told me that they do this so that the copies cannot be resold. I've always felt that it was a bit overkill. Really unnecessary."

We'd get a couple of interviews. The ones with Mike typically asked more about Hawkwind and BÖC songs or earlier Moorcock albums. We reminded them to include questions about *Terminal Café*. For interviews via email, I provided grammar and punctuation edits to Mike's responses, and sometimes the questions too.

○ ○ ○ ○ ○ ○

I spent May to July rolling out mixes of each *Hollow Lands* song for Al to listen to and comment on. By December, we completed remaining new parts. We had saved many vocals for last or were only now taking the time to assemble our best singers. Al recorded Tony Mann for *Conflict*. Dana McCoy for the *Delicious* female vocals, as well as parts on three songs with a theatrical approach—multiple singers to cover multiple characters. This included two narrator parts by Eric Bloom that Al previously recorded offstage after a BÖC concert. David Hirschberg did Mr. Underwood in *Memorable Night At Café Royal*. Al got incoming vocals from Andy Shernoff (*We May Yet Be Saved*) and Joe Bouchard (*Playing at Ships*), and then uploaded them for me to intake. And Al convinced me to keep my *Robot Nurse* lead vocals. (Originally, I wanted a female singer, or have Al convince his brother to do it.)

Work was ongoing now for the third album. For example, I was working with Andy Dalby on *Try and Try Again*, a song I started. We discovered that the Pro Tools session had some auto-tempo changes in the middle of some measures. This resulted in tempo hiccups when trying to play to a click. I never noticed this before because the actual song—click muted—played back fine. Andy also suggested adding extra measures and a specific chord pattern to end the solo section. He sent a few measures of his guitar (with temp bass and drums), and I then expanded the piece on my end with the needed bars.

We were fast-tracking this piece as I had met Arthur Brown at a Mountain Winery show ("Royal Affair Tour," with Yes, Asia, John Lodge, and Carl Palmer's ELP Legacy). Arthur sang vocals during the Legacy set, and he was now onboard. The bass and drums for this piece would eventually be done by Steve York and Al, respectively. Steve's involvement was a nice touch, as he played on Arthur's 1974 *Dance* album. For the drums, Al changed his drum kit, close to an exact replica of the kit he used on *Burning For You*.

In the end, Arthur's participation wasn't meant to be. There were potential issues of where to record him. I offered to pay for any transportation and studio time. Arthur and his manager eventually went email silent.

Try & Try Again lived up to its title. One of the last songs to get vocals as I would try and try again to procure a strong vocalist to replace my guide track. It started with Arthur (yes, then no), moved to David Cousins (yes for about a year, then pulling out due to publicized health issues, plus David didn't feel the song was in his style, which seemed odd to me as I thought my vocals were channeling him…), Nick Saloman (who didn't want to sing on any song), John Hudson (another Strawbs connection—he thought my vocals were fine, while I didn't), Keith Christmas (too low for him, and he thought my vocals sounded fine), Kev Ellis (bad timing, if I remember correctly), Al and then David Hirschberg (their takes a different interpretation, distant from my original vision), and Jerry Jeter (this worked, emotive, smooth, almost like Arthur minus any high wire moments). I was happy.

To The Time Machine At Last, the song started by Al and Richie came in. This was the penultimate song for *The Hollow Lands*. All that remained: completing the last song—sticking the landing.

Back in July, I wrote to Al: "I've come up with a pretty complicated, simple piece to end the album. Complicated because at one point there are four different vocals lines at once. The voice is Amelia, start to finish. I also did specific keyboard passages for each part.

To make it work, we need a great singer…who is willing to take my starter vocals and create better melodies (as opposed to excessive "talk" vocals). We also need a director (you) to lead her through this. Mixing this will also be a challenge."

Al reworked my vocal arrangement to bring my idea to life—first, alternating parts by Amelia and Jherek, and then presenting the multiple parts concurrently. Dana McCoy would be the female singer, completing her parts in late December; Al, the male vocalist.

I initially titled the song *We Must Build A Fire*. I mentioned an alternate Title—*Two Spirits Burning*, a phrase I included in the song (reminiscent of when Al snuck BÖC album title *Secret Treatise* in *Isn't It Delicious* on *The Hollow Lands*). I followed up with our final title: *We Must Make A Fire*. This matched Mike's text. Plus, build was already used in the song and book line—"we must build a hut."

Besides incorporating a slew of vocal tracks, I started to trim heads and tails of songs, and search for parts of songs to cut. We were creeping towards the CD time length limit.

We did mix tweaks into the first week of January. This included my sawtooth synth for bite on *On The Hunt*, in response to Al's mention that it needed something, "maybe percussion or some kind of 16th note pattern"; I also added wind chimes, plucky synth, and reverbed piano given Al's suggestion for "some sparkle on top."

By January 6, 2021, we had almost everything in place for a successful release. Al: "I must say I really love the sequence of the last 3 songs. I can't help smiling after the last one."

○ ○ ○ ○ ○ ○

I was now working with Gonzo on a release plan.

- Release date: If I deliver the audio and artwork by February, the album will release in May/June.
- 12-page booklet: Yes. We can include all the lyrics.
- No box set. PledgeMusic no longer existed and Gonzo didn't have a substitute service in place.
- No vinyl. A double album would be too costly.

A few weeks later, Rob at Gonzo emailed me. Gonzo could no longer support physical formats for SB. The message: With the huge decline in physical sales, titles like mine really suffered. They could do a digital release. I declined.

Epilogs...Snapshots at The End of Time

March 6, 2020: Al asked If I could play piano on a song for his new Imaginos project. I said yes. I delivered organ and piano for *Half Life*

Time, the last song on *Imaginos II - Bombs Over Germany*. On the same day, I shared with him: "On the *Hollow Lands* front, some big news. Cleopatra will release it, and it looks like there will be a limited run of vinyl too."

I was already deep into the third *Dancers* album. We didn't have a song for *Dregs*, the poem by Ernest Dowson that opens the third book. Al commented: "I also listened to all the mixes for what you have for *End Of All Songs*. Some great tracks there. I had a thought about the first song, maybe we should offer Don Roeser the opportunity to write the song to Dowson's poem. He may not have time or not be interested but I'm sure he would not be offended if asked. Another thought is how are we going to fit 27 songs (chapters) on a single disk? Should there be a part 1 and part 2?"

Buck would take Dowson's poem and write an inspired song (titled *The End Of Every Song*), and share tracks by him, Al, and Danny. The SB version opened our 2023 *Part 1* release. In 2024, Buck released his own version, along with a video.

I believe Buck interprets the end of all songs literally, as presented in the poem. An ending. Inevitable. His video is moving, with images of BÖC friends and family, some no longer with us. Following BÖC's *Ghost* album, some fans wondered if this was Buck's last song.

My interpretation differs. On the *Part 2* album, I wrote these lines for the opener: "When will we hear the end of all songs?" On one hand, I was playing with the idea that we hadn't gotten to the last album, last song. The answer: "When we complete our journey at the end of time."

In my mind, there is always a possibility of hope. In terms of an ending...I was more attached to my take on Mike's last chapter, seeing the end as the beginning, a return to the beginning. Where Amelia and Jherek are a new Adam and Eve.

Buck adds "I wrote the song from what I saw as Dowson's perspective, not from any understanding of Michael Moorcock's expansion on the forward. Yet I feel my vision of *End* is somehow hopeful and inspirational beyond recognizing the despair and gloom of Dowson's circumstance. My video is a bit of dramatic license, and makes for a good story."

In September 2024, The Cure released their first new song in 16 years: *Alone*. The opening vocal line is "This is the end of every song that we sing," a line from the Dowson poem. Further in Robert Smith's lyrics are three other words from the poem: fires, dregs, ghosts.

In a statement (shared online by AV Club), Smith says: "I had been struggling to find the right opening line for the right opening song for a while, working with the simple idea of 'being alone', always in the back of my mind this nagging feeling that I already knew what the opening line should be," he continued. "As soon as we finished recording, I remembered the poem *Dregs*, by the English poet Ernest Dowson...and that was the moment when I knew the song—and the album—were real."

I wonder if Smith first came upon the poem via the Moorcock book.

First The Year of Covid

To Robert Rich:

> *On the work front, I've been working at home the last week, and into the foreseeable future. On the plus side, technology makes it work well. I do need to remember to take breaks, get fresh air, play with the dog in the back yard. Last bit is easy to do. :-)*

To Al:

> *I've been working at home for seven weeks now, and it's quite hard to turn off the day job. I am lucky that we have a back yard, and our dog helps us keep things sane and playful. The last few weekends, I've managed to start a cadence where I'm getting back into music.*

Don Falcone

To Jack Gold-Molina:

> *My attention to music has been extra diverted for the last two months or so. Day-job included doing documentation for a half-dozen Dolby projects, most of which have now released. I've also been working at home since the first week of March, and it's often hard to turn off work, and differentiate work from home...I'm still working out how best to deal with that.*

To Doug Erickson (Grindlestone):

> *Over the last week, the air quality nearby has been better for the most part. It was extremely bad for a couple of weeks, and put a dent on going to outdoor restaurants, or even spending too much time in the back yard. Plus, we had that one day [Wednesday, September 9, 2020] where it was dark until late afternoon, and the sky was orange all day and night. Much of the bad air quality in the Bay Area has been due to smoke from Oregon, and not Ca. fires. All very weird.*
>
> *Covid-wise, we did our first get-together since February with a couple of friends. We met at a fish place in Half Moon Bay, each sitting at different tables. We'll be doing that again at a different place in a few weeks. It was good to see them, and talk, etc.*
>
> *The Berklee Music course ended two weekends ago. Dolby is kind of putting a hold on like expenditures for a while, and I need to take a semester off any ways. I have already talked to my boss, and her boss, and they know that I'll ask to do another class in January. They both support it but may not be able to get approval at that time. To be continued...Karen recently reminded me that Kim (Cascone) went to Berklee. I had forgotten.*
>
> *I do have access to the LinkedIn (formerly lynda.com)*

classes free, via Dolby. I think I mentioned Lynda courses to you a few years ago. You do them at your own pace. They have lots of audio courses, including Live and other DAWs. [They also have mixing and mastering courses.]

I have redone the music room a bit. I think the class got me thinking a bit... And sitting there during Dolby meetings... This includes working on a new Pro Tools session template, and all the audio and MIDI connections. Lots of testing. I do now have the surround speakers working again, and am working on getting all the keyboards always hooked up and available.

I'm still working on the instrumental album, and it is coming along well. I think I have David Cross onboard... Additionally, he asked Cyrille a lot of questions to vet me (and to make sure that I wasn't still working with Voiceprint / Gonzo).

SB & MM II album official release date is probably December 4.

In the one-sheet, Mike noted:

The Hollow Lands is a beautiful piece of work, building on An Alien Heat with musical subtlety and intelligence. I am delighted by the interpretation and can't wait to hear the resolution to this amazing project! They are a wonderful complement to what is one of my own favourite sequences and I could not hope for a better interpretation.

10/21: Al's Imaginos II album was about to come out, and he wrote:

My album is out in a little over 2 weeks and I am in the top 20 of all amazon pre-sales releases. I've done 31 interviews in the last 2 weeks and a half. And the most is yet to come. I've been talking up the SB Moorcock release as much as I can. Sometimes I get to talk for an hour, but

radio wants 15 or less. Anyway, I can't wait to crank the
HL disc in the car as I'm cruising down the highway,
That's the true test.

○ ○ ○ ○ ○ ○

In 2021, Al and I would re-read the third book, chart out the chapters and possible songs. We agreed that we couldn't cover the book in one album. Plus, Matt Green, my contact at Cleopatra confirmed they wouldn't do a double album. This would result in 2023's *Part 1*, and then *Part 2*. Hopefully, in mid-to-late 2025.

With Al busier during the gestation time for these albums—second and third *Imaginos* albums and joining The Dictators—the SB & MM album workflows…and results…would be different in that I (or another musician and me) would start most of the songs.

I was also now doing most of the transcriptions of Mike's text, developing lyrics and vocal lines. These let me weave in some of my lyrics and secondary concepts (usually about art, the process of making music, or life).

Perhaps noticeable in titles I created throughout the series: *Learning the Art, Try and Try Again, Second Thoughts, Building A Bad Scene, Bring Back The Living, Remember Those Who Have Died (At Least Once), Each Vehicle Has Two Eyes, Don't Concern Yourself With The End Of The World.*

Al continued to contribute drums and other instruments: 8 songs on *Part 1*, 10 songs on *Part 2*.

Feb 14, 2021, Al noted:

I haven't written anything for the record yet, but I can if
necessary. I have found that many of my favorites on the
last 2 records have been songs where you wrote the music,
and I added a vocal on top. It's also fun for me because I
approach that aspect of the songwriting in a non-
mathematical way. I don't even know what key many of
those songs are in.

○ ○ ○ ○ ○ ○

The 2022 session with Mike in Texas covered *Part 1* songs and some *Part 2* ones.

With concerns of Covid, Mike and Linda preferred my option of getting someone local to do the session.

I brought in my former Digidesign co-worker Nick Pellicciotto (now living in Texas, working for Apple and writing about Dolby Atmos with Apple Logic, while I wrote Dolby Atmos guides at Dolby). Nick was a fan of Mike's work, and I knew I could trust him to be professional and respectful at the Moorcock homestead.

I gave Nick the tracks and guidance for what I wanted Mike to try: background vocals, humming, shorter lead phrases, narration, whistling, some harmonica.

I prepared one Pro Tools session. For each song, I created clips with markers for where he would sing, along with muted clips for sections he wasn't touching. They were available, if Mike needed a longer lead in, or wanted to listen to the song.

The session went well, and I got what was needed for the songs. Although, I, of course, wish I could have been there in the room. Able to suggest some on-the-fly, out-of-box ideas.

Nick helped again in 2024, as he and Mike did another session to address the remaining *Part 2* songs.

○ ○ ○ ○ ○ ○

Don Falcone

July 1, 2023, Blue Öyster Cult at the Marin Country Fair. After the show, I met Buck for the first time. I gave him a copy of *The Hollow Lands* to give to Jules.

Buck Dharma and Don, Marin Country Fair, 2023 (photo by Karen Anderson)

September 20, 2023, Tangerine Dream w/encore guest Robert Rich, at the Regency Ballroom, San Francisco. After the show, I talked to Robert while the band were tearing down. I introduced myself to violinist Hoshiko Yamane, who was on the *Part 1* album.

December 8th, 2023, Cleopatra releases *The End Of All Songs - Part 1*.

May 20th, 2024, The Damned w/The Dictators, Regency Ballroom, San Francisco. After Al played drums for The Dictators, he called me and visited Karen and me in the balcony. This was the first time we met. After the show, Monty of the Damned and contributor to our *Dancers* project, texted me, and we met downstairs near the bar.

Al Bouchard's Thoughts on the Dancers at the End of Time

I first heard of Don Falcone and Spirits Burning in December of 2006 when he invited me to contribute to a new recording called Internal Detective. There were members of Hawkwind and other space rock and prog groups I had heard of involved so I was naturally intrigued. At that time, I sent him CDs of the tracks through the mail. I was homeless at the time, so I had to record the tracks at the school where I was teaching after the students had gone home. He expected to have all the recordings for this album by February of the next year. It took almost 4 years coming out in the summer of 2010. I was thinking that maybe Don didn't want to use the track because what I sent him was not very good because of the circumstances under which it was recorded but the results were surprisingly viable.

In the meantime, I worked on another project—a Motorhead tribute record—with a band I had with Les Braunstein where we did a version of their song Funny Farm in the style of Django Reinhardt. It was a lot of fun even if the results were confusing. Don and Spirits

Burning were also on the album, doing a cover of Ace Of Spades.

In 2013 I was asked to contribute another piece to a Spirits Burning record, some kind of tribute to John Coltrane. This was something I could sink my teeth into, and I had a much better recording setup because I was living with my friend Mark Barkan at the time, and I had a studio in his house. What I sent him was not bad and the result was quite good. It is something I'm proud to have made. (The song ended up on a Spirits Burning & Clearlight album.)

In January of 2016 I was asked to contribute some song sketches to a new project, Michael Moorcock's Dancers At The End of Time trilogy. This was a dream assignment for me. I had just had surgery for Prostate Cancer and was undergoing radiation therapy. I was in a lot of pain, so I had been prescribed medical marijuana. While under the influence I started recording hundreds of little riffs on guitar and piano. I had also bought a baritone guitar and was finding all sorts of cool things to do with that. I had also been able to rent my own tiny apartment and had a recording setup that was competitive to what a high-end studio would have but just one input channel.

I bought An Alien Heat (the first book of the Dancers trilogy) and enjoyed it thoroughly. I hadn't read any of Mike's books except for the Elric & Stormbringer series which Eric Bloom had turned me on to during my BÖC days. What struck me was the rich and colorful wordplay in the books. I was delighted by it. When Don Falcone told me that most of the album was going to be instrumental, I was disappointed. I urged him to consider more vocals. (Years later, I learned that I had misunderstood. He was suggesting a handful of songs, if lyrics didn't work out.) I chose some chapters and started writing lyrics that I culled from the text. The results were very satisfactory for me and Don urged me to do more. I realized that singing most of the songs myself would not be in the spirit of the Spirits Burning collective, so I started getting my friends to contribute vocals. At the same time, I was doing some gigs with Blue Öyster Cult to commemorate the 40th anniversary of Agents of Fortune, our first platinum album. I was able to talk Don, Richie and Eric into contributing to the album. I realized I was getting excited about the whole project and when all the songs were completed and mixed, I was extremely happy with the result.

As soon as that first record was completed, I purchased a copy of the complete Dancers At The End Of Time trilogy in one soft cover book. I started thinking of lyrics for the next volume before any of the music was written. In the last days of 2017, we started work in earnest on The Hollow Lands, the second in the series. Don had some music written in a Dropbox folder we would be using for the rest of the project. Somewhere in the middle of that whole process I realized that one of the reasons why it was so satisfying to me was that it was exactly like what I hoped the Imaginos trilogy would be like.

I began casting a bigger net of friends to contribute and thinking about creating a complete arc of music where the beginning and the ending were equally memorable. The Hollow Lands record took some time to complete. By 2020 I was also getting involved in many other projects like the Dictators and my own trilogy of Imaginos, so I was not able to work as consistently on the project, but the songs kept coming. The End Of All Songs - Part 1 came out and Part 2 is nearing completion as I write this. There will be more in the future, but I am extremely grateful to Don Falcone for getting me started on these new adventures in music and lore.

Definition of Don(e)

FOR 33 YEARS, I was a technical writer for companies producing audio hardware and software. It was at Digidesign (Avid) that I was able to buy, or inherit tools (which had been discarded, or abandoned by former employees). That's how I continued to build a home studio. None of these tools last forever, so it would be necessary to sometimes replace or update them. Financially, it was also prudent to put off making changes to one's studio for as long as possible.

That's why I still have an older Mac tower with an older version of Pro Tools software running with older I/O boxes. However, I also have the latest software on a Mac laptop.

At Digidesign, and then at Dolby, I experienced two types of manufacturing methodologies: Waterfall and Agile (specifically, Scrum).

Waterfall: The product manager sets a date for general availability (GA) and the team drives towards it. You create a product requirements document (PRD), do analysis and design to meet those requirements, develop and test the product, and then package it for real-world use. I worked in Waterfall at Orban and Digidesign.

Home Studio Music Rack, 2013; Pictured from Left, Kiara, Don
(photo by Karen Anderson)

A music analogy...set a release date and stick to it. Reality checks: If you have a day job or live gigs, you might need more time. Planning CDs? Manufacturing can take up to three months.

Vinyl? Longer. Maybe up to nine months.

Agile: The product team works out smaller, iterative completion dates. For example, complete a software feature in a month and then release it.

A music analogy…do a single and release it digitally the next month.

Scrum (a subset of Agile) provides specific team structures, events, and requirements. I worked in a scrum environment when it was introduced at Avid and Dolby. The term scrum comes from rugby teams and their scrum formation used when they restart play.

Scrum, when done well, feels more collaborative.

It starts with an interactive team: product management, developers, testers, technical writers, graphics designers. Everyone has a voice, even one outside a standard role.

For example, a writer can provide design input, do testing, question team decisions, touch code. (One Dolby engineer and his wife use scrum for household chores!)

There are recurring scrum events for creating and managing a backlog—the user "stories" (features you want to provide), and "issues" (bugs) that need fixing for that story to be happy.

The team works in an agreed upon cycle (called a "sprint"), for example, two weeks, on each planned story and issue. The "definition of done" is when the story or issue has been developed and tested, and the product is ready for real-world use (or to be demoed to stakeholders).

When I was at Dolby in San Francisco, one of my scrum teams was in Barcelona.

For their daily meetings (called a standup), they used a white board to track items for the current sprint. There were columns for different milestones. The last column was "Done." For a time, they posted a picture of me over the last letter.

Thus, was born the "Definition of Don."

Dolby Atmos Team White Board in Barcelona (photo by Pau Arumi)

Personal Side Notes

- A scrum "standup" originally meant standing up; where each team member states what they did yesterday, planned to do today, and any blockers—things in the way of their plans. Standing implied a quick meeting, under 15 minutes. I challenged standing up at Avid after my second knee surgery. The team complied; I sat on a couch. With remote teams, it's likely that multiple people sit around a table facing a large monitor displaying teammates. During Covid 2020, everyone was at home…sitting, unless standing up, stretching.

- There are other scrum events besides backlog planning and starting a new sprint: sprint review (where you demo what is done), and sprint retrospective (how did we do, what could we do differently?). These events are managed by a member of the team, deemed a "scrum master." I was a scrum master for almost a year. I thought it cool that a tech writer could guide a team through its plans. (Music analogy: A bass player can lead a band.)

- Backlog planning was originally called backlog grooming. I was part of an inclusive language group at Dolby; it took a while for me to move teams in my purview to replace the use of the word grooming; the national Scrum Alliance organization had already done so. (Music analogy: Consider the meaning of words you use in art and day-to-day discussions.)

In my scrum experience, we worked on products that included multiple features, and we drove towards a single end date when the collection of all features was done. That always felt like we were using scrum to achieve waterfall.

In a way, I do scrum with SB. Or at least I'm aware of the connections. My whiteboard and digital text files track the albums and songs I work on—the stories I want to tell. The whiteboard includes initials of who is doing the next part. The file has the fuller backlog—the parts needed to complete a song, the songs needed to complete an album; and, for each song, any recording or mixing issues to address. I do self-reviews (retrospectives) of songs and plans every week. For deeper collaborations, I expand the scrum team to include the main collaborator.

It's about moving the project along. In a healthy and happy way, driving towards getting things done.

The Gift of Change

In 1990, Orban decided to open a second building (in San Leandro, Ca), eventually replacing the one on Bryant Street in San Francisco, This led to Karen and I moving to San Leandro and a larger house.

(I met Thessalonians Kim and Paul at the San Francisco Orban. The warehouse sat at one end of the block, Hotel Utah Saloon, where I once played, occupied the other.)

A few years later, Orban underwent new ownership (from AKG to Harmon), and they needed to dispense old inventory and unneeded gear previously used for testing. Someone had a great idea. Instead of throwing gear away, why not do an employee giveaway? On giveaway day, I was near the front of the line. As you moved into the warehouse, you could pick something, bring it back to your desk, and then return to the line. Many employees took an AKG headphone or mic. I knew of two very special pieces of gear. On my first trip, I grabbed the Eventide H3000SE Ultra Harmonizer, which I still use as an outboard effects device. Original price $2500. On my next trip, I picked one of a few dbx prototype, unreleased effects boxes. These had Lexicon-based verbs and delays, developed by Paul. Wonderful effects, which I incorporated into early albums I produced (before giving it away as payment for mastering). On subsequent trips, I got an AKG mic and headphones.

While this was a great experience, getting gear and giving a perk to employees, I later realized the event foreshadowed future layoffs.

In 2000, Harmon decided to jettison Orban. They were leaving the broadcast market, and sold Orban to a competitor, the smaller CRL. A year earlier, under my manager's leadership, I began training to move from a technical writing position to a product management position for the Audicy (or a combination of the two). The Audicy was the DAW I was using for my music projects.

When the new owner gathered the managers and leads in a room, my previous manager gone, he asked who the next product manager for the Audicy would be. A coworker said it was him. I was stunned. I stated I was in training for the position, and everyone knew that. No one in the room spoke up. Stunned again. Everyone seemed afraid of the new owner. No one did the right thing. Very sad. The new owner decided to talk to the two of us in his office. He then did a very "biblical" thing. He decided to give the position to a third person. To this day, no one in that room has apologized for what happened. Before the year ended, I left for Digidesign; bigger company, better pay, and much better gear for my music adventures.

The Melting Euphoria Trio Ends

1994 was closing, and after two years, the Melting Euphoria trio of Anthony, Don, and Mychael was showing real signs of progress. We had recorded our songs in a real studio, Kim Cascone mixing one song, artwork completed by Al Stutrud (who did work for Orban and would later do layout for some of my future albums). We were anticipating the delivery of physical CDs. Anthony had covered the manufacturing costs.

End-of-year vacation time beckoned. I needed it. No practices. No gigs. I was also in a couple of Silent projects, and they were on a break as well. This was a chance to finish day job responsibilities and prepare for a week of rest over the holidays. At the top of my to-do list: See my undergraduate school advisor John Taggart, coming to San Francisco for a rare poetry reading. I had not seen John in years. His reading was scheduled for a Friday night.

Anthony called and informed me he had just booked a show on that Friday night, during our off time. I said I could not do it.

We decided to meet at his apartment. I lived at the city's edge. It took me about 30 minutes to get to his place, deeper into the city, and find parking. Our discussion immediately started to get heated, and I suggested we continue talking in the hallway, outside his apartment. My reason: His wife was there. His young son was there. She was supportive of the band, and his time in the band. She might have even helped to pay for the new CD. Still, it felt like we needed some privacy, and a moment to lower the temperature.

I probably said something like "let's discuss this privately, outside, away from your wife and kid." Anthony responded with an unexpected "She's in the band as much as anyone else." This was my Spinal Tap moment. And I didn't react well. The only band discussion where I really lost it and cursed more than a few times. I then quit.

I was so upset that I never did make it to John's poetry reading.

Black Sabbath & Dating

I dated Victoria Fricchione for nine months in high school. June 1973 to February 1974. Vikkie was older, a sophomore when I was a freshman. We met at the program teaching students how to play trombone. We hit it off. We both liked hard rock: Black Sabbath, Blue Öyster Cult, Deep Purple.

As the 1973 school year ended, we began dating. My parents didn't want me dating, feeling I was too young, so we concealed the depth of our relationship. They knew I liked a girl in another town, and she played trombone. We were on the phone a bit too. Eventually, they probably got wind that we were smooching in the corners of the Catholic high school hallways. Father Gotwalt, the principal, was friends of the family. He was part of a card group that met monthly: my mom, dad, two uncles, two aunts, two priests.

They played a progressive rum game called Shang-hai. (My mom and dad taught our family. We had games with them, my siblings, everyone's partner, and eventually my nieces and nephew.)

In June of 1973, I was 14, turning 15 in November. No driver's license for another year and a half. Vikkie visited me in Steelton at least once. We met a couple of blocks from my house, at the Steelton-Highspire Steamrollers football field. There was a playground within the field fences, below the actual football field. I remember us sitting on a seesaw. Not really seesawing, just sitting there, talking.

I was a huge Marvel comics fan. There was a moment where I was buying their entire catalog. Super-hero books, war books (Sgt. Fury and His Howling Commandos), horror books, westerns (including Ghost Rider), sword & sorcery (Conan and King Kull), comedy books (like Spoof), and even Patsy Walker (briefly). I used to walk from home to downtown Steelton, a half mile to the Taxi Stand on Front Street. They had the best selection of incoming titles. Other places on Front Street (like Ray's Diner) had books. They just got them slower. My dad's office at 4 S. Front Street was at the town's center, two doors from a Bethlehem Steel Plant entrance, and across the street from the main bank. When the lunch whistle blew, the town flooded with workers. My dad was the owner of Steelton Coal & Oil. In his office, he and his friends sat and talked in a sea of cigarette smoke. I would often visit during my comic book trips. (Next door was Bernardo's Store, a steelworker hangout). One of the Bernardo brothers, Tony, was my godfather.)

The best place for me to buy comics in nearby Harrisburg was a store in the Kline Village shopping center. A few blocks away, my parents bought groceries at A&P or Giant. The block of eateries across the street included Gino's (whose Sirloiner and Gino Giant probably preceded McDonald's quarter pounder and Big Mac, respectively), a family pub named Lum's, and Amity House—the first place I remember chocolate chip ice cream in a stainless-steel bowl.

When my parents went to get groceries, I sometimes tagged

along. In my younger years, my dad drove me to Kline Village. By my teens, I walked to Kline Village while they did their shopping. On some occasions, I brought my friend, fellow comic book collector Scott Baer, with me.

In the summer of '73, the stars aligned. Vikkie lived directly between the grocery stores and Kline Village. Scott and I would walk to the playground near her house and meet up with her. Scott would take his place on a swing. Vikkie and I would French kiss and so on. And Scott would hum or whistle…I must thank Scott for his part in this. It allowed my relationship with Vikkie to grow, so that we were a real couple into the new school year. (I told my parents about this many, many years later.)

My sophomore year began with Vikkie sharing a locker with Shari Thomas (another new trombone player), and me sharing a locker with her younger brother Toni Thomas (also a new trombone player). We exchanged locker mates. In band, I don't remember sitting next to Vikkie. I suspect that Mr. Frey, the band director might have tried to prevent that. At football games, we were free.

Our dating always felt curtailed, limited to grocery store visits, hallway meetups between classes, band practice, and football games. We did have one class together. Typically, students from different levels didn't have class together. The exception: A language class. We sat next to each other in Spanish class.

Years later, when Karen, my future wife and I began to date and I was staying at her place overnight, I awoke one morning and touched her. She said, "Don't touch me, I'm a Persian cat." I wrote a song—one specifically for a female singer.

Persian Cat (Original Lyrics)

I find a branch that hurts when I light it
I find a place to send sweet signals
one hundred yards, one hundred homes
just a few more seconds of alone

One of the Spirits Burning

If I, if I was a Persian cat
I would lay cash on that
find me a Jack of Hearts
who was a king
and if I, if I was a God of War
and I was always strong
I would slow down the score
and I wouldn't need no more
I get stuck on the seesaw
when I want to be on the swing

I find a brush to paint my body
I'm ready to show my true colors
me and my mate behind the bleachers
root on the team like there's no tomorrow

If I, if I was a Persian cat...

I get stuck on the seesaw
when I want to be on the swing

Somehow...I incorporated the past relationship with Vikkie into the song. The lines "one hundred yards, one hundred homes, just a few more seconds of alone" refer to the Steel-Hi football field and surrounding homes (my childhood home's large backyard tree, visible from the football field). This was the field where a younger me sat with my dad for his alma mater team and loved getting caramel taffy apples (probably made at the chip factory—Utz, then Charles Chips—two backyards behind our house, a warehouse smack dab in a residential section, and whose gravel parking lot was next to my grandparent's house).

The lines about "true colors" refers to the "blue and gold" of my high school vs. the "silver and blue" of my dad's. McDevitt was now playing against Steel-Hi. Or maybe the "brush to paint" and "colors" refers to the Halloween show where I had my body painted, and

Karen was the sound person for the band, and now I was nurturing a relationship with her, with honesty.

And the "me and my mate behind the bleachers" was literal. This was the nature of my time with Vikkie. A football game was an opportunity to kiss. Privacy in a public place.

And the "seesaw" and "swing" made their appearance. This was the key. In the same way that I wanted a deeper, moving relationship with Vikkie in high school, I now wanted one with Karen.

Note: The 1988 version of SB performed *Persian Cat*. The guitarist often called lead singer Catherine Foreman "Persian Cath," I don't think he knew the song referred to Karen. I did write a couple of songs specifically from Catherine's life moments (like *The Train*, on SB album *Behold The Action Man*).

January 31, 1974, Black Sabbath and Blue Öyster Cult playing at the Hersheypark Arena. Vikkie and I wanted to go. Scott was a possible (albeit younger chaperone). His parents wouldn't let him go. My dad said ok with the caveat that he drive Vikkie and I to the concert and then pick us up afterwards. He later commented that the post-concert parking lot looked like "the end of the world."

On the way back to Vikkie's house, nearing Kline Village, we decided to have a bite to eat at Lum's.

This had been a great night for me. The concert was exceptional. From the five-guitar moment of BÖC's *Born To Be Wild* encore to Ozzy peace signs and Black Sabbath's onslaught of their album catalog, including *Sabbath Bloody Sabbath*. On the arena floor, we felt at one with the band and audience. And I was getting extra time with Vikkie at a restaurant.

After we sat, I excused myself and went to the restroom. It was then that my dad had a conversation with Vikkie. He told her that he didn't want me dating.

Soon after, Vikkie broke up with me. If I remember correctly, she dropped out of the band as orchestra season was starting. We also had to deal with the issue of being locker mates.

In the fall of 1977, my first month at Shippensburg, I attended a fraternity toga party. Vikkie was there, standing on the balcony of the apartment housing the party. We were both in togas. We talked. I saw her on campus just a few more times during her 1-2 years there.

(I thought the toga party that night was influenced by the film *Animal House*. However, *Animal House* was released the next year. For some additional fun: The group I was with that night had all attended a school in Harrisburg, Pa. In the film, character Kent Dorfman is described as "a legacy from Harrisburg.")

My dad was a special person. Family and friends visited him at our house or in his office to get financial advice or words or wisdom. A great father. Except for how he dealt with my first girlfriend. My mom later asked me if I would have stayed in Steelton if he had handled it differently. (I added: Or, if I had decided to date more, despite his wishes.) I believe I was destined to move away. The call of poetry and music was growing, as was the influence to take that interest elsewhere.

There were optional elsewheres. I was accepted for a Graduate program that operated in England, on the campus of Oxford University. As someone who loved British music and literature, this was amazing. My dad was unwilling to provide the necessary money, and I had little savings. He was concerned I would go there and join a band. So, he paid for me to go to San Francisco and SF State University…where I joined a band.

The Bane of Bain

For a moment, working at Digidesign was the coolest thing in the world. I was introduced to Pro Tools. Built up chops reading and editing guides. More importantly, I was touching the software daily. I remember when co-writer Mike Freitas (Dot 3 drummer, and percussionist on the SB cover of Santana's *Soul Sacrifice*) said that I didn't understand what a VCA track was and its importance. He was right. I'd rectify that. I could use a single VCA track fader to adjust the gain of a group of tracks (a stem), like the drum stem or keyboard stem, while maintaining the differential of each track's level. I could also use the VCA track to mute the stem or solo it. This introduced a whole new tool to mixing.

I knew from magazines like Future Music that Pro Tools was the Darth Vader of the DAW world. Not the new, cool, loop-based or live DAW. I also knew from Sound On Sound that Pro Tools was the industry leader. They even mentioned my team's documentation as being some of the best in the business. The power and reach were furthered when my team visited Lucasfilm's Skywalker Ranch. They had a room with row upon row of Pro Tools HD systems. Former Digidesign product manager Danny Caccavo (who did mixes of SB songs when I needed help, like *Alien Injection* and *Live Forever*) now worked there and put together the visit for my Tech Comms team. The lunchroom food was great too!

Digidesign employees could purchase gear at manufacturing cost. One of my early raises included a computer tower and some add-ons. I quickly built a professional-level DAW setup for a home studio and produced quality mixes and recordings. It was a good business practice. Eating, sleeping, and breathing Pro Tools resulted in improving my writing and editing, and gave more weight to my voice at meetings and standups. When Avid acquired M-Audio, I soon had two Sputnik mics and bought a Solaris mic for Daevid Allen. I purchased a field recorder (great for recording one of my MRIs, even though the attendants initially said I couldn't have it in the room). I would use the MRI sounds for my Grindlestone project and in a new mix of SB's *Second Degree Soul Sparks*. And I inherited a prototype purple Venom keyboard, which I used as a MIDI controller for the 2017 UK gigs. When Avid acquired Wizoo (A.I.R.), I had a new slew of processing plug-ins and virtual instruments.

With time, came change. Avid, the parent company, was having issues with its video side, and looked to Bain Capital for help. Bain is known for looking toward outsourcing, moving job roles and responsibilities offshore, for example, Ukraine or India. As the years passed, the outsourcing ratio towards overseas work increased, as did layoffs. What the leaders had implied might be a 60-40 split of local to outsource at most, soon reached a ratio with more outsourced personnel. The 2010 day that the Digidesign brand was phased out arrived—the employees hearing this in a crowded lunchroom meeting, yelling in disbelief. Soon after, the letters spelling out Digidesign on top of the Daly City office building were removed.

On a cool morning in late 2011, a week after we celebrated GA for a release, I was informed that I was being laid off that day, one of over a 100, two who reported to me. The HR rep and my boss gave me a strange offer: Do you want to be present when they are informed? I may have surprised them. I didn't hesitate. Yes, I'm still here for this day, and I want to do my job. This includes being there for them. Throughout the day, I talked to those leaving, and those who prepared to remain without us.

I had a fourth-floor office. I briefly closed its door as I talked to my wife on the phone. My office had multiple windows behind me, revealing the street below, the freeways to San Francisco or the peninsula, and the sky that approached a Pacific Ocean that was out of sight. My office slightly overhung from the building offices below me. It felt like my office would totter straight down if there was an earthquake. Looking inward, my office had a large window. You could see anyone approaching. I remember the shape of Thomas Dimuzio…QA tester at Avid by day; well known for his experimental music work; he did some mastering for me, and in the next century would be in The ClimateMusic Project with Cartoon's Scott Brazieal.

Thomas had long hair. He had a larger frame in those days. A friendly giant. A welcome sight. He was peering in with a macabre look. He raised his outstretched hands high into the air in disbelief.

Spirits Burning '87

The definition of done begins with a backlog of lives to live.

Karen Anderson Remembers…

…Where It Began, Went, and Continued Onward

Imagine an 18-yr old freshman [October 1982]. I was in Laura Weber's guitar class at SFSU. Bob is in the class too and he speaks of a band he's in, No Poetry. The lead singer is Meg Lee Chin. She's quite the dynamo—lyrics, vox, stage presence. He talks me into running the sound board at a gig in the Haight. He picks me up in his green MG and drives me to the gig. Heaven's Gate is the first club in SF I've been to and I'm underage. Their former keyboard guy Don is there with Karen West and Hollie Berman. Afterward Bob was too inconvenienced to drive me all the way back to the dorms, so he arranges a ride for me with Karen, Hollie, Tracy (not Tracy Williams), and Don. Got back safe and sound.

In the Fall of '83, I applied for a job at Pizza Boat in the Student Union. The manager guy looked familiar—couldn't put my finger on it. Anyway, I was hired. Was months later we both had an "aha!" moment. We knew each other from the ride to the dorms from the Haight a year ago. I worked at Pizza Boat for 2+ semesters before I left to work at Technical Services in the Student Union of SFSU.

The story of Spirits Burning is one of rising, then crashing and burning, then regenerating again like the mythical phoenix.

In 1987, I was typing my graduation application in the production office at SFSU Student Union, when Don and Tracy (Williams) stopped by (demo tape in hand) to solicit a gig. I hadn't seen them for maybe three years. We exchanged pleasantries, and I told Don I did live sound there. Don gets an idea—he invited me to the Hudson Street rehearsal studio to listen to a practice of his band Spirits Burning. Later, he asked me to work live sound for the band. Since my brief and yet unsatisfying work with No Poetry in 1982, I hadn't worked with a band one-on-one. SB seemed like a good fit—couple people I know from my Pizza Boat days, the others were nice and, more importantly, I liked their music.

Since '86, I was working for trade time (studio hours

in exchange for $) to sit at the front desk/assistant engineer at Hyde Street Studios. Coincidentally, producer Sandy Pearlman (BÖC) was working in Studio C. Anyway, I thought Spirit Burning's demo tape was a little shaggy, so I offered my trade time to make a "proper" demo for the band. Garry Creiman (who produced bands: Specimen, Flipper, Bonnie Hayes, The Mr T Experience) produced and I assisted.

I worked more and more on the band's behalf getting gigs, posting flyers, running sound board live. Don and I grew closer. We have many aligned goals and shared respect. Don and I started living together in '88.

This incarnation of the SB band eventually breaks up, in the meantime Tracy takes the reins of her own band Creative Element, then later Red Rain and her own solo career. I got to produce some of her music, recording on my analog Fostex M80 8 Track Multi-Track 1/4" Reel-to-Reel Tape Recorder at Hudson Street.

Don starts again with a lead singer, Cathy Foreman, then a series of musicians follows. I recorded demos here and there. More tryouts for bandmates. They settle on Doug gtr, Julia bass/vox, Denis Murphy drummer.

We get married August 1989. I remember them there at the reception. Ok, so they work on their band stuff, and months go by and there's frustration. If they got a gig once a month, they were lucky. Little to no airplay and scant fan base. No interest from a manager. 9 or so months into this, the band were ready for a change. Little by little I was getting pushed out. Since I was a little less-than-thrilled with them this was fine by me. They eventually ganged up on Don and quit en masse and even tried to commandeer the rehearsal studio. He told them to get lost or words to that effect. Crash-burn.

All in all, it was a good run working with SB. No regrets.

About KA

I came to San Francisco in 1982 to attend college at San Francisco State University majoring in Broadcast Communication Arts. Learned audio engineering and live sound engineering on-the-job at SFSU Student Union Tech Services for three years. My goal was to be a studio producer. That ran its course around 1991. Came back to State to learn Graphic Arts (analog edition). I continue to use my self-taught digital skills to this very day.

Final Practice

In a letter to my parents, written after an SB 1990 practice, I wrote:

Spirits Burning has broken up. I'm getting back with Tracy (vocals). Kiersten is going to play bass. The old band was creatively stifling for the last year or so, and even though it was my songs (my group?), I didn't feel a part of it. Karen hadn't been supportive of SB for a long time either. She's really happy I'm working with Tracy again. We're calling ourselves Creative Element. We're going to do half my material / half hers. The last SB was starting to feel like work—it wasn't very family like. Tracy and Kiersten are a lot more like family. So that's what's going on musically.

By 1993, the Tracy bands stopped. The collection of musicians, sound people, and even friends of the band, fell to two. Kiersten on bass and me on keys. I was now paying the full monthly rent for our share of the studio. We had one remaining flicker.

We did tryouts for a new SB. Graham Clarke (U.S. Graham, from the Rhythm Monkeys) blew us away. A guitar sound somewhere between U2 and Until December. A bit of echo and cool. A very new, fresh take on my songs. After a practice or two, he brought in drummer Chuck Rimsby. Again, the songs propelled, with sound bouncing off the egg cartons littered on the walls for sound diffusion. It was magical.

After a couple of practices, Graham and Chuck decided against joining. This was the end. I had a day job, and could no longer afford to have a practice space, especially one that had no band, no one to share the cost with, and no one to invest the energy in a local band going nowhere.

Towards the end of that letter to my parents, I added:

> *Spirits Burning doing its last gig. Sunday, Feb 11 (1990). It's being videotaped, and then I'm laying the name to rest.*

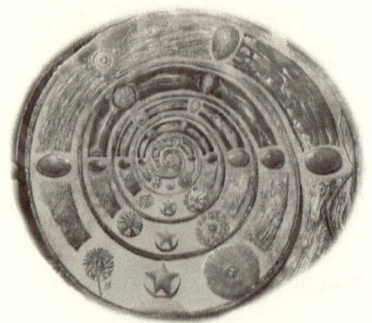

The Crew (295 and Counting)

THIS CHAPTER ACKNOWLEDGES the musicians and writers—the crew—who have contributed to the modern Spirits Burning. When preparing this book, I contacted many of them and asked them to briefly describe their SB experience.

I saw this as somewhere between a thank you, along with a possible learning moment. I was open to whatever they wanted to share. The results reveal some of the behind-the-scenes happenings and thoughts of each contributor.

The crew numbers almost 300. This fed into why I placed this chapter towards the end. In tech writing lingo, it is reference material, as opposed to a concept or task, and should usually be in the back of the documentation.

For a list of which albums each person appears on, see the spreadsheet available at www.spiritsburning.com/thecrew. For information about each person and their music, visit the internet.

Igor Abuladze: Guitar

I was contacted by Don with an offer to record guitar parts on one of his songs [My Life Of Voices]. I believe he heard about me from my friend Doug Erickson with whom we had a guitar trio called Zesty Enterprise. Doug and I met at one of the Guitar Craft courses and shared a genuine love for the music of King Crimson, Genesis, and Yes.

I listened to the rough demo of the song and said 'yes' to Don. It took me about a week to write a guitar arrangement for the tune, and after experimenting with some overdubbed layers, I finally recorded all the guitar parts, created a stereo mix of all guitars, and sent the Wave file to Don.

Don listened to what I recorded and liked it immediately, and I was happy that I didn't receive an email asking me to change anything.

When the album was released and I listened to it, it was almost shocking how well the guitar parts I recorded sat in the mix with the rest of the band and the vocals!

Extra bonus was to hear the drummer Ken Pustelnik from English band The Groundhogs playing on the track! I was very lucky to have their album called Split, when I was only 14 years old, which I still listen to and love. I would never believe it if anyone had told me that one day, I would end up being on the same recording with the drummer from The Groundhogs!

Dave Adams: Bass

As I remember, I got involved because, at the time, I was part of Osiris the Rebirth and, amongst others, we collaborated with Bridget Wishart who also works with Spirits Burning. I was asked to contribute bass to one track [The Real Time] on the Behold The Action Man album. My bass parts were recorded at the home studio we used to record the OTR albums, fairly basic facilities. To be honest, I was a little disappointed with the results on hearing the track. I don't think I played my best and the sound seems thin, possibly why I wasn't asked to contribute again.

Daevid Allen: Guitar, Vocals, Bass, Lyrics

From the *Elevenses* one-sheet:

> *Christopher David Allen (13 January 1938–13 March 2015), better known as Daevid Allen, sometimes credited as Divided Alien, was an Australian and had a brilliant career as a poet, musician, artist, and one-time cab driver that spanned over fifty years. Daevid was constantly pushing boundaries and was always the center of activity. He continually inspired those around him to be creative and to achieve their best.*

The Daily Telegraph said:

> *Allen revelled in being the court jester of hippie rock and never lost his enthusiasm for the transcendent power of the psychedelic experience. He once remarked, 'Psychedelia for me is a code for that profound spiritual experience where there is a direct link to the gods.' That he never attained the riches and fame of many of his contemporaries did not concern him.*

Andy Anderson: Percussion

When I first contacted Andy, I wrote:

> *I'm married to Karen (Anderson), one of your newer Facebook friends and 'long lost' cousins.*

They used to joke online about being related, which they weren't. "Actually, don't know if she mentioned this, but her dad's nickname was Andy (from Anderson), so he was an Andy Anderson of sorts." Andy responded that "My Dad was a pro boxer (Cliff Anderson) here in the UK, way back in 1948-51, And my nickname is Andy (from Anderson) too."

While preparing to replace drums on a song I was working on,

Andy's Mac died. He purchased a new laptop, updated his version of Reason software, and then recorded his drums. He initially sent an mp3 for review, and then sent the .wav version.

Andy died 26 February 2019.

Bruce Anderson: Guitar

Bruce played on *The Eagle Has Landed*, a Malcolm Mooney & The Tenth Planet song that Mal provided to the first album.

Dave Anderson: Bass

Dave is an example of a contributor who is on a couple of albums, is busy when next invited, and then returns to the crew a few years later (once, four albums later).

Karen Anderson: Vocals, Guitar, Percussion, Lyrics

Karen remembers four of the many songs she contributed to:

Salome - Alien Injection

Don demoed the song for me, and I thought it lacked guitar scrunchiness. He was ok with me trying something on my black Strat. I came up with a crunchy sound for the chorus and some weird metallic sounds.

Sarah's Surprise - Earth Born

Indy, my chow chow and I went into a hot recording room. I was to supply background vox for Sarah's Surprise—and on a lark, I had Indy pant into the mic as a percussive element.

Stellar Kingdom - Starhawk

Don didn't have anything—so I came up with Stellar Kingdom on my own. He added a sentence at the end to get writing cred. Loser! (LOL).

Xara's Poem - Starhawk

Words were already written by Mack Maloney, so I concocted an English kinda melody.

For Karen's special entry, see *Definition of Don(e)*; Additional words in *17. Tips - $ense*.

Yanik Lorenzo Andreatta: Bass

For the *Healthy Music* album, Yanik was my contact for members of Universal Totem Orchestra, a band that I was briefly label mates with on Black Widow Records. Yanik and two of his bandmates started the song *Infinite City*. Yanik also delivered vocal and guitar parts for a second song—*Our Secret Cloud*—which he didn't play on.

Deb Angelosanto (formerly Nash): Guitar, Organ

It was such a thrill to be part of Behold the Action Man. I remember being both thrilled and terrified to be part of it, afraid I wasn't worthy, but privileged to play on the tracks Every Space Opera and This Mark You Make with such notable musicians. Don is a mixing master; he blended my acoustic guitar and iron organ parts in so precisely. Both songs have such a cool groove!! A true honor!

Carroll Ashby: Trombone

Carroll was part of the Mushroom jams that Pat Thomas provided for use on the *Reflections* album.

Jsun Atoms (Jason Adams): Vocals

The opportunity to contribute to this musical interpretation of Michael Moorcock's legendary novel with members of Blue Öyster Cult, Chrome, Helios Creed, and The Groundhogs was a true gift. When listening back to In The Future, it makes me feel like we did An Alien Heat cosmic justice. There's a Bowie Starman feel

that would make any music lover proud. I love that
Michael Moorcock added to the vocals himself. Don
Falcone did an incredible job of bringing these world class
musicians together to create this incredible experience.

Takahashi Atsuki: Drums

Takahashi played on a version of *Pink Lady Lemonade* that Makoto sent to me, and I reworked into an SB song. This included me sampling his exposed drums to create a new tribal intro to the song.

Ryan Avery: Violin

Don first invited me to collaborate while we were both
working at Avid. I tend to record violin tracks in my home
studio and provide the stems to artists so they can do what
they want with that. And I believe that's what we did
with Spirits Burning.

Don's style of music is different than what I normally
play violin on (which is mostly electronic). And it's
always fun spreading my wings to see what sort of fun
style mishmashes can occur when playing different styles.
Between some initial ideas Don had for where a violin
might sit, and a few takes of improved lines and
additional backing violins, I think that's how the
collaboration tended to occur.

Ileesha Bailey (now Collins): Vocals

Ileesha sang on two albums: *Crazy Fluid* and *Starhawk*.

Harvey Bainbridge: Synth

Harvey's first SB input was for *Bloodlines*. After that album, Bridget and I commissioned Harvey to provide a lengthy track of synth performances that we could use as starter material for future songs. These found their way into the third Spirits Burning & Bridget album, plus two SB & Michael Moorcock albums.

Mark Barkan: Lyrics

Al considered Mark skillful in songwriting and brought him onboard for *Seven Finger Solution*. Mark was previously credited for co-writing songs for The Archies and The Monkees. Mark also wrote songs for Olivia Newton-John's first film, 1970's *Toomorrow*, quite likely the first sci-fi space musical. Olivia's band features an instrument, the tonaliser, which creates sonic vibrations that get the attention of aliens. Shades of the musical instruments as weapons in the 1976 book *Time Of The Hawklords*.

Giuliano Beber: Guitar

Giuliano adds spice to my favorite song on the *Healthy Music* album— *Our Secret Cloud*.

Steve Bemand: Guitar

Spirits Burning was brought to my attention by Bridget, my long-time musical collaborator, through Facebook around 2008. I was not playing in a live band at the time, although I was periodically recording music with Richard Chadwick.

I contributed guitar to a track [Hit The Moon] and from then recorded for a number of tracks over the years to Don's internet musical collective.

The music was multifarious, but well played and produced. By having so many diverse influences it was multifaceted.

Some tracks I've played on have been with some great musicians who I'd be unlikely to meet to play music with, in the flesh. Quite an assemblage!

For Steve's special entry, see *Bridges to the Plumley House & Extended Hawkwind Family*.

K. Soren Bengtsson: Guitar

darXtar were busy writing and recording our Tombola album at the time. I did however want to contribute with something since a lot of great musicians were onboard, so I did the lead guitar and e-bow for the track Snakebite Serum, utilizing a completely different style from what I did in darXtar. I also used an earlier recording of Dr. Patric on saxophone which didn't fit on the Tombola album. I believe it ended up on Delicious Marsupials. It's always fun to be part of projects like these, but sometimes the planets won't align.

K. Soren also contributed to two other first album songs: *The Unknown* and *Solar Campfires / CellularPhonics*.

Erin Bennett: Vocals

It was a real pleasure working with Don and Spirits Burning. It's always nice to get an insight into the process of other artists and I was glad to be a part of this project alongside such legends such as Michael Moorcock.

Bond Bergland: Guitar

Bond provides one of the "stealth" instruments to the intro of *Beautiful Stealth, In A Church* on the debut album.

Robert Berry: Vocals

When Don wrote me to see if I'd sing a song on his new album, I was intrigued but of course wanted to hear the music and read the lyrics to make sure I could do it justice. Interesting to me, We Move You reminded me of something I had done for Geoff Downes when he was working on a stage show of Video Killed the Radio Star. The key was lower than I usually sing, and the melody was smoother in presentation which lent to me using a bit more vibrato than usual. Great finished track, cool big production style and sound, success by all that participated.

Louise Bialik: Vocals

Silene's Light was passed to me in 2007 through an .MP3 file over a Dropbox link messaged to me on Myspace. I was then collaborating with Simon House and Alan Davey, Comitatus and 17 Pygmies. I fed the audio file into my Pro Tools processor utility then recorded three-part harmonies in soprano, falsetto, contralto. "In the end it's done, then comes the sun" reminded me of The Flintstones' Pebbles and Bam Bam Let The Sun Shine In, Face It With A Grin tune, so I evoked that sunny angel hippie energy, compiled the vocals, then bumped a vocals mix which I shared with collaborators Davey, House, Michael Mayr and Simone Bardazzi. Mayr and Bardazzi and I were finishing up on Comitatus' Portable Casanova with producer Kramer.

Jon Birdsong: Trumpet, Whistle

Jon was part of the Mushroom jams that Pat Thomas provided for use on the *Reflections* album.

Eric Bloom: Vocals

Eric provided narration to two songs on *The Hollow Lands*. Al recorded him offstage, at a Blue Öyster Cult gig.

Andy Bole: Guitar

I met Don at Kozfest, a great little psychedelic rock festival in England. A lot of the musicians that play at Kozfest are part of the global Gong family and Don was there checking things out.

Don [previously] asked me to contribute to the album Make Believe It Real. A few weeks later, he sent me the track Embers, which I contributed some Bouzouki and Glissando Guitar to. I just revisited the album a few weeks ago and I'm very proud to have contributed.

Paul Booth: Flute

Ian East put me in touch with Paul while Paul was on the road with Steve Winwood. I had asked Ian for a Celtic flute part for the *Roadmap* piece *Fuel For The Gods*, and he felt that Paul could help. Paul had a low D whistle with him (metal not wood), which was the right key for the song, and was able to record from his hotel room.

Albert Bouchard: Drums, Vocals, Multiple Instruments, Lyrics

Al debuted with SB on *Behold The Action Man*, followed by *Healthy Music In Large Doses*. He then became a major collaborator for the Spirits Burning & Michael Moorcock albums.

For Al's special entry, see *In a Deeper Fix with Michael Moorcock*.

Joe Bouchard: Vocals, Guitar, Trumpet, Lyrics

When I first heard of the Spirits Burning project, I didn't know what to expect. My brother Albert sent me demos of the songs and I started working on vocals post haste. The melodies and phrasing were challenging, almost like contemporary classical music. It took me maybe a week to find the style of singing needed for those songs, but I was very happy with the results. Also, it was a great honor to be featured on those recordings along with so many great singers and musicians.

Paul Braunbehrens: Bass

I have no idea if Paul knows that he is on an album. I've been unable to locate him. He was in a late 80's SB, and I used an instrumental loop from one of our demos in a new version of our *Every Opera*, retitled *Every Space Opera*.

Scott Brazieal: Keys

Scott and I were bandmates in the Third Floor project in the 80s and contributed to Gary Parra's Trap in the 90s. We reconnected in the 2000s at a get-together for Kellie Campbell, Scott's former girlfriend and third-floor roommate, who now had cancer. We performed a song or two at the ceremony for her after she passed away.

Subsequently, Scott contributed keys to the *Crazy Fluid* and *Healthy Music* albums. For *Part 2,* I asked Scott to create the initial rhythms and tracks for *The Parade* piece—perhaps in a Haydn style, since he was mentioned in the book. I gave Scott the lyrics, which mentioned instruments in the parade. The final song includes eight musicians and over a dozen instruments, plus Mike's reading. When Joe Bouchard added trumpet, he noted that it had a Bartok feel.

Alan Sitar Brown: Sitar

My experience of being part the Spirits Burning and Clearlight album The Roadmap In Your Head was magical and one of the most comfortable recording sessions I've ever attended. It was great to collaborate with fine musicians from around the world. The album is a masterpiece from the cover artwork to the brilliantly produced and arranged compositions. I was more than thrilled with the finished product. It was an honor to be part of the album.

Roz Bruce: Vocals

Roz sings lead vocals on *Part 2* track *Put The Kettle On*. Her YouTube band videos convinced me that she had the voice I needed for *Kettle*. (I missed her Kozfest 2017 performance; she played on Sunday, after I had left.)

Vaughan Burton: Guitar

My involvement began as a result of my having worked with Albert Bouchard. I'm very fond of Michael

Moorcock's Dancers trilogy; I started writing a song about a moment in The End of All Songs, the final book in the series. Albert felt that the track could fit and asked that I send the demo to Don Falcone. I recorded a more pristine version that Don framed between his own moody, dreamy passages. Sometime afterward, Don invited me to contribute to two other songs in the concept.

J. J. Cache: Drums

J.J. was part of the Spirits Burning vs. Spaceship Eyes live ensemble. He also played on SB's cover of Genesis' *Return of the Giant Hogweed*.

Robert Calvert: Vocals, Lyrics

From Wikipedia:

Robert Calvert's Centigrade 232 tape recitation was first used with music on the second Spirits Burning album Reflections In A Radio Shower, released in 2001. Don Falcone took the original recording of Calvert reading his poem Centigrade 232 and integrated it into the track Drive-By Poetry. Lines from another Centigrade 232 poem (Ode To A Crystal Set) appear on the CD's opening track Second Degree Soul Sparks.

Once upon a time…"Robert Calvert, Art Hero and Inventor" by Don Falcone, November 15th, 1997. Originally written for the Robert Calvert "spirit of the p/age" website produced by Knut Gerwers, now housed on the Aural Innovations site; also republished in Progression magazine, issue 36, Summer/Fall 2000. Visit http://www.aural-innovations.com/robertcalvert/oncalvert/onmain/falcon.htm.
    Calvert died 14 August 1988.

Michael Camaro (Mikko Savolainen): Drums

Michael was part of the recording with Dark Sun bandmates Santtu and Juha that laid the foundation of the song *Alien Injection*.

Dave Cameron: Drums

Dave was part of ST 37 recordings provided for use on two albums.

Marc Capelle: Keys

Marc was part of the Mushroom jams that Pat Thomas provided for use on the *Reflections* album.

Kevin Carnes: Drums

Kevin worked at The Pizza Boat at SF State a few years after I managed there.

And Kevin's 80's bands practiced at the Hudson Street space across the hall from my bands. Decades later, I reached out to him to play drums on two *Healthy Music* tracks.

Along with Karen, Sam Herzberg, Tracy Williams, and myself, that makes four Pizza Boaters to have been on SB releases.

Nat Carsten: Percussion

Don asked me to play on Spirit Burning's Starhawk album about one year after I had been laid off from where we had once shared a neighboring cubicle wall at Dolby. I showed up at his lovely home studio in San Bruno in an admittedly downtrodden and severely stoned state, having still been unemployed for the entire prior year.

Don asked me to play on three songs, of which he already had a few ideas for me to play some unconventional percussion upon. During the session, I was feeling particularly inadequate, and that I had provided sloppy, platitudinous performances that I had left feeling a bit ashamed of myself with, at the end of the day. However, once I received and listened to the final record, I was floored to hear how Don had managed to use just about every sound that we had recorded to great effect!

On the Peter Gabriel-esque JigSawMan Flies A

JigSawShip, we came up with a few simple patterns and tracks using various home objects (like tapping a pen cap on a can of compressed air), and then he also seemed to snazz up a pretty fitting lick of my rat-tat-tapping upon "checkers and backgammon" (...boards with drumsticks, I presume? I honestly only vaguely remember recording that particular part, today, but it sounds great)!

Stellar Kingdom sees me playing some snare drum bits that Don floated just on top of the mix, like Cool Whip on ice cream, whilst also answering along with some of his own apt soft-electronic kick drum punctuation points.

When I arrived at This Time, This Space, I was (and still am!) extremely flattered, impressed, and moved to immediately discover that Don had very lovingly arranged the first twenty seconds of the intro into a dedicated percussion piece, solely using tracks which I had recorded separately, yet still hadn't heard layered together at all, until that moment!

When I finished listening to what Don had magically done to my performances, all of my residual shame dissolved, for Don had healed it with his magical mixing powers; a mix of which still stands up quite strongly today, ten years after its release!

Daniel Todd Carter: Drums

I was contacted by Spirits Burning leader/producer Don Falcone regarding whether I would be interested in contributing to Spirits Burning as a drummer. My experience was positive, though it did take quite a long time for the original drum tracks to appear on a Spirits Burning album. I contributed two original drumtracks via my Roland V-Drums to two songs for the Crazy Fluid album. Don made them even better, polishing the drumtracks up to a high gleam, and when I finally heard the end result, I was quite impressed.

A few years later, I reached out to Don, and he extended an invitation for me to contribute an electronic Wavedrum tabla part for In Search of Friends On the Day of Masks, which ended up on an album titled Healthy Music In Large Doses. Although I tracked the electronic tabla track quite well, I felt my track was quite buried in the mix and it was rather hard to hear my final performance on that track. Though…again, I was quite happy to be on this album in the Spirits Burning fold, because I've always felt that this particular title was one of the better releases that this collective has released.

This band/collective/project has always strived to significantly improve itself and grow, and progress forward, and that is why some of the best musicians from legendary bands and projects have contributed their talents.

Cotton Casino: Voice

Cotton's contribution was included on a version of *Pink Lady Lemonade* that Makoto sent to me, and I reworked into an SB song. Makoto credited Cotton with vocals.

To this day, I cannot hear any voice, except for Karen's singing that I added locally. Maybe Cotton's voice was processed to the point that it sounds like something else. Maybe they were so low in the mix they are lost.

There is an AMT version of their song that credits her with "Voice, Other (Beer & Cigarette)."

Richie Castellano: Guitar, Vocals, Percussion, Lyrics

I got involved with the Spirits Burning project through Albert Bouchard. He and I got to work together on Blue Öyster Cult's anniversary shows and we both wanted to do more. At first, he and Don Falcone would send me tracks to play and sing on. That was fun, but I really enjoyed getting to write with Albert. I went to Albert's apartment, and I was amazed by how quickly he worked. We wrote To The Time Machine, At Last in under 2 hours. Both Albert Bouchard and Don Falcone are incredibly prolific guys and it's always a pleasure being part of their musical visions.

Richard Chadwick and Steve Bemand, onstage with Spirits Burning, 2017
(photo by Jack Gold-Molina)

Richard Chadwick: Drums, Percussion

I didn't know much about Spirits Burning, I'm not on the internet and don't like writing letters and chatting to people I don't know on forums.

Steve my old mate asked me if I'd join in what I subsequently realised would be a rare live performance of the project in England and happily agreed.

We rehearsed the band at Rockaway Park, a brilliant place.

Don turned up for final rehearsal before we did two gigs, one in Bath as a warmup and then Kozfest—both were shambolic masterpieces of futuristic space rock… mmm… Nice.

Keith Christmas: Vocals, Guitar

I invited Keith to sing lead on a *Starhawk* song, *JigSawMan*. I told him the in-progress song currently had instrument parts by Cyrille, Steve (York), and me, and there would be some background singers.

Keith accepted the invitation, and let me know that he used Logic Pro. When he delivered his vocals, he surprised me with a guitar track—it was exactly what the piece needed.

Michael Clare: Bass

I came to Spirits Burning because of my association with Daevid Allen. I had been working with Daevid as his US representative (which doesn't mean as much as you might read into it) and was road manager for Gong's first ever US tour in 1996. At the end of 1998, we started a band: University of Errors. Around that time, Daevid did some recording with Don for the first Spirits Burning album; when it came time to make the second one, Don asked me if I would like to contribute to it. 'Sure' I said. Don gave me some basic rhythm tracks to work with and then I went to his studio in San Leandro, CA and recorded. This would be the same pattern for all of my contributions to

Spirits Burning until I moved away from the Bay Area in 2004. After that, I contributed my parts remotely. Don would send me the basic tracks and I would record the bass part and send it back to him. I was always pleased with how Don integrated my bass parts into the songs.

For more from Michael, see *Two Weird & Other New Spells with Daevid Allen*.

Graham Clark: Violin

I don't really remember much—I know that Michael Clare picked me up and drove me over. That is all I remember really.

Andy Colquhoun: Guitar

Andy provided guitar for the song *Peace and Love* for *Part 2*. During research, I discovered in the PoliceWiki that "Andy Colquhoun played guitar in the Rockets and was considered as The Police's guitarist when Stewart Copeland started the band. Andy Colquhoun however wanted Stewart to join the Rockets."

Alisa Coral: Percussion, Synth

I bought the first two Spirits Burning CDs when they were released so I knew about the project right from the beginning.

When Don contacted me about recording for it in 2019, I was very surprised but also flattered because I thought he didn't rate me high actually. Of course I agreed to join his amazing ensemble of great musicians and my favourite writer Michael Moorcock.

I was moving my recording studio to another apartment at that time so basically had only a laptop and soundcard at the moment. But I think the recordings turned out alright. Don Falcone is a legend!

Jaime Cortinas: Bass

I remember Strafed By a UFO, and how wonderful it was to be involved with musicians spanning different continents. I believe Daevid Allen was in Australia, yourself and others from the US. I thought that was pretty cool. It was interesting laying down a bass track and hearing the final results was a delight. In essence it allowed me to be a part of a musical collective that I never believed possible.

Chas Cronk: Bass

My contributions were recorded remotely (as I guess most people's were). It was a shame not to meet other folk involved, though of course that would have been entirely impractical! It was, however, a wonderful experience to be asked to take part in an SB project along with so many people I greatly admire, and I thank you sincerely for asking me. I'm honoured to be a crew member!!

David Cross: Violin

David was one of nine violinists featured on the acoustic-based *Evolution Ritual* album. He was also part of one of my favorite King Crimson line-ups.

Crum (Julian Crimmins): Synth

When I had a request from Don to use one of my songs for the magnificent Spirits Burning The End of All Songs, I was ecstatic as I knew the high standards of his previous releases were very well respected by folk here in the UK. It was a pleasure collaborating with Don from start to finish & how he keeps so many musicians 'happy' is a testament to his attitude, which is first class.

Carlton Crutcher: Drums

Carlton was part of ST 37 recordings provided for use on the *Reflections* album.

Joel Crutcher: Guitar

Joel was part of ST 37 recordings provided for use on two albums.

Andy Dalby: Guitar, Vocals, Bass

My brief time with the Spirits Burning: I think we must have been 'friends' on Facebook. Don messengered me to see if I'd like to be involved with his Spirits Burning/Michael Moorcock project. Presumably he was aware of my work in the distant past with Arthur Brown's Kingdom Come. The first two KC albums could be called progressive and were quite complex musically, the third was more space rock.

After my hippy prog time with ABKC ended in the mid 70s, I did quite a lot of session work, you never really know what's involved until you turn up, you have to be prepared for everything. You also have to take as many instruments and toys as you can carry because if you forget the (insert appropriate effects pedal, acoustic, dobro, slide, wah wah, etc.) you can guarantee that will be the one thing they can't do without!

So, the opportunity to work on songs/music from the comfort of my home studio was very appealing. I'd done a bit of file swap work, so I knew what to expect. At first, I was sent a list of chords, time signatures and tempos to work with. Later I would be working to anything, from just keyboard parts to everything except my guitar bits. Don seemed to like what he heard so I kept on keeping on.

I've always enjoyed working with time signatures, so I wasn't fazed by any of the weird stuff. I find the challenge enjoyable, in fact the whole process has been very enjoyable. It's a bit nerve racking working on something for days, to then send it off to a different time zone and have to wait for it to be 'marked'. At least in the studio they tell you straight away if they hate it! Anyway, as I said, Don has liked pretty much everything I've done so all good there.

I think the project is now complete so who knows what's next. I am 75 after all!

Tom Dambly: Trumpet, EVI

When Don first invited me to participate in a Spirits Burning project, I really wasn't sure what I could contribute to a progressive rock outing as an avant classical trumpet player. But after checking out a few tracks, I realized that he wasn't looking for traditional horn lines and that there was a lot of room for creative experimentation. The working mixes came with very little in the way of instructions. Each track was like a self-contained puzzle that presented its own challenges.

I usually started by looking for ways to play along with the sounds that were already laid down. Early on, I spent a lot of time trying to analyze the structure of the tunes and either double or answer lines played by flute, sax, violin, guitar, or percussion. Later, I stopped trying to fit in and stretched out a bit, with countermelodies or harmony parts where they made sense. Some tracks with electronic textures were ideal for muted effects, analog EVI sounds and other extended timbres, like playing a trumpet with a clarinet mouthpiece or an oboe reed.

Little did I know that I was joining a huge collective—a virtual band of sorts—of accomplished musicians from all over the map, geographically and musically. In addition to Spirits Burning, I had the pleasure of playing on other projects with Don, such as Weird Biscuit Teatime and Quiet Celebration, which I remember had a really nice ambient vibe. I usually sent a good bit of material in response to these projects, and it was always fun to get the finished tracks and hear what Don chose to do with the sounds I lobbed his way. I never anticipated that such sonic alchemy was possible!

DarkSanttu, a.k.a. Santtu Laakso: Bass

I had been following Spirits Burning from the beginning and reviewed their albums for our psychedelic music site Psychotropic Zone. Don also knew Dark Sun, my space rock band at the time. I had this tune in my head that we recorded for the project with our drummer Mike Camaro (Mikko Savolainen) and guitar player Yur Zappa (Juha Häikiö). I can't even remember the initial name, but after some hard work by Don, Kev Ellis, & Capt. Black etc. it became the title track of the album Alien Injection.

The whole project went really smoothly with Don giving some info along the way.

I was really happy and proud of being part of the Spirits Burning community. The best thing was that Alien Injection was released not only on CD but also on vinyl by Italian label Black Widow Records. I still cherish the fact that me and my Dark Sun buddies got to be part of this.

The Spirits Burning project was also very influential for me when I started my own psychedelic project Astral Magic in 2020. The idea to collaborate with musicians from all over the world online was very useful during the pandemic as most of us were locked in. It really works well with most people who have the ability and energy to record their parts at home. Some of the Spirits Burning family members are also now part of Astral Magic Cult. I recorded a whole album (Ad Infinitum) with Bridget Wishart, for example. Kev Ellis also recorded vocals for a few of my songs for the album Cosmic Energy Flow that also features Nik Turner on the title track.

Don has also given me the opportunity to add some bass to two of the recent Spirits Burning albums and I will be willing to collaborate for as long as possible! Always a pleasure to work with Don and the Spirits Burning family.

Roger Davenport: Guitar

Roger provided acoustic guitar on *Reflections*, the disc 1 end of *Make Believe*. Roger probably came onboard via Bridget; the Plumleys used to live a couple of houses away.

I got to meet Roger when Bridget and I passed his house during a jaunt to a grocery and saw him through a window in his kitchen. (Roger and I also did an unreleased track; he played all or most of the instruments and I wrote and sang lyrics, which include the line "I've got a backlog of lives to live.")

Alan Davey: Bass, Synth

Alan initially came onboard via Bridget (for the first two Spirits Burning & Bridget Wishart albums). He subsequently played on five more albums.

Marcus Davis: Kick Drum, Snares, Hi Hat

Marcus was the leader of DRUMCART Mardi Gras 2019, recorded in New Orleans by my Dolby coworker Marc LoCascio. When I expressed interest in using two of their performances, Marcus okayed their use, and Marc provided the multitrack. The tracks became the rhythms for two songs on the *Evolution Ritual* album.

Caron de Burgh, formerly Hansford: Oboe

I remember recording on Richard's tiny studio at the end of a Karda Estra session. The kind of chair that once settled in, there was no room for much moving around! Some great music came out of that room though.

Dead Fred: Violin, Guitar, Bass, Vocals

We diverse artistes and artisans blithely sent our chunks of time-stamped musical concrete to the great crusher Mr. Don Falcone. It is he who skillfully re-combines and blends our wayward notes into many a tasty album.

Len Del Rio: Synth

Tommy Grenas wrote most of the track, Arcturus (for the first Spirits Burning album). I mixed the track at our home studio in LA. I may have added some synths.

Herb Diamant: Reed

I felt honored to be included, I've enjoyed seeing the new releases and I'm impressed by your on-going commitment.

Joe Diehl: Guitar

I 'auditioned' for a band that had an ad in BAM magazine. I declined… and it was mutual, but I got along well with the band leader (Tony Zollar) who passed my name along to Don.

The new band was Kameleon. Joe would later play with me in an 80's version of SB. We would stay in touch in the 90s, Joe playing on a Spaceship Eyes album and a few gigs. When SB started recording as a space rock collective, Joe was onboard again.

For more words from Joe, see *So, You Have Chosen a Band Name*.

Matt Dowse: Trombone

I'd been playing trombone with Citizen Fish for a good while and Jasper put me in touch. When I arrived (I think in the front room of a house in Bath?) I was given free rein to add a part to an expansive soundscape [Storm Shelter]…all of which sounded pretty good already…I'd

*just done a recording with Echobelly, and the vocal
reminded me of that vibe. It was a totally relaxing
experience...in a home...making sounds...I'm listening
to the track sitting on an early morning train with the
sun skipping over the Herefordshire hills. It's making me
smile.*

Jim Dunn: Drums

Jim played on two songs on the Spirits Burning & Bridget Wishart
album *Make Believe It Real*.

Judy Dyble: Autoharp

In 2009, I responded to a question on Judy's Facebook page. I said I
had a music collective called SB and would love to have her
contribute. It ended up taking 7 years. At the time of my invite, I was
working on five albums, and none of them felt right for her autoharp
or vocals. Plus, she was starting to work on lots of projects. In 2015,
we reconnected, and she suggested doing some "random swirls and
tinklings" on autoharp. I was able to incorporate what she sent on *The
Roadmap In Your Head* title track. Judy died 12 July 2020.

Ian East: Sax

I invited Ian to two SB & Clearlight songs. A soprano or alto sax for
Birth of Belief, and for *Fuel For The Gods*, an Irish flute part (kind of the
Titanic movie sound). Ian accepted the invite for the first track. He
noted that he didn't do Celtic flutes and put me in touch with Paul
(Booth), who was touring with Steve Winwood.

When Ian asked for more *Birth* guidance, I collected Cyrille's
suggestions: Flurry place: 4:11.076 to 5.10.211: fast notes in the
treble range. Choruses: 2:35.76 to 3:1.538, 6:009.230 to 7:15.692:
more orchestrated, emotional phrasing. I added "If you want to try
something in the last one minute or so, I can try to weave it in."

Paul Eggleston: Synth

Chris (Green) and I were an improvisational synthesizer band that was generating a ton of material in the late 1990s. 6-8 hour sets in NYC were the rule at a once-a-month residency in SOHO, all brand-new stuff every show. We sounded like a hybrid of tripped out 1970's Tangerine Dream mixed with Klaus Schulze of the same era. The fact that I grew up listening to/worshipping Gong and Daevid Allen and ended up being mixed into the collaboration on one of the Spirits Burning Daevid Allen solo albums is still fairly mind blowing!

John Ellis: Guitar

John provided rhythm and surf guitar for *We Move You* on the *Starhawk* album. An instrumental version of this piece was remixed for the *Recollections* album. John was a special connection for me; besides his work with Gabriel and The Stranglers, he was also part of the K band that backed Peter Hammill, my favorite artist for many years.

Kev Ellis: Vocals, Harmonica

Don first contacted me in 2007, when I was just starting to experiment with home recording with GarageBand on the iPad. The first track he sent me was Alien Injection, a killer space rock tune that had been put together by Santtu and some of the guys from Dark Sun in Finland. I added a vocal and off went the track around the world again with a multitude of amazing folk adding their stuff to it. It ended up as the title track of the CD, which came out in 2008.

In 2016, Don said he wanted to do a couple of gigs in the UK, so rehearsals were organised. Practices for the live band consisted of me, Bridget Wishart, Martin Plumley, Steve Bemand, Colin Kafka, and Richard Chadwick. It was fun to rehearse with these guys, who had all been friends since they were young, they had an almost telepathic musical bond that only comes from long friendships. The day before the first rehearsal I'd had a fairly large day rehearsing with Dubbal, in a pub soon to be closed down and we'd drunk the bar dry...my guys were convinced I'd get sacked from the Spirits Burning gig, but it wasn't the case.

Rehearsals went well, and eventually Don came over from the US and we played a couple of gigs, one in Bath and one at Kozfest. Much fun was had, Don hired a stick drive camper and managed to drive it successfully to the top of a muddy field, I was impressed!

Doug Erickson: Guitar

A mutual friend, Jeff Melton, suggested I reach out to Don, saying he could see us working together like Fripp and Eno. Guitar and synths/studio work/ambient. So, I called Don and we set up a time to meet at his studio. I believe our piece Balsamic Fringe Decoy from our first Grindlestone album one came from that first day, which went well musically and personality wise. After a bit of getting to know each and making sure we could work together, if I remember correctly, our sessions at first either were let's try this and record more as experiments with no expectations or were for me to record additional guitar on songs for his project Spirits Burning.

Then it moved more to Don having a basic tempo or rhythm or idea for a new Spirits Burning song and I would be the initial instrument recorded for the track. Typically, I would have some riffs or chord changes prepped, and then have a session with Don and record in one or two takes, or he might introduce something to me, and I would come up with my part during the session. Like the kids' game of telephone, I would record and then wouldn't hear it again until the other musicians had recorded their parts. Don might have edited or *rearranged my recorded parts so it would go in a new direction that a couple of times I didn't remember recording my part. Because this was Don's studio project, I understood whatever changes he made or the direction the piece went in were like that last kid in the telephone line. No judgement, just different.*

It would have been great to be in the same room with one or more of the other musicians, especially the many professional musicians that I can name drop I "recorded with" lol. First, just to actually meet many of them, and secondly, I might have changed bits of my parts because the bass player came up with this riff or the drummer did that. Adding some variations to my parts due to what the other musicians recorded would have been great as a musician working with other musicians, but in this situation with the Spirits Burning crew all over the US and Europe that's not happening. Overall, a musical adventure I treasure.

At some point in our sessions, we decided to record as Grindlestone with a focus on an ambient album, which eventually became two albums plus soundtrack work ending up on a documentary and a bit of incidental music on random TV shows.

Sarah Evans: Vocals

Bridget invited Sarah, her former Hippy Slags bandmate and guitarist to provide background vocals on the *Bloodline* album.

Thom Evans: Percussion, Jew's Harp

Thom played on two tracks that Melodic Energy Commission started for *Behold The Action Man*.

He also played on a *Healthy Music* track.

Detlev Everling & Renate Everling: French Horn, Double Bass, Respectively

Once upon a time on MySpace, Frank Hensel hosted a series of samplers called myouterspace. There he asked musicians around the world to collaborate. So, Bridget and me collaborate for the song On and On. Later, Renate and I met Bridget and Martin in England. Bridget asked us to take part on Bloodlines.

We made recordings with French horn and double bass and also vocals with our neighbour and friend Gitta Mackay for 3 songs. I wrote a bass-solo for Renate and she complained about how complicated it was. We recorded it...and we are still married! I recorded a very complicated horn solo for Holding Hands, and I was asked by Bridget: "Professor Detlev, could you please record a solo with much less notes?"

I was part of the crew for A Tower Struck Down. I think it was crazy to choose this song for the [Steve Hackett] tribute-album! But it went very well! I did the sequenzer-arpeggios on French horn, only possible to do this in a studio! I like that you used Gitta's 'tooooot!'

David Falcone: Acoustic Guitar

David is my brother and a fixture in the Philadelphia folk scene. For David's special entry, see *Tips - Things That Start with S*.

Don Falcone: Keys, Bass, Percussion, Lyrics

Here, I understand the challenge presented to collaborators when I asked for a few sentences about their Spirits Burning experience. A challenge magnified when I address my entry after completing most of this book.

Spirits Burning has proven to be a good name for most of my music. Forever flexible, regardless of expectations from others.

It has proven to be a special place to collaborate and grow

musically, side-by-side with others from around the world. A gathering place for musicians of different skills and notability, united with like interests or musical openness. It was and continues to be about trying (the attempts), patience (to let things play out), and following through (to put it all together as best one can). Then sharing the results globally. Listening and enjoying.

I am at the life stage where it's clear that music is part of who I am. If I had to choose two words to capture that: Spirits Burning.

My niece Suzanne introduced me to the word ikigai during a family Christmas Zoom call. Wikipedia reads "*Ikigai* (生き甲斐, lit. 'a reason for being') is a Japanese concept referring to something that gives a person a sense of purpose, a reason for living." Google adds: "It represents the intersection of what you love, what you are good at, what the world needs, and what you can be paid for. These four elements combine to help individuals find purpose and satisfaction in their lives."

My day job, my technical writing career, checked those four boxes. Spirits Burning? It never paid much. And I usually think I'm good at it. Well, checking three out of four more boxes is pretty good too. I can live with that.

Ernie Falcone: Pinball, Voice

My cousin Ernie was part of a Maryland basement jam by three Mars Everywhere members and me. I used snippets in the *Crazy Fluid* song *Pinball Symphonics*.

For more from Ernie, see *Tips - Sharing an Event*.

Stella Ferguson: Violin

Stella answered the call when I needed a violin for the *Healthy Music* track *Raised On Coal & Oil*.

Francesco Festi: Vocals

The vocal interplay of Universal Total Orchestra's Francesco Festi and Ana Torres Fraile are part of the elixir that shapes *Our Secret Cloud*—my favorite song on the *Healthy Music* album.

Dave Andre Figoli: Guitar

Dave and Steve Taylor co-wrote the original version of the *Alien Injection* instrumental *Augustus*. They delivered their multi-track recording, and I weaved in additional new material (from Doug Erickson, Purjah, and me).

Don Fleming: Vocals

It was great to work with Al [on Fall In Love] and really just to get to hang with him and record some music together, which is something we have done a few times before (my band Gumball did a cover of BÖCs Beautiful As A Foot that Al joined us on). I was, and continue to be disappointed in the mix that was released. I never get it with mixes that bury the vocal and make it impossible to hear the words. To me the point of mixes is to let the singer tell the story and the music back that up. Especially on a project that is built around the words it is a bit baffling. Mine wasn't the only low vocal, but honestly, I can't make it through the song, it's too disappointing. The process was great, the result leaves me cold.

Catherine Foreman: Vocals

...recording Every Opera at your place...Other than that, it was fun to see you and Karen again and to meet your new dog! It was a pretty quick recording session that day as I recall.

For Catherine's special entry, see *So, You Have Chosen a Band Name*.

Paul Fox: Synth, Sample

I actually don't have a lot of memory around this [recording Behold The Action Man song The Train], but I recall that I'd relocated to the SF Bay area, and was living in Burlingame, right next to the CalTrain station.

There was a friend of mine (Jason Grisell), who was living down in Palo Alto, and he would often come up on the train and I'd meet him at the station. (He and I were doing musical stuff and eating donuts from the donut shop next to the station.) As a sound effects designer for my day job (at Sony PlayStation in those days) I often carried a small recording device with me, and after hearing the train warning bells as well as the passing train, I decided to capture it. I think I'd already done so when you asked me to participate on that track, so it was good timing! I remember that bit more than the bassline.

Ana Torres Fraile: Vocals

The vocal interplay of Universal Total Orchestra's Francesco Festi and Ana Torres Fraile are part of the elixir that shapes *Our Secret Cloud*—my favorite song on the *Healthy Music* album.

Michael Freitas: Percussion

I got involved w/ Spirits Burning when Don asked me if I could add some percussion to a song he was working on. I really liked his Grindlestone project, especially the album one, so was excited to hear what this song might be like. When he told me it was for a Santana tribute album, I was excited, percussion for a Santana tune, hell yeah! Then he told me he'd like me to play Dumbek on it... I thought "OK, that could be cool" and asked what song is it? I assumed something from the more recent (at that time) catalog like maybe Aqua Marine (on the album Marathon) or something else a little outside the main Santana sound. Of course not "It's Soul Sacrifice" he tells me. After a few minutes of me muttering "wtf?" I got to work on it, and it was really fun reinterpreting the song the way Don envisioned it! Thanks again for asking me to participate, Don!

Amy Fry (formerly Hedges): Clarinet

I was lucky enough to be involved in the recording of this Spirits Burning track through being a regular musician for Richard Wileman and his Karda Estra project.

When recording the clarinet parts, I don't always get to hear the whole piece. During the recording process, there is a focus on the lines that I am playing. So, it is wonderful and exciting when I get to hear the finished piece! Holy Water And The Sea Movers is a great piece of musical art and it was a pleasure to be involved.

Craig Fry: Violin

Craig was one of nine violinists featured on the acoustic-based *Evolution Ritual* album. Craig has also contributed to two Spirits Burning & Bridget Wishart albums, and one Spirits Burning & Michael Moorcock album.

Erin Fusco: Vocals

Erin was brought onboard via her husband, Karl E. H. Seigfried. She is part of the choir on *Bloodlines* song *Czaritsa*.

Knut Gerwers: Vocals, Lyrics

A few words about my involvement with Don and his burning orchestra of spirits.

I got involved through my work on the late great Robert Calvert. I'd been working on that website [the spirit of the p/age] for a while, way back in the 90s, when kindred spirits found each other very quickly. I also got in touch with Kenneth Magnusson and his band The Moor, for whom I wrote a couple of lyrics/spoken word pieces, which I performed during two tours through Germany, joined by Mr. Nik Turner. Don asked me if I could do something similar—just via the web and the Atlantic between us. I did two of my own pieces and two lyrics Don had sent me. One of his in particular (In a Church), a dizzying nonesense-rhyme-play, including lots of assing and oofing sounds, was a bit puzzling at first, but after I tried my tongue at it, it turned into great fun. After all: A little Dadaistic injection can't hurt. Those futuristic-space-rock-visions are all too often in danger of getting a bit over-pompous, a little deflation of mindless laughter should be a suitable antidote. The best thing, of course, is the surprise element, when the finished albums come back, and you discover which kind of sounds are surrounding your voice and lyrics. And yes, it was a delight to discover how In a Church and my own pieces Dark Theatre and The Idle Hours of the Fruit Fly had turned out—to hear how a number of musicians— who I had never met—were not just plastering those words in sound but had really listened to them, coming up with sounds and ideas which created a new kind of architecture, new rooms of sound and suggestions around them, thus expanding the whole thing on several levels: ideas, images, emotions, atmospheres…

And another wonderful surprise that came out of Don's online-orchestra approach: I found myself on the same album with the fantastic Mr. Malcolm Mooney, former singer of the mighty CAN. So, Don, keep those spirits cooking.

Steve Gianolio-Jones: Vocals

My first learning of Spirits Burning was through watching Bridget Wishart at a number of festivals we (Electric Cake Salad) were fortunate to be billed at and through playing a number of shows with Alan Davey, for when conversation led to Spirits Burning.

Following that, it was a message from Don Falcone who asked if I would be interested in doing lead vocals on a song for the musical adaptation of The End of All

Songs. This sounded intriguing due to the weight of the other names planned for the album and it wasn't long before I had accepted, and Don had sent me over some lyrics for Don't Concern Yourself with the End of the World and the music. I had to admit that I wasn't familiar with Michael Moorcock's work, but a quick look on eBay brought me to a copy of The End of all Songs for some homework!

After some direction from Don on vocal style, I headed for my home studio and laid down some vocals—this was strange for me to sing someone else's lyrics in a different style to what I have been used to, but now the lyrics and characters made sense, thanks to the book I was able to put some expression into the vocals. Don got back to me after hearing the first take and thankfully was happy with what he heard, so after a few messages back and forth across the Atlantic, the track was completed, and I was really happy with the result.

It was definitely a different experience to what I have been used to but has opened my mind to different ways of working in the studio and with musicians other than my usual bandmates.

Andy Glass: Guitar

Andy played guitar on the opening song of *Part 2*. After his band Solstice opened for Hawkwind, I checked out their YouTube video, and then invited Andy. He was unfamiliar with Spirits Burning and I was previously unfamiliar with his band.

Jack Gold-Molina: Drums

One of the things that I like about working with the Spirits Burning collective is that, after I have submitted my drum or percussion tracks, I never know what to expect for the final outcome. While I am usually provided a basic composition structure as a creative reference, the completed version of the song always remains a mystery until the album is released. And then, it is nothing like what I imagined it would be. There was a track on The Roadmap In Your Head that I was asked to start by playing an avant jazz ride with only a cymbal and snare drum. When it was finished, it was a beautiful psychedelic jazz-rock thing with Cyrille Verdeaux and Didier Malherbe doing these incredible piano and saxophone improvisations. I am always amazed by the album when it is released.

For more from Jack, see *Mistakes Are Made*.

Fabio Golfetti: Guitar

Daevid Allen once told me "Fabio is the best glissando player on the planet!" While I try to avoid inviting people just before or during a recording session or tour, I seem to do the opposite with Fabio. The good news: He says yes, and then contributes when he's available.

Uto G. Golin: Drums, Vocals

On the *Healthy Music* album, Uto and two of his Universal Totem Orchestra bandmates started *Infinite City*; and he provided chorus vocals on *Our Secret Cloud*.

Claire Grainger: Vocals

Bridget invited Claire, her former Hippy Slags bandmate and bassist to provide background vocals on the *Bloodline* album.

Sebastian Grande: Guitar

Sebastian was featured on the Omenopus remix of SB's *Always* (on the Omenopus *Portents* album).

Grawer (Eric Johnson): Drums

Grawer played on the second and third albums, most notably providing the drums for *The Hawk*. I used to listen to his radio show on KFJC 89.7 FM when commuting to work.

Chris Green: Synth

I was happy when Don reached out asking for contributions to the Spirits Burning project that became Found In Nature. Bionaut was in the midst of a creative outburst, and the only question was what to send!

Around that time, Paul Eggleston and I traveled regularly to New York where we performed a long-running series of shows we called Somnaphelia. We would set up huge stacks of electronic gear and play until everyone, including ourselves, were asleep. It was all improvised, and we recorded loads of it. We also often recorded sessions before and after our trips to New York.

I remember a long session of going through recordings and culling out a few pieces for Don. It might have gone for days! I was in the end phase of a years-long sleep experiment I conducted on myself to see how little I needed to function, so that whole time seems to be one long electronic soundscape!

Tommy Grenas: Synth, Guitar

Melting Euphoria, Pressurehed, Farflung, Nik, were bonded by Cleopatra and Purple Pyramid as being the rare structure of Spacerock in California in the late 80s early 90s. When Don mentioned the concept of Spirits Burning, I could not help but think of Daevid's and Gilli's G.A.S [Gong Appreciation Society], cosmic couriers, and of course, and most obviously, Hawkwind Friends and Relations series, where all the HW fam contributed to Frenchy's vision at Flicknife. Now many years down the line, that vessel has remained true for Don and his vision. Back on that early record, Don asked me for a track when everyone I worked with was off on other adventures and what not. We had just finished working on a Farflung record and all the gear was still mic'd up. Basically, I laid down a real shit drum track, put on a guitar, bass, oscillator, ect., ect. I thought Don was going to use the raw track for loops ect. I had no idea what he was going to do with the track. I would not have cared if he had slowed it down backwards and had had his adorable chow chow gnaw on the tape through his mosh before loading it back up. Just had respect he would do what he needed to use it for. It was recorded very quickly, ha ha, I was totally thinking of a Frenchy thing (like i said). Don kept it rather cool and open to mystery. I always loved those HW bootleggy things back in the day. He, Twas, Clever keeping us crustys on our space punk toes. Blessings Don for keeping Spirits Burning alive around the globe. What Nik, Daevid, Damo, Huw, Joel, ect ect would have wanted.

Mike Grimes: Keys

I met Mike through my Exposé magazine contacts and saw his band Puppet Show play live. When it came time to do a cover with some challenging keyboards, I invited Mike. The song: Yes' *South Side Of The Sky* on *Tales From The Edge, A Tribute To The Music Of Yes*.

Rick Hake: Synth

Rick and fellow F/I bandmember Brian Wensing appeared on three songs on the debut album, including *The Ticking of Science*, which features Steven Wilson.

Ami Hassinen: Synth

Ami and his Nemesis partner Jyrki Kastman contributed to four songs on the debut album, two of which I sang lead vocals on: *Speak To The Wind* and *Secret Invention*.

Steve Hayes: Synth

I was excited to be asked to contribute to the tune [La Rue Inconnue, on The Roadmap In Your Head album] and to be part of the Spirits Burning family.

Paul Hayles: Keyboards

When doing parts in 2011, Paul wrote:

> *I'm a great believer on just jammin with what I'm listening to. I put on your track and record a track that I play live to it. Sometimes it works immediately—first take and only take. Some trax, 'cuz of their nature do require a few takes but all 'cept one was recorded live i.e., a take from start to finish. Good fun!!*

Paul died 12 February 2024.

Tom Heasley: Tuba

Ken played on *The Eagle Has Landed*, a Malcolm Mooney & The Tenth Planet song that Mal provided to the first album. I once saw Tom play solo at the Luggage Factory, opening for Thomas Dimuzio, a former Digidesign coworker.

Scott Heller: Synth

Don and I, our paths have crossed here and there over the years and many of my friends have appeared on one or many of his Spirts Burning projects. When I was in SF in Nov 2022, we met in person at a local bar, near where I was staying for the first time, and talked about our space rock projects. Sometime after, Don invited me to play some synths on a track [Part 2 song On Her Island] and it was an honour.

Frank Hensel: Guitar, Synth

Those were the days—the MySpace days! At the beginning of the noughties, I contacted a lot of my musical heroes on that long forgotten "social networking service" (when that word still meant a good thing).

As a strictly amateur musician, I was happy beyond belief to be able to work via internet with people like Harald Großkopf (drummer for Klaus Schulze in the 70s) and ex-members of my beloved all time fave HAWKWIND. Most fun of all was to work with Bridget Wishart then and I guess that's why Don Falcone mailed me to ask for a contribution to his SPIRITS BURNING project.

I ended up being on Bloodlines and Healthy Music... and on ASTRALFISH. These were very small contributions, but I am quite proud to have been a tiny comet passing the SPIRITS BURNING galaxy for a nano second!

Sam Herzberg: Percussion

Sam is one of the few SB contributors who I've known over four decades. He was probably a freshman in college when we met at SF State and the Pizza Boat, where we both worked. I got to see him join his first club band, be the bass part of a rhythm section for his next band's demo, and then see him get signed and tour, and get married. As he lives nearby, he's perfect for home studio percussion recordings.

For some words from Sam, see *So, You Have Chosen a Band Name*.

Keith Hill: Guitar

I got involved with Spirits Burning when Don contacted me about contributing to the Spirits Burning & Bridget Wishart Bloodlines album. It was also great to be on the same track & with a writing credit with the late great Daevid Allen & also appearing on the Spirits Burning &

Clearlight The Roadmap In Your Head album too! Recording wise, everyone contributed a lot & every Spirits Burning album I have heard has a strong eclectic flow through it.

Steve Hillage: Guitar

Steve contributed via his work for Cyrille's *Impressionist Symphony* album. There were unused guitar parts that I was given an ok to include in an SB piece on the *Roadmap* album.

Higashi Hiroshi: Guitar

Higashi played on a version of *Pink Lady Lemonade* that Makoto sent to me, and I reworked into an SB song.

David Hirschberg: Vocals, Guitar, Bass, Lyrics

I from the start admired your insight, courage and vision. Give a project with some parameters, i.e. lyrics to music and throw faith to the small universe of musicians then go ahead and make it work! Kudos to you for an amazing collaborative approach that invites all the players' takes and insights as to what this is and what it could be and ultimately what it became.

I remember after the first day of working on the MM project as Mr. Underwood...I had no prior knowledge when Al presented the lyrics that we then edited to create a little more of a meter and rough rhyme scheme. I was intrigued and a little intimidated at first. By the end of the day, I remember distinctly feeling...what a great day! We wrote lyrics, mostly edited from the text, created harmonies and recorded... What a satisfying day! When can we do more? And there was more and again was interesting, creative and quite a cool buzz!

I was incredibly flattered that you asked me to do a bass part for Bring Back the Living [for Part 2]. I had to let it ruminate for a bit which entailed listening a bunch of times and letting the piece itself tell me what it needed. Once that happened it came together in pretty much a weekend with a couple of requests for solutions to Al. He seemed surprised and pleased with what I had come up with and very quickly helped with the little parts with square corners in need of shaving...I think we were done in two or three takes. I really enjoyed learning the piece and I hope giving it what it needed on the bottom end...it did feel right. And again, really appreciated the opportunity to grow and contribute as well as again marveling at this way of making a recording that in the end hung together pretty danged well!

I appreciate you Don!

Michael Holt: Keys

Michael was part of the Mushroom jams that Pat Thomas provided for use on the *Reflections* album.

Niall Hone: Bass

Niall plays bass on *Part 2* track *The Sun Had Risen*.

Chris Hopgood: Guitar

Chris provided the guitar solo in the title track of the *Alien Injection* album. It's possible that Chris was introduced to me via Kev Ellis, as they both played with Magick Cat. Or maybe the other way around.

Simon House: Violin

Simon contributed to three Spirits Burning & Bridget Wishart albums, via Bridget's invite. Simon's arrival in Hawkwind was really the moment I connected with the band. His violin, mellotron, and synth parts. It was fun and rewarding to follow his career, as he moved onward with Bowie, and then Thomas Dolby (*Blinded By Science*), Michael Oldfield, and yes, Spirits Burning. Or look backwards...when he played with Third Ear Band and High Tide.

Carl Howard: Synth

I met Carl at Strange Daze 99. In my review of that festival for Exposé magazine, I wrote that "Born To Go inherited the Friday headline spot. With a Hawkwind live 1979 snappiness, I'd swear during *Space Rock City* the dual synths of Boone and Howard were bouncing off surrounding trees." Carl would contribute to three of the first four albums.

Ron Howden: Drums

Ron was part of a jam that Lux Vibratus provided for use on the *Hollow Lands* album. Ron died 29 September 2023.

Mike Howlett: Bass

> *The experience was so transcendental I must have entered an enchanted realm, and all memory was erased—for security reasons!*

Mike recorded bass for two songs and then sent them to me via WeTransfer. Given the structure of *The Birth Of Belief*, he said he did a "sort of bass tabla part with a few twiddles here and there. With both parts, please feel free to loop any section or fiddle about as you like—or not use if you don't like it."

Warren Huegel: Drums

> *It was such a treat to be asked to participate in a Spirits Burning recording. Even more special was the chance to connect with Daevid Allen again through something we shared in a deep way—music. I recorded my drum track at El Studio in San Francisco, with Phil Becker as engineer.*

Edward Huson: Percussion

When I worked at Orban, I was surprised to learn that my boss' husband, Edward, played tablas (which he taught me were tabla and bayan). I had come to appreciate Larry Thrasher's tabla parts with Thessalonians, and I was excited to have Edward bring that sound into many of my bands: Spaceship Eyes, Quiet Celebration, SB.

Indy (Indigo): Vocals, Percussion

Of all our dogs, Indy showed the most interest and comfort in my home studios (San Francisco, San Leandro, San Bruno). Always comfortable around a microphone, the musician of our dog daughters.

David Jackson: Sax, Flute

David came onboard for the acoustic-based Evolution Ritual album. He technically provided parts for two songs. There were so many tracks that I was able to spread some of them across two different variations built over Mike Moorcock's harmonica parts.

David has since contributed to *Part 2*, and we are halfway into a Spirits Burning & David Jackson instrumental album.

> *Don Falcone is a mysterious catalyst! As well as being an inspiring musician and musical communicator, Don Falcone is an International conduit through which really interesting musicians from across time periods and continents combine forces and create fascinating pieces of new music with especially evocative and wonderful titles.*
>
> *We have unfortunately never met—yet—but Don knew who I was and got in touch through the wonders of www! He offered me some fascinating music to listen to and contribute to—if sufficiently inspired—and so I was. The titles always get me started and interested; but the space and unusual orchestrations always get me involved—and drive me on to work on a piece I could never have imagined!*
>
> *A 'falcon' (Falco peregrinus—the bird born to stun!) has been important in my musical life for a long, long time, because of a tune called Corpus Christi Carol (by Benjamin Britten). I recorded it for Tonewall Stands. I*

had recently performed this tune live in Guastalla, (Italy) with an impassioned actor telling the vivid story—which features a wounded knight from the Crusades, his may, (maiden), a miraculous standing stone—and a falcon, who hovers above.

As I left that ancient seven-pointed-star-shaped walled town—driving along the River Po embankments with my guide—a Peregrine falcon swooped on the car and flanked us for miles.

It was an unforgettable experience. And so is the music of Don Falcone.

David James: Guitar

I received a mix of a work-in-progress from Don, with a strange, seemingly unmoored vocal.

It took a few listens to find a way in past the voice to really hear the other music and find my way to guitar parts that wouldn't obtrude. Plugging, plunging, subtracting, until I had bits I thought worthy of sending off to Don. Happily, he said he liked the parts for Child of the Moon.

Later, when I was given the final result, I was pleasantly surprised to hear so many voices—including the slightly more moored lead voice—so many layers; and to hear the parts, electric and acoustic, that I had offered being used to make up the final song.

Jerry Jeter: Guitar

I've known Jerry since the early 80s. He has always had a great voice. I'm still trying to figure out why I was Kameleon's main lead vocalist. And he always has a nice touch to various guitar styles.

Some fiery.

Some simply cool.

He lives nearby, such that I can record him here. (He's one reason I finally purchased a Neumann mic, a TB3664 Tripod Mic

Stand w/Boom, and a StedmanXL 6" Metal Pop Filter w/Goose-neck.)

For some words from Jerry, see *So, You Have Chosen a Band Name.*

Jerry and Don, San Bruno Home Studio, 2024 (photo by Karen Anderson)

Barney Jones: Guitar, Synth

Barney was part of a Maryland basement jam by three Mars Everywhere members and me. I used snippets in the *Crazy Fluid* song *Pinball Symphonics.* Barney died 3 July 1996.

Langdon Jones: Piano

Langdon was part of a Michael Moorcock & The Deep Fix demo session track, *The Entropy Tango*, which was used on the *Alien Injection* album.

Mason Jones: Guitar

Mason played on three tracks on the debut album, including orchestral guitar samples on the final track, *ARC - A Real Creeper*.

Nigel Mazlyn Jones: Guitar, Vocals

Nigel provided the lead vocals for *Our Crash*, the opening song of the *Starhawk* album. He also played the lead, rhythm, and gliss guitar on the *Make Believe It Real* song *Cyber Spice*.

Colin Kafka: Bass

Colin was brought onboard for two 2017 live performances, the Kozfest one subsequently released as a live album.

Jyrki Kastman: Synth

Jyrki and his Nemesis partner Ami Hassinen contributed to four songs on the debut album, two of which I sang lead vocals on: *Speak To The Wind* and *Secret Invention*.

Makoto Kawabata: Guitar, Organ

Makoto sent me a version of *Pink Lady Lemonade* with the understanding that I could use their band performance to create a new song.

I met Makoto when he and Cotton played with Daevid Allen in San Francisco at The Hemlock.

Kenny Kearney: Guitar

Kenny played on *The Eagle Has Landed*, a Malcolm Mooney & The Tenth Planet song that Mal provided to the first album.

Simon Keevil: Guitar

Another musician from one of Bridget's former neighborhoods. Simon plays EBow guitar on two *Make Believe* songs: *Journey Past The Stars*, and the remix, retitled *No One Cries In Space*.

Keith The Bass (Keith Bailey): Bass

So, it was Bridget Wishart who contacted me, to ask if I could provide a bassline for one of the tracks for Spirits Burning. I'd just trashed my rather ancient computer at the time, so had to take the file round to a small demo studio near me and record my offering there. It was a bouncy, dubby kind of piece [Skyline Signal], and after trying several different approaches to it, I finally took Miles Davis's advice—less is more—and laid down a very simple line... As soon as I started, it all fell into place beautifully, and I felt like I'd found that missing piece of a jigsaw... I really enjoyed doing it after that— and it only took 3 takes! Proud to have been able to contribute!

Keith ended up contributing to two songs on the *Make Believe* album.

Suharo Keizo: Bass

Suharto played on a version of *Pink Lady Lemonade* that Makoto sent to me, and I reworked into a new song.

Peter Knight: Violin

When the Covid weirdness entered our lives back in 2020, I decided that instead of generally saying 'No' to offers of session work, I would generally say 'Yes'. Tours were cancelled, and the young people immediately began doing concerts from their homes, most of them with not great visuals or a great sound. I didn't fancy that.

Don Falcone got in touch asking me to play Fiddle on a track, and my answer was 'Yes' and thank you.

The track arrived, and there is always that moment when you wonder if you will like it or not. As soon as the track started, I was intrigued. I played as I play and sent my part to Don.

Don has asked me to write a few lines for this book,

and in his email, he included a link to the track I played on, which I haven't heard since playing on it. I tend not to listen to music after I have made it. Of course, working on new albums, mixing, mastering etc., it takes a lot of listening. Once the album is released, I never listen to it again unless it's for reference. So, ten minutes ago I played the track Your Better Angels, and smiled.

Thanks, Don, for sending me good music to play on.

Keith Kniveton, a.k.a. Capt. Black: Synth

Besides playing with Hawkwind in 1999, and from 2000–2002, Keith may have more knowledge about Hawkwind history and equipment than anyone else I have collaborated with. Keith appears on the *Alien Injection* and *Crazy Fluid* albums.

William Kopecky

I remember reading a lot about Don and his prog/ psych/space rock adventures in the prog magazines in the 2000s. I decided to contact him and ask if he needed a bassist for one of his albums. He got back to me straight away and said he was thinking of getting in touch with me as he'd been reading about me and my projects too. Cool.

The first album I did with Spirits Burning was Crazy Fluid, which was released in 2010. Since then, I've played on several SB records, including collabs with Michael Moorcock and Clearlight, and I've been in some awesome company: members of Blue Öyster Cult, Hawkwind, and Gong (to name a few) have all been featured on the same tracks. At the time of this writing, I'm working on new songs for one of his forthcoming releases, and I'm happy to be doing it. The raw tracks he sends me are always full of floating improv moments and strange twists and turns, so they can be hard to navigate, but he always makes everything sound great in the end.

He's a very talented and prolific artist, and it's a pleasure to be on this wonderful, cosmic musical trip with him.

Chris Kovacs: Percussion, Synth

Chris came onboard via Cyrille.

He contributed synth and tabla to the opening track of the *Healthy Music* album.

David L: Guitar

David wrote or cowrote and plays on every song of the *Golden Age Orchestra* album.

He reminiscences:

Ideas and sketches turned into sound
Thom the world poet's words swirling around
The will to create was about all that we had
In the time before, the world had gone mad
An auditory surprise to hear what had been gleaned
From one afternoon in one shared day dream

Tiffany Lamson: Hi Toms, Cowbell, Jam Block

Tiffany was part of the DRUMCART Mardi Gras 2019 performance that was provided for use on two *Evolution Ritual* songs.

Rich Landar: Synth, Mandolin

I was introduced to Don, when our mutual friend Roger Neville-Neil suggested that me and my King Black Acid bandmate, Daniel Riddle might be worthy additions to upcoming Spirits Burning tracks. I received tracks, which typically only had one or two other instruments already in place and was given carte blanche to add what I felt worked. As there were often substantial keyboards to start the tracks, I sent over some spacey mandolin parts, which happily made it onto some recordings. It was always so cool, to see what other players had added to the songs and how our parts would interact. Quite an atypical but excellent approach to arranging and recording.

Jon Leidecker, a.k.a. Wobbly: Loops

Jon got to see and appreciate my early drum 'n' bass work with Spaceship Eyes and was open to providing samples for a song on the second album. Although Jon and I worked together at three different companies (Orban, Digidesign, Dolby), I suspect I was lucky to get his contribution when I did, as most of my experimentations went in a different (what I would call song-oriented) direction than his experimental, electronic adventures.

Alison Lewis: Vocals

I first got involved with Spirits Burning while working with you at Digidesign. Perhaps I'd shared that I was a singer, and/or you'd heard something of mine, and eventually invited me to record background vocals on one of the tunes. My biggest memory of that session was that we discovered, shortly after completing my parts, that the microphone had been facing the wrong way! But we decided that it sounded good that way, and so we left it as is.

I then did some research and found that it was an optional method.

Susie Loraine: Vocals

Al recorded Susie for *Part 2* song *Remember Those Who Have Died (At Least Once)*. She sang parts for both Amelia Underwood and the Iron Orchid.

I don't even know the name of the song, believe it or not! I can tell you that it was a big surprise that I was on the album at all. I think I understood the emotion of the women I was portraying even though I did not really know the whole story. It seems one of the male characters had made some decisions unbeknownst to her and she was angry. It was quite an experience recording because I had never done it before.

Gitta MacKay, a.k.a. Jackie Robinson, Simone, and Gitta Walther: Vocals

Gitta came onboard via the Everlings. A surprise. Yes, there is something extra fun about having one of the voices of Silver Convention. The famous scream in Penny McLean's *Lady Bump*; a backup singer to Donna Summer. More exciting for me though, was her openness to newer, space rock-based songs.

Her haunting vocals on the *Behold The Action Man* song *Rendezvous At Lava Lounge* and the cover of Steve Hackett's *A Tower Struck Down* are wondrous!

Gitta died 10 October 2014.

Bert Mackenzie: Vocals

I got involved indirectly through our mutual friend, ex-Hawkwind Bassist/Vocalist, Alan Davey. Who recommended my daughter, Emma to yourself to do some vocals on the album. You then asked if I would do a very small spoken part as her father as part of the story, as I was her real father anyway, and could I do it in an Irish accent. This I was delighted to do, and it was so easy, as we could do our parts over our mobile phones, and you would incorporate them into the recording process!

Emma Mackenzie: Vocals

After Alan Davey recommended Emma for SB, I contacted her and said I'd like to get her on an album. It took a few years...and I found the perfect place: three songs on the *Starhawk* album where the voice of Princess Xara, the story's love interest, made sense. For good measure, her father, Bert Mackenzie, voiced the part of the king on one of those songs.

Kenneth Magnusson: Mellotron

In 2000, or maybe 2001, I was contacted by one Don Falcone who wanted to ask me about playing mellotron with a project called Spirits Burning. I think he got my name from Knut Gerwers who at the time was closely connected to my band The Moor. There is no way that I would say no to such a suggestion. I played on two songs, one of which was later used on Glissando Grooves by daevid allen and don falcone. Over the years I had the joy to play on some more albums. The highlight for me, who started out as a bassist, was when I on The Roadmap In Your Head (album and song) ended up playing music with Mike Howlett. Just wow! The low point was when I discovered I was invited to play on the Jherek Carnelian trilogy (Dancers at the End of Time really) but due to a mail fuck up (on my part I'm afraid) I missed that boat. When I was young, I often signed with Jherek Carnelian. Good thing they (Post Office etc.) didn't try to decipher the signature. The trilogy was penned together with author Michael Moorcock. Yeah, the same Michael Moorcock we named the band after, The Moor was initially called The Michael Moorcock Experience but was shortened to The Moor. Dumb thing, shortening names.

Oh dear, I really did miss that one. . . I still wake up in the middle of the night, screaming.

Didier Malherbe: Sax

Didier contributed via his work for Cyrille's *Impressionist Symphony* album.

There was an unused sax part that I was given an ok to include in a Spirits Burning piece on the *Roadmap* album.

Matt Malley: Bass

Hearing the songs again—I really loved your Fripp/Eno vibe. I also miss the bass [guitar] I tracked for you—it was a Lakland Decade, black with original factory installed Dark Star pickups, (discontinued and very sought after in the bass player world). It had a Fender P-bass vibe but darker. Kicking myself for selling that one.

I remember really liking your energy—buoyant and otherworldly. Very musical. Working with you was a breeze—you weren't the nit-picky type and you had a trust with the musicians you put together, so you let us fly. It comes through in your recordings; no heavy or tired vibes there...just an uplifting, hopeful look into what the future might bring for humanity. It was a real pleasure to be a small part of this vision!

Mack Maloney: Lyrics

It was such a tremendous feeling when I first heard the music that evolved from the printed words of the Starhawk book. Same characters, same story, just told in another way, through a different medium. I remember thinking, this sure doesn't happen to everyone. And I have Don and SB to thank.

For more from Mack, see *Discography*.

Tony Mann: Vocals

Albert Bouchard is a friend and an inspiration. I had written some songs and he offered to record some demos for me to help finish the tunes. He played all the instruments on the demos and did a wonderful job.

I didn't even drum on them—he did! I just sang. Albert mentioned that he liked my voice, and asked if I would sing on a tune for Spirits Burning that was connected to Michael Moorcock. I knew that name from

BÖC—*Black Blade was a favorite. I discovered there was a whole creative world of Michael Moorcock. I also discovered that Michael had a band called The Deep Fix, who in 1978 played at The Roundhouse in London with The Lightning Raiders—a band I actually played in at some point! Even Michael was surprised at that.*

Albert told me Don Falcone was putting this all together, and that this was the 2nd part of a trilogy. Albert gave me a demo of the song to rehearse to, but the song Conflict and Illusions was more like a dream sequence to me than a typical song. It didn't have a chorus, and it was a challenge for me to get some feel going. The lyrics were written by Michael Moorcock, and the music by Albert and the very talented David Hirschberg. I recorded my vocal track at Albert's home studio. Luckily, Albert produced and guided me through. He said he could tell I had rehearsed it. We made quick work of it, and Albert contributed some other voices to the track, as did Dana McCoy. I know Dana and had seen her perform.

Eventually Don put it all together and I received the CD. Don does a fantastic job organizing the project and making sense of it all. I really like the packaging and the layout of the album. It helps bring the fantasy to life. Don also promoted each song on his page.

It was a great feeling to be recognized among such legendary and talented performers. It's an honor to be among the illustrious alumni of Spirits Burning. Among the 'cast' are some of the most mind bending and thought-provoking individuals. It's a group I respect immensely.

Thank you, Don Falcone, Michael Moorcock, Albert Bouchard, and all the members of Spirits Burning. May you continue to create and inspire. Imagination is a great and powerful thing.

Toby Marks a.k.a. Banco de Gaia: Bass

An unexpected SB contribution: Toby's bass parts for *Rocket To The End Of The Line* on the *Bloodlines* album. Surprising because Toby, better known as Banco de Gaia, typically does eclectic global dance and chill-out music.

Toby writes:

> *I was asked to add a bass part to this track and, listening to it I thought it needed bass guitar rather than synth, but I didn't have one at the time. An electric 6-string and pitch shifter seemed to do the job ok though. Being an old Hawkwind fan it was a pleasure to get to meet Bridget who turned out to live not far from me.*

Fabrizio Mattuzzi: Keys

Fabrizio and two of his Universal Totem Orchestra bandmates started the *Healthy* song *Infinite City*.

Nick May: Guitar

> *What an eclectic mix of styles and influences that [Make Believe It Real] project was! It was really difficult to know where to go with it but at the same time very inspiring to have such a window of wide-open possibilities, a sort of journey into the unknown with only the guitar as a rudder. Interesting also, because it very much involved working with the proverbial 'cast of thousands'—only they were all invisible, so you never knew who you were going to end up playing on a track with. There was a lot of freedom, though that in itself can be a bit challenging because it can easily lead to 'option paralysis' (which admittedly it did a couple of times along the way). Got there in the end though. Overall, the whole thing was a lot of fun, which of course is what counts most in the end.*

Don Falcone

Michael Mayr: Synth

Michael appeared on the Spirits Burning & Bridget Wishart song *Storm Shelter*.

Dana McCoy: Vocals

I have never met Don Falcone and let me be clear. I'm not happy about it.

I have had the honor of singing many characters over a handful of years for this unbridled project. Albert Bouchard brought me in, and I have so enjoyed working with him, he composed the songs I sang on, and the way of it was, Albert would have me in to his studio in his teensy NY apartment, I'd squish between the mic and a couch or a bureau, wherever the mood struck, and Albert would put on these crazy genius tracks which can't really be described. Trying would be reductive, but if I had to under pain of death, I'd say Progressive Sci Fi Fusion Opera Adventure? Nope, that's a total fail, but best I can do. I did not read the book(s?); I did not know the characters; Albert masterminded his part of this world of 'Spirits Burning' and used my voice like splashes of neon color for his otherworldly canvases.

I've never felt so wild and free on any project. There were no rules, no limits, I was continually allowed, no, encouraged! To paint outside the lines. Whatever came to me was welcomed. So, I would hear the tracks for the first time, start singing before we'd even listened all the way through, and Albert and I would get really excited and riff together, fanning the flames of inspiration.

It didn't have to sound pretty, though some of it was heartbreakingly delicate, some sounded like screeching crows fighting over carrion. And the flow of the music was like a long ride on a rollercoaster that roared through interplanetary landscapes.

Don, Albert, Thank you. I really do need to read the

Dancers at the End of Time trilogy by Michael Moorcock, don't I? I've obviously been deeply positively affected by the music the books inspired. It would be amazing to make the acquaintance of all the brilliant artists involved...

George McDonald: Guitar, Theremin

I got involved in the project through Don Xaliman, who I met in the early 1970s. In 1975, he became sound engineer for a fusion jazz band I was playing in called Lion & the Child, also the band where I began my descent down the synthesizer Rabbit Hole. After that band ran its course, we started playing experimental music and collaborating together which evolved into the Melodic Energy Commission. The Franklin Bros Paul & Mark, Randy Raine-Reusch, Donnie [Don Xaliman] and myself. It's always been more of a collective than a band with new members coming and others going on every release. After Del Dettmar & Paul Rudolph contributed to the first and second albums, we kind of became part of the greater Hawkwind family. Which probably led us to Spirits Burning.

Recordings were almost always started from improvisation with one or more musicians done on multitrack, then a good part was selected, and overdub tracks were added. Some of it at Donnie's studio, some at mine. Then Donnie did endless mixing and editing.

I always liked the results of the Spirts Burning releases, the variations that the different artists provided to a single theme.

Pierce McDowell: Bass, Stringed Instruments

I met Pierce when Daevid was staying at his place in San Francisco. I picked up Daevid and took him to my home studio, in San Leandro.
Regarding Spirits Burning, Pierce writes:

I have nothing but positive experiences, other than the issues of working with sound files as opposed to face-to-face players.

When I first met Daevid, it was backstage at the first Gong show at GAMH. It was after the show so there were a lot of people backstage. When I walked in Daevid immediately crossed the room, pointing at me with a revolving index finger. He said, 'I think we have met before'. I found out later from Gilli that they had a French friend, named Pierre that looked a lot like I do. She often called me Pierre instead of Pierce.

For more from Pierce, see *Two Weird & Other New Spells with Daevid Allen.*

Buck McGibbony: Synth, Beats

This former Farflung and Nik Turner tour musician teamed up with Melissa Trancess to produce a completed dance track for the debut album.

Mac McIntyre: Bass

Mac played bass guitar on *Bloodlines* song *Lady Jane.*

Greg McKella: Guitar

Don approached me in 2017 to lay some guitar down on To Steal a Space Traveller for Spirits Burning & Michael Moorcock. At the time, I didn't know who else would be contributing, but was really made up with the finished track when the album came out the following year, hearing my rhythm and glissando guitar play on the track, and with a cast of stellar luminaries.

Michael Merrill: Drums, Percussion

Michael usually went by Mychael in credits. We played in a couple of bands alongside Anthony Budziszewski, most notably Melting Euphoria. As that band was in hiatus or winding down, Michael and I reconnected. Besides contributing to three SB albums and a Weird Biscuit Teatime song, he, Luis Davila and I did an album under the name Fireclan (with me on bass).

Michael was one of a couple of people in my life who died at a younger age, who I had no idea that they were ill, and who left behind one or more children. It's that 'no idea' part that I can only wonder about. The choice of whether to communicate one's health, who to let in on one's final journeys.

Michael died 7 July 2006, of cancer, at the age of 42.

Judy Merryweather: Vocals, Lyrics

For the synth-based trippy dance piece *Be Careful What You Wish For* (on *Bloodlines*), Bridget brought Judy onboard to do the vocals. Judy wrote the lyrics and vocal lines, and then did the vocals. This is the only Spirits Burning & Bridget Wishart vocal piece that Bridget doesn't sing on.

Sindisiwe Mhlnaga: Vocals, Translations

For the *Bloodlines* song *Chaminuka*, Sindisiwe translated Bridget's English lyrics into Shona and Ndbele, and then sang on the piece with Bridget and Daevid.

Dave Mihaly: Percussion

Dave was part of the Mushroom jams that Pat Thomas provided for use on the *Reflections* album.

Bob Mild: Drums

Bob is another Portland musician to contribute to Spirits Burning. Two songs for the *Action Man* album, including the mysterious closing instrumental, *Underworld Messiah*. When I couldn't connect with Bob's bandmate, Jsun Atoms, for his copy of the CD, Bob was kind enough to accept two copies in the mail, and then hand one off to Jsun.

Danny Miranda: Bass

*Albert Bouchard reached out to me and Don Falcone—
Donald Roeser also told me that it would be fun if I got
involved. Everything went well from the beginning. I was
really impressed with the amount of harmonic and
rhythmic freedom that I had, and I was able to really
experiment with different things than I would normally
be able to do, like using echoes on bass, and overdubbing
several bass parts and making a collage of it was very
fulfilling to me and continues to be.*

*I love the variety of the music and the musicians, you
have woodwinds, you have electric guitars, acoustic
guitars, Spacey atmospheres, and these are all of the
things that I am very interested in and it's one of the
most fulfilling things I've done.*

Gabriel Monticello: Bass

*I always feel honored when Don asks me to record for
Spirits Burning. There are so many brilliant musicians
from all over the globe to choose from. I am proud to
count myself as one of them. I came to Spirits Burning
through Bridget Wishart's recommendation on the album
Make Believe It Real. The recording process is one that I
wouldn't have dreamed of until recently. Technology
allows us to record our parts and submit digital copies.
Don serves as that master marionette who gathers our
submissions and ensures that they tell a cohesive and
interesting story. It wasn't that long ago that this process
was impossible and collecting so many musicians from so
many locations would have been financially unfeasible.
What a glorious time to be alive.*

Mal Mooney: Vocals, Lyrics

Mal and I talked about how best for him to contribute to the debut
album. We decided to use my choice of one of the songs from his

Malcolm Mooney & The Tenth Planet album. As is, no additions.

Michael Moorcock: Vocals, Harmonica, Guitar, Lyrics

Perhaps the initial surprising aspect of my correspondence with Mike was when he signed off with "PARD!" Short for partner, particularly in the American southwest, where Mike was spending at least half of each year.

Besides the Spirits Burning journeys he supported and would contribute to, and letting me produce a Deep Fix album, there were some things to learn along the way.

Communication is what's important.

As we get older and our eyes are stressed, larger fonts improve readability. At first, that meant that I made sure to increase the font size in my emails to Mike. And, at some point, I found myself increasing the size of responses from others for my own reading experience. As we get older, our typing skills are challenged. All caps doesn't always mean that you are shouting. It can mean that it's simply an easier way to get the message out. When reading Mike's emails, I try not to over-emphasize my reading of any upper-case content.

For some words from Mike, see the *Foreword*.

Mike Moskowitz: Guitar

I had been a colleague of Don at Digidesign for a few years when the two of us decided to get together and jam at a local practice facility in San Francisco. With Don on electric bass, and myself on electric guitar, we played around with a few ideas and landed on a cool rhythm track. I recorded my guitar track with electronic drum accompaniment to Don to work with, and I was very pleased to see him turn it into a track (Stand & Deliver) with vocals and full instrumentation. The highlight was the lead guitar by Daevid Allen—what a treat to share a track with him!

Mr. Dibs (J. Hulme): Vocals

Dibs provides vocals for *Flurry of New Worlds,* on *Part 2.* I had tried for years to get Dibs onboard, when his Krel and Spacehead bands were often mentioned in Andy Gee reviews, when he joined Hawkwind, and after. I invited him to play bass, and then cello, and then vocals.

Anne Marie Nacchio, formerly Castellano: Vocals

Anne Marie came onboard for the first Spirits Burning & Michael Moorcock album, *An Alien Heat*, via Al. Her multi-faceted vocals on *Soirée Of Fire* and *Quest For Bromley* are two of the vocal highlights of the album.

Giorgio Cesare Neri: Guitar

I have never met Don Falcone in person, but I knew the Spirits Burning collective because I have always loved progressive rock and psychedelia (from the ancient Greek psyche anima and delos to show) and this musical reality was recommended to me by the boss of my label, Massimo Gasperini of Black Widow.

In fact, in 2009, my album Logos was released for Black Widow, and I think that somehow Don became aware of this album and through Black Widow we started a long-distance collaboration.

I collaborated on three Spirits Burning records, including the acoustic project. The song he gave me, prouder and happier is So Strong Is Desire with Daevid Allen, my legend since always and inside me I thank Don for making my guitars and Daevid possible...

I asked Don if he wanted to be on my new album and Don gave me some killer synth parts... So, I can honestly say that I am grateful to Don for having me participate in this wonderful sonic family...and I sincerely hope to participate again.

Roger Neville-Neil: Lyrics

I met Roger at the 1999 Strange Daze space rock festival held in Ohio. Afterwards, we started a 15-year correspondence. He sent haikus and Action Man manuscripts, and I provided feedback and edits. I did the same for stories he wrote for Exposé magazine, where his Action Man detective persona attended live shows in Oregon, including ones with Nik Turner, Lemmy, and others, like Jsun Atoms (which led to his participation in Spirits Burning).

I surprised Roger when I decided to do a Noir-based album with his detective as the focus. He was also surprised that I included him in the planning and review of each song for what became *Behold The Action Man*.

Our last collaboration was with the Spirits Burning adaptation of Mack Maloney's *Starhawk* book. I started the music for a song with a psychedelic lounge feel (based on a location described in the book), titled it *Tripping With The Royal Family*, and asked Roger to write the lyrics. His words wonderfully captured the main character's trips to meeting royal family members one by one.

Perhaps Roger's best SB lyrics were *Stand and Deliver*. On the *Behold* studio album, and then featured as the final song of the 2017 Kozfest gig.

David Newhouse: Sax, Keys

I probably started following Dave's Facebook page, via his former Muffins bandmate Paul Sears. I didn't realize until later that Dave was the long-haired dude with my cousin Diane at some of our family picnics when I was in my teens.

I invited Dave to the *Roadmap* album. First song: *Outsiders Parachute In*. I asked for sax. Dave provided soprano, alto, tenor, and baritone saxes, clarinet, alto flute, electric piano, organ. It literally took the song into new directions. Quite cool ones, in fact. Next song: *Some Demon Cloak Time*. Soon after: *Black Squirrel At The Root Of The Staircase*. Dave wrote "Don! I am LOVING *Black Squirrel*!!! So much fun to play on! Exceptional!" And Dave again found a way to steer the song into new territory, using most of the same instruments he used on *Parachute*.

Dave next contributed to the acoustic-based *Evolution Ritual* album, and then *The End Of All Songs - Part 1* and *Part 2*.

Juliette Norrmen-Smith: Shaker, Glockenspiel, Vocals

Juliette was part of the DRUMCART Mardi Gras 2019 performance that was provided for use on two *Evolution Ritual* songs.

Sean Orr: Violin

> *My experience with Spirits Burning is one of the more unique recording experiences I've had. I had to let go of my usual approach to playing and just let go. I had to envision texture and color as much or more than timing or what notes I was playing. It was much like painting a musical picture. It did help me grow as a musician.*

Monty Oxymoron (Laurence Burrow): Percussion

> *I was very pleased to be asked to contribute to Don's project: I'd known his work with Daevid Allen of Gong, who I'd known since I attended his 'Zero-Initiation' workshops near Glastonbury in the late 1980s. And what a prestigious company Don had involved! I recall a cooking pot was one of the things I used to create sounds with: I like playing objects not designed as instruments. Don later kindly filmed me performing at the 'Flower Piano' project in the Golden Gate Park Botanical Gardens in 2019. My astrologer friend had told me 'something big' would happen the following year (2020) that would disrupt just about everything, so I was determined to take opportunities like that one during time off from touring with the Damned: he wasn't wrong! It's an honour to be asked to join in projects such as those: hopefully there will be more to come!*

John Pack: Vocals

John provided backing vocals to the *Make Believe* song *Demonkind*.

Alex Palao: Guitar

Alex was part of the Mushroom jams that Pat Thomas provided for use on the *Reflections* and *Alien Injection* albums.

Stephen Palmer: Synth, Guitar

Steve is one of the few Spirits Burning connections that I reciprocated his contribution; by providing synth for his Mooch project. Karen sang on both his Mooch and Blue Lily Commission projects. And Steve and I teamed up for an ambient album, *Gothic Ships*.

Ursula Pank, formerly Smith: Cello

I was able to locate and contact Ursula via Luca Ferrari's site: *Ghettoraga Third Ear Band's Official Archive*. I decided to send her *Strolling Into The Future*, a song started by Andy Dalby that was folkier and less experimental compared to other tracks.

As Ursula wasn't familiar with home recording, I encouraged her to try Audacity (or GarageBand). Her subsequent delivery was recorded with a mic in front of an iPad. She was concerned that the quality might be awful. I wrote, "in context, most of the incidental sounds will not be heard. That said, I can eq out any of the sounds that are noticeable. Plus, I will silence the silent spaces between parts, which I normally do." Pro Tools provides many ways to silence parts of a track.

Jasper Pattison: Bass

Jasper played on three Spirits Burning & Bridget Wishart albums. In 2016, I contacted him to play with a live version of the band at Kozfest. He declined as he was in two other bands, both of which played at U.K. festivals.

Gary Parra: Drums

Gary was instrumental in my move to make Spirits Burning a collective. Co-producing and playing on his *Trap* album opened the door for me to work with many musicians in a multi-track environment. Playing live with Gary in the Spaceship Eyes live ensemble got me to reconsider where I was at musically and where I wanted to go next. Gary contributed to five of the first nine albums. Gary died 30 July 2016.

Pete Pavli: Cello, Bass, Guitar

Pete played viola on *Our Secret Cloud*, my favorite *Healthy Music* song. Plus, he was on the *Alien Injection* pieces built from Moorcock demo sessions.

> *I liked very much the viola track I did with you...quite beautiful, and the work you did with Mike turned out very well.*

For more from Pete, see *In a Deep Fix with Michael Moorcock*.

Doug Pearson: Synth, Violin, Bass

Doug contributed to two early albums. He also played violin on the SB cover of Hawkwind's *High Rise*, recording his parts in my home studio.

Erik Pearson: Guitar

Erik was part of the Mushroom jams that Pat Thomas provided for use on the *Reflections* and *Alien Injection* albums.

Stefanie Petrik: Vocals

Stefanie's vocals were included on a bounced vocal track of her and Daevid Allen, provided by Daevid for the *Roadmap* vocal piece.

John Pierpoint: Guitar, Bass

John is part of material Lee Potts delivered to me for some future Spirits Burning & Bridget Wishart songs.

Neil Pinnock: Didgeridoo

Neil was another member of Mooch that contributed to Spirits Burning via my connection with Stephen Palmer.

Martin Plumley: Guitar, Vocals

Martin has contributed to Spirits Burning studio and live recordings. Martin is married to Bridget. Together, they perform as Chumley Warner Bros.

For Martin's special entries, see *Bridges to the Plumley Household & Extended Hawkwind Family*.

Martin, onstage with Spirits Burning, 2017 (photo by Jack Gold-Molina)

John Pluth: Guitar

John was in the Spirits Burning vs. Spaceship Eyes live ensemble. He also played on SB covers of Genesis' *Return of the Giant Hogweed* and King Crimson's *Red*.

Josh Pollock: Guitar

Josh was part of the Mushroom jams that Pat Thomas provided for use on the *Reflections* album.

Nic Potter: Bass

Nic was the first family member of Van der Graaf Generator to contribute to Sprits Burning. Given my historical love of that band, Hammill albums, and the *Long Hello* series, Nic was a special invite. His acceptance of that invite, his always congenial communications, and his wonderful basslines for the *Bloodlines* song *Heavens Hide* are forever.

Nick died 16 January 2013.

Nigel Potter: Acoustic Guitar

I was honoured to be asked by Don to contribute to a new Spirits Burning album [Our Best Trips]. I was asked if I would like to contribute to a track or start one of my own. I chose one of my own. A simple acoustic-based piece. What returned to me sometime later was a fully-fledged musical composition [Alpha Happiness], built around my simple acoustic. The finished piece was astounding, so much so I remember asking Don if it could really be my simple guitar that had been at the heart of it. It made me realise for the first time just what music could be, given the touch of hands that knew already how to shape the very fabric of music. It was an amazing experience for me. One I will never forget.

Lee Potts: Guitar, Percussion

I first bumped into Don through Bridget (Wishart). I believe I did the first ever remix/reworking of a Spirits Burning track, the track was called Always from the Earth Born album. Side note: I consider Earth Born to be their best album, so check it out. Obviously, Don watched over the whole process while it was being put together and gave a little input here and there. The track later retitled Always (Spirit Free) was released on a couple of albums and got to No.1 in the Sound Awesome charts. Thanks, Don, for all your help over the years. - Lee (of Omenopus).

Lee's 2010 remix/reworking was the first by someone other than me. I did Spirits Burning remixes for 2006's daevid allen & don falcone album and one for 2002's Bay Prog CD.

Mark Poulin: Guitar

Mark was part of Mack Maloney's Sky Club band. When I decided to adapt Mack's *Starhawk*, Mark was invited to two songs.

John Purves, a.k.a. Purjah: Wind, Reed, Guitar

If John was still with us, I'm sure he'd say he was surprised that I invited him to Quiet Celebration and Spirits Burning and continued to invite him.

At heart, John was about jazz, and most of my invites, promotion, and reviews emphasized ambient or space rock. When it came to QC, jazz was the tail of our ambient-ethno-jazz. For Spirits Burning, it was space rock occasionally with a jazz flavor. However, John heard my full message—I always wanted to stretch definitions. The medieval sounds of the Moorcock songs on *Alien Injection* a good example.

This is where we can see the prowess of John.

Besides jazz, he had a large collection of ethnic instruments and played them well. SB gave him a place to experiment with sound, something he would do in a different way in his jazz sextet. And then I discovered that John played guitar. And he could distort.

I always hoped that John enjoyed these adventures as much as I enjoyed inviting him, and then experiencing his contribution. I could count on him to make each song he touched better, interesting. He is missed. I can only wonder what other music we could have concocted had his life been different.

John died 3 August 2018.

Ken Pustelnik: Drums

Ken asked Jonathan Downes (Gonzo magazine) to recommend him to me, as he would love to get involved with Spirits Burning. Ken provided drums to the *Starhawk* and *Alien Heat* albums. He was also in the audience for the Spirits Burning live show in Bath.

Jay Radford: Saz, Guitar

Jay contributed to multiple albums. He was also part of Mushroom, who appeared on two early albums.

> *When asked to participate in a Spirits Burning project, you're never sure where in the stream you're jumping in, who else will be riding the rapids, and what the final destination will be. It is always an adventure and an honor to be aboard.*

Jules Radino: Drums

Jules came onboard via Al Bouchard. Jules has proved hard for me to contact.

When I got a copy of the SB & Moorcock CD for him, I took his copy with me to a BÖC show, and after the show, asked Don Roeser to pass it onward to him.

Randy Raine-Reusch: Flute, Zither

Randy played on two tracks that Melodic Energy Commission started for *Behold The Action Man*, plus the opening track.

Ken Randolph: Bass

Ken played on *The Eagle Has Landed*, a Malcolm Mooney & The Tenth Planet song that Mal provided to the first album.

Robert Rich: Synth, Flute

I feel honored to have contributed in some small way to over a decade of Spirits Burning projects, either as the mastering engineer or with an instrumental part or two. I love how Don Falcone has managed to pull together this global community of space-rock magicians and lunatics, many of whom have played a large role in my own personal artistic development (Daevid Allen and Michael Moorcock, to name two.) These projects celebrate the nostalgia of concept albums and lyrical storytelling, and they convey a spirit of playfulness and the joy of crazy new ideas. I have no clue how Don manages to herd all these cats together into so many long-distance collaborations, but he is certainly a masterful cat-herder!

Jerry Richards: Guitar

Jerry's first venture into Spirits Burning was via Steve Swindells, for *One Way Trip* on *Earth Born*. A few years later, when I contacted Jerry to contribute to the *Starhawk* album, he was busy with a Hawklords DVD and an upcoming show in Wales. He asked if I could give him something that begins and ends with the existing arrangement and is complete with tempo and chords. The result: *Right On The Mark*, with Jerry's rhythm and leads, some of which weave around the end song jam with him, violinist Cyndee Lee Rule, and my synth. Almost like it was recorded live, with all of us in the same room!

Teed Rockwell: Stick, Guitar

One of the toughest things about Spirits Burning was playing with Bridget Wishart, the singer from Hawkwind. The chord changes in our foundation track didn't follow any of the traditional patterns. I don't think she had any idea what she wanted the chords to be. They would be different for each verse, even though the melody was the same, so I had to make up my own chords. By the time I heard all the tracks layered on top of each other, they were different both from her version and from my version. And yet somehow it all fit.

Donald "Buck Dharma" Roeser: Guitar, Vocals

Working with the Spirits Burning project has been fun and rewarding in a unique way for me. This is the first time I'd contributed to a musical production I had no idea how it would come out before hearing it. It's neat that everyone contributing stirred their ingredient into the stew, then got to taste it when it was done. It has a unique energy and synergy, to my ear. Proud to have participated in it.

For more words from Buck, see *In a Deeper Fix with Michael Moorcock*.

Paul Rudolph: Guitar

I believe Nik Turner somehow introduced me to Spirits Burning and it has been an honour to be associated with so many cool and talented people. I love what Don has done with all the different styles of music and his production is awesome. Well Done and Thanks for the opportunities to be involved.

Cyndee Lee Rule: Violin

My early online chats with Cyndee had lots of sibilance: sssspaceeee and sssssstrange. We also shared a bond in that she lived in Pennsylvania, where I grew up.

I was fond of violin, and she was one of the first violinists to regularly contribute to Spirits Burning. She played a Viper, an electric violin, which weaved in nicely. (She was one of twelve "Viper

Vixens" featured in a calendar.)

We got to meet in person at two NEARfests. We got together again when she was in the Bay Area for the American String Teachers Association (ASTA), my first time in a vegan restaurant in decades.

Trey Sabatelli: Drums, Percussion

After realizing that Don and I both had common interests and history of being fans of Gong and the Gong family, I took him up on his generous offer to explore and create new original music he was doing in this vein. We had the advantage of the latest music recording technology and were able to piece together performances and mix them into complete collaborations with other fantastic musicians. Don was the alchemist—putting together the musical stew—I was a solid ingredient. Super fun to do the recordings and was amazed at the final results. My favorite moments were when the Weird Biscuit Teatime group got together for a glorious session in person. I got to meet, jam and collaborate with a hero (Daevid) and spend time with him, working together in real time. Super fun indeed!

Nick Salomon: Guitar

I first contacted Nick in 2014. While he expressed a theoretical interest, he didn't have any digital recording equipment. We decided his involvement wasn't meant to be, at least at this time. Jumping to 2022, I invited Nick to do lead vocals on the song *Try and Try Again*. He responded that he hates singing, even though he obviously does it for his own material. Two months later, I invited him to play guitar on an in-progress song, which didn't have vocals yet. He suggested I get it closer to completion, and then get back to him. Seven months later—January of 2023—all the parts were in place. Nick now had gigging and recording to do. He wouldn't be able to do his guitar parts until September of 2023. The good news: The song was for a 2025 release. His parts were well worth the wait.

Dean Santomeiri: Synth

Dean played on *The Eagle Has Landed*, a Malcolm Mooney & The Tenth Planet song that Mal provided to the first album.

Andrew Scott: Guitar

Andrew appears on *The Hollow Lands* song *Awful Dilemma*.

Paul Sears: Drums

I first met Don at NEARfest some years ago back in the mid 2000s. I knew he was Ernie Falcone's (founder of MARS EVERYWHERE) cousin, but we had never met before and I really had no clue how productive this guy was with Spirits Burning, Daevid Allen, and other musos & bands. Not long after I moved to Arizona in 2010, he asked me to play on HEALTHY MUSIC IN LARGE DOSES, a Spirits Burning record with Steve York (!!!) on bass and many others, including Daevid Allen.

By working with Don, I was able to appear on records with many folks I would not have gotten to otherwise.

In the case of Daevid Allen, I had already met him during the first week of October 1978 via Giorgio Gomelsky's Zu Manifestival where we both played. Sometime after that during 1979 I was asked by Daevid to be part of New York Gong which I declined due to lack of a coherent plan. That band was Bill Laswell on bass, Al Hertzberg (Manster) on guitar, Kramer on trombone, Mike Beinhorn on synths, Daevid on guitar and myself on drums. I recorded our single rehearsal, took the tape and deck home, and have only let 2 copies out: One to Daevid's son and one to Don.

Despite my bailing on this (and Al Hertzberg did too), Daevid and I remained friendly, and I saw him again some years later with University of Errors that had Michael Clare on bass. Great high energy stuff! Daevid, Michael, and Don had already done a record called

Weird Biscuit Teatime with another drummer named Trey Sabatelli and were going to do a 2nd one around 2015 and Trey was not available, so I got the call to play on several tracks. Daevid's health was on the decline by the time we finished it, and David passed away not long after it was done. It came out as Daevid Allen Weird Quartet, and it was a real thrill to work on.

In the case of Clearlight, I had already played live with them at Progday festival in 2003, so Cyrille Verdeaux and I were already acquainted. Again, there was a record in progress with Don and another drummer, (no clue on that story) and so Cyrille & Don asked me if I wanted in. OF COURSE! They sent me the music and I studied it for a couple of months. Cyrille's daughter was living in San Francisco, and he had a trip planned (from Brasilia at that time) so why not stop on the way and conduct me in my Arizona studio while I record? This worked out really well and I got my parts done in 2 days. Great having the composer right there! I suggested we bring in my friend Linda Cushma to play bass on 2 tracks which she did. One of the prettiest records I have ever played on.

Jonathan Segel: Violin

Well, there is definitely some overlap in musicians in the wider space/psychedelic rock world, numerous coincidences, and crossovers. I think in my specific case it was Don having heard a track I made for Daevid Allen after his transcendence and wondering if I would add some sound to something he had done with Daevid, though in both cases the back story would be more interesting than that simple explanation (I'll leave his to him, mine is simple: most of my life I was a fan, got to open for Gong in the early 90s with my band Hieronymus Firebrain, finally got to play with the guy with Big City

Orchestra much later. Numerous anecdotes will have to wait.)

I moved from the SF Bay Area to Sweden back in 2012, so our collaborations have all been via the internet. That makes it easy enough for me to record at home and send tracks back to add into Don's mixes. And to be honest, it's been very easy to work that way, if my tracks work, they work and if not, he can mute them. (I've tried not to make too much to overwhelm him!) It's been pretty funny for me learning who else is playing or singing on these tracks as many of these people are musical icons to me—or literary icons!

Of course, I would love to play with the folks involved in real time and space someday!

Karl E. H. Seigfried: Bass, Double Bass

The whole process of recording with Spirits Burning has always been absolutely surreal. Playing duet solos with people I obsessively listened to as a teenager nearly half a century ago—like Hawkwind's Simon House and Gong's Steve Hillage—was definitely a trip. The fact that it all takes place virtually, without ever meeting the players involved, takes it to an even more surreal level.

Steffe Sharpstrings (Stephan Lewry): Guitar

I really enjoyed being involved with the Spirits Burning track [Live Forever]! My approach to the request to add guitar was first to augment the very intriguing melodic framework, then fill the very spacious track with curtains of fuzz power chord guitar. The track spoke to me of early San Fran psychedelic crossed with Hawkwind. It was a gas to be involved.

Adrian Shaw: Bass

I was approached by Don Falcone some years ago to contribute to his "Spirits Burning" projects, which I've always found to be interesting to work on. He drew together a lot of artists from a similar background to myself, mainly Space Rock and Psychedelia, and the results were universally challenging and rewarding.

Andy Shernoff: Vocals, Lyrics

Albert Bouchard brought me onto the project. If my memory serves me well, I liked the song he thought I should sing but I was more interested in doing something more left field and completely different from my normal approach, so I suggested Dark Dominion from Alien Heat. Albert approved and I returned with a vocal unlike any I've ever sung and had a ball recording it.

Billy Sherwood: Guitar

I think I first contacted Billy via Cleopatra Records. He provided scorching leads for the two opening tracks of the *Starhawk* album, which weave into each other: *Our Crash* and *I Have Two Names*.

Fabienne Shine: Vocals

The first time I heard of Don Falcone and Michael Moorcock was in 2018 in NYC through the mouth of Albert Bouchard! Albert is a longtime friend of mine since 1979 and the Black and Blue Tour, featuring Black Sabbath, Blue Öyster Cult, and our band Shakin' Street. The tour was produced by Sandy Pearlman, who was managing all three bands.

Albert asked me to come to his studio to sing a song for Don's album! Referring to a psychedelic vision from the Victorian era. My favorite era! The song: Time Machine Cabriolet.

I got overwhelmed to participate to such a trippy project. I also sang on another album, enjoying Don and Albert's fusion in a sense of Music and Poetry...they are really "clicking"—a special sound full of imaginary landscapes where you enter, floating, exploring a Different Galaxy, made of Love, Wilderness, Sounds, and Perfumes.

In 2022, I asked Fabienne to sing a second song that I felt was perfect for her: *It Is Everything*, a song for *The End Of All Songs - Part 1*. When she was unable to secure a recording solution in Southern California, we made plans for her to fly northward into San Francisco and record at my home studio. The results: One of my favorite songs on the album. Plus, Fabienne recorded backing vocals for *Part 2* songs.

Fabienne and Don at the Home Studio, 2023

Craig Shropshire: Percussion

I mentioned to Dave Willey that I was looking for a percussionist and he recommended Craig. He proceeded to provide parts for seven songs over three albums.

An assortment of rhythmic instruments: Cajón, Kanjira, and Udu. *Far & Away The Lands Escape, Bias Of Recency* was extremely fun to mix as I combined all four tracks of Udus that Craig provided, and then added my keyboard dumbek, dulcimer, harp, and piano.

Mick Slattery: Guitar

Mick was receptive to play guitar on *An Alien Heat*, and then returned for *Evolution Ritual*. His first delivery had the rhythm and lead on a single track. I asked him to re-deliver separate tracks for each part, and he did that. Mick died 17 March 2023.

Jessie May Smart: Violin

I went to the July 16, 2015, Steeleye Span show at Great America Music Hall with Michelle Kolota; neither of our partners were interested in attending. Following the show, we went downstairs to the stage front before leaving. I talked to Jessie, told her how great she and the band were, told her about Spirits Burning, and we exchanged contact info.

After a couple of invites and candidate songs, Jessie finally said yes when I asked her in December of 2020 to contribute fiddle to *Strolling Into The Future*, the *Evolution Ritual* song that Andy Dalby started.

Bruce Smith: Drums

Bruce was the first drummer I played with in San Francisco, and one of the best.

We connected rhythmically when I played bass, and then when I switched to keyboards. Bruce is on a song via use of one of our Kameleon demos. I have been unable to locate Bruce since our 80's days.

Graham Smith: Violin

A few years back, Don Falcone asked me to take part in his Spirit Burning project and contribute a violin part for a song called Far and Away The Lands Escape. I only had a laptop to record over the soundtrack, but I scraped something together and sent it on.

Don did a good job with the mix. It was an interesting experience to return to the spirit of prog and space rock and the feeling of that era. In the 70s, I had shared gigs with a number of the artists involved, including Hawkwind. When I was in Van der Graaf, we shared top bill with Hawkwind in Berlin, and much later during a reunion with String Driven Thing in a revival gig with Hawkwind in Blackpool. Far and Away sums it up nicely.

Judge Smith: Vocals

Jonathan Downes (Gonzo magazine) suggested getting Judge to contribute to Spirits Burning. Jonathan contacted Judge for me and reported back that he was interested.

Judge remembers:

Singing for you on Spirits Burning was a good experience; excellent tunes and interesting lyrics, and fascinating musicians to sing to.

Scotty Smith: Drums, Percussion

Around 2008, when I was looking for a drummer, I was given Scotty's name. Probably from one of his former Giraffe bandmates, as two of them worked with me at Digidesign.

Scotty contributed to Spirits Burning releases from 2009 until 2015.

This included quickly stepping in when we lost the drummer for a cover of Pink Floyd's *Take Up Thy Stethoscope and Walk*.

David Speight: Drums

I began my involvement with Don in 2010, leading to the release of Behold the Action Man. From the get go, I was really attracted to the idea of having a blank slate regarding what I contributed to this, and the following Spirits Burning collaborations. Equally attractive was not knowing what sort of project would arrive next, nor which of the many diverse musicians within the SB family it would involve!

I recorded the sessions either in my home-made studio room, occasionally in a larger hall due to its acoustics (Cool Can...), and at least once in a country garden in summer! (Yes' South Side...) I remember eagerly awaiting an email from Don containing the latest track. I would usually listen to the song for the first time and play along until I was happy with my interpretation of it.

All the tracks were a welcomed challenge and were rewarding in terms of finding the right approach and sound, others just seemed to 'click' (the track Italian Lake was second hearing / first take!). I initially used electric drums for the diversity of sounds and percussion it provided. In later sessions, I used my Sonor 3000 series acoustic kit. Whichever kit I used, all recording was onto a zoom R16 from which WAV files were sent off for Don.

Karen Stackpole: Gongs

Don Falcone and I had the good fortune to both work at Dolby Laboratories and got to talking in earnest about music back in 2016 while standing out on the SF Civic Center lawn in front of the Bill Graham Auditorium during a company fire drill one fine sunny morning. We knew some of the same musicians and Don told me about Spirits Burning and asked if I'd be willing to contribute some of my gongs and percussion work to some of the pieces. Of course, I was intrigued, and that's how my involvement began.

The first couple of tunes that Don thought could benefit from my particular sounds—working with large metal and found percussion—were the tracks Roadmap and College Sky. It was the modern collaborative method of sending layered mixes back and forth through file sharing, downloading and creating a session, listening and getting inspired, and improvising and recording some takes for the tunes, and sending the tracks back to Don for mixing. It worked really well, this approach, and gave me the time and space to sit with the tunes and get inspired to create some sounds that would enhance the piece.

I contributed to several tunes over the years, and really enjoyed the adventure of the process and experiencing the finished work after Don did his magic.

Kurt Statham: Bass

Kurt was part of the Mushroom jams that Pat Thomas provided for use on the *Reflections* album.

Craig Stewart: Synth

Craig was part of ST 37 recordings provided for use on *Found In Nature*.

Mark Stone: Guitar

Mark was part of ST 37 recordings provided for use on two albums.

Dave Sturt: Bass

Dave appeared on *Roadmap* song *Early Evening Rain*, which also included flute by Nik Turner.

Steve Swindells: Keys, Vocals, Lyrics, Percussion

One Way Trip: This was recorded quite a while before the pandemic, but it certainly pioneered 'remote, collaborative, working'.

I certainly recorded my contributions alone in my studio in London, and I imagine many of the people involved did the same, wherever they might have been.

The result is a pleasingly eclectic, esoteric, spacey disconnected... connect!

Rocket To The End Of The Line: I never thought I'd play with the legendary Daevid Allen, but here it is in all its gritty glory.

A magnificent, magnum opus from all corners of the earth, and an amazing joint effort.

I was particularly impressed by how tightly Bridget synched with my vocals—in unison.

And I love that epic ending. Spine-tingling and tantalising.

Jay Tausig: Guitar

The Spirits Burning collective was the first time I had collaborated with anyone online. The required Technology was still kind of new to me in a way, and it was a very exciting time musically back then. Dan Carter had turned me on to a Spirits Burning track he had contributed drums to, and I really enjoyed it. Being a mutual friend of Daevid Allen's I reached out to Don and expressed interest in collaborating/contributing to Spirits Burning. Don sent me some tracks to work on soon after and it began. I ended up contributing 12 string acoustic and electric guitar to 2 songs on Spirits Burning and Clearlight Healthy Music in Large Doses. Down the road I also contributed guitars and synthesizer to Spirits Burning Starhawk and Spirits Burning and Bridget Wishart Make Believe It Real. It cannot be overstated how amazing it was to be included on these albums, surrounded by some of my favorite musicians, from some of my favorite bands.

Brian Tawn: Vocals, Lyrics

Hawkfan magazine scribe and publisher! For Brian's special entry, see *In a Deep Fix with Michael Moorcock*.

Shannon Taylor-Wishart: Drums

Shannon contributed to a cover of *A Tower Struck Down*.

Steve Taylor: Bass, Drums, Guitar

Steve's first appearance with Spirits Burning was on the *Alien Injection* instrumental *Augustus*. Steve and Dave Figoli co-wrote the original version of the song. They delivered their multi-track recording, and I weaved in additional new material (from Doug Erickson, Purjah, and me). Steve's next input was acoustic guitar for a cover of Gong's *Opium For The People*, a bonus track on *Our Best Trips*.

Scott Telles: Bass Guitar

I'm pretty sure I caught wind of Spirits Burning at one of the Strange Daze festivals we played in 1998-2000, but the event that keeps sticking in my mind is the ST 37 gig at Cafe du Nord on 7/28/1999. I remember Kurt Stenzel and Beyond-O-Matic and how terrific they were, and what a great club that was, and how lucky we were to get to play there, and I do believe it was that night that somebody slipped me a copy of the Melting Euphoria CD Through the Strands of Time and I was pretty fucking impressed. What a great record! So, the name of Don Falcone was introduced to my brain, and it must have had a pretty serious impact, cuz later on in the same year, we were already on a Spirits Burning record, the wonderful Reflections in a Radio Shower!! Even though long-distance collaboration was certainly not so easy in those days, Don somehow made it all work seamlessly. We sent him some fragments we'd been working on, he sent us some ideas we developed—and it came out great!

Mr. Falcone is a genius at collaboration. We couldn't have had a nicer experience contributing to the incredible Spirits Burning mythos. The stuff he has done in uniting diverse members of the Hawkwind/space rock/psych rock community from all over the world is, frankly, amazing. The other night I was in Chicago watching the Damned and the Dictators, and there was proud Spirits Burning member Albert Bouchard on the drums and Monty Oxymoron [keys for The Damned]! Don has taken the Dancers at the End of Time trilogy by one of my favorite SF writers, Michael Moorcock, in the same direction ST 37 is working towards on our forthcoming record Ballardesque, dedicated to the writing of another British SF great. 2020's The Hollow Lands certainly would have been in my top 5 records of the Plague Year, if I was a rock critic type that made such lists.

Thom The World Poet: Vocals, Lyrics

By magic GONG tribe evolves into eclectic Muse Tribes worldwide… Fortunate to be performing with Divided Alien a.k.a Daevid Allen (Hero with a Thousand Faces), Gilli Smyth and Harry Williamson, and to be thereby linked to Golden Age musicians, representing the very best and brightest harmony helpers from circles in cities world-wide. Ripples in the world pool, i got to improvise with cheerfilled Muse Makers of brilliance.

Time will treasure their amazing and eclectic productions—i can only recommend all aspects of Spirits Burning musicians, and the astonishing wisdom of Don Falcone, in birthing such brightness into this most necessary lifetime.

Huw Thomas: Guitar, Bass

Huw and Bridget's song *Evening* was reworked with new material by Daevid and me for the Spirits Burning & Bridget Wishart album *Earth Born*.

Pat Thomas: Percussion

Besides recording percussion at my home studio, Pat gave me the multi-tracks of a half dozen or so Mushroom jams, with the understanding that I could use the performances in whole or piece-meal to create new songs.

For Pat's special entry, see *Reincarnation in the Time of Spirits Burning*.

PJ Thomas: Low Toms, Alarm Bell

PJ was part of the DRUMCART Mardi Gras 2019 performance that was provided for use on two *Evolution Ritual* songs.

Dan Thompson: Drums

Dan had recorded some drum and percussion pieces, which he provided for use as starter rhythms.

These helped create four songs and a remix for the Spirits Burning & Bridget Wishart *Make Believe* album.

Trevor Thoms, a.k.a. as Judge Trev: Guitar

Trev helped launch Spirits Burning, providing fiery guitar on the first two albums. In 2002, he sent me a copy of *God and Man*, his solo acoustic project, which I loved. It led to me inviting Trev to sing lead vocals and play guitar on our cover of The Moody Blues song *The Story In Your Eyes*.

Trev died 8 December 2010.

Larry Thrasher: Percussion, Guitar

Larry and I were bandmates in Thessalonians. We also worked together at Digidesign. Larry contributed to songs on two albums.

Vicente L Tiburcio: Guitar

I got involved in this project because of Albert Bouchard. He was my H.S. music teacher and we've been good friends for about 24 yrs now. I was over at his place laying down some bass and guitar tracks for his record Surrealist. While there, he showed me a project he was working on which was Spirits Burning. He played me a track [Hothouse Flowers], which ended up being the one I'm on. I was fiddling around on guitar. When the song ended, I realized he had recorded it. We dug what I was doing at the end of the song. So, he kept it and told you he has a friend who played the end solo.

The end result was pretty cool. I really dig the concept of the record. I'm very happy to have been and always will be a part of the project.

Kavus Torabi: Guitar

Kavus played on *Coffee For Coltrane*, the song started by Albert Bouchard for the Spirits Burning & Clearlight album *The Roadmap In Your Head*. The song was also included on *Recollections Of Instrumentals*.

Melissa Trancess: Vocals, Synth

Melissa teamed up with Buck McGibbony to produce a completed dance track for the debut album.

Theo Travis: Sax, Flute

The first Spirits Burning piece that Theo contributed to was *Healthy Music* song *Coffee for Coltrane*.

When Theo asked what I was looking for, along with sax start and finish locations. I responded:

With the new guitar part, there are less areas for sax. Here are the main sections that need sax: Start to .37, 2.16 to 3.06, 4.06 to 5.04. There's also a 'band' riff

that happens three times: 2.08 to 2.16, 3.56 to 4.06,
and 5.04 to 5.12. If you feel inspired to play anywhere
else, that's fine.

Theo recorded three full sax takes, including the riffs, which he doubled in octaves to make them thicker and stronger.

Nik Turner: Sax

Connecting with Nik felt like a maze.

He had multiple Facebook pages and websites, all in different states, which made it hard to tell if they were active or not. Email addresses would sometimes appear, and then seem to go extinct. Sometimes Nik would answer in one place and then go quiet, and then answer in another place.

We eventually made solid contact, with official plans for me to do a recording session at my home studio. I was incredibly happy with the results.

Nik's sax parts on *We Move You* are stunning.

Nik died 10 November 2022.

Twink (Mohammed Abdullah, born John Charles Edward Alder): Tambourine

It was great to have Twink onboard to do tambourine on a Spirits Burning & Bridget Wishart album. He has a special place in music history. He was the drummer for these bands:

- Tomorrow, with pre-Yes Steve Howe.
- Santa Barbara Machine Head, with future Deep Purple keyboardist Jon Lord.
- Pretty Things, *S.F. Sorrow* album, generally considered the first rock opera.
- Pink Fairies, alongside guitarist Paul Rudolph, who plays on a couple of Spirits Burning & Michael Moorcock albums.
- Post-Pink Floyd band with Syd Barrett, which played live a few times.

Unknown: Drums

We have a mystery. Around 1997, I was commissioned by Cleopatra Records to do a cover of *Red* for a King Crimson tribute album.

My Spaceship Eyes solo project was on the label's electronica sublabel, Hypnotic. This tribute was for their space/prog label, Purple Pyramid.

The Spaceship Eyes live ensemble, which had previously performed my pre-Hypnotic songs, had a more space/prog flavor, so a good option for the song. However, our drummer, Gary Parra, was no longer available. Along with the guitarist and bassist from the ensemble, we decided to move forward…resurrecting the band name Spirits Burning.

Here, the mystery ensues: We needed a drummer, quickly. I worked at Orban, as did Carol, our bass player. Renee, an employee there, had a drum contact. We did the recording and didn't continue to play with the drummer.

What was his name?

The release didn't include band members in the credits. Was it Renee's drummer acquaintance Jimmy? Another of her acquaintances, a drummer named Sammy? Someone else?

I located her Jimmy on Facebook—Jimmy Wells, the John Bonham drummer for Zeppelin Live. He does remember Renee. He has no memory of the *Red* session. (One aside: Karen and I, drummer Sam Herzberg and his wife, and my friend Rob Burns saw Zeppelin Live in Redwood City, in 2023.)

Carol then discovered a photo of her, me and the drummer, taken during our recording.

Unfortunately, the drummer had his back to the camera. You can see a mustache, a mullet haircut, and a "Guitar Center, The Musician's Choice" shirt with no sleeves. While Jimmy used to look a little like the person in the photo and did have that shirt, he didn't think it was him. When he heard the recording, he confirmed: He wasn't the drummer.

The mystery remains.

Jean van den Elsen: Vocals, Translations

Jean provides male vocals to the piano-based, 14-minute-plus *Reflections*, the *Make Believe It Real* song closing disc 1.

> *I first heard about Spirits Burning through my dear friends Bridget Wishart and Martin Plumley. Martin and I had been playing and performing together for a few years when Bridget asked me if I would like to add backing vocals to a couple of her songs for a project she'd been working on with Don. I happily agreed and enjoyed the whole process of experimenting with Bridget's lyrics and adding some lines in Dutch. I loved how our vocals complemented each other, and we were really pleased with the result. I had no idea what was going to happen with the songs, but I was totally blown away when hearing the songs on the finished Make Believe It Real album. Don's arrangements and production really lifted the songs and the whole album is just a feast for the ears!*

Cyrille Verdeaux: Keys, Vocals, Lyrics

Cyrille has recorded at my studio numerous times, contributing to multiple albums, including two under the name Spirits Burning & Clearlight.

For Cyrille's short entry, see *Healthy Music & Twisting Roadmaps with Cyrille Verdeaux*.

Lux Vibratus: Bass

> *Don usually sends me a rough demo with a brief background of the feel that he has in mind. He's open to ideas, as well as working together on a track that I'd submitted for the project. It was great meeting up with Don and Karen at the Michael Moorcock book signing while we were working on the first record from the Dancers at the End of Time trilogy. I'm a big fan of the storyline and it's been an honor to be a part of the*

recordings of this project among such distinguished and talented contributors.

Alan Wall: Acoustic Guitar

Alan is mostly known as a British novelist and writer. He provided original music for the closing number on the *Alien Injection* album.

> *I always wanted to write a guitar tune that would never end. Just in case I was ever kidnapped. So, this is it. You can play this one until your fingers drop off. Then I sent it to Don, and he sent it into outer space.*

Mike Walsh: Drum, Guitar, Keys

Miles and Bridget created the song *Chain Of Thought* and donated it to the *Make Believe* album. From there, Gabe Monticello and I recorded bass guitar and mellotron, respectively, and then I mixed the song for the album.

Tim Walters: Recorders

> *You sent me the raw demo, I wrote and played some recorder harmonies, pretty straightforward. If I'd known you were going to add a bunch more instruments I probably would have played less. Pretty cool to be on a Michael Moorcock song! btw: I still have your Mars Everywhere cassettes.*

Darryl Way: Violin

> *I recorded the violin part in my own studio, after Don sent me the backing track. The only person I interacted with, was Don. I enjoyed working on the track and the freedom he allowed me to put my own stamp on the recording. It was a very atmospheric piece of music, so it was right up my strasse.*

Carol Weeks: Bass

Carol was in the Spirits Burning vs. Spaceship Eyes live ensemble. She also played on Spirits Burning's covers of King Crimson's *Red* and Genesis' *Return of the Giant Hogweed*.

Carol writes:

> *Regarding my time performing and recording with Don Falcone and friends: It's been a really long time since I've thought about this! What I remember most is being pushed way out of my comfort zone towards a type of music and style of playing that had been unfamiliar and somewhat uncomfortable for me. I was also not accustomed to or comfortable with improvisational playing, mostly because I was still a novice. Although learning came quickly and easily in many ways and I really enjoyed playing and performing, I was always extremely nervous, whether performing live or during a recording. Don was patient and took the time to make it as comfortable as possible, which I appreciated. I also appreciated the trust he had in me, when I wasn't sure of myself. I'll always be grateful for all of my experiences with Don and his band mates.*

Marc Weinstein: Drums

Marc played on *The Eagle Has Landed*, a Malcolm Mooney & The Tenth Planet song that Mal provided to the first album.

Brian Wensing: Synth

Brian and fellow F/I bandmember Rick Hake appeared on three songs on the debut album, including *The Ticking of Science*, which featured Steven Wilson.

Peter Wetherbee: Drums

Peter contributed to a special mix of *Clear Audient* for the daevid allen & don falcone album.

> *I remember it was an exciting challenge because I didn't know the prog rock world at all, but the music was cool, and the time changes were musical, so I dove in pretty hard on this track. My studio at the time was very industrial, raw sheetrock and concrete, but I had some nice microphones and preamps and kept it live, without much damping material. I remember thinking (perhaps naïvely) that the kit should sound 'industrial' for this track. I did several takes over a day and ended up using a fairly early one, which made me happy (that my primitive music theory mind seemed to grok the material without undue deliberation or even thinking). I'm proud to hear this track and have my name associated with such epic names in progressive rock and to be part of this cool Spirits Burning project. Daevid Allen is particularly special because I was initially exposed to him by my early mentor Bill Laswell, who said Gong and Soft Machine were a big influence on Material and other early Laswell productions in the 1980s. I didn't use a lot of microphones, but I remember being very pleased with the way an omnidirectional B&K 4006 microphone, through a Demeter tube preamp, was able to capture the entire kit in a nice round way.*

Richard Wileman: Guitar

> *Don approached me around 2007 to play bouzouki on the song Crafted From Wood on the Spirits Burning & Bridget Wishart Earth Born album. I had bought a Transylvanian bouzouki to record on my Karda Estra concept album Voivode Dracula in 2004 and I assumed Don made the connection from this and decided to get in*

touch. I loved the song, especially the beautiful thoughtful lyrics and I submitted a simple arrangement that suited its folk atmosphere. Don liked what I'd done and so began a series of requests from him to contribute to further Spirits Burning tracks (plus the Astralfish album).

Sometimes this would be my own playing electric/acoustic guitars, folk instruments, occasional fx/guitar synth etc., and other times I arranged woodwinds or vocals from people involved in my own Karda Estra or solo projects. It's always fascinating to see who Don asks to play on these albums as quite often they are musicians from the psych/prog world that I grew up listening to. Don gives minimal instructions and seems happy to let me work up my own contributions. A recent recording suggestion was for the guitar writing to sound like Peter Gabriel meets P J Harvey. Well, my playing still sounded like me, but I knew exactly where he was coming from, and I found it a very helpful mindset.

Two massive influences for me when I was a teenager were author Michael Moorcock and the band Blue Öyster Cult and Don asked me around 2015 to work on his first Dancers At The End Of Time album. Now, not only were Moorcock and some BÖC members going to be on it, but the Dancers series are one of my all-time favourite books. And to my dismay, I had to decline because I was completely snowed under with wrestling my Time & Stars album into shape, amongst other things! Fortunately, Don didn't hold this against me, and I was delighted to work on the second album in the series The Hollow Lands, plus I have done work on the forthcoming End Of All Songs - Part 2.

In 2020 and still so enamoured with the lyrics, I returned to that first SB song I worked on Crafted From Wood and recorded my own rearranged version for my *album Arcana. I also play it live quite often too. So far, I am on seven of Don's albums with the eighth Part 2 yet to be released at the time of writing. It's a real pleasure to have contributed to Spirits Burning for so long now. It has such a wonderful kaleidoscopic mixture of styles and musicians. You never know what (or who) will be next!*

Dave Willey: Accordion

I was honored to appear alongside Don and his amazing musicians! It's true that 2013 was especially busy for me, so my recollections are kind of a blur.

When I received Dave's parts, I commented that "you do a nice little run a couple of minutes into the piece that I think would make a nice intro." Dave ok'd that I "cut and move as need be!"

Paul Williams: Drums, Synth

Don (you) reached out to me at one of the first Strange Daze festivals in Ohio. I assume you heard of Quarkspace as part of the burgeoning USA spacerock scene. You played me a tape of some of the material currently in progress and asked if I would be interested in providing drums and synth work. After answering in the affirmative, I received a CD-R with stereo mixes and added my own tracks, sending it back to you.

It served as a nice introduction to possibilities of remote music collaboration. I enjoyed being on tracks with luminaries like Daevid Allen, Michael Moorcock, and others. I still missed the feel of sharing a musical space with others in real-time, remote real-time jamming remains a possibility for the future as network bandwidth and latency continue to improve.

It's been an honor to be part of this unique chapter in psychedelic music. The world's largest geographically dispersed spacerock band!

Tracy Lee Williams: Vocals, Guitar, Lyrics

Don Falcone is a poet, an amazing lyricist, a prolific songwriter, singer, music lover and a very talented musician. He seems to love and appreciate many styles of music, which helps make him such a wonderful songwriter. He is not inhibited or constricted by musical boundaries.

Don introduced me to such great music that I had not listened to. I remember going over to Don's house and us listening to albums. He introduced me to Hawkwind, Kate Bush, the Stranglers and many others...

I met Don in the Fall of 1984. I started SFSU that year and got a job on-campus at the Pizza Boat. Don worked there along with a bunch of other college students who were also musicians. Don's presence in my life during the 1980s and 90s was a wonderful creative collaboration from which many songs were written. Over the years in the 1980s and 90s, we wrote many wonderful songs together and I still listen to them to this very day. I think the first song we wrote together and recorded was Who's Foolin' Who. And the first time I ever sang a song on stage was with a version of Don's band, Spirits Burning, at Mabuhay Gardens ('The Fab Mab') and the song was Who's Foolin' Who. It was a magical night.

From the very beginning of our musical friendship, it was easy to collaborate with him. I remember many fun nights out at the Hunters Point studio just jamming and creating wonderful songs with Don and the other musicians. For several years during the 80s, I played with Don in his band, Spirits Burning. We played many fun gigs throughout San Francisco including many, many gigs at the Chi Chi Club. In later years, we created Creative Element and then we worked together on Red Rain.

Upon joining Spirits Burning, our first professional recording at Hyde Studios was an all-nighter I will never forget. Somewhere in the middle of the night / morning, we were short $200, and we needed it to finish the recording session. I think my dad gave me the money. From that session, we recorded wonderful songs such as Future Memories, Spirits Burning and Silver Chains! Don has always been such an amazing songwriter and collaborator.

Harry Williamson: Guitar

As a starter, I am really peripheral to the process (from my perspective) so I am not really sure how useful anything I could contribute was going to be. However, I accept you may have had a different view.

In general, I found the process quite strange, to be given a recorded track or tracks with an invitation to add more or less anything to it, is a really unusual process for me. I have produced over 200 CDs and many DVDs over the past 26 years and of course lots of vinyl and other formats. Seldom have I encountered a brief like this. I commend you for being brave enough to create this in the first place.

My Experiences: More than anything else my experiences were really varied and determined by the organisation of the material presented.

For example, a-rhythmic pieces present a completely different challenge to something done to a clear rhythm. This was the most obvious distinction. Creating another texture for a cloud-like dream sequence is much easier than meticulously adding detail to a complex structure bound by tempo. In either case, the first step for me was to listen carefully to what had gone before and see which direction the path lead. Sometimes it was clear that most of the tracks worked together and one or two were set at a different angle—sometimes it was hard to hear what the final intention was, when listening to everything at once. So, sorting out the parts that worked vs. those that probably did not was the first job.

When I had the luck to be presented with a piece more or less at the start, it was in some ways easier, as the field was less constrained, but conversely the possibilities were vastly more numerous.

The process of adding a notional sub-mix was I thought a great and obvious idea, where it worked, to tell the next person in line how the last person had heard what had just been created—how it sat in the mix.

The Results: I am not sure whether I got to hear the final results of all my contributions. Possibly because I moved house and studio a few times, I don't know. What I did hear was intriguing. Sometimes my contribution appeared obvious and seemed to lead the music in a particular direction, other parts were used in a peripheral or decorative way, for example. Again others, as I'd expect, were not featured. That is clearly going to be part of this process. Much water under many bridges.

Randy Wilson: Keys, Vocals

I first met Don when we worked for Digidesign / Avid near San Francisco and was introduced to the Spirits Burning CDs. The diversity of experimental styles from a single band was very impressive. Don had established relationships with many other musicians, artists, and other creative folks around the world. Some of these people were well known or played with established bands.

Don recognized that because of the change to digital recording, musicians could collaborate unrestrained by the sync and timing problems that plagued the recording industry when using taped tracks from different sources. Don's approach in the early years of the 21ˢᵗ century was new and original, enabling international collaborations that would have been previously impossible.

Don and a few key crew members provided the album planning and musical direction, as well as compiling, mixing, and mastering the tracks. This made the process very easy for contributors.

I was enthused to work with Daevid Allen, Don, and other fantastic musicians from around the world whose main common thread was our admiration of experimental and progressive music. It was a great opportunity to take a musical puzzle and add pieces along with many creative contributors to produce something unique and unexpected.

Steven Wilson: Guitar

A fellow Scorpio, who contributed guitar to the song *The Ticking Of Science*.

Wikipedia describes Steven as a "British musician, who is best known as the founder, lead guitarist, singer and songwriter of Porcupine Tree. He is involved with many other bands and musical projects, both as musician and producer, whilst also maintaining a solo career. Also known as successful sound recordings restorer."

The pdf of Steven's music output (2021 edition) is staggering: http://www.voyage-pt.de/swdisco.pdf.

Bridget Wishart (Bridget Plumley): Vocals, EWI, Lyrics

Since her Spirits Burning arrival on the *Alien Injection* album, Bridget has contributed to every album except one (the SB & Thom ensemble that was recorded in California). She is featured on the Spirits Burning & Bridget Wishart albums and was part of the 2017 live band.

For Bridget's special entry, see *Bridges to the Plumley Household & Extended Hawkwind Family*.

Bridget, onstage with Spirits Burning, 2017 (photo by Jack Gold-Molina)

Alisa Wood: Vocals

I really enjoyed singing on SB. The story and music were mesmerizing, and it was an enchanting creative experience.

Alisa sings a duet with me on *Part 2* song *On Her Island*.

Brook Lynn Wright: Shaker, Vocals

Brook Lynn was part of the DRUMCART Mardi Gras 2019 performance that was provided for use on two *Evolution Ritual* songs.

Pete Wyer: Acoustic Guitar

Pete appears on the last track of the second album. Neither of us can remember how that came to be. Was it via Steve Palmer, who is a common acquaintance? Was it via MySpace, which once upon a time fostered collaborations in the space rock community?

Max Wynter: Trumpet

Max was invited by Bridget. He provided the trumpet flair to the mysterious *Mother Of The Dragon* on *Bloodlines*.

Don Xaliman: Synth, Bass, Chimes, Gong

Don played on and delivered two tracks that Melodic Energy Commission started for *Behold The Action Man*. He also played on four other SB albums.

Hoshiko Yamane: Violin

Hoshiko was one of nine violinists featured on the acoustic-based *Evolution Ritual* album. She is also on *The End Of All Songs - Part 1*.

April 28, 2024: Hoshiko Yamane, residency performance, at the Headlands Center for the Arts, Sausalito. Karen and I attend and greatly enjoy Hoshiko's solo performance.

Pete Yarbrough: Cello Bass

I believe Pete came onboard via his former Netherworld bandmate Randy Wilson (who I worked with at Digidesign, and who probably knew I was on the hunt for string players for the more medieval-sounding Moorcock/Pavli songs on *Alien Injection*).

Greg Yaskovic: Guitar, Pinball

Greg was part of a Maryland basement jam by three Mars Everywhere members and me. I used snippets in the *Crazy Fluid* song *Pinball Symphonics*.

Steve York: Bass

In a 10 June 2020 interview for It's Psychedelic Baby Magazine, Klemen Breznikar asks Steve "What currently occupies your life? Any future projects we should expect?"

> *I have been involved with the space rock project Spirits Burning and have played on three of their CDs. In 2019, I recorded five tracks for them. Three are to be included in an upcoming release in the Spirits Burning / Michael Moorcock series... Two are for an acoustic album.*

Steve died 13 October 2020.

Yur Zappa (Juha Häikiö): Guitar

Yur was part of the recording with Dark Sun bandmates Santtu and Mikko that laid the foundation of the song *Alien Injection*.

Duane Zarakov (Patrick Faigan): Percussion

Duane appears on two songs on the *Reflections* album.

Zero (Luis Davila): Synth

Luis went by Zero in Melting Euphoria credits. He was one of my replacements when I quit that band. When they went into hiatus or were winding down, I reconnected with Michael, their drummer, and soon met Luis. He would contribute to two SB albums, and we did an album with Michael under the name Fireclan (with me on bass).

Discography

THIS CHAPTER COVERS my primary albums and singles.

Besides playing keyboards, bass guitar, and a variety of sound-making instruments on these releases, I produce all the Spirits Burning albums and many of the other bands or projects where I'm a musician. Beginning with the first SB album, I started listing my producer credit with my middle name—"Produced by Don Marino Falcone." One way for my dad's name (Marino) to continue onward.

Full discography (including albums I guested on and compilations I appear on): www.donfalcone.com/discography.html

Albums (In Release Order)

Thessalonians - Soulcraft (1993)

My debut album. A chance to play my Roland D-50 tweaked synth patches in an experimental ambient playground with ethnic elements (like Larry Thrasher's tabla).

The booklet says mixed and recorded at Sergays Recording Emporium and Jhopdi Studios. My memory: I was recorded at an Oakland mansion that Larry is housesitting. Upstairs corner room.

UFA (Unidentified Floating Ambience) (1994)

With the larger Thessalonians group semi-disbanded, Kim, Paul, and I continue onward as a trio, recording in a small, rectangular room in Paul's apartment near Divisadero Street, in SF.

Concept: Record with different band names to imply different approaches. Unfortunately, the list of songs by Spice Barons, Hydrosphere, Astralfish, and Patternclear leads listeners to think this is a compilation.

My liner notes:

> We trace our deepest reactions to the ambient sound around us through non-invasive imaging. Highlighting the blood, so it can be seen in the brain at the moment of listening, we can study the patterns that emerge over time. Patterns formed during a single listening experience (e.g., a song) can be considered a map to understanding our aural sensors. By placing various maps side by side, we discover similar maps, similar reactions. This repetition may suggest a plural intelligence within each of us, or the revelation of past lives, or astrological potentials, or simply a like moment in time of which we are an integral part.
>
> In this spirit exists Spice Barons, Patternclear, Satellite IV, etc., combining natural and electronic sounds so that they make a perfect sense. All that we are emanates from the same seed. But how the flower is picked and assimilated remains random. In listening to the ambience that surrounds us, there is always the potential for shared experience. There is also the potential for individualized impressions which are constantly redefining the ambience. This occurs when an aural composition moves further and further from the maps formed by its initial listeners (i.e., its godly or human creators). For better or worse, our ambience will float away from us, toward the plural you—in enough directions to keep it eternally unidentified.

Spice Barons - Future Perfect State (1995)

The Cascone/Falcone/Neyrinck trio hits a new gear. We move further from the non-MIDI arpeggios of my Juno 60, incorporating multiple MIDI boxes and devices capable of syncing to the same beat. The results: A more mature ambient music.

My liner notes:

Ambient music is a living spice, weaving through each earth-mind. We hear its tune when human beings recreate the sounds of ritual, the weightlessness and void of the solar system, or any energy that is heavenly. It is a phenomenon that usually begins with a naïveté. Instead of levitation, we fall. Instead of opening doors to new rooms, we discover walls that keep us in the old ones. We cannot deny who and what we are. Yet, we invent the wheel, turn it upside down, inside out, and continue to create a new ambiance.

Some minds may feel the natural disasters of the late 20th century signify a coming Armageddon. That if Babel was the watershed where communication went awry, then the science of modern civilization that preaches a telecommunications superhighway, is in fact food for the gods to show renewed wrath.

Other minds, unite in a belief that the ever-growing ambient soul of society can be interpreted as a tribute to the best that is human. And that understanding between different entities can only be achieved through a communication that weaves in more than one direction.

What has always been our strength, our excitement, is the spices around us. From the taste of ginger, to the crisp sound of autumn leaves beneath a gentle walk, to the pulsating white of a full moon. Spices are everywhere, forever weaving. Ambient music is one of these spices, and as one, is inherently shared. Built from the perceptions of musicians, incorporating sounds that occur in the world,

naturally and unnaturally, it begins as an open door.
Listeners are invited to assimilate floating ambient
sounds in the traditional way: listen, dream, levitate.
Furthermore, listeners can communicate more intimately
with the music by becoming part of the music. Ambient
music is a voice which attempts to inspire listeners to
become pro-active, to help breathe new life into its
eternal dialogue, by ceasing to be a listener only. It is
time to speak a voice and become part of the ambient
weave: be it via acoustic or electronic instruments, be it
with skill or naïveté, be it with television or radio, be it
with any sound or non-sound.

The Ambient room is an open room, now and forever.

Melting Euphoria - Through The Strands of Time (1995); re-released as From The Madness We Began (2013)

The original trio version of this band. I primarily play keyboards and handle vocals. We record at Conscious Sound, in San Rafael, CA.

The album includes my experimental ambient composition, *Disappearance Of A Friend*. Beside keys, I do record player needle drops, slow down a turntable playing Melanie, and add percussion. For extra hype, Kim Cascone mixes the piece.

The re-release is held hostage by a label for seven years. When I get that deal untethered, we put together a release on Voiceprint that includes bonus tracks of demos from previous bands. This includes my composition *One Spirit Burning*.

Trap - Beyond The Status Quo (1996)

Drummer Gary Parra's experimental prog album launches Musea sub label Gazul. My role escalates from additional keyboardist to: co-writing five tracks; appearing on and mixing most songs; co-producer. We mix the album on the centerpiece of my home studio—Orban's DSE7000FX workstation—on loan from work (later rebranded as the Audicy).

I play with members of Cartoon, as Gary is joined by Scott, Herb, and Craig. Plus, the challenge of working with different line-ups song-to-song and bringing together 11 musicians under one project foretells the creation and sound management of Spirits Burning.

Spaceship Eyes - Kamarupa (1997)

I produce a solo album highlighting my synth playing and use it as a resume to get signed to a label. I record and save keyboard MIDI performances via Passport's Master Tracks Pro (on Windows), and then output the audio to my Orban DSE workstation for mixing.

Spaceship Eyes - Truth In The Eyes Of A Spaceship (1998)

Concept: Cleopatra Records owner Brian Perera asks me to do drum 'n' bass. I produce an experimental version of the genre.

I had sent the label a letter and copy of the *Kamarupa* CD. In response, Brian asked me to record multiple songs for compilations, and then offered a three-album contract.

The title track opens the film *Better Living Through Circuitry*. Three Spaceship Eyes songs in total are used throughout the film.

The album includes my first collaboration with a Hawkwind family member, Harvey Bainbridge—on *The Great Yew Hedge*—plus a remix by Freaky Chakra (Daum Bentley).

Spirits Burning - New Worlds By Design (1999)

The tray reads "A Gathering In Space...organized by Don Falcone (Spaceship Eyes)"

Concepts: Celebrate space rock; invite as many people as possible from the space rock community.

After two Spaceship Eyes solo albums that include guests, I do a more band-oriented album with space rock as its foundation. Gazul, the label that released Gary's *Trap* album, expresses interest in releasing this and the next SB album.

Steven Wilson (Porcupine Tree) contributes guitar to *The*

Ticking Of Science. Daevid Allen performs on seven songs, including
Arc - A Real Creeper.

The 2017 SB live ensemble performs three songs from this
album: *By Design*, *Snakebite Serum*, *The Unknown*.

Quiet Celebration - Quiet Celebration (2000)

Concepts: Celebrate ambient music via a quartet (keys, winds/reeds,
contrabass, tabla); name each song after a color and date. For
example, *Salmon (December 27)*.

The songs are originally keyboards only for a planned second
Spaceship Eyes album. When Cleopatra offers a contract for that
project with the caveat to do drum 'n' bass, I now have an album
worth of songs for another band.

Songs from the album are used on TV shows, including *Beyond
The da Vinci Code*, *Conspiracy Files: Mystery of Roswell*, *The Secret Life of
Vampires*, *Pamela Anderson: Driven*.

Spaceship Eyes - Of Cosmic Repercussions (2000)

Concept: Combine drum 'n' bass with space and prog rock.

> *With one of the more original rhythmic palettes of recent
> electronica, Falcone's percussion designs sound like a
> Rube Goldberg contraption on acid, taking ambient
> tablas and morphing them into jungle grooves on Big
> Martian Dog Hop, and alternating jazz with a heavy-
> metal death march on Keep Yourself Healthy.*
> —Michael Paoletta, Billboard, Nov. 18, 2000

We list my credits in the album liner notes under "Camouflage,"
separate from guests, under "Contributors." Some online services
and reviewers exclude my name in content.

The song *Vapor (Spaceship Eyes vs. Spice Barons)* remixes an unused
piece by Spice Barons. One of the best pieces we ever did now has a
home.

My decisions on the artwork are disconnected, a lesson for

future releases. The under tray is an image of my knee's arthroscopic surgery. The cover background image is from an Orban Audicy ad—yes, that "ban" at the bottom of the cover is part of an "orban." The disc tray, while vibrant, looks like a background for a Nick Fury video game. The image that should have been the cover, the *Spiral Dance* painting by David Gulotta, is on CD booklet page four.

Disappointingly, Cleopatra decides to end the contract after this release.

Spirits Burning - Reflections In A Radio Shower (2002)

The tray reads: "Communications through Space...received by Don Falcone (Spaceship Eyes)." Concept: Space rock celebration, continued.

I am ready to take more risks, as Gazul Records is actively promoting "the cause of new musics."

For this album, Jill Calvert gives me permission to use Robert Calvert readings. Plus, I locate the legendary Isle of Wight concert chatter about Nik Turner. I bring it all together in *Second Degree Soul Sparks*.

New Spell is performed by the trio of Daevid, Michael Clare, and me. The seed for our Weird bands.

Fireclan - Sunrise to Sunset (2004)

Michael Merrill and Luis Davila of Melting Euphoria are now contributing regularly to SB. We decide to record an album as a trio. I have the equipment to record and mix us. And I will be the bass guitarist.

My new Carvin 5-string bass and still-functioning Phase 90 stomp box inspire me to play some creative bass parts. Digidesign co-worker Stan Cotey (Giraffe) lends me his Neumann mic for recording the drums; I use it as a single overhead mic. Daevid guests on two tracks.

Thessalonians - Solaristics (2005)

The final album by Thessalonians Don/Kim/Larry/Paul doesn't get released by Silent Records after Kim sells the label. A decade later, we agree to release it on my Noh Poetry Records label.

The album includes two short solo pieces by each member. Highlighted by Larry's tabla-esque performance of water in a bathtub.

Weird Biscuit Teatime - DJDDAY (2005)

The first Weird quartet: Daevid, Michael, and me recruit drummer Trey Sabatelli (Starship). Early recording and mixing are done with the Orban Audicy and then moved to Pro Tools as I fully transition to Digidesign hardware and software.

Artist Hawk Alfredson provides cover and interior art pieces. He will do the same for the future Weird album and two Spirits Burning & Clearlight albums.

Falcone & Palmer - Gothic Ships (2006)

Steve Palmer and I team up to create ambient space music. We release it as a CD-R, probably for a smaller manufacturing run (as you couldn't do small CD runs in those days).

Cheaper too.

In retrospect, I feel it makes the release appear less professional to reviewers and others.

Spirits Burning - Found In Nature (2006)

The tray reads: "Patterns & Mysteries in Space…interpreted by Don Falcone (Spaceship Eyes)." Concepts: Instrumentals; incorporate acoustic instruments into space and prog.

With a new label (Mellow), the album is stuck in the release queue for months before finally being available. Otherwise, they give me 60 copies: more copies of a release than any other label.

daevid allen & don falcone - Glissando Groove (SFO Soundtribe 3) (2006)

Part of Daevid's *Bananamoon Obscura* series. Concept: Best-of highlighting Daevid's work with SB. Includes two new ambient pieces, created from recordings of Daevid's gliss guitar at my home studio.

> *The 12ᵗʰ in a series of 17 recordings released by Daevid Allen, the founder of the experimental progressive group Gong, consists of a variety of ambient and electronic pieces that drift between trippy psychedelic freakouts like ARC - A Real Creeper and graceful, stately pieces like New Spell and Lionization, all of which combine the talents of Allen and his collaborator, the synthesizer musician Don Falcone.*
> —Allmusic

Quiet Celebration - Sequel (2007)

With Ashley (contrabass) no longer available, I invite a guest to each song to maintain a quartet. The one non-quartet piece—*Henna (November 15)*—features Purjah and me contributing to my brother David's original composition *Behind Your Eyes*. We continue naming each song after a color and date.

Grindlestone - one (2008)

Concepts: Dark ambient with some experimentation; three-word song titles whose acronym is a real-world acronym. Example: *Online Emergency Molasses*, which equates to OEM.

Doug Erickson and I work on this project for almost a decade. We even throw out most of the first dozen songs we create, and then start over. Result: the second, and last Noh Poetry release on CD-R.

Spirits Burning—Alien Injection (2008)

The tray reads: "Space rock remedies…prepared by Don Falcone."

Italy's Black Widow Records releases it in two formats: CD and double LP.

The album features five Hawkwind family members, including the return of Bridget Wishart to music. And Michael Moorcock—I work out a deal to clean up his *Gloriana* and *Entropy Tango* demo sessions and use four of the songs with additional instruments.

At work, I discover product manager Danny Caccavo owns a mellotron. We end one workday with his mellotron semi-blocking my office door, connected by a short cable to a Pro Tools box on my desk. Danny runs Pro Tools inside my office while I stand in the hallway, playing mellotron parts for multiple songs.

Don Playing Mellotron Parts Outside His Digidesign Office in Daly City

Spirits Burning & Bridget Wishart - Earth Born (2008)

The tray reads: "A song-oriented journey by a cosmically festive crew...presented by Bridget Wishart (Hawkwind) and Don Falcone."

Concepts: First all-vocal Spirits Burning album; feature Bridget. I list song credits in reverse alphabetical order so that Wishart is usually first.

I had signed a larger licensing deal with Voiceprint, which supports the Daevid Allen Weird Biscuit Teatime project and multiple SB albums (including this one). With Bridget's help, we procure contributions from eight Hawkwind family members.

I dedicate the album to my mom, who hears the in-progress songs when I visit PA in 2007, a few months before she passes away. I brought a boom box with me, and we listen to a cassette of the songs while we play Scrabble in the kitchen.

Spirits Burning - Our Best Trips: 1998 to 2008 (2008)

The tray reads: "A space rock archaeological dig...assembled by Don Falcone." Concept: A best-of album.

My Voiceprint contract includes one best-of album. I add three bonus tracks; one is a cover of Gong's *Opium For The People*.

Spirits Burning & Thom the World Poet - Golden Age Orchestra (2009)

Concept: Let the band play while Thom improvises lyrics.

I am invited to record an impromptu session with Thom, Jay Radford, Michael Clare, and David L at Jay's house. I record the core band and vocals live via my laptop, small Pro Tools system, and some mics. I record my keys afterwards, and we suddenly have an SB folk album.

Spirits Burning & Bridget Wishart - Bloodlines (2009)

The tray reads: "A historical jaunt by a cosmically festive crew... presented by Bridget Wishart (Hawkwind) and Don Falcone." Concepts: Vocal songs with Bridget; songs about historical figures (real or fictional).

The second album with Bridget includes the first SB appearance of Harvey Bainbridge.

Spirits Burning - Crazy Fluid (2010)

The tray reads: "Crazy turns taken at the space rock border... navigated by Don Falcone."

Concept: Space rock meets rock in opposition (RIO). Originally, an instrumental album.

Grindlestone - tone (2011)

Doug (Erickson) and I collect field recordings (from my MRI to machinery near his work), and he adds some guitar. We create an entire album without me playing a note. Instead, I play with Pro Tools and its sound design capabilities.

It's one of my favorite Noh Poetry releases. Also, one of our worst selling albums. I wish we had found an established label to give it proper promotion and distribution.

Spirits Burning - Behold The Action Man (2011)

The tray reads: "A Space Rock Journey Into Film Noir...investigated by Don Falcone & Roger Neville-Neil." Concept: Space rock meets film noir.

The song *Stand and Deliver* starts as a jam between Mike Moskowitz (a coworker), me, and a drum machine at a practice space in San Francisco. In 2017, it closes our Kozfest live set.

Astralfish - Far Corners (2012)

Concepts: Showcase Bridget's EWI (Electronic Wind Instrument); instrumental album; ambient, with some experimentation.

This album continues our collaboration, and a chance to touch new territory. It also has a smaller crew (15 musicians) compared to a standard SB album.

While composing songs, Bridget surprises me with *Seven 8*, a non-lyric vocal piece.

Spirits Burning & Clearlight - Healthy Music In Large Doses (2013)

The tray reads: "An aural panacea...prescribed by Don Falcone & Cyrille Verdeaux." Concepts: Instrumentals that showcase Cyrille Verdeaux (on 10 of 13 tracks); song titles reflect panaceas.

Cyrille records at my San Bruno home studio. Daevid adds vocals to what becomes the end song *Bring It Down*.

Spirits Burning & Bridget Wishart - Make Believe It Real (2014)

The tray reads: "A World Full of Make Believe...woven by Bridget Wishart & Don Falcone." Concepts: Showcase Bridget; lyrics about the world of make believe.

This is the first SB double CD. It includes contributions from eight Hawkwind family members, and Twink.

I talk to Bridget about doing some acoustic-sounding songs. We do that with the disc one bookend songs. The album opens with *Make Believe (It Acoustic)*, featuring violinist Craig Fry (Cartoon); and I get to play a harmonium (that Gary Parra gave me years earlier).

The disc ends with the 14-minute 15-second piano-based *Reflections*, where my piano channels my inner Kate Bush; Bridget runs with it lyrically and vocally.

Clearlight – Impressionist Symphony (2014)

The tray features Cyrille's story of this album, including "When I found out that Don's equipment and technique of collecting tracks from Musicians living all around the World was exactly what was needed to complete my impressionist project, I proposed for him to become a partner in this impressionist saga."

Concept: "Music aimed at the glory of all the impressionists, audio as well as visual."

Spirits Burning - No One Cries In Space (2015)

Concepts: Celebrate first 15 years of SB; most songs feature Hawkwind family members.

Gonzo head Rob Ayling asks me to prepare a promotional album to accompany some orders for the Hawkwind 2DVD/2CD *Space Ritual Live* release.

Spirits Burning - Starhawk (2015)

The tray reads: "A sci-fi adventure…resurrected by Don Falcone & Mack Maloney."

Concept: Musical adaptation of Mack Maloney's *Starhawk* novel.

Mack does promotion for some Gonzo artists, and Rob Ayling puts us in touch. Mack brings onboard Matt Malley (Counting Crows) and *Sky Club* guitarist Mark Poulin. He tries to bring in Jon Anderson, who he was doing promotion for, and Patrick Moraz; neither Yes family member is meant to be.

I write most of the lyrics and try to make them universal, avoiding character names as much as possible. I felt this was an issue with a concept album like Hawkwind's *The Chronicle Of The Black Sword*, which was based upon the adventures of Michael Moorcock's Elric character.

The album includes an eight-page comic by Steve Lines to accompany the songs and tell the story minus words. And I get to be Editor in Chief.

Mack adds:

> *When Don first approached me about translating the Starhawk book into an SB album, I wasn't sure how it would work. The book is a sprawling space opera that literally spans the Milky Way galaxy and has lots of characters, action, romance, adventure and an F-16 jet fighter that can go two light years a second. How could someone tell that story in just three or four chords?*
>
> *I remember talking to Don about how much involvement I should have in creating the project. He was very generous to the point of offering to include a song of my own on the album. But in a moment of clarity, I made what I came to learn was the right decision. I just left it to Don and the great musicians of SB to interpret the book their way, to write the music and sing the songs about how they saw and felt the story. Hands off was the way to do it and for me, the results were stunning.*

Daevid Allen Weird Quartet - Elevenses (2015)

Follow up to the Weird Biscuit Teatime album. We create some of the songs when I reserve a studio where I work, available to all Digidesign employees. We record Daevid, Michael, and Trey live. They play to a couple of pre-recorded keyboards songs that I started, do some jams, and play a song I teach them, called *Alchemy*.

Drummer Trey Sabatelli isn't available when we begin completing the album; we recruit Paul Sears.

Spirits Burning & Clearlight Verdeaux - The Roadmap In Your Head (2016)

The tray reads: "Sonic paths for a new day…envisioned by Don Falcone & Cyrille Verdeaux."

Concepts: Showcase Cyrille—this time he's on every track; instrumental album (well, mostly, as Bridget and Daevid each unexpectedly send me vocals); cover a roadmapped 24 hours in a life;

create a sense of cool, like a 60's spy movie; and with Daevid's death, celebrate his life with Gong family and friends: Daevid Allen, Michael Clare, Ian East, Fabio Golfetti, Steve Hillage, Didier Malherbe, Pierce McDowell, Mike Howlett, Kavus Torabi, Theo Travis, Harry Williamson.

Spirits Burning & Michael Moorcock - An Alien Heat (2018)

The tray reads: "An Alien Heat at the End of a Multiverse... reimagined by Don Falcone, Albert Bouchard (BÖC), & Michael Moorcock." Concepts: Adapt book one of Mike's *Dancers At The End Of Time* trilogy; Mike sings or plays harmonica (13 of 16 songs).

After Albert joins the project and becomes a primary collaborator (15 of 16 songs), he brings onboard members of BÖC and The Dictators.

The label does a boxed version that Karen and I design; containing a poster (signed by Al, Mike, and me), postcards, a sticker, main CD, bonus CD with instrumental versions, and a lyric book. Subsequent pressings are the main CD only.

Artist Jilaen Sherwood provides cover and interior art pieces. She previously did the artwork for the Michael Moorcock & The Deep Fix *Demo Sessions* album we released on Noh Poetry.

Michael Moorcock & the Deep Fix - Live At The Terminal Café (2019)

I produce and play on Mike's 21st century Cajun-influenced album, an adaptation of his *Blood: A Southern Fantasy* novel. Contrary to the album title, the recording is not live.

After I get multi-tracks of the six songs recorded by Mike, Martin Stone, and their band in France, I create three more songs from the longest piece. Plus, Mike does an a cappella version of *St. James's Infirmary* during our recording session in Texas, and I add piano. Marvel Comics/Thor artist Walter Simonson provides interior art pieces.

Spirits Burning & Michael Moorcock - The Hollow Lands (2020)

The tray reads: "Hollow Lands, at the Center of a Multiverse… reimagined by Don Falcone, Albert Bouchard (BÖC), & Michael Moorcock." Concepts: Adapt book two of Mike's *Dancers* trilogy; Mike sings or plays harmonica (16 of 18 songs).

The album features seven Blue Öyster Cult family members: Eric Bloom, Al Bouchard, Joe Bouchard, Richie Castellano, Danny Miranda, Jules Radino, Donald Roeser.

Artist Keith Donald provides cover and interior art pieces.

Spirits Burning - Evolution Ritual (2021)

The tray reads: "An Evolving Ritual in an Acoustic Brew…prepared by Don Falcone." Concepts: Acoustic space rock; everyone plays an acoustic or acoustic-sounding instrument—no distortion or unnatural effects; perhaps a cross between Third Ear Band and *The Long Hello* albums by Van der Graaf members. As the album develops, it becomes a celebration of violinists.

The album is the SB debut of some special prog and folk instrumentalists: David Cross (King Crimson), Daryl Way (Curved Air), Steeleye Span family members Peter Knight and Jessie May Smart, Van der Graaf family members David Jackson and Graham Smith.

Of special note: Finding and onboarding Ursula Pank (formerly Ursula Smith), of early Third Ear Band.

Spirits Burning - Recollections Of Instrumentals (2022)

Concept: SB's best instrumentals.

This album results after discussing my catalog with Brian at Cleopatra. I include four songs that are not streaming or part of a download album yet: *The Ticking Of Science* featuring Steven Wilson; *New Spell* featuring Daevid Allen; *Coffee For Coltrane* featuring Albert Bouchard and Theo Travis; and a song built from Acid Mothers

Temple's *Pink Lady Lemonade*. After licensing these songs to Cleopatra for the length of the contract, I must exclude the songs when I subsequently release digital albums of the respective releases the songs were originally on. It's a trade-off. I'm happy to give these songs new exposure on a great start-to-finish instrumental album.

I include two instrumental remixes of vocal songs. This doesn't affect my use of the vocal versions elsewhere.

Originally planned as a 2020 CD/LP to piggybank off the *Hollow Lands* release, the label switches gears to distance it from that release. When Covid happens, the release date slips further, and the vinyl version is dropped.

Spirits Burning & Michael Moorcock - The End Of All Songs - Part 1 (2023)

Concepts: Adapt book three of Mike's *Dancers* trilogy; Mike sings or plays harmonica (16 of 17 songs). As songs develop, we decide to split book three songs into two albums.

Rodney Matthew provides the cover and interior art pieces, some that I had as posters during my teens.

Spirits Burning - Live At Kozfest (2024)

A live album of our 2017 festival performance. It takes seven years to complete the mixes. We include two bonus tracks—studio versions of songs that we play at our warmup show in Bath and remove from the set at Kozfest due to time restraints.

Live line-up: Steve Bemand (electric guitar, backing vocals), Richard Chadwick (drums, backing vocals), Kev Ellis (Kaoss Pad, lead vocals), Don Falcone (keyboards, lead vocals), Colin Kafka (bass guitar), Martin Plumley (acoustic guitar, backing vocals), Bridget Wishart (lead and backing vocals, EWI).

The set includes songs from the SB catalog, plus a cover of Hawkwind's *Images*.

Vinyl Singles/EPs

Spaceship Eyes - Cheebahcabra (Freaky Chakra Remix)/Dreaming Without The Right Side (Extended Jung Mix) (1998)

The age of the 12-inch dance mix. Drum 'n' bass style.

The A side Cheebahcabra remix by Freaky Chakra (Daum Bentley) incorporates voice samples by my Orban coworker Luis Endara, the company's sales manager for Latin America and the Caribbean. We recorded his signature phrase "Check It Out!," a few lines about "getting down with some ganga man," and the Spanish and English version of the album title "La verdad en los ojos de una nave especial…Truth in the Eyes of a Spaceship!"

The B side features samples of acoustic guitar and a Jung lecture, both by my brother David (which he provided to me on a cassette).

Spirits Burning & Daevid Allen - The Roadmap In Your Heart/Another Roadmap In Your Head/ An Ambient Heat (2017)

A 7-inch, 45 RPM EP for Record Store Day. Concepts: Feature Daevid. I remix the *Roadmap* instrumental and vocal songs from the second Spirits Burning & Clearlight album and create one new track from a gliss session with Daevid.

One of the Spirits Burning CD

BOOKS PURCHASED DIRECTLY from Stairway Press include a CD inside the back cover. The CD includes released and unreleased recordings mentioned in the book.

Track Listing and Credits

All songs produced by Don Marino Falcone, except: *Far*, produced by Falcone and Wishart; *Loralyn*, produced by SF State students (including Robin Burns) with instructor John Barsotti; *Spirits Burning*, produced by Garry Creiman, with Karen Anderson assisting. New mastering by Robert Rich

All songs used by permission of Don Falcone and Noh Poetry Records, unless noted otherwise
> *Used by Permission of Cleopatra Records
> **Used by Permission of Deko Records

1. **Spirits Burning & Michael Moorcock** — *Hothouse Flowers* **(4:10)**
(Featuring Blue Öyster Cult family members Albert Bouchard, Donald "Buck Dharma" Roeser, Richie Castellano, plus Michael Moorcock); From An Alien Heat, October 2018
(Lyrics: Theodore Wratislaw, Reworked by A. Bouchard; Music: Falcone & A. Bouchard, with Avery, R. Castellano, Moorcock, Roeser, Tiburcio, Vibratus)

Ryan Avery: Violin
Al Bouchard: Drums, Cowbell, Shaker, Tambourine,
    Acoustic Gtr, End Vocals
Richie Castellano: Guitar
Don Falcone: Piano, Synth, Virtual Drums
Michael Moorcock: End Vocals
Donald "Buck Dharma" Roeser: Lead Vocals
Vincente Tiburcio: Guitar Solo
Lux Vibratus: Bass Guitar

2. Spirits Burning — *Alien Injection* (5:25)
From Alien Injection, 2008
(Lyrics: Falcone; Music: Santtu & Zappa; Final Mix: Danny Caccavo)

Michael Camaro: Drums
Captain Black: Distant Synth Pads
Dark Santtu: Bass Guitar
Kev Ellis: Lead Vocals
Don Falcone: Mellotron, Rhythm & Acid Bass Guitars,
     Backing Vocals
Chris Hopgood: Guitar Solos
Carl Howard: Synth Arpeggios
Yur Zappa: Rhythm Guitar

3. Spirits Burning & Bridget Wishart — *Earth Born* (5:32)
(Featuring Hawkwind Family Members Bridget Wishart, Simon
House, Alan Davey, Richard Chadwick); From Earth Born, 2008
*(Original Song "Earthborn" by Bemand, Chadwick, Davey, Wishart; Rewrite
by Plumley & Wishart, with Chadwick, Falcone, House, Sabatelli)*

Bridget Wishart: Vocals
Trey Sabatelli: Acoustic Drums
Martin Plumley: Acoustic Guitar
Simon House: Violin
Don Falcone: Organ, Synth, M-Tron, Backing Vocals, Loops,
     Virtual Drums
Alan Davey: Bass Guitar
Richard Chadwick: Space Drums

4. Daevid Allen Weird Quartet — *Imagicknation** (3:56)
(Featuring David Allen); From Elevenses, 2016
(Lyrics: Allen; Music: Allen, Clare, Falcone, Sears)

Daevid Allen: Vocals
Michael Clare: Bass
Don Falcone: Keyboards (Organ, Synth, Cello, Sine Wave),
    1/4-inch Jack, Filtered Click Track
Paul Sears: Drums

5. Michael Moorcock & The Deep Fix — *Lou** (3:07)
(Featuring Martin Stone, Michael Moorcock); From Live At The
Terminal Café, 2019
(Lyrics & Music: Moorcock; Mixed & Produced by Don Marino Falcone)

Martin Stone: Guitars
Michael Moorcock: Lead & Backing Vocals
Dan Baudrillart: Drums
Brad Scott: Bass
    With
Catherine Foreman: Female Vocals
Sean Orr: Fiddle

6. Spirits Burning — *Your Better Angels* (4:01)
(Featuring Steeleye Span family member Peter Knight); From
Evolution Ritual, 2021
(Music: Gold-Molina & Falcone, with Erickson, Knight, Kopecky, Plumley)

Doug Erickson: Acoustic Guitar
Don Falcone: Keyboards (Mallets, Glockenspiel, Piano)
Jack Gold-Molina: Drums
Peter Knight: Fiddle
William Kopecky: Bass Guitar
Martin Plumley: Mandolin

7. Spirits Burning — *Oak, Elm, and Spruce* **(4:10)**
From Found In Nature, 2006.
(Music: Dambly, David Falcone, Don Falcone, Landar, Merrill; Guitar from the original composition The Little Turtle, by David Falcone)

Tom Dambly: Flugelhorn
Dave Falcone: Acoustic Guitar
Rich Landar: Synth
Don Falcone: Keyboard Strings, Bass Guitar
Mychael Merrill: Djembe, Kettle Drum

8. Astralfish — *Far* **(2:08)**
(Featuring Bridget Wishart, Daevid Allen); From Far Corners, 2012
(Music: Wishart, Seigfried, Falcone, Allen)

Bridget Wishart: EWI Clarinets
Karl E. H. Seigfried: Bowed Bass
Don Falcone: Synths
Daevid Allen: Gliss Guitars

9. Spirits Burning & David Jackson — *Ebb Of Flow* **(5:39)**
(Featuring Van der Graaf Generator family member David Jackson);
Unreleased, for future album
(Music: Falcone, with Jackson, Kopecky)

Don Falcone: Piano
David Jackson: Saxes (Tenor, Alto, Sopranino, Soprano,
    Double Horns)
William Kopecky: Bass

10. Spirits Burning & Clearlight — *Our Secret Cloud* (8:14)
(Featuring Pete Pavli & Cyrille Verdeaux); From Healthy Music In Large Doses, 2011
(Music: Beber, Falcone, Festi, Fraile, Golin, Pavli, Seigfried, Verdeaux)

Giuliano Beber: Guitar
Don Falcone: Strings, Synth Rumblies, Samples
Francesco Festi: Male Vocals
Ana Torres Fraile: Female Voice
Uto G. Golin: Chorus
Pete Pavli: Viola
Karl E. H. Seigfried: Double Bass
Cyrille Verdeaux: Piano, Organ

11. Spaceship Eyes — *Vapor (Spaceship Eyes Vs. Spice Barons)** (5:01)
(Featuring Kim Cascone); From Of Cosmic Repercussions, 2000
(Music: Cascone, Falcone, Neyrinck)

Don Falcone: Synth, Audicy
Edward Huson: Tabla & Bayan
Jerry Jeter: Lead & Rhythm Guitar
Spice Barons (Kim Cascone/Don Falcone/Paul Neyrinck): Synths, Samples, Electronic Percussion

12. Spirits Burning — *Arc - A Real Creeper* (6:33)
(Featuring Daevid Allen); From New Worlds By Design, October 1999 *(Lyrics & Music: Falcone)*

Daevid Allen: Voice (Poetry Improv), Gliss Guitars
Karen Anderson: Female Voices
Don Falcone: Keyboards, Samples
Mason Jones: Orchestral Guitar Sample

13. Spirits Burning — *By Design*** (6:09)
(Featuring Hawkwind's Richard Chadwick); From Live at Kozfest, 2024 *(Music: Falcone & Bruce Smith)*

Steve Bemand: Electric Guitar
Richard Chadwick: Drums
Kev Ellis: Kaoss Pad
Don Falcone: Keyboards (Synths, Organ)
Colin Kafka: Bass Guitar

14. Kameleon — *Loralyn* (3:34)
1981 Cassette Demo
(Lyrics & Music: Falcone)

Don Falcone: Bass Guitar, Piano
Jerry Jeter: Vocals, Acoustic Guitar
Bruce Smith: Drums

15. Spirits Burning — *Persian Cat* (4:41)
Unreleased Spirits Burning song, written in 1988, recorded parts from 2003 "US band" session
(Lyrics & Music: Falcone)

Karen Anderson: Vocals, Acoustic Guitar
Michael Clare: Bass Guitar

16. Spirits Burning — *Spirits Burning* (4:09)
1987 Demo Cassette
(Lyrics & Music: Falcone)

Jane Bryan: Vocals
Joe Diehl: Guitars
Don Falcone: Keyboards
Rick Gauvreau: Drums
Tracy Williams: Vocals

Procuring a Copy of the One of the Spirits Burning CD

If the CD was not included in your book, and you want one, do this:

1. Carefully cut off the bottom of the page.
2. Send the cutout and your address to Stairway Press along with USD $10 to cover printing and shipping.

Stairway Press
1000 West Apache Trail, Suite 126
Apache Junction, AZ 85120

Note: The $10 is a not-for-profit contribution. All profits (if there are any) will be donated to Seattle Music Partners.

For questions, email Ken@StairwayPress.com

================cut here=================

Enclosed is USD $10 for a copy of the *One of the Spirits Burning* CD

Don Falcone